PRAISE FOR

People We Meet on Vacation

"Emily Henry is my newest automatic-buy author, and *People We Meet on Vacation* is the perfect getaway: a heartfelt, funny, tender escape that you wish could last forever."

—**Jodi Picoult,** #1 *New York Times* bestselling author of *The Book of Two Ways*

"*People We Meet on Vacation* is a gorgeous slow-burn romance, full of sexual tension and tantalizing possibility. I fell head over heels for Alex and Poppy, and loved traveling all over the world with them both."

—**Beth O'Leary,** *Sunday Times* bestselling author of *The Flatshare*

"A compulsively readable book full of sparkling wit, dazzling prose, and a romance that grabbed me by the heart and wouldn't let me go."

—**Abby Jimenez,** *USA Today* bestselling author of *Life's Too Short*

"Emily Henry is a STAR! Deeply emotional and starkly funny, *People We Meet on Vacation* cements [her] as the Queen of Banter. Rom-com fans will swoon over this slow burn friends-to-lovers romance. Poppy and Alex are real and flawed and ultra-lovable, and their summer trips will scratch an itch for those of us who've missed traveling. A perfect summer read!"

—**Alexis Daria,** bestselling author of *You Had Me at Hola*

"An absolute delight: swoony, legitimately moving, and packed with witty banter that makes Alex and Poppy jump off the page. We are already waiting impatiently for whatever Emily writes next."

—**Heather Cocks and Jessica Morgan,** *USA Today* bestselling authors of *The Royal We* and *The Heir Affair*

PRAISE FOR
Beach Read

———

"It's in [the] tension that Henry's writing truly sings—the accidental touches that linger, the hand-caressing beneath an Olive Garden table. Very few writers can capture this kind of pretending it didn't happen while desperately wishing it would happen again, and it's not only convincing but infectious."

—***The New York Times Book Review***

"Once I started *Beach Read* I legit did not put it down."

—**Betches**

"That Henry can manage to both pack a fierce emotional wallop and spear literary posturing in one go is a testament to her immense skill."

—***Entertainment Weekly***

People We Meet on Vacation

EMILY HENRY

JOVE
New York

A JOVE BOOK
Published by Berkley
An imprint of Penguin Random House LLC
penguinrandomhouse.com

Copyright © 2021 by Emily Henry
Readers Guide copyright © 2021 by Emily Henry

A JOVE BOOK, BERKLEY, and the BERKLEY & B colophon
are registered trademarks of Penguin Random House LLC.

Library of Congress Cataloging-in-Publication Data

Names: Henry, Emily, author.
Title: People we meet on vacation / Emily Henry.
Description: First Edition. | New York: Jove, 2021.
Identifiers: LCCN 2020036305 (print) | LCCN 2020036306 (ebook) |
ISBN 9781984806758 (trade paperback) | ISBN 9781984806765 (ebook)
Subjects: GSAFD: Love stories.
Classification: LCC PS3608.E5715 P46 2021 (print) | LCC PS3608.E5715
(ebook) | DDC 813/.6—dc23
LC record available at https://lccn.loc.gov/2020036305
LC ebook record available at https://lccn.loc.gov/2020036306

First Edition: May 2021

Printed in the United States of America

5th Printing

Book design by Ashley Tucker

I wrote the last one mostly for me.
This one's for you.

PROLOGUE

Five Summers Ago

O N VACATION, YOU can be anyone you want.

Like a good book or an incredible outfit, being on vacation transports you into another version of yourself.

In your day-to-day life, maybe you can't even bob your head to the radio without being embarrassed, but on the right twinkly-light-strung patio, with the right steel drum band, you'll find yourself whirling and twirling with the best of them.

On vacation, your hair changes. The water is different, maybe the shampoo. Maybe you don't bother to wash your hair at all, or brush it, because the salty ocean water curls it up in a way you love. You think, *Maybe I could do this at home too. Maybe I could be this person who doesn't brush her hair, who doesn't mind being sweaty or having sand in all her crevices.*

On vacation, you strike up conversations with strangers, and forget that there are any stakes. If it turns out impossibly awkward, who cares? You'll never see them again!

You're whoever you want to be. You can do whatever you want.

Okay, so maybe not whatever you want. Sometimes the weather forces you into a particular situation, such as the one I'm in now, and you have to find second-rate ways to entertain yourself as you wait out the rain.

On my way out of the bathroom, I pause. Partly, this is because I'm still working on my game plan. Mostly, though, it's because the floor is so sticky that I lose my sandal and have to hobble back for it. I love everything about this place in theory, but in practice, I think letting my bare foot touch the anonymous filth on the laminate might be a good way to contract one of those rare diseases kept in the refrigerated vials of a secret CDC facility.

I dance-hop back to my shoe, slip my toes through the thin orange straps, and turn to survey the bar: the press of sticky bodies; the lazy whorl of thatched fans overhead; the door propped open so that, occasionally, a burst of rain rips in off the black night to cool the sweating crowd. In the corner, a jukebox haloed in neon light plays the Flamingos' "I Only Have Eyes for You."

It's a resort town but a locals' bar, free of printed sundresses and Tommy Bahama shirts, though also sadly lacking in cocktails garnished with spears of tropical fruit.

If not for the storm, I would've chosen somewhere else for my last night in town. All week long the rain has been so bad, the thunder so constant, that my dreams of sandy white beaches and glossy speedboats were dashed, and I along with the rest of the disappointed vacationers have spent my days pounding piña coladas in any crammed tourist trap I could find.

Tonight, though, I couldn't take any more dense crowds, long wait times, or gray-haired men in wedding rings drunkenly winking at me over their wives' shoulders. Thus I found myself here.

In a sticky-floored bar called only BAR, scouring the meager crowd for my target.

He's sitting at the corner of BAR's bar itself. A man about my age, twenty-five, sandy haired and tall with broad shoulders, though so hunched you might not notice either of these last two facts on first glance. His head is bent over his phone, a look of quiet concentration visible in his profile. His teeth worry at his full bottom lip as his finger slowly swipes across the screen.

Though not Disney World–level packed, this place is loud. Halfway between the jukebox crooning creepy late-fifties tunes and the mounted TV opposite it, from which a weatherman shouts about record-breaking rain, there's a gaggle of men with identical hacking laughs that keep bursting out all at once. At the far end of the bar, the bartender keeps smacking the counter for emphasis as she chats up a yellow-haired woman.

The storm's got the whole island feeling restless, and the cheap beer has everyone feeling rowdy.

But the sandy-haired man sitting on the corner stool has a stillness that makes him stick out. Actually, everything about him screams that he doesn't belong here. Despite the eighty-something-degree weather and one-million-percent humidity, he's dressed in a rumpled long-sleeve button-up and navy blue trousers. He's also suspiciously devoid of a tan, as well as any laughter, mirth, levity, etc.

Bingo.

I push a fistful of blond waves out of my face and set off toward him. As I approach, his eyes stay fixed on his phone, his finger slowly dragging whatever he's reading up the screen. I catch the bolded words **CHAPTER TWENTY-NINE**.

He's fully reading a book at a bar.

I swing my hip into the bar and slide my elbow over it as I face him. "Hey, tiger."

His hazel eyes slowly lift to my face, blink. "Hi?"

"Do you come here often?"

He studies me for a minute, visibly weighing potential replies. "No," he says finally. "I don't live here."

"Oh," I say, but before I can get out any more, he goes on.

"And even if I did, I have a cat with a lot of medical needs that require specialized care. Makes it hard to get out."

I frown at just about every part of that sentence. "I'm so sorry," I recover. "It must be awful to be dealing with all that while also coping with a death."

His brow crinkles. "A death?"

I wave a hand in a tight circle, gesturing to his getup. "Aren't you in town for a funeral?"

His mouth presses tight. "I am not."

"Then what brings you to town?"

"A friend." His eyes drop to his phone.

"Lives here?" I guess.

"Dragged me," he corrects. "For vacation." He says this last word with some disdain.

I roll my eyes. "No way! Away from your cat? With no good excuse except for enjoyment and merrymaking? Are you sure this person can really be called a *friend*?"

"Less sure every second," he says without looking up.

He's not giving me much to work with, but I'm not giving up. "So," I forge ahead. "What's this friend like? Hot? Smart? Loaded?"

"Short," he says, still reading. "Loud. Never shuts up. Spills on every single article of clothing either of us wears, has horrible romantic taste, sobs through those commercials for community college—the ones where the single mom is staying up late at her computer and then, when she falls asleep, her kid drapes a blanket over her shoulders and smiles because he's so proud of her? What else? Oh, she's obsessed with shitty dive bars that smell like salmonella. I'm afraid to even drink the *bottled* beer here—have you seen the Yelp reviews for this place?"

"Are you kidding right now?" I ask, crossing my arms over my chest.

"Well," he says, "salmonella doesn't have a smell, but yes, Poppy, you are short."

"Alex!" I swat his bicep, breaking character. "I'm trying to help you!"

He rubs his arm. "Help me how?"

"I know Sarah broke your heart, but you need to get back out there. And when a hot babe approaches you at a bar, the number one thing you should not bring up is your codependent relationship with your asshole cat."

"First of all, Flannery O'Connor is not an asshole," he says. "She's shy."

"She's evil."

"She just doesn't like you," he insists. "You have strong dog energy."

"All I've ever done is try to pet her," I say. "Why have a pet who doesn't want to be petted?"

"She wants to be petted," Alex says. "You just always approach her with this, like, wolfish gleam in your eye."

"I do not."

"Poppy," he says. "You approach *everything* with a wolfish gleam in your eye."

Just then the bartender approaches with the drink I ordered before I ducked into the bathroom. "Miss?" she says. "Your margarita." She spins the frosted glass down the bar toward me, and a ping of excited thirst hits the back of my throat as I catch it. I swipe it up so quickly that a fair amount of tequila sloshes over the lip, and with a preternatural and highly practiced speed, Alex jerks my other arm off the bar before it can get liquor splattered on it.

"See? Wolfish gleam," Alex says quietly, seriously, the way he delivers pretty much every word he ever says to me except on those rare and sacred nights when Weirdo Alex comes out and I get to watch him, like, lie on the floor fake-sobbing into a microphone at karaoke, his sandy hair sticking up in every direction and wrinkly dress shirt coming untucked. Just one hypothetical example. Of something that has exactly happened before.

Alex Nilsen is a study in control. In that tall, broad, permanently slouched and/or pretzel-folded body of his, there's a surplus of stoicism (the result of being the oldest child of a widower with the most vocal anxiety of anyone I've ever met) and a stockpile of repression (the result of a strict religious upbringing in direct opposition to most of his passions; namely, academia), alongside the most truly strange, secretly silly, and intensely softhearted goofball I've had the pleasure to know.

I take a sip of the margarita, and a hum of pleasure works its way out of me.

"Dog in a human's body," Alex says to himself, then goes back to scrolling on his phone.

I snort my disapproval of his comment and take another sip. "By the way, this margarita is, like, ninety percent tequila. I hope you're telling those unappeasable Yelp reviewers to shove it. *And* that this place smells nothing like salmonella." I chug a little more of my drink as I slide up onto the stool beside him, turning so our knees touch. I like how he always sits like this when we're out together: his upper body facing the bar, his long legs facing me, like he's keeping some secret door to himself open just for me. And not a door only to the reserved, never-quite-fully-smiling Alex Nilsen that the rest of the world gets, but a path straight to the weirdo. The Alex who takes these trips with me, year after year, even though he despises flying and change and using any pillow other than the one he sleeps with at home.

I like how, when we go out, he always beelines toward the bar, because he knows I like to sit there, even though he once admitted that every time we do, he stresses out over whether he's making too much or not enough eye contact with the bartenders.

Truthfully, I like and/or love nearly everything about my best friend, Alex Nilsen, and I want him to be happy, so even if I've never particularly liked any of his past love interests—and especially didn't care for his ex, Sarah—I know it's up to me to make sure he doesn't let this most recent heartbreak force him into full hermit status. He'd do—and has done—the same for me, after all.

"So," I say. "Should we take it from the top again? I'll be the sexy stranger at the bar and you be your charming self, minus the cat stuff. We'll get you back in the dating pool in no time."

He looks up from his phone, nearly smirking. I'll just call it smirking, because for Alex, this is as close as it gets. "You mean the stranger who kicks things off with a well-timed 'Hey, tiger'? I think we might have different ideas of what 'sexy' is."

I spin on my stool, our knees *bump-bump*ing as I turn away from him and then back, resetting my face into a flirtatious smile. "Did it hurt . . ." I say, ". . . when you fell from heaven?"

He shakes his head. "Poppy, it's important to me that you know," he says slowly, "that if I ever *do* manage to go on another date, it will have absolutely nothing to do with your so-called help."

I stand, throw back the rest of my drink dramatically, and slap the glass onto the bar. "So what do you say we get out of here?"

"How are you more successful at dating than me," he says, awed by the mystery of it all.

"Easy," I say. "I have lower standards. And no Flannery O'Connor to get in the way. And when I go out to bars, I don't spend the whole time scowling at Yelp reviews and forcefully projecting *DON'T TALK TO ME*. Also, I am, arguably, gorgeous from certain angles."

He stands, setting a twenty on the bar before tucking his wallet back into his pocket. Alex always carries cash. I don't know why. I've asked at least three times. He's answered. I still don't know why, because his answer was either too boring or too intellectually complex for my brain to even bother retaining the memory.

"Doesn't change the fact that you're an absolute freak," he says.

"You love me," I point out, the tiniest bit defensive.

He loops an arm around my shoulders and looks down at me, another small, contained smile on his full lips. His face is a sieve, only letting out the smallest amount of expression at a time. "I know that," he says.

I grin up at him. "I love you back."

He fights the widening of his smile, keeps it small and faint. "I know that too."

The tequila has me feeling sleepy, lazy, and I let myself lean into him as we start toward the open door. "This was a good trip," I say.

"Best yet," he agrees, the cool rain gusting in around us like confetti from a cannon. His arm curls in a little closer, warm and heavy around me, his clean cedarwood smell folding over my shoulders like a cape.

"I haven't even minded the rain much," I say as we step into the thick, wet night, all buzzing mosquitoes and palm trees shivering from the distant thunder.

"I've preferred it." Alex lifts his arm from my shoulder to curl over my head, transforming himself into a makeshift human umbrella as we sprint across the flooding road toward our little red rental car. When we reach it, he breaks away and opens my door first—we scored a discount by taking a car without automatic locks or windows—then runs around the hood and hurls himself into the driver's seat.

Alex flicks the car into gear, the full-tilt AC hissing its arctic blast against our wet clothes as he pulls out of our parking space and turns toward our rental house.

"I just realized," he says, "we didn't take any pictures at the bar for your blog."

I start to laugh, then realize he's not kidding. "Alex, none of my readers want to see pictures of BAR. They don't even want to read about BAR."

He shrugs. "I didn't think BAR was that bad."

"You said it smelled like salmonella."

"Other than that." He ticks the turn signal on and guides the car down our narrow, palm-tree-lined street.

"Actually, I haven't really gotten *any* usable pictures this week."

Alex frowns and rubs at his eyebrow as he slows toward the gravel driveway ahead.

"Other than the ones you took," I add quickly. The pictures Alex volunteered to take for my social media are truly terrible. But I love him so much for being willing to take them that I already picked out the least atrocious one and posted it. I'm making one of those awful midword faces, shriek-laughing something at him as he tries— badly—to give me direction, and the storm clouds are visibly forming over me, as if I'm summoning the apocalypse to Sanibel Island myself. But at least you can tell I'm happy in it.

When I look at that photo, I don't remember what Alex said to me to elicit that face, or what I yelled back at him. But I feel that same rush of warmth I get when I think about any of our past summer trips.

That crush of happiness, that feeling that *this* is what life's about: being somewhere beautiful, with someone you love.

I tried to write something about that in the caption, but it was hard to explain.

Usually my posts are all about how to travel on a budget, make the most of the least, but when you've got a hundred thousand people following your beach vacation, it's ideal to show them . . . a beach vacation.

In the past week, we've had approximately forty minutes total on the shore of Sanibel Island. The rest has been spent holed up in bars and restaurants, bookstores and vintage shops, plus a whole lot of time in the shabby bungalow we're renting, eating popcorn and counting lightning streaks. We've gotten no tans, seen no tropical fish, done no snorkeling or sunbathing on catamarans, or much of anything aside from falling in and out of sleep on the squashy sofa with a *Twilight Zone* marathon humming its way into our dreams.

There are places you can see in their full glory, with or without sunshine, but this isn't one of them.

"Hey," Alex says as he puts the car in park.

"Hey, what?"

"Let's take a picture," he says. "Together."

"You hate having your picture taken," I point out. Which has always been weird to me, because on a technical level, Alex is extremely handsome.

"I know," Alex says, "but it's dark and I want to remember this."

"Okay," I say. "Yeah. Let's take one."

I reach for my phone, but he already has his out. Only instead of holding it up with the screen facing us so we can see ourselves, he has it flipped around, the regular camera fixed on us rather than the front-facing one. "What are you doing?" I say, reaching for his phone. "That's what selfie mode's for, you grandpa."

"No!" he laughs, jerking it out of reach. "It's not for your blog—we don't have to look good. We just have to look like ourselves. If we have it on selfie mode I won't even want to take one."

"You need help for your face dysmorphia," I tell him.

"How many thousands of pictures have I taken for you, Poppy?" he says. "Let's just do this one how I want to."

"Okay, fine." I lean across the console, settling in against his damp chest, his head ducking a little to compensate for our height difference.

"One . . . two—" The flash pops off before he ever gets to three.

"You monster!" I scold.

He flips the phone around to look at the picture and moans. "Noooo," he says. "I *am* a monster."

I choke over a laugh as I study the horrible ghostly blur of our faces: his wet hair sticking out in stringy spikes, mine plastered in frizzy tendrils around my cheeks, everything on us shiny and red from the heat, my eyes fully closed, his squinted and puffy. "How is it possible we're both so hard to see *and* so bad-looking simultaneously?"

Laughing, he throws his head back against his headrest. "Okay, I'm deleting it."

"No!" I fight the phone out of his hand. He grabs hold of it too, but I don't let go, so we just hold it between us on the console. "That was the point, Alex. To remember this trip how it really was. And to look like ourselves."

His smile is as small and faint as ever. "Poppy, you don't look anything like that picture."

I shake my head. "And you don't either."

For a long moment, we're silent, like there's nothing else to say now that this has been settled.

"Next year let's go somewhere cold," Alex says. "And dry."

"Okay," I say, grinning. "We'll go somewhere cold."

1

This Summer

"POPPY," SWAPNA SAYS from the head of the dull gray confer-ence table. "What have you got?"

For the benevolent ruler of the *Rest + Relaxation* empire, Swapna Bakshi-Highsmith could not possibly exude any less of our fine magazine's two core values.

The last time Swapna rested was probably three years ago, when she was eight and a half months pregnant and on doctor-mandated bed rest. Even then, she spent the whole time video-chatting with the office, her laptop balanced on her belly, so I don't think there was a ton of relaxation involved. Everything about her is sharp and pointed and smart, from her slicked-back high-fashion bob to her studded Alexander Wang pumps.

Her winged eyeliner could slice through an aluminum can, and her emerald eyes could crush it afterward. In this moment, both are pointed squarely at me. "Poppy? Hello?"

I blink out of my daze and skootch forward in my chair, clear-ing my throat. This has been happening to me a lot lately. When you have a job where you're only required to come into the office once a week, it's not ideal to zone out like a kid in algebra for fifty percent of that time, even less so to do it in front of your equal parts terrifying and inspiring boss.

I study the notepad in front of me. I used to come to the Friday meetings with dozens of excitedly scribbled pitches. Ideas for stories about unfamiliar festivals in other countries, locally famous restaurants with colloquial deep-fried desserts, natural phenomena on particular beaches in South America, up-and-coming vineyards in New Zealand—or new trends among the thrill-seeking set and modes of deep relaxation for the spa crowd.

I used to write these notes in a kind of panic, like every experience I hoped to someday have was a living thing growing in my body, stretching branches out to push on my insides, demanding to break out of me. I'd spend three days before pitch meetings in something of a sweaty Google trance, scrolling through image after image of places I'd never been, a feeling something like hunger growling in my gut.

Today, however, I spent ten minutes writing down the names of countries.

Countries, not even cities.

Swapna is looking at me, waiting for me to pitch my next big summer feature for next year, and I'm staring at the word *Brazil*.

Brazil is the fifth-largest country in the world. Brazil is 5.6 percent of the earth's mass. You cannot write a short, snappy piece about vacationing in Brazil. You have to at least choose a specific region.

I flip the page in my notebook, pretending to study the next one. It's blank. When my coworker Garrett leans toward me as if to read over my shoulder, I snap it closed. "St. Petersburg," I say.

Swapna arches an eyebrow, paces along the head of the table.

"We did St. Petersburg in our summer issue three years ago. The White Nights celebration, remember?"

"Amsterdam?" Garrett throws out next to me.

"Amsterdam's a spring city," Swapna says, vaguely annoyed. "You're not going to feature Amsterdam and not include the tulips."

I once heard she's been to upwards of seventy-five countries and many of those twice.

She pauses, holding her phone in one hand and tapping it against her other palm as she thinks. "Besides, Amsterdam is so . . . trendy."

It is Swapna's closely held belief that to be *on trend* is to be *already late to that trend*. If she senses the zeitgeist warming to the idea of Toruń, Poland, then Toruń's off the docket for the next ten years. There's a literal list pushpinned into a wall by the cubicles (Toruń is not on this list) of Places *R+R* Will Not Cover. Each entry is in her handwriting and dated, and there's something of an underground betting pool on when a city will be freed from the List. There's never so much quiet excitement in the office as those mornings when Swapna marches in, designer laptop bag on her arm, and strides up to the List with a pen already out, ready to cross off one of these banned cities.

Everyone watches with bated breath, wondering which city she's rescuing from *R+R* obscurity, and once she's safely in her office, door shut, whoever's closest to the List will run up to it, read the scratched-out entry, and turn to whisper the name of the city to everyone in editorial. There's usually silent celebration.

When Paris was relinquished from the List last fall, someone broke out champagne and Garrett pulled a red beret out of a drawer in his desk, where he'd apparently been hiding it for just such an occasion. He wore it all day, jerking it off his head every time we heard the click and whine of Swapna's door. He thought he'd gotten away with it too, until she paused beside his desk on her way out for the night and said, "*Au revoir*, Garrett."

His face had gone as bright as the beret, and though I didn't think Swapna had meant it to be anything but funny, he'd never quite recovered his confidence since then.

Having Amsterdam declared "trendy" has his cheeks flushing past beret red straight to beet purple.

Someone else throws out Cozumel. And then there's a vote for Las Vegas, which Swapna briefly considers. "Vegas could be fun." She looks right to me. "Poppy, don't you think Vegas could be fun?"

"It could definitely be fun," I agree.

"Santorini," Garrett says in the voice of a cartoon mouse.

"Santorini is lovely, of course," Swapna says, and Garrett heaves an audible sigh of relief. "But we want something inspired."

She looks at me again. Pointedly. I know why. She wants *me* to write the big feature. Because that's what I came here to do.

My stomach twists. "I'll keep brainstorming and work something up to pitch you on Monday," I suggest.

She nods acceptance. Garrett sags in the chair beside me. I know he and his boyfriend are desperate for a free trip to Santorini. As any travel writer would be. As any human person probably would be.

As I definitely should be.

Don't give up, I want to tell him. *If Swapna wants inspiration, she's not getting it from me.*

I haven't had any of that in a long time.

"I THINK YOU should push for Santorini," Rachel says, swirling her glass of rosé on the mosaic top of the café table. It's a perfectly summery wine, and because of her platform, we got it for free.

Rachel Krohn: style blogger, French bulldog enthusiast, born-and-bred Upper West Sider (but mercifully not the kind who acts like it's so *adorable* that you're from Ohio, or even that Ohio exists—has anyone even *heard* of it?), and professional-grade best friend.

Despite having top-of-the-line appliances, Rachel hand-washes all her dishes, because she finds it soothing, and she does so wearing four-inch heels, because she thinks flat shoes are for horseback riding and gardening, and only if you haven't found any suitable heeled boots.

Rachel was the first friend I made when I moved to New York. She's a social media "influencer" (read: gets paid to wear specific brands of makeup in pictures at her beautiful marbled vanity), and while I'd never had a friendship with a Fellow Internet Person, it turned out to have its perks (read: neither of us has to feel embarrassed when we ask the other to wait while we stage photos of our sandwiches). And while I might've expected not to have much in common with Rachel, it was during our third hangout (at the same wine bar in Dumbo where we're currently sitting) that she admitted she takes all of her photos for the week on Tuesdays, changing outfits and hair in between stops at different parks and restaurants, then spends the rest of the week writing essays and running social media for a few dog rescues.

She fell into this job by way of being photogenic and having a photogenic life and two very photogenic (if constantly in need of medical attention) dogs.

Whereas I set out to build a social media following as a long game to turn travel into a full-time job. Different paths to the same place. I mean, she's still on the Upper West Side and I'm on the Lower East Side, but we're both living advertisements.

I take a mouthful of the sparkling wine and swish it around as I turn over her words. I haven't been to Santorini, and somewhere in my parents' overcrowded house, in a Tupperware box full of things that have absolutely nothing in common, there's a list of dream destinations I made in college, with Santorini near the top. Those clean white lines and great swaths of glittering blue sea were about as far from my cluttered bi-level in Ohio as I could imagine.

"I can't," I finally tell her. "Garrett would spontaneously combust if he pitched Santorini and, once I got on board, Swapna approved it for me."

"I don't get it," Rachel says. "How hard can it be to pick a vacation, Pop? It's not like you've been saving your pennies. Pick a place. Go. Then pick another one. That's what you do."

"It's not that simple."

"Yeah, yeah." Rachel waves a hand. "I know, your boss wants an 'inspired' vacation. But when you show up somewhere beautiful, with the *R+R* credit card, inspiration will appear. There is literally no one on earth better equipped to have a magical vacation than a travel journalist with a big-ass media conglomerate's checkbook. If you can't have an inspired trip, then how the hell do you expect the rest of the world to?"

I shrug, breaking a piece of cheese off of the charcuterie board. "Maybe that's the point."

She arches one dark eyebrow. "What's the point?"

"Exactly!" I say, and she gives me a look of dry disgust.

"Don't be cute and whimsical," she says flatly. To Rachel Krohn, *cute and whimsical* is nearly as bad as *trendy* is for Swapna Bakshi-Highsmith. Despite the softly hazy aesthetic of Rachel's hair, makeup, clothes, apartment, and social media, she's a deeply pragmatic person. For her, life in the public eye is a job like any other, one she's kept because it pays the bills (at least when it comes to cheese, wine, makeup, clothes, and anything else businesses choose to ship her), *not* because she relishes the kind of manufactured semifame that comes with the territory. At the end of every month, she does a post with the worst, unedited outtakes from her photo shoots, the caption reading: *THIS IS A FEED OF CURATED IMAGERY MEANT TO MAKE YOU PINE FOR A LIFE THAT DOES NOT EXIST. I GET PAID FOR THIS.*

Yes, she went to art school.

And somehow, this kind of pseudo performance art has done nothing to curb her popularity. Whenever I'm in town for the last day of the month, I try to schedule a wine date so I can watch her check her notifications and roll her eyes as the new likes and follows pour in. Every once in a while she'll stifle a shriek and say, "Listen to this! 'Rachel Krohn is so brave and real. I want her to be my mom.' I'm *telling* them they don't know me, and they still don't get it!"

She has no patience for rose-colored glasses and even less for melancholy.

"I'm not being cute," I promise her, "and I'm definitely not being whimsical."

The arch of her eyebrow deepens. "Are you sure? Because you're prone to both, babe."

I roll my eyes. "You just mean I'm short and wear bright colors."

"No, you're *tiny*," she corrects me, "and wear loud patterns. Your style is, like, 1960s Parisian bread maker's daughter bicycling through her village at dawn, shouting *Bonjour, le monde* whilst doling out baguettes."

"Anyway," I say, pulling us back on track, "what I mean is, *what's the point* of taking this ridiculously expensive vacation, then writing all about it for the forty-two people in the world who can afford the time and money to re-create it?"

Her brows settle into a flat line as she thinks. "Well, first of all, I don't assume most people use *R+R* articles as an itinerary, Pop. You give them a hundred places to check out, and they choose three. And secondly, people want to see idyllic vacations in vacation magazines. They buy them to daydream, not to plan." Even as she's being Pragmatic Rachel, cynical Art School Rachel is creeping in, giving her words an edge. Art School Rachel is something of an old man screaming at the sky, a stepdad at the dinner table, saying, "Why don't you unplug for a while, kids?" while holding out a bowl to collect everyone's phones.

I love Art School Rachel and her Principles, but I'm also unnerved by their sudden appearance on this sidewalk patio. Because right now words are bubbling up that I haven't said aloud yet. Sensitive, secret thoughts that never fully exposed themselves to me in the many hours I've spent lying on the still-like-new sofa of my uncozy, unlived-in apartment during the downtime between trips.

"What's the point?" I say again, frustrated. "I mean, don't you ever feel like that? Like, I worked so hard, did every single thing right—"

"Well, not *everything*," she says. "You did drop out of college, babe."

"—so I could get my dream job. And I actually got it. I work at one of the top travel magazines! I have a nice apartment! And I can take cabs without worrying too much about what that money *should* go to, and despite all of that"—I take a shaky breath, unsure of the words I'm about to force out even as the full weight of them hits me like a sandbag—"I'm not happy."

Rachel's face softens. She sets her hand on mine but stays silent, holding space for me to go on. It takes me a while to make myself. I feel like such an ungrateful jerk for even having these thoughts, let alone admitting them aloud.

"It's all pretty much how I pictured it," I finally say. "The parties, the layovers in international airports, the cocktails on the jet, and the beaches and the boats and the vineyards. And it all looks how it should, but it feels different than I imagined it. Honestly, I think it feels different than it used to. I used to bounce off the walls for weeks before a trip, you know? And when I got to the airport, I'd feel like—like my blood was humming. Like the air was just vibrating with possibility around me. I don't know. I'm not sure what's changed. Maybe I have."

She brushes a dark curl behind her ear and shrugs. "You *wanted* it, Poppy. You didn't have it, and you wanted it. You were hungry."

Instantly, I know she's right. She's seen right through the word vomit to the center of things. "Isn't that ridiculous?" I groan-laugh. "My life turned out how I hoped it would, and now I just miss *wanting* something."

Shaking with the weight of it. Humming with the potential. Staring at the ceiling of my crappy, pre-*R+R* fifth-floor walk-up, after a double shift serving drinks at the Garden, and daydreaming about the future. The places I'd go, the people I'd meet—who I'd *become.* What is there left to want when you've got your dream apartment, your dream boss, and your dream job (which negates any anxiety over your dream apartment's obscenely high rent, because you spend most of your time eating at Michelin-starred restaurants on the company's dime anyway)?

Rachel drains her glass and globs some Brie onto a cracker, nodding knowingly. "Millennial ennui."

"Is that a thing?" I ask.

"Not yet, but if you repeat it three times, there'll be a *Slate* think piece on it by tonight."

I throw a handful of salt over my shoulder as if to ward off such evil, and Rachel snorts as she pours us each a fresh glass.

"I thought the whole thing about millennials was that we don't get what we want. The houses, the jobs, the financial freedom. We just go to school forever, then bartend 'til we die."

"Yeah," she says, "but you dropped out of college and went after what you want. So here we are."

"I don't want to have millennial ennui," I say. "It makes me feel like an asshole to not just be content with my amazing life."

Rachel snorts again. "Contentment is a lie invented by capitalism," Art School Rachel says, but maybe she has a point. Usually, she does. "Think about it. All those pictures I post? They're selling something. A lifestyle. People look at those pictures and think, 'If only I had those Sonia Rykiel heels, that gorgeous apartment with the French oak herringbone floors, *then* I'd be happy. I'd swan about, watering my houseplants and lighting my endless supply of Jo Malone candles, and I'd feel my life in perfect harmony. I'd finally *love* my home. I'd *relish* my days on this planet.'"

"You sell it well, Rach," I say. "You seem pretty happy."

"Damn right I am," she says. "But I'm not content, and you know why?" She plucks her phone off the table, flips to a specific picture she has in mind, and holds it up. A shot of her reclined on her velvet sofa, laden in bulldogs with matching scars from their matching lifesaving snout surgeries. She's dressed in SpongeBob SquarePants pajamas and isn't wearing a lick of makeup.

"Because every day there are back-alley puppy mills breeding more of these little guys! Getting the same poor dogs pregnant over and over again, producing litter upon litter of puppies with genetic mutations that make life hard and painful. Not to mention all the pit bulls doubled up in kennels, rotting in puppy prison!"

"Are you saying I should get a dog?" I say. "Because the whole travel-journalist thing kind of precludes pet ownership." Truthfully, even if it didn't, I'm not sure I could handle a pet. I *love* dogs, but I also grew up in a house teeming with them. With pets come fur and barking and chaos. For a fairly chaotic person, that's a slippery slope. If I went to a shelter to pick up a foster dog, there's no guarantee I wouldn't come home having adopted six of them and a wild coyote.

"I'm saying," Rachel replies, "that purpose matters more than contentment. You had a ton of career goals, which gave you purpose. One by one, you met them. *Et voilà*: no purpose."

"So I need new goals."

She nods emphatically. "I read this article about it. Apparently the completion of long-term goals often leads to depression. It's the journey, not the destination, babe, and whatever the fuck else those throw pillows say."

Her face softens again, becomes the ethereal thing of her most-liked photographs. "You know, my therapist says—"

"Your mom," I say.

"She was being a therapist when she said this," Rachel argues, by which I know she means, Sandra Krohn was being decidedly Dr. Sandra Krohn, in the same way that Rachel is sometimes decidedly Art School Rachel, not that Rachel was actually in a therapy session. Beg as Rachel might, her mother refuses to treat Rachel as a patient. Rachel, however, refuses to see anyone else, and so they remain at an impasse.

"Anyway," Rachel continues, "she told me that sometimes, when you lose your happiness, it's best to look for it the same way you'd look for anything else."

"By groaning and hurling couch cushions around?" I guess.

"By retracing your steps," Rachel says. "So, Poppy, all you have to do is think back and ask yourself, when was the last time you were truly happy?"

The problem is, I don't have to think back. Not at all.

I know right away when I was last truly happy.

Two years ago, in Croatia, with Alex Nilsen.

But there's no finding my way back to that, because we haven't spoken since.

"Just think about it, will you?" Rachel says. "Dr. Krohn is always right."

"Yeah," I say. "I'll think about it."

2

This Summer

DO THINK ABOUT it.

The whole subway ride home. The four-block walk after that.
Through a hot shower, a hair mask, and a face mask, and several
hours of lying on my stiff new sofa.

I don't spend enough time here to have transformed it into
a home, and besides, I'm the product of a cheapskate father and a
sentimental mother, which means I grew up in a house filled to the
brim with junk. Mom kept broken teacups my brothers and I had
given her as kids, and Dad parked our old cars in the front yard just
in case he ever learned to fix them. I still have no idea what would
be considered a *reasonable* amount of bric-a-brac in a house, but I
know how people generally react to my childhood home and figure
it's safer to err on the side of minimalism rather than hoarding.

Aside from an unwieldy collection of vintage clothes (first rule
of the Wright family: never buy anything new if you can get it used
for a fraction of the price), there isn't much else in my apartment to
fixate on. So I'm just staring at my ceiling, and thinking.

And the more I think about the trips Alex and I used to take together, the more I long for them. But not in the fun, daydreamy, energetic way I used to *long* to see Tokyo in cherry blossom season, or the Fasnacht festivals of Switzerland, with their masked parades and whip-wielding jesters dancing down the candy-colored streets.

What I'm feeling now is more of an ache, a sadness.

It's worse than the *blah*-ness of not wanting anything much from life. It's wanting something I can't convince myself is even a possibility.

Not after two years of silence.

Okay, not *silence*. He still sends me a text on my birthday. I still send him one on his. Both of us send replies that say "Thank you" or "How are you doing?" but those words never seem to lead much further.

After everything happened between us, I used to tell myself it would just take time for him to get over it, that things would inevitably go back to normal and we'd be best friends again. Maybe we'd even laugh about this time apart.

But days passed, phones were turned off and on in case messages were getting lost, and after a full month, I even stopped jumping every time my text alert sounded.

Our lives went on, without each other in them. The new and strange became the familiar, the seemingly unchangeable, and now here I am, on a Friday night, staring at nothing.

I push off the sofa and grab my laptop from the coffee table, stepping out onto my tiny balcony. I plop into the lone chair that fits out here and prop my feet on the guardrail, still warm from the sun despite the heavy cloak of night. Down below, the bells chime over the door to the bodega on the corner, people walk home from long nights out, and a couple of cabs idle outside my favorite neighborhood bar, Good Boy Bar (a place that owes its success not to its drinks but to the fact that it allows dogs inside; this is how I survive my petless existence).

I open my computer and bat a moth away from the fluorescent glow of its screen as I pull up my old blog. The blog itself *R+R* couldn't care less about—I mean, they evaluated my writing samples from it before I got the job, but they don't care whether I maintain it. It's the social media influence they want to keep cashing in on, not the modest but devoted readership I built with my posts on shoestring-budget travel.

Rest + Relaxation magazine doesn't specialize in shoestring-budget travel. And though I'd planned to keep up *Pop Around the World* in addition to my magazine work, my entries petered off not long after the Croatia trip.

I scroll back to my post about that one and open it. I was already working at *R+R* by then, which meant every luxurious second of the trip was paid for. It was supposed to be the best one we'd ever taken, and small slivers of it *were*.

But rereading my post—even with every hint of Alex and what happened scrubbed out of it—it's obvious how miserable I was when I got home. I scroll further back, scouring for every post about the Summer Trip. That was what we called it, when we texted about it throughout the year, usually long before we'd nailed down where we would go or how we'd afford it.

The Summer Trip.

As in, *School is killing me—I just want the Summer Trip to be here already*, and *Pitch for our Summer Trip Uniform*, with an attached screenshot of a T-shirt that says YEP, THEY'RE REAL on the chest, or a pair of overall shorts so short as to be, essentially, a denim thong.

A hot breeze blows the smell of garbage and dollar-slice pizza up off the street, ruffling my hair. I twist it into a knot at the base of my neck, then shut my computer and pull out my phone so fast you'd think I actually planned to use it.

You can't. It's too weird, I think.

But I'm already pulling up Alex's number, still there at the top of my favorites list, where optimism kept him saved until so much time had passed that the possibility of deleting him now seems like a tragic last step I can't bear to take.

My thumb hovers over the keyboard.

Been thinking about you, I type. I stare at it for a minute, then backspace to the beginning.

Any chance you're looking to get out of town? I write. That seems good. It's clear what I'm asking, but pretty casual, with an easy out. But the longer I study the words, the weirder I feel about being so casual. About pretending nothing happened and the two of us are still close friends who can plan a trip in such an informal forum as a postmidnight text.

I delete the message, take a deep breath, and type again: Hey.

"Hey?" I snap, annoyed with myself. Down on the sidewalk, a man jumps in surprise at the sound of my voice, then looks up at my balcony, decides I'm not talking to him, and hurries off.

There's no way I'm going to send a message to Alex Nilsen that just says *Hey*.

But then I go to highlight and delete the word, and something horrible happens.

I accidentally hit send.

The message *whooshes* out.

"Shit, shit, shit!" I hiss, shaking my phone like maybe I can make it spit the text back up before that measly word starts to digest. "No, no, n—"

Chime.

I freeze. Mouth open. Heart racing. Stomach twisting until my intestines feel like rotini noodles.

A new message, the name bolded at the top: **ALEXANDER THE GREATEST**.

One word.

Hey.

I'm so stunned that I almost just text *Hey* back, like my whole first message never happened, like he just *hey*'d me out of the blue. But of course he didn't—he's not that guy. I'm that guy.

And because I'm that guy, who sends the worst text message in the world, I've now gotten a reply that gives me no natural inroad to a conversation.

What do I say?

Does *How are you?* sound too serious? Does that make it seem like I'm expecting him to say, *Well, Poppy, I've missed you. I've missed you BAD.*

Maybe something more innocuous, like *What's up?*

But again I feel like the weirdest thing I could do right now is willfully ignore that it *is* weird to be texting him after all this time.

I'm sorry I sent you a text message that said hey, I write out. I erase it, try for funny: You're probably wondering why I've brought you here.

Not funny, but I'm standing at the edge of my tiny balcony, actually shivering with nervous anticipation and terrified to wait too long to respond. I send the message and start to pace. Only, because the balcony's so tiny and the chair takes up half of it, I'm basically just spinning like a top, a tail of moths chasing the blurry light of my phone.

It chimes again, and I snap down into the chair and open the message.

Is this about the disappearing sandwiches in the break room?

A moment later, a second message comes in.

Because I didn't take those. Unless there's a security camera in there. In which case, I'm sorry.

A smile blooms across my face, a flood of warmth melting the anxious knot in my chest. There was a brief period of time when Alex was convinced he was going to get fired from his teaching job. After waking up late and missing breakfast, he'd had a doctor's appointment over lunch. He hadn't had time to grab food after, so he'd gone to the teachers' lounge, hoping it was someone's birthday, that there might be donuts or stale muffins he could pick over.

But it was the first Monday of the month, and an American History teacher named Ms. Delallo, a woman Alex secretly considered his workplace nemesis, insisted on cleaning out the fridge and counter space on the last Friday of every month—and then making a big deal about it like she expected to be thanked, though oftentimes her coworkers lost a couple of perfectly good frozen lunches in the process.

Anyway, the only thing left in the fridge was a tuna salad sandwich. "Delallo's calling card," Alex had joked when he recounted the story to me later.

He'd eaten the sandwich as an act of defiance (and hunger). Then spent three weeks convinced someone was going to find out and he'd lose his job. It's not like it was his dream to teach high school literature, but the job paid okay, had good benefits, and was in our hometown back in Ohio, which—though to me, a definite negative—meant he got to be close to two of his three younger brothers and the children they'd started churning out.

Besides, the kind of university job Alex *really* wanted just didn't come up very often these days. He couldn't afford to lose his teaching job, and luckily he hadn't.

SandwichES? PLURAL? I type back now. Please, please, please tell me you have become a full-fledged hoagie thief.

Delallo's not a hoagie fan, Alex says. Lately she's been hot for Reubens.

And how many of these Reubens have you stolen? I ask.

Assuming the NSA is reading this, none, he says.

You're a high school English teacher in Ohio; of course they're reading.

He sends back a sad face. Are you saying I'm not important enough for the U.S. government to monitor?

I know he's joking, but here's the thing about Alex Nilsen. Despite being tall, fairly broad, addicted to daily exercise and healthy eating and general self-control, he also has this hurt puppy face. Or at least the ability to summon it. His eyes are always a little sleepy, the creases beneath them a constant indication that he doesn't love sleep the way I do. His mouth is full with an exaggerated, slightly uneven cupid's bow, and all of this combined with his straight, messy hair—the one part of his appearance he pays no attention to—gives his face a boyishness that, when wielded properly, can trigger some biological impulse in me to protect him at all costs.

Seeing his sleepy eyes go big and watery and his full mouth open into a soft O is like hearing a puppy whimpering.

When other people send the frowny emoji, I read it as mild disappointment.

When Alex uses it, I know it's the digital equivalent of him pulling Sad Puppy Face to tease me. Sometimes, when we were drunk, sitting at a table and trying to make it through a game of chess or Scrabble that I was winning, he'd deploy the face until I was hysterical, caught between laughing and crying, falling out of my chair, trying to make him stop or at least cover his face.

Of course you're important, I type. If the NSA knew the powers of Sad Puppy Face, you'd be in a lab getting cloned right now.

Alex types for a minute, stops, types again. I wait a few more seconds.

Is this it? The message he finally stops responding to? Some big confrontation? Or, knowing him, I guess it's more likely to be an inoffensive *Nice talking but I'm headed to bed. Sleep well.*

Ding!

A laugh breaks out of me, the force of it like an egg cracking in my chest, spilling out warmth to coat my nerves.

It's a photo. A blurry, ineffectual selfie of Alex, under a street-light, making the infamous face. As with nearly every picture he's ever taken, it's shot slightly from below, elongating his head so it comes to a point. I throw my head back with another laugh, half-giddy.

You bastard! I type. It's one a.m. and now you've got me headed to the pound to save some lives.

Yeah right, he says. You'd never get a dog.

Something like hurt pinches low in my stomach. Despite being the cleanest, most particular, most organized man I know, Alex loves animals, and I'm fairly sure he sees my inability to commit to one as a personal defect.

I look up at the lone dehydrated succulent in the corner of the balcony. Shaking my head, I type out another message: How's Flannery O'Connor?

Dead, Alex writes back.

The cat, not the author! I say.

Also dead, he replies.

My heart stutters. As much as I loathed that cat (no more or less than she loathed me), Alex adored her. The fact that he didn't tell me she died slices through me in one clean cut, a guillotine blade from head to foot.

Alex, I'm so sorry, I write. God, I'm sorry. I know how much you loved her. That cat had an amazing life.

He writes only, Thanks.

I stare at the word for a long time, unsure where to go from there. Four minutes pass, then five, then it's been ten.

I should get to bed now, he says finally. Sleep well, Poppy.

Yeah, I write. You too.

I sit on the balcony until all the warmth has drained out of me.

3

Twelve Summers Ago

THE FIRST NIGHT of orientation at the University of Chicago, I spot him. He's dressed in khaki pants and a U of Chicago T-shirt, despite having been at this school for all of ten hours. He looks nothing like the sort of artistic intelligentsia I imagined befriending when I chose a school in the city. But I'm here alone (my new roommate, it turns out, followed her older sister and some friends to college, and she ducked out of O-Week events ASAP), and he's alone too, so I walk up to him, tip my drink toward his shirt, and say, "So, do you go to University of Chicago?"

He stares at me blankly.

I stammer out that it was a joke.

He stammers something about spilling on his shirt and a last-minute outfit change. His cheeks go pink, and mine do too, from secondhand embarrassment.

And then his eyes dip down me, sizing me up, and his face changes. I'm wearing a neon orange and pink floral jumpsuit from the early seventies, and he reacts to this fact as if I'm also holding a poster that says FUCK KHAKIS on it.

I ask him where he's from, because I'm not sure what else to say to a stranger with whom I have no shared context apart from a few hours of confusing campus tours, a couple of the same boring panels on life in the city, and the fact that we hate each other's clothes.

"Ohio," he answers, "a town called West Linfield."

"No shit!" I say, stunned. "I'm from East Linfield."

And he brightens a little, like this is good news, and I'm not sure why, because having the fact of the Linfields in common is sort of like having had the same cold: not the worst thing in the world, but nothing to high-five over.

"I'm Poppy," I tell him.

"Alex," he says, and shakes my hand.

When you imagine a new best friend for yourself, you never name him Alex. You also probably don't imagine him dressing like some kind of teenage librarian, or barely looking you in the eyes, or always speaking just a little bit under his breath.

I decide that if I'd looked at him for five more minutes before crossing the globe-light-strewn lawn to talk, I would've been able to guess both his name and that he was from West Linfield, because these two facts match with his khakis and U of Chicago shirt.

I'm sure that the longer we talk, the more violently boring he'll become, but we're here, and we're alone, so why not be sure?

"So what are you here for?" I ask.

His brow furrows. "Here for?"

"Yeah, you know," I say, "like, I'm here to meet a wealthy oil baron in need of a much younger second wife."

That blank stare again.

"What are you *studying*?" I clarify.

"Oh," he says. "I'm not sure. Prelaw, maybe. Or literature. What about you?"

"Not sure yet." I lift my plastic cup. "I mostly came for the punch. And to not live in southern Ohio."

Over the next painful fifteen minutes, I learn he's here on academic scholarships, and he learns that I'm here on loans. I tell him that I'm the youngest of three, and the only girl. He tells me he's the oldest of four boys. He asks if I've seen the gym yet, to which my genuine reaction is "*Why?*" and we both go back to shifting awkwardly on our feet in silence.

He is tall, quiet, and eager to see the library.

I'm short, loud, and hoping someone comes by and invites us to a real party.

By the time we part ways, I'm fairly confident we'll never speak again.

Apparently, he feels the same way.

Instead of *goodbye* or *see you around* or *should we swap numbers*, he just says, "Good luck with freshman year, Poppy."

4

This Summer

"D ID YOU THINK about it?" Rachel asks. She's pounding away on the stationary bike beside me, sweat droplets flying off her, though her breathing is even, as if we were moseying through Sephora. As usual, we found two bikes at the back of spin class, where we can keep up a conversation without being scolded for distracting other cyclists.

"Think about what?" I pant back.

"What makes you happy." She lifts herself to pedal faster at the teacher's command. For my part, I'm basically slumped over the handlebars, forcing my feet down like I'm biking through molasses. I hate exercise; I love the feeling of having exercised.

"Silence," I gasp, heart throbbing. "Makes. Me. Happy."

"And?" she prompts.

"Those raspberry vanilla cream bars from Trader Joe's," I get out.

"And?"

"*Sometimes* you do!" I'm trying to sound cutting. The panting undermines it.

"And rest!" the instructor screams into her microphone; thirty-some gasps of relief go up around the room. People fall slack at bikes or slide off them into a puddle on the floor, but Rachel dismounts like an Olympic gymnast finishing her floor routine. She hands me her water bottle, and I follow her into the locker room, then out into the blazing light of midday.

"I won't pry it out of you," she says. "Maybe it's private, what makes you happy."

"It's Alex," I blurt out.

She stops walking, gripping my arm so that I'm held captive, the foot traffic ballooning around us on the sidewalk. "What."

"Not like that," I say. "Our summer trips. Nothing has ever topped those."

Nothing.

Even if I ever get married or have a baby, I expect the Best Day of My Life to still be something of a toss-up between that and the time Alex and I went hiking in the mist-ridden redwoods. As we were pulling into the park, it started to pour, and the trails cleared out. We had the forest to ourselves, and we slipped a bottle of wine into our backpack and set off.

When we were sure we were alone, we popped the cork and passed the bottle back and forth, drinking as we trudged through the stillness of the woods.

I wish we could sleep here, I remember him saying. *Like just lie down and nap.*

And then we came to one of those big, hollowed-out trunks along the trail, the kind that's cracked open to form a woody cave, its two sides like giant cupped palms.

We slipped inside and curled up on the dry, needly earth. We didn't nap, but we rested. Like, instead of absorbing energy through sleep, we drew it into our bodies through the centuries of sunshine and rain that had cooperated to grow this massive tree protecting us.

"Well, you obviously have to call him," Rachel says, effectively lassoing me and yanking me out of the memory. "I've never understood why you didn't just confront him about everything. Seems silly to lose such an important friendship over one fight."

I shake my head. "I already texted him. He's not looking to rekindle our friendship, and he *definitely* doesn't want to go on a spontaneous vacation with me." I fall into step again beside her, jogging my gym bag higher on my sweaty shoulder. "Maybe you should come with me. That'd be fun, wouldn't it? We haven't gone anywhere together in months."

"You know I get anxious when I leave New York," Rachel says.

"And what would your therapist say about that?" I tease.

"She'd say, 'What do they have in Paris that they don't have in Manhattan, sweetie?'"

"Um, the Eiffel Tower?" I say.

"She gets anxious when I leave New York too," Rachel says. "New Jersey is about as far as the umbilical cord stretches for us. Now let's get some juice. That cheese board has basically formed a cork in my butthole and everything's just piling up behind it."

AT TEN THIRTY on Sunday night, I'm sitting in bed, my soft pink duvet piled up on my feet and my laptop burning against my thighs. Half a dozen windows sit open in my web browser, and in my notes app I've started a list of possible destinations that only goes to three.

1. Newfoundland
2. Austria
3. Costa Rica

I've just started compiling notes on the major cities and natural landmarks of each when my phone buzzes on my side table. Rachel's been texting me, swearing off dairy, all day, but when I reach for my phone, the top of the message alert reads **ALEXANDER THE GREATEST**.

All at once, that giddy feeling is back, swelling so fast in me I feel like my body might pop.

It's a picture message, and when I tap it open, I find a shot of my hilariously bad senior photo, complete with the quote I chose for them to print beneath it: *BYE.*

Ohhhhhhh nooooo, I type through laughter, shoving my laptop aside and flopping down on my back. Where did you find this?

East Linfield library, Alex says. I was setting up my classroom and I remembered they have yearbooks.

You have defied my trust, I joke. I'm texting your brothers for baby pictures right now.

Right away, he sends back that same Sad Puppy shot from Friday, his face blurry and washed out, the hazy orange glow of a streetlight visible over his shoulder. Mean, he writes.

Is that a stock photo that you keep saved for occasions such as these? I ask.

No, he says. Took it Friday.

You were out pretty late for Linfield, I say. What's open apart from Frisch's Big Boy at that hour?

It turns out that once you're 21 there's plenty to do after dark in Linfield, he says. I was at Birdies.

Birdies, the golf-themed dive bar "and grill" across the street from my high school.

Birdies? I say. Ew, that's where all the teachers drink!

Alex fires off another Sad Puppy Face shot, but at least this one's new: him in a soft gray T-shirt, his hair sticking up all over the place and a plain wooden headboard visible behind him.

He's sitting in bed too. Texting me. And over the weekend, when he was working on his classroom, he not only thought about me, but took the time to go find my old yearbook shot.

I'm grinning hugely now, and buzzing too. It's surreal how much this feels like the early days of our friendship, when every new text seemed so sparkly and funny and perfect, when every quick phone call accidentally turned into an hour and a half of talking nonstop, even when we'd seen each other a few days before. I remember how, during one of the first of these—before I would've considered him my *best friend*—I had to ask him if I could call him back in a second so I could go pee. When we got back on the phone, we talked another hour and then he asked me the same thing.

By then it seemed silly to get off the phone just to avoid hearing pee hitting a toilet bowl, so I told him he could stay on the phone if he wanted. He did *not* take me up on it, then or ever, though from then on, I often peed mid–phone call. With his permission, of course.

Now I'm doing this humiliating thing, touching the picture of his face like I can somehow feel the essence of him that way, like it will bring him closer to me than he has been for two years. There's no one to see it, and still I feel embarrassed.

Kidding! I reply. Next time I'm home, we should go get sloppy with Mrs. Lautzenheiser.

I send it without thinking, and almost immediately my mouth goes dry at the sight of the words on-screen.

Next time I'm home.

We.

Was that too far? Suggesting we should hang out?

If it was, he doesn't let on. He just writes back, Lautzenheiser's sober now. She's also Buddhist.

But now that I haven't gotten a direct reply to the suggestion, positive or negative, I feel an intense desire to push the matter. Then I guess we'll have to go get enlightened with her instead, I write.

Alex types for way too long, and the whole time I'm crossing my fingers, trying to forcefully will away any tension.

Oh, god.

I thought I'd been doing fine, that I'd gotten over our friend breakup, but the more we talk, the more I miss him.

My phone vibrates in my hand. Two words: Guess so.

It's noncommittal, but it's something.

And now I'm on a high. From the yearbook photos, from the selfies, from the idea of Alex sitting up in bed texting me out of the blue. Maybe it's pushing too hard or asking too much, but I can't help myself.

For two years, I've wanted to ask Alex to give our friendship another shot, and I've been so afraid of the answer that I've never gotten the question out. But not asking hasn't brought us back together either, and I miss him, and I miss how we were together, and I miss the Summer Trip, and finally, I know that there *is* one thing in my life that I still really want, and there's only one way to find out if I can have it.

Any chance you're free until school starts? I type out, shaking so much my teeth have started to chatter. I'm thinking about taking a trip.

I stare at the words for the span of three deep breaths, and then I hit send.

5

Eleven Summers Ago

OCCASIONALLY, I SEE Alex Nilsen around on campus, but we don't speak again until the day after freshman year ends.

It was my roommate, Bonnie, who set the whole thing up. When she told me she had a friend from southern Ohio looking for someone to carpool home with, it didn't occur to me that it might be that same boy from Linfield I'd met at orientation.

Mostly because I'd managed to learn basically nothing about Bonnie in the last nine months of her stopping by the dorm to shower and change her clothes before heading back to her sister's apartment. Frankly, I wasn't sure how she even knew I was from Ohio.

I'd made friends with the other girls from my floor—ate with them, watched movies with them, went to parties with them—but Bonnie existed outside our all-freshman squad-of-necessity. The idea that her friend could be Alex-from-Linfield didn't even cross my mind when she gave me his name and number to coordinate our meetup. But when I come downstairs to find him waiting by his station wagon at the agreed-upon time, it's obvious from his steady, uncomfortable expression that he was expecting me.

He's wearing the same shirt he had on the night I met him, or else he's bought enough duplicates that he can wear them interchangeably. I call out across the street, "It's you."

He ducks his head, flushes. "Yep." Without another word, he comes toward me and takes the hampers and one of the duffle bags from my arms, loading them into his back seat.

The first twenty-five minutes of our drive are awkward and silent. Worst of all, we barely make any progress through the crush of city traffic.

"Do you have an aux cable?" I ask, digging through the center console.

His eyes dart toward me, his mouth shaping into a grimace. "Why?"

"Because I want to see if I can jump rope while wearing a seat belt," I huff, restacking the packets of sanitary wipes and hand sanitizers I've upended in my search. "Why do you think? So we can listen to music."

Alex's shoulders lift, like he's a turtle retracting into his shell. "While we're stuck in traffic?"

"Um," I say. "Yes?"

His shoulders hitch higher. "There's a lot going on right now."

"We're barely moving," I point out.

"I know." He winces. "But it's hard to focus. And there's all the honking, and—"

"Got it. No music." I slump back in my seat, return to staring out the window. Alex makes a self-conscious throat-clearing sound, like he wants to say something.

I turn expectantly toward him. "Yes?"

"Would you mind . . . not doing that?" He tips his chin toward my window, and I realize I'm drumming my fingers against it. I draw my hands into my lap, then catch myself tapping my feet.

"I'm not used to silence!" I say, defensive, when he looks at me.

It's the understatement of the century. I grew up in a house with three big dogs, a cat with the lungs of an opera singer, two brothers who played the trumpet, and parents who found the background noise of the Home Shopping Network "soothing."

I'd adjusted to the quiet of my Bonnie-less dorm room quickly, but this—sitting in silence in traffic with someone I barely know—feels wrong.

"Shouldn't we get to know each other or something?" I ask.

"I just need to focus on the road," he says, the corners of his mouth tense.

"Fine."

Alex sighs as, ahead, the source of the congestion appears: a fender bender. Both cars involved have already pulled onto the shoulder, but traffic's still bottlenecking here.

"Of course," he says, "people just slowing down to stare." He pops open the center console and digs around until he finds the aux cable. "Here," he says. "You pick."

I raise an eyebrow. "Are you sure? You might regret it."

His brow furrows. "Why would I regret it?"

I glance into the back seat of his faux-wood-sided station wagon. His stuff is neatly stacked in labeled boxes, mine piled in dirty laundry bags around it. The car is ancient yet spotless. Somehow it smells exactly like he does, a soft cedar-and-musk scent.

"You just seem like maybe you're a fan of . . . control," I point out. "And I'm not sure I have the kind of music you like. There's no Chopin on this thing."

The furrow of his brow deepens. His mouth twists into a frown. "Maybe I'm not as uptight as you think I am."

"Really?" I say. "So you won't mind if I put on Mariah Carey's 'All I Want for Christmas Is You'?"

"It's May," he says.

"I'll consider my question answered," I say.

"That's unfair," he says. "What kind of a barbarian listens to Christmas music in May?"

"And if it were November tenth," I say, "what about then?"

Alex's mouth presses closed. He tugs at the stick-straight hair at the crown of his head, and a rush of static leaves it floating even after his hand drops to the steering wheel. He really honors the whole ten-and-two wheel-hand-positioning thing, I've noticed, and despite being a massive sloucher when he's standing, he has upheld his rigidly good posture as long as we've been in the car, shoulder tension notwithstanding.

"Fine," he says. "I don't like Christmas music. Don't put that on, and we should be fine."

I plug my phone in, turn on the stereo, and scroll to David Bowie's "Young Americans." Within seconds, he visibly grimaces.

"What?" I say.

"Nothing," he insists.

"You just twitched like the marionette controlling you fell asleep."

He squints at me. "What does *that* mean?"

"You hate this song," I accuse.

"I do not," he says unconvincingly.

"You hate David Bowie."

"Not at all!" he says. "It's not David Bowie."

"Then what is it?" I demand.

An exhale hisses out of him. "Saxophone."

"Saxophone," I repeat.

"Yeah," he says. "I just . . . really hate the saxophone. Any song with a saxophone on it is instantly ruined."

"Someone should tell Kenny G," I say.

"Name one song that was improved by a saxophone," Alex challenges.

"I'll have to consult the notepad where I keep track of every song that has saxophone."

"No song," he says.

"I bet you're fun at parties," I say.

"I'm fine at parties," he says.

"Just not middle school band concerts," I say.

He glances sidelong at me. "You're really a saxophone apologist?"

"No, but I'm willing to pretend, if you're not finished ranting. What else do you hate?"

"Nothing," he says. "Just Christmas music and saxophone. And covers."

"Covers?" I say. "Like . . . book covers?"

"Covers of songs," he explains.

I burst out laughing. "You hate covers of songs?"

"Vehemently," he says.

"Alex. That's like saying you hate vegetables. It's too vague. It makes no sense."

"It makes perfect sense," he insists. "If it's a good cover, that sticks to the basic arrangement of the original song, it's like, *why?* And if it sounds nothing like the original, then it's like, *why the hell?*"

"Oh my god," I say. "You're such an old man screaming at the sky."

He frowns at me. "Oh, and you just like everything?"

"Pretty much," I say. "Yes, I tend to like things."

"I like things too," he says.

"Like what, model trains and biographies of Abraham Lincoln?" I guess.

"I certainly have no aversion to either," he says. "Why, are those things you hate?"

"I told you," I said. "I like things. I'm very easy to please."

"Meaning?"

"Meaning . . ." I think for a second. "Okay, so, growing up, Parker and Prince—my brothers—and I would ride our bikes up to the movie theater, without even checking what was playing."

"You have a brother named *Prince*?" Alex asks, brow lifting.

"That's not the point," I say.

"Is it a nickname?" he says.

"No," I answer. "He was named after Prince. Mom was a huge fan of *Purple Rain*."

"And who's Parker named after?"

"No one," I answer. "They just liked the name. But again, not the point."

"All your names start with *P*," he says. "What are your parents' names?"

"Wanda and Jimmy," I say.

"So not *P* names," Alex clarifies.

"No, not *P* names," I say. "They just had Prince and then Parker, and I guess they were on a roll. But again, that's not the point."

"Sorry, go on," Alex says.

"So we'd bike to the theater and we'd just each buy a ticket to something playing in the next half hour, and we'd all go see something different."

Now his brow furrows. "Because?"

"That's also not the point."

"Well, I'm not going to just *not* ask why you'd go see a movie you didn't even want to see, by yourself."

I huff. "It was for a game."

"A game?"

"Shark Jumping," I explain hastily. "It was basically Two Truths and a Lie except we'd just take turns describing the movies we'd seen from start to finish, and if the movie jumped the shark at some point, just took a totally ridiculous turn, you were supposed to tell how it actually happened. But if it didn't, you were supposed to lie about what happened. Then you had to guess if it was a real plot point or a made-up one, and if you guessed they were lying and you were right, you won five bucks." It was more my brothers' thing; they just let me tag along.

Alex stares at me for a second. My cheeks heat. I'm not sure why I told him about Shark Jumping. It's the kind of Wright family tradition I don't usually bother sharing with people who won't get it, but I guess I have so little skin in this game that the idea of Alex Nilsen staring blankly at me or mocking my brothers' favorite game doesn't faze me.

"Anyway," I go on, "that's not the point. The point is, I was really bad at the game because I basically just like things. I will go anywhere a movie wants to take me, even if that is watching a spy in a fitted suit balance between two speedboats while he shoots at bad guys."

Alex's gaze flickers between the road and me a few more times.

"The Linfield Cineplex?" he says, either shocked or repulsed.

"Wow," I say, "you're really not keeping up with this story. Yes. The Linfield Cineplex."

"The one where the theaters are always, like, mysteriously flooded?" he says, aghast. "The last time I went there, I hadn't made it halfway down the aisle before I heard splashing."

"Yes, but it's *cheap*," I said, "and I own rain boots."

"We don't even know what that liquid is, Poppy," he says, grimacing. "You could have contracted a disease."

I throw my arms out to my sides. "I'm alive, aren't I?"

His eyes narrow. "What else?"

"What else . . ."

". . . do you like?" he clarifies. "Besides seeing *any* movie, alone, in the swamp theater."

"You don't believe me?" I say.

"It's not that," he answers. "I'm just fascinated. Scientifically curious."

"Fine. Lemme think." I look out the window just as we're passing an exit with a P.F. Chang's. "Chain restaurants. Love the familiarity. Love that they're the same everywhere, and that a lot of them have bottomless breadsticks—ooh!" I interrupt myself as it dawns on me. The thing I hate. "Running! I *hate* running. I got a C in gym class in high school because I 'forgot' my gym clothes at home so often."

The corner of Alex's mouth curves discreetly, and my cheeks heat.

"Go ahead. Mock me for getting a C in gym. I can tell you're dying to."

"It's not that," he says.

"Then what?"

His faint smile inches higher. "It's just funny. I love running."

"Seriously?" I cry. "You hate the very concept of cover songs yet *love* the feeling of your feet pounding against pavement and rattling your whole skeleton while your heart jackhammers in your chest and your lungs fight for breath?"

"If it's any consolation," he says quietly, his smile still mostly hidden in the corner of his mouth, "I hate when people call boats 'she.'"

A laugh of surprise bursts out of me. "You know what," I say, "I think I hate that too."

"So it's settled," he says.

I nod. "It's settled. The feminization of boats is hereby over-turned."

"Glad we got that taken care of," he says.

"Yeah, it's a load off. What should we eradicate next?"

"I have some ideas," he says. "But tell me some of the other things you love."

"Why, are you studying me?" I joke.

His ears tinge pink. "I'm fascinated to have met someone who'd wade through sewage to see a movie they've never heard of, so sue me."

For the next two hours we trade our interests and disinterests like kids swapping baseball cards, all while my driving playlist cycles through on shuffle in the background. If there are any other saxophone-heavy songs, neither of us notices.

I tell him that I love watching videos of mismatched animal friendships.

He tells me he hates seeing both flip-flops and displays of affection in public. "Feet should be private," he insists.

"You need help," I tell him, but I can't stop laughing, and even as he mines his strangely specific tastes for my amusement, that shade of humor keeps hiding in the corner of his mouth.

Like he knows he's ridiculous.

Like he doesn't mind at all that I'm delighted by his strangeness.

I admit that I hate both Linfield and khakis, because why not? We both already know the measure of things: we're two people with no business spending any time together, let alone spending an extended amount of it crammed into a tiny car. We are two funda-mentally incompatible people with absolutely *no* need to impress each other.

So I have no problem saying, "Khakis just make a person look like they're both pantsless *and* void of a personality."

"They're durable, and they match everything," Alex argues.

"You know, sometimes with clothes, it's not a matter of whether something *can* be worn but whether it *should* be worn."

Alex waves the thought away. "And as for Linfield," he says, "what's your problem with it? It's a great place to grow up."

This is a more complicated question with an answer I don't feel like sharing, even with someone who's going to drop me off in several hours and never think of me again.

"Linfield is the khakis of Midwestern cities," I say.

"Comfortable," he says, "durable."

"Naked from the waist down."

Alex tells me he hates themed parties. Leather cuff bracelets and pointy shoes with squared-off toes. When you show up somewhere and some friend or uncle makes the joke "They'll let anyone in here!" When servers call him *bud* or *boss* or *chief.* Men who walk like they just got off a horse. Vests, on anyone, in any scenario. The moment when a group of people are taking pictures and someone says, "Should we do a silly one?"

"I love themed parties," I tell him.

"Of course you do," he says. "You're good at them."

I narrow my eyes at him, put my feet on the dashboard, then take them back down when I see the anxious creases at the corners of his mouth. "Are you stalking me, Alex?" I ask.

He shoots me a horrified look. "Why would you say something like that?"

His expression makes me cackle again. "Relax, I'm kidding. But how do you know I'm 'good at' themed parties? I've seen you at *one* party, and it was *not* themed."

"It's not about that," he says. "You're just . . . always sort of in costume." He hurries to add, "I don't mean in a bad way. You're just always dressed pretty . . ."

"Amazing?" I supply.

"Confidently," he says.

"What a surprisingly loaded compliment," I say.

He sighs. "Are you misunderstanding me on purpose?"

"No," I say, "I think that just comes naturally for us."

"I just mean that for you, it seems like a themed party might as well just be a Tuesday. But for me, it means I stand in front of my closet for, like, two hours trying to figure out how to look like a dead celebrity out of my ten identical shirts and five identical pants."

"You could try . . . not buying your clothes in bulk," I suggest. "Or you can just wear your khakis and tell everyone you're going as a flasher."

He makes a repulsed grimace but otherwise ignores my comment.

"I hate the decision making of it all," he says, waving the suggestion off. "And if I try to go *buy* a costume it's even worse. I'm so overwhelmed by malls. There's just too much. I don't even know how to choose a store, let alone a rack. I have to buy all my clothes online, and once I find something I like, I'll order five more of them right away."

"Well, if you ever get invited to a themed party where you're sure there will be no flip-flops, PDA, or sax and thus you're able to attend," I say, "I'd be happy to take you shopping."

"Are you being serious?" His eyes flick from the road to me. It started getting dark out at some point without my noticing, and Joni Mitchell's mournful voice is cooing out over the speakers now, her song "A Case of You."

"Of course I'm serious," I say. We might have nothing in common, but I'm starting to enjoy myself. All year I've felt like I had to be on my best behavior, like I was auditioning for new friendships, new identities, a new life.

But strangely, I feel none of that here. Plus . . . I love shopping.

"It'd be great," I go on. "You'd be like my living Ken doll." I lean forward and turn the volume up a bit. "Speaking of things I love: this song."

"This is one of my karaoke songs," Alex says.

I bust into a guffaw, but from his chagrined expression, I quickly gather that he's not joking, which makes it even better.

"I'm not laughing *at* you," I promise quickly. "I actually think it's adorable."

"Adorable?" I can't tell if he's confused or offended.

"No, I just mean . . ." I stop, roll the window down a little to let a breeze into the car. I pull my hair up off my sweaty neck and tuck it up between my head and the headrest. "You're just . . ." I search for a way to explain it. "Not who I thought, I guess."

His brow creases. "Who did you think I was?"

"I don't know," I say. "Some guy from Linfield."

"I am some guy from Linfield," he says.

"Some guy from Linfield who sings 'A Case of You' at karaoke," I correct him, then devolve into fresh, delighted laughter at the thought.

Alex smiles at the steering wheel, shaking his head. "And you're some girl from Linfield who sings . . ." He thinks for a second. "'Dancing Queen' at karaoke?"

"Only time will tell," I say. "I've never been to karaoke."

"Seriously?" He looks over at me, broad, unfiltered surprise on his face.

"Aren't most karaoke bars twenty-one and up?" I say.

"Not all bars card," he says. "We should go. Sometime this summer."

"Okay," I say, as surprised by the invitation as by my accepting it. "That'd be fun."

"Okay," he says. "Cool."

So now we have two sets of plans.

I guess that makes us friends. Sort of?

A car flies up behind us, pressing in close. Alex, seemingly un-bothered, puts on his signal to move out of his way. Every time I've checked the speedometer, he's been holding steady precisely at the speed limit, and that's not about to change for one measly tailgater.

I should've guessed what a cautious driver he'd be. Then again, sometimes when you guess about people, you end up very wrong.

As the sticky, glare-streaked remains of Chicago shrink behind us and the thirsty fields of Indiana spring up on either side of us, my shuffling driving playlist moves nonsensically between Beyoncé and Neil Young and Sheryl Crow and LCD Soundsystem.

"You really do like everything," Alex teases.

"Except running, Linfield, and khakis," I say.

He keeps his window up, I keep mine down, my hair cycloning around my head as we fly over flat country roads, the wind so loud I can barely make out Alex's pitchy rendition of Heart's "Alone" until he gets to the soaring chorus and we belt it out together in horrendous matching falsettos, arms flying, faces contorted, and ancient station wagon speakers buzzing.

In that moment, he is so dramatic, so ardent, so absurd, it's like I'm looking at an entirely separate person from the mild-mannered boy I met beneath the globe lights during O-Week.

Maybe, I think, Quiet Alex is like a coat that he puts on before he walks out the door.

Maybe this is Naked Alex.

Okay, I'll think of a better name for it. The point is, I'm starting to like this one.

"What about traveling?" I ask in the lull between songs.

"What about it?" he says.

"Love or hate?"

His mouth presses into an even line as he considers. "Hard to say," he replies. "I've never really been anywhere. Read about a lot of places, just haven't seen any of them yet."

"Me neither," I say. "Not yet."

He thinks for another moment. "Love," he says. "I'm guessing love."

"Yeah." I nod. "Me too."

6

This Summer

MARCH INTO SWAPNA'S office the next morning, feeling wired despite the late night I had texting Alex. I plop her drink, an iced Americano, down on her desk and she looks up, startled, from the layout proofs she's approving for the upcoming fall issue.

"Palm Springs," I say.

For a second, her surprise stays fixed on her face, then the corners of her razor-edged lips curl into a smile. She sits back in her chair, folding her perfectly toned arms across her tailored black dress, the overhead light catching her engagement ring so that the behemoth ruby set at its center winks fantastically.

"Palm Springs," she repeats. "It's evergreen." She thinks for a second, then waves her hand. "I mean, it's a desert, of course, but as far as *R+R*, there's hardly any place more restful or relaxing in the continental United States."

"Exactly," I say, as if that had been what I was thinking all along. In reality, my choice has nothing to do with what *R+R* might like and everything to do with David Nilsen, youngest brother of Alex and a man set to marry the love of his life this time next week.

In Palm Springs, California.

It was a hiccup I hadn't expected—that Alex already *had* a trip scheduled next week: his brother's destination wedding. I'd been crushed when he told me, but I said I understood, asked him to congratulate David, and set my phone down, expecting the conversation to end.

But it hadn't, and after two more hours of texting, I'd taken a deep breath and pitched the idea of him stretching his three-day trip to spend a few extra days on an *R+R*-funded vacation with me. He'd not only agreed but invited me to stick around for the wedding after.

It was all coming together.

"Palm Springs," Swapna says again, her eyes glossing as she slips into her mind and tries the idea out. She breaks suddenly from her reverie and reaches for her keyboard. She types for a minute, then scratches her chin as she reads something on her screen. "Of course, we'd have to wait to use that for the winter issue. The summer's low season."

"But that's why it's perfect," I say, spitballing and a little panicked. "There's all kinds of stuff going on in the Springs in the summer, and it's less crowded and cheaper. This could be a good way to kind of get back to my roots—how to do this trip on the cheap, you know?"

Swapna's lips purse thoughtfully. "But our brand is aspirational."

"And Palm Springs is peak aspiration," I say. "We'll give our readers the vision—then show them how they can have it."

Swapna's dark eyes light up as she considers this, and my stomach lifts hopefully.

Then she blinks and turns back to her computer screen. "No."

"What?" I say, not even on purpose, just because my brain can't compute that this is happening. There is no way that this, my job, is where the train goes off the rails.

Swapna gives an apologetic sigh and leans over her gleaming glass desk. "Look, Poppy, I appreciate the thought that went into this, but it's just not *R+R*. It will translate as brand confusion."

"Brand confusion," I say, apparently still too stunned to come up with my own words.

"I thought about it all weekend, and I'm sending you to Santorini." She looks back to the layout proofs on her desk, her face shifting gears from Empathetic but Professional Manager Swapna to Concentrating Magazine Genius Swapna. She's moved on, the signal so strong that I find myself standing even though, inside, my brain is still caught on a refrain of *but, but, but!*

But this is our chance to fix things.

But you can't give up that easily.

But this *is what you want.* Not gorgeous whitewashed Santorini and its sparkling sea.

Alex in the desert, in the dead of summer. Wandering into places before checking them out on Tripadvisor, unstructured days and late, late nights and full hours of sunshine lost to the inside of a dusty bookstore he couldn't pass by, or a vintage shop whose clutter and germs have him standing, rigid yet patient, near the door as I try on dead people's hats. That's what I want.

I stand in the doorway of the office, heart racing, until Swapna looks up from the proofs, her eyebrow arched inquiringly, as if to say, *Yes, Poppy?*

"Give Santorini to Garrett," I say.

Swapna blinks at me, evidently confused.

"I think I need some time off," I blurt out, then clarify. "A vacation—a real one."

Swapna's lips press tight. She's confused but not going to push for more information, which is good because I wouldn't know how to explain anyway.

She gives a slow nod. "Send me the dates, then."

I turn and walk back to my desk feeling calmer than I have in months. Until I sit down and reality forces its way in.

I've got some savings, but taking a trip that's affordable by $R+R$'s standards—and on their dime—is a *very* different thing from taking a trip that *I* can afford with my own money. And as a high school English teacher with a doctorate and all of its associated debt, there's no way Alex could afford to split costs with me. I doubt he'd agree to take the trip at all if he knew I was funding it myself.

But maybe this is a good thing. We always had so much fun on those trips we cobbled together on cents. Things only started going downhill once $R+R$ got involved in our summer trips. I can do this: I can plan the perfect trip, like I used to; remind Alex how good things can be. The more I think about it, the more this makes sense. I'm actually excited by the idea of having one of our old-school, dirt-cheap trips. Things were so much simpler back then, and we always had a blast.

I pull out my phone and take my time trying to craft the perfect message.

Fun thought: Let's do this trip the way we used to. Cheap as shit, no professional photographers tailing us, no five-star restaurants, just seeing Palm Springs like the impoverished academic and digital-age journalist that we are.

Within a few seconds, he replies: R+R's okay with that? No photographer?

I unconsciously start waggling my head back and forth like the tiny angel and devil on my shoulder are taking turns tugging it from left to right. I don't want to outright lie to him.

But they *are* okay with it. I'm taking a week off, so I'm free.

Yep, I say. Everything's all set if you're okay with it.

Sure, he writes. Sounds good.

It does sound good. It'll be good. I can make it good.

7

This Summer

A S SOON AS the plane touches down, the four babies that spent the full six-hour flight screaming stop at once.

I slip my phone from my purse and turn off airplane mode, waiting out the flood of incoming text messages from Rachel, Garrett, Mom, David Nilsen, and—last but absolutely not least—Alex.

Rachel says, in three different ways, to please let her know as soon as I land that my plane didn't crash or get sucked into the Bermuda Triangle, and that she's both praying for and manifesting a safe landing for me.

Safe and sound and already missing you, I tell her, then I open up the message from Garrett.

Thank you SO MUCH for not taking Santorini, he writes, then, in a separate message: Also . . . Pretty weird decision IMHO. I hope you're okay . . .

I'm fine, I tell him. I just had a wedding come up last minute and Santorini was your idea. Send me lots of pics so I can regret my life choices?

Next, I open the message from David: SO happy you're coming with Al! Tham's excited to meet you, and of course you are invited to EVERYTHING.

Of all of Alex's brothers, David has always been my favorite. But it's hard to believe he's old enough to get married.

Then again, when I said that to Alex, he texted back, Twenty-four. I can't imagine making a decision like that at that age but all my brothers got married young, and Tham's great. My dad's even on board. He got a bumper sticker that says I'M A PROUD CHRIST FOLLOWER WHO LOVES MY GAY SON.

I snorted laughter into my coffee as I read that one. It was so supremely Mr. Nilsen, and also perfectly played into Alex's and my running joke about David being the family favorite. Alex hadn't even been allowed to listen to secular music until he was in high school, and when he decided to go to a secular university, there had been weeping.

In the end, though, Mr. Nilsen really *did* love his sons, and so he pretty much always came around on matters that concerned their happiness.

If you'd gotten married at twenty-four, you'd be married to Sarah, I texted Alex.

You'd be married to Guillermo, he said.

I sent him back one of his own Sad Puppy selfies.

Please tell me you're not still carrying a torch for that dick, Alex said.

The two of them had never gotten along.

Of course not, I wrote back. But Gui and I weren't the ones in a torturous on-and-off relationship. That was you and Sarah.

Alex typed and stopped typing so many times I started to wonder if he was doing it just to annoy me.

But that was the end of that conversation. When he next texted me, the following day, it was with a non sequitur, a picture of BeDazzled black robes that said SPA BITCH on the back.

Summer Trip Uniform? he wrote, and we've dodged the topic of Sarah ever since, which makes it pretty damn clear to me that there's something going on between them. Again.

Now, sitting on the cramped and sweltering plane, taxiing toward LAX, in the post-baby-scream silence, it still makes me a little sick to think about. Sarah and I have never been each other's biggest fans. I doubt she'd approve of Alex taking another trip with me if they were back together, and if they aren't properly but are on their *way* to being, then this could very well be the last summer trip.

They'd get married, start having kids, take their whole family to Disney World, and she and I would never be close enough for me to be a real part of Alex's life anymore.

I push the thought away and answer David's text message: I'M SO EXCITED AND HONORED THAT I GET TO BE THERE!

He sends back a gif of a dancing bear, and I tap open the text from my mom next.

Give Alex a big hug and kiss for me:), she writes, with the smiley face typed out. She never remembers how to use emojis and becomes impatient immediately when I try to show her. "I can type them out just fine!" she insists.

My parents: not the biggest fans of change.

Do you want me to grab his butt while I'm at it? I write back to her.

If you think that will work, she replies. I'm getting tired of waiting for grandbabies.

I roll my eyes and exit out of the message. Mom has always adored Alex, at least partly because he moved back to Linfield and she's hoping we'll wake up one day and realize we're in love with each other and I'll move back too and get pregnant immediately.

My father, on the other hand, is a doting but intimidating man who has always terrified Alex so much that he's never let one ounce of personality out while in the same room as Dad.

He's brawny with a booming voice, mildly handy in the way so many men of his generation are, and he has a tendency to ask a lot of blunt, bordering-on-inappropriate questions. Not because he's hoping for a certain response but because he's curious and not very self-aware.

He is also, like all members of the Wright family, not *amazing* at modulating his voice. To a stranger, my mother shouting "Have you tried these grapes that taste like cotton candy? Oh, you'll *love* them! Here, let me wash some off for you! Oh, let me wash a bowl first. Oh, no, all our bowls are in the fridge with Saran Wrap covering our leftovers—here, just grab a fistful instead!" might be mildly overwhelming, but when my father's brow crinkles and he blasts out a question like "Did you vote in the last mayoral election?" it's easy to feel like you've just been shoved into an interrogation room with an enforcer the FBI pays under the table.

The first time Alex picked me up at my parents' house for a karaoke night that first summer of our friendship, I tried to shield him from my family and my house, as much for his sake as for my own.

By the end of our first road trip home I knew enough about him to understand that his walking into our tiny house filled to the brim with knickknacks and dusty picture frames and dog dander would be like a vegetarian taking a tour of a slaughterhouse.

I didn't want him to be uncomfortable, sure, but just as badly, I didn't want him to judge my family. Messy and strange and loud and blunt as they were, my parents were amazing, and I'd learned the hard way that that *wasn't* what people saw when they came through our front door.

So I'd told Alex I'd meet him in the driveway, but I hadn't

stressed the point, and Alex—being Alex Nilsen—had come to the door anyway, like a good 1950s quarterback, determined to introduce himself to my parents, so they "wouldn't worry" about me riding off into the sunset with a stranger.

I heard the doorbell and went running to head off the chaos, but in my vintage pink-feathered house shoes, I wasn't fast enough. By the time I got downstairs, Alex was standing in the front hall between two towers of stacked storage containers, getting batted back and forth by our two very old and badly behaved husky mixes, as a slew of unseemly family photos stared down at him from every side.

At the moment I came skittering around the corner from the stairs, Dad was booming out, "Why would we *worry* about her going out with you?" and then, "And when you say 'going out,' do you mean that you two are—"

"Nope!" I interrupted, dragging the hornier of our dogs, Rupert, back by the collar before he could mount Alex's leg. "We are *not* going out. Not like that. And you definitely don't need to worry. Alex is a *really* slow driver."

"That's what I was trying to say," he stammered. "I mean, not the driving speed. I drive . . . the speed limit. I just meant, you don't *need* to worry."

Dad's brow furrowed. Alex's face drained of blood, and I wasn't sure whether he was more unnerved by my father or by the layer of dust visible along the baseboards in the hallway, which, frankly, I'd never noticed until that moment.

"Did you see Alex's car, Dad?" I said quickly, a diversion. "It's *very* old. His phone too. Alex hasn't gotten a new phone in, like, seven years."

Alex's face went red even as my father's relaxed into interest and approval. "Is that so?"

Still, all these years later, I can remember with vivid clarity the way Alex's gaze flickered to mine, searching my face for the correct answer. I gave him a little nod.

"Yes?" he answered, and Dad clapped a hand on his shoulder so hard Alex flinched.

Dad gave a big, no-holds-barred grin. "It's always better to repair than to replace!"

"Replace what?" Mom shouted from the kitchen. "Did something break? Who are you talking to? Poppy? Does anyone want some chocolate-dipped pretzels? Shoot, let me just find a clean plate . . ."

When we finally finished the twenty-minute goodbye required to leave my house and made it back to Alex's car, he said only of the whole affair, "Your parents seem nice."

I responded, with accidental aggression, "They *are*," like I was daring him to bring up the dust or the humping husky or the two billion childhood drawings still magnetized to our fridge or anything else, but of course he didn't. He was Alex, even if I didn't understand everything that meant back then.

In all the years I've known him since, he's still never said an unkind word about any of it. He even sent flowers to my dorm when Rupert, the husky, died. *I always felt we had a special connection after that night we shared*, he joked in the card. *He will be missed. If you need anything at all, P, I'm here. Always.*

Not that I have the note memorized or anything.

Not that, in the lone shoebox's worth of saved cards and letters and scraps of paper I allow myself to keep in my apartment, this one made the cut.

Not that there were full days during our friendship's hiatus when I tortured myself with the thought that maybe I should throw that card away since, as it turned out, *always* had ended.

Toward the back of the plane, one of the babies starts screaming again, but we're pulling up to the gate now. I'll be off in no time.

And then I'll see Alex.

A thrill zings up my spine, and a nervous flutter works back down into my stomach.

I open the last unread message in my inbox, the one from him: Just landed.

Same, I type back.

After that, I don't know what to say. We've been texting for over a week, never broaching the topic of the ill-fated Croatia trip, and everything's felt so normal until right now. Then I remember: I haven't seen Alex in real life in over two years.

I haven't touched him, haven't even heard his voice. There are so many ways this could be awkward. Almost certainly we'll experience some of them.

I'm excited to see him, of course, but more than that, I realize I'm terrified.

We need to pick a meeting point. Someone has to suggest it. I summon the layout of LAX to mind from the soup of hazy memories of every dully carpeted gate and electric walkway I've seen in the last four and a half years of working at *R+R*.

If I ask to meet at baggage claim, will that mean a long stretch of walking toward each other silently until we're close enough to actually talk? Am I supposed to hug him?

The Nilsens aren't a huggy bunch, as opposed to the Wrights, who are known to grab, elbow, slap, rustle, squeeze, and nudge for emphasis during any conversation, no matter how mundane. Touching is such second nature to me that once I accidentally hugged my dishwasher repairman when I let him out of the apartment, at which point he graciously told me he was married, and I congratulated him.

Back when Alex and I were close, we hugged all the time; but that was then, when I knew him. When he was comfortable with me.

I fight my roller bag free from the overhead bin and push it along ahead of me, sweat gathering in my armpits beneath my light sweater and under the blunt little approximation of a ponytail swept off my neck.

The flight took forever; every time I checked the clock, it seemed like full hours had been condensed into a minute or two. I was bouncing-up-and-down-in-my-very-small-seat eager to get here, but now it's like time is making up for the ballooning it did during the flight, shrinking so that I travel the whole length of the jet bridge in an instant.

My throat feels tight. My brain feels like it's sloshing around in my skull. I step out into the gate, move sideways out of the path of everyone coming off the jet bridge behind me, and slip my phone out of my pocket. My hands are sweaty as I start to type: *Meet at bag*—

"Hey."

I spin toward the voice just as the owner of it sidesteps the stroller parked between us.

Smiling. Alex is smiling, his eyes puffy in that sleepy way, his laptop bag slung over one shoulder and earbuds hanging around his neck, his hair an utter mess compared to his dark gray trousers and button-up and his scuffless leather boots. As he closes the gap between us, he drops his carry-on bag behind him and pulls me into a hug.

And it's normal, so natural to push up on my tiptoes and wrap my arms around his waist, burrow my face into his chest, and breathe him in. Cedar, musk, lime. There is no greater creature of habit than Alex Nilsen.

Same inscrutable haircut, same cleanly warm scent, same basic wardrobe (though enhanced a little over time with better tailoring and shoes), same way of squeezing me around the upper back and drawing me in and up against him when we hug, almost pulling me off the ground but never tightening so much that the embrace could be considered *bone-crunching*.

It's more like *sculpting*. Gentle pressure on all sides that briefly compresses us into one living, breathing thing with twice as many hearts as we should have.

"Hi," I say, beaming into his chest, and his arms slide down to my midback, tightening.

"Hi," he says, and I hope he heard the smile in my voice the way I hear it in his. Despite his general aversion to any form of public affection, neither of us lets go right away, and I have the sense that we're thinking the same thing: it's okay to hold on for an inappropriately long time when it's been two years since you've hugged.

I shut my eyes tight against rising emotion, pressing my forehead into his chest. His arms fall down to my waist and lock there for a few seconds. "How was your flight?" he asks.

I draw back enough to look up into his face. "I think we had some future world-class opera singers on board. Yours?"

His control over his small smile wavers, and his grin fans wide. "I almost gave the woman next to me a heart attack during some turbulence," he says. "I grabbed her hand by accident."

A high-pitched laugh shivers through me, and his smile goes wider, his arms tighter.

Naked Alex, I think, then push the thought away. I really should've come up with a better way of describing this version of him a long time ago.

As if he's reading my thoughts and fittingly mortified, he tamps his smile back down and releases his hold on me, stepping back for good measure. "You need to get anything from baggage claim?" he asks, grabbing the handle of my bag along with his.

"I can get that," I offer.

"I don't mind," he says.

As I follow him away from the crowded gate, I can't stop staring at him. In awe that he's here. In awe that he looks the same. Awed that this is real.

He glances down at me as we walk, his mouth twisting. One of my favorite things about Alex's face has always been the way that it allows two disparate emotions to exist on it at the same time, and how legible those emotions have become to me.

Right now, that twist of his mouth is saying both *amused* and *vaguely wary*.

"What?" he says, in a voice that rides that same line.

"You're just . . . tall," I say.

He's cut too, but commenting on that usually leads to embarrassment on his part, like having a gym body is somehow a personality flaw. Maybe to him it is. Vanity is something he was raised to avoid. Whereas my mom used to write little notes on my bathroom mirror in dry-erase marker: *Good morning to that beautiful smile. Hello, strong arms and legs. Have a great day, lovely belly that feeds my darling daughter.* Sometimes I still hear those words when I get out of the shower and stand in front of the mirror, combing my hair: *Good morning, beautiful smile. Hello, strong arms and legs. Have a great day, lovely belly that feeds me.*

"You're staring at me because I'm tall?" Alex says.

"*Very* tall," I say, as if this clears things up.

It's easier than saying, *I have missed you, beautiful smile. It's so good to see you, strong arms and legs. Thank you, freakishly taut belly, for feeding this person I love so much.*

Alex's grin ripens to the point of splitting open as he holds my gaze. "It's good to see you too, Poppy."

8

Ten Summers Ago

A YEAR AGO, WHEN I met Alex Nilsen outside my dormitory with a half dozen bags of dirty laundry, I wouldn't have believed we'd be taking a vacation together.

It started with the occasional text after our road trip home—blurry pictures of the Linfield movie theater as he drove past, with the caption *don't forget to get vaccinated*, or a shot of a ten-pack of shirts I'd found at the supermarket, *birthday present* typed beneath it—but after three weeks, we'd graduated to phone calls and hangouts. I even convinced him to see a movie at the Cineplex, though he spent the whole time hovering over the seat, trying not to touch anything.

By the time summer ended, we'd signed up for two core requirement classes together, a math and a science, and most nights, Alex came to my dorm or I went to his to struggle through the homework. My old roommate, Bonnie, had officially moved in with her sister, and I was rooming with Isabel, a premed student who'd sometimes look over Alex's and my shoulders and correct our work while crunching on celery, her alleged favorite food.

Alex hated math as much as I did, but he loved his English

classes and devoted hours each night to their assigned reading while I aimlessly perused travel blogs and celebrity gossip rags on the floor beside him. My courses were uniformly boring, but on nights when Alex and I walked the campus after dinner with cups of hot chocolate, or weekends when we wandered the city on a quest for the best hot dog stand or cup of coffee or falafel, I felt happier than I ever remembered. I loved being in the city, surrounded by art and food and noise and new people, enough that the school part of it was bearable.

Late one night, when snow was piling up in my windowsill and Alex and I were stretched out on my rug studying for an exam, we started listing places we wished we were instead.

"Paris," I said.

"Working on my American Lit final," Alex said.

"Seoul," I said.

"Working on my Intro to Nonfiction final," Alex said.

"Sofia, Bulgaria," I said.

"Canada," Alex said.

I looked at him and erupted into slaphappy exhaustion-laughter, which triggered his trademark chagrin. "Your top three vacation destinations," I said, lying back on the rug, "are two separate essays and the country nearest to us."

"It's more affordable than Paris," he said seriously.

"Which is what really matters when you're daydreaming."

He sighed. "Well, what about that hot spring you read about? The one in a rain forest? That's in Canada."

"Vancouver Island," I supplied, nodding. Or a smaller island near it, actually.

"That's where I'd go," he said, "if my travel companion weren't so disagreeable."

"Alex," I said, "I will happily go to Vancouver Island with you.

Especially if the other options are just watching you do more homework. We'll go next summer."

Alex lay back beside me. "What about Paris?"

"Paris can wait," I said. "Also we can't afford Paris."

He smiled faintly. "Poppy," he said, "we can barely afford our weekly hot dogs."

But now, months later, after a semester of picking up every possible shift at our campus jobs—Alex at the library, me in the mailroom—we've saved enough for this very cheap red-eye (complete with two layovers), and I'm buzzing with excitement as we finally board.

As soon as we lift off and the cabin lights dim, though, the exhaustion kicks in and I find myself being lulled to sleep, head resting on Alex's shoulder, a small pool of drool accumulating on his shirt, only to jolt awake when the plane hits a pocket of air that makes it dip and Alex accidentally elbows me in the face in response.

"Shit!" he gasps as I sit bolt upright, clutching my cheek. "Shit!" His white knuckles are clamped around the armrests, the rise and fall of his chest shallow.

"Are you afraid of flying?" I ask.

"No!" he whispers, considerate of the other sleeping passengers even in his panic. "I'm afraid of dying."

"You're not going to die," I promise. The jet settles into a rhythm, but the seat belt light comes on and Alex keeps gripping the armrests like someone's flipped the plane upside down and started trying to shake us out.

"That doesn't seem good," he says. "It sounded like something broke off the plane."

"That was the sound of your elbow smashing into my face."

"What?" He looks over. The two simultaneous expressions on his face are surprise and confusion.

"You hit me in the face!" I tell him.

"Oh, shit," he says. "Sorry. Can I see?"

I pull my hand away from my throbbing cheekbone, and Alex leans in close, his fingers hovering over my skin. His hand falls away without ever landing. "It looks okay. Maybe we should see if a flight attendant can bring some ice."

"Good idea," I say. "We can call her over and tell her you hit me in the face, but I'm *sure* it was an accident and also it's not your fault—you were surprised and—"

"God, Poppy," he says. "I'm really sorry."

"It's okay. It doesn't hurt that bad." I nudge his elbow with mine. "Why didn't you tell me you were afraid of flying?"

"I didn't know I was."

"Meaning?"

He tips his head back against the headrest. "I hadn't flown before tonight."

"Oh." My stomach clenches guiltily. "I wish you'd told me."

"I didn't want to make it a thing."

"I wouldn't have made it a thing."

He looks over at me skeptically. "And what do you call this?"

"Okay, fine, yes, I made it a thing. But look." I slide my hand under his and tentatively fold my fingers into his. "I'm here with you, and if you want to sleep for a little, I'll stay awake to make sure the plane doesn't crash. Which it won't. Because this is safer than driving."

"I hate driving too," he says.

"I know you do. But my point is, this is better than that. Like, way better. And I'm here with you, and I've flown before, so if there's a reason to panic, I'll know. And I promise you, in that situation, I *will* panic and you'll know something's wrong. Until then, you can relax."

He stares at me through the dark of the cabin for a few seconds. Then his hand relaxes into mine, his warm, rough fingers settling. It gives me a surprising thrill to hold his hand. Ninety-five percent of the time, I see Alex Nilsen in a purely platonic way, and I'd guess his number hovers a bit higher. But for that other five percent of the time, there's this *what-if*.

It never lasts long or pushes too hard. It just sits there, cupped between our hands, a gentle thought without much weight behind it: What would it be like to kiss him? How would he touch me? Would he taste the way he smells? No one has better dental hygiene than Alex, which isn't exactly a *sexy* thought but certainly sexier than the opposite end of the spectrum.

And that's about as far as the thought ever goes, which is perfect, because I like Alex *way* too much to date him. Plus we're entirely incompatible.

The plane judders through another quick stretch of turbulence, and Alex's grip tightens.

"Time to panic?" he asks.

"Not yet," I say. "Try to sleep."

"Because I need to be well rested when I meet Death."

"Because you need to be well rested when I get tired in Butchart Gardens and make you carry me the rest of the way."

"I knew there was a reason you brought me with you."

"I didn't bring you with me to be my mule," I argue. "I brought you with me to be my patsy. You're gonna cause a diversion as I run through the dining room of the Empress Hotel during high tea, stealing tiny sandwiches and priceless bracelets off unsuspecting guests."

He squeezes my hand. "I guess I'd better sleep, then."

I squeeze back. "Guess so."

"Wake me up when it's time to panic."

"Always."

He rests his head on my shoulder and pretends to sleep.

When we land, he will have a horrible kink in his neck and my shoulder will ache from sitting in this position for so long, but right now I don't mind. I have five glorious days of travel with my best friend ahead of me, and deep down, I know: nothing can go wrong, not really.

It's not time to panic.

9

This Summer

D O WE HAVE a rental car?" Alex asks as we head out of the airport into the windy heat.

"Sort of." I chew on my lip as I fish my phone out to call a cab. "I sourced a ride from a Facebook group."

Alex's eyes narrow, the jet-induced gusts rolling through the arrivals area making his hair flap against his forehead. "I have no idea what you just said."

"Remember?" I say. "It's what we did on our first trip. To Vancouver? When we were too young to legally rent a car?"

He stares at me.

"You know," I say, "that women's online travel group I've been in for, like, fifteen years? Where people post their apartments for sublet and list their cars for rent? Remember? We had to take a bus to pick up the car outside the city and walk, like, five miles with our luggage?"

"I remember," he says. "I've just never stopped to wonder why anyone would rent their car to a stranger before this moment."

"Because a lot of people in New York like to leave for the winter and a lot of people in Los Angeles like to go somewhere else for the summer." I shrug. "This girl's car would've been sitting unused for, like, a month, so I got it for the week for seventy bucks. We just have to take a cab to pick it up."

"Cool," Alex says.

"Yeah."

And here is the first awkward silence of the trip. It doesn't matter that we've been texting nonstop for the past week—or maybe that's made it worse. My mind is unforgivingly blank. All I can do is stare at the app on my phone, watching the car icon creep closer.

"This is us." I tip my chin toward the approaching minivan.

"Cool," Alex says again.

Our driver takes our bags and we pile in with the two other people we're ridesharing with, a middle-aged couple in matching BeDazzled visors. WIFEY, says the hot-pink one. HUBBY, says the lime-green one. Both of them are wearing flamingo-print shirts, and they're so tanned already they look something like Alex's shoes. Hubby's head is shaved, and Wifey's is dyed a bright bottle-red.

"Hey, y'all!" Wifey drawls as Alex and I settle into the middle seats.

"Hi." Alex twists in his seat and offers a smile that's almost convincing.

"Honeymoon," Wifey says, waving between her and Hubby. "What about you two?"

"Oh," Alex says. "Um."

"Same!" I loop my hand through his, turning to flash them a smile.

"Ooh!" Wifey squeals. "How do you like that, Bob? A car full of lovebirds!"

Hubby Bob nods. "Congrats, kids."

"How'd you meet?" Wifey wants to know.

I glance at Alex. The two expressions his face is making right now are (1) terrified and (2) exhilarated. This is a familiar game for us, and even if it's more awkward than usual to have my hand tangled in and dwarfed by his, there's also something comforting about slipping out of ourselves in this way, playing together like we always have.

"Disneyland," Alex says, and turns to the couple in the back seat.

Wifey's eyes widen. "How magical!"

"It really was, you know?" I shoot Alex hearty eyes and poke his nose with my free hand. "He was working as a VS—that's what we call vomit scoopers. Their job is just to sort of linger outside all those new 3D rides and clean up after seasick grandparents."

"And *Poppy* was playing Mike Wazowski," Alex adds dryly, upping the ante.

"Mike Wazowski?" Hubby Bob says.

"From *Monsters, Inc.*, hon," Wifey explains. "He's one of the main monsters!"

"Which one?" Hubby says.

"The short one," Alex says, then turns back to me, affecting the dopiest, most over-the-top look of adulation I've ever seen. "It was love at first sight."

"Aww!" Wifey says, clutching her heart.

Hubby's brow wrinkles. "When she was in the costume?"

Alex's face tints pink under Hubby's appraisal, and I cut in: "I have *really* great legs."

Our driver drops us on a street of stucco houses surrounded by jasmine in Highland Park, and as we climb out onto the hot asphalt, Wifey and Hubby wave us a fond farewell. The instant the cab's out of view, Alex releases his hold on my hand, and I scan the house numbers, nodding toward a reddish-stained privacy fence. "It's this one."

Alex opens the gate, and we step into the yard to find a boxy white hatchback waiting in the driveway, its every edge rusted and chipping.

"So," Alex says, staring at it. "Seventy bucks."

"I might've overpaid." I duck around the front driver's-side wheel, feeling for the magnetic box where the owner, a ceramicist named Sasha, said the key would be. "This is the first place I'd check for a spare if I were stealing a car."

"I think bending that low might be too much work to steal this car," Alex says as I pull the key out and straighten up. He walks around the back of the car and reads the tailgate: "Ford Aspire."

I laugh and unlock the doors. "I mean, 'aspirational' *is* the *R+R* brand."

"Here." Alex takes out his phone and steps back. "Let me get a picture of you with it."

I pop the door open and prop my foot up, striking a pose. Immediately, Alex starts to crouch. "Alex, no! Not from below."

"Sorry," he says. "I forgot how weird you are about that."

"*I'm* weird?" I say. "You take pictures like a dad with an iPad. If you had glasses on the end of your nose and a UC Bearcats T-shirt on, you'd be indistinguishable."

He makes a big show of holding the phone up as high as possible.

"What, and now we're going for that early-2000s emo angle?" I say. "Find a happy medium."

Alex rolls his eyes and shakes his head, but snaps a few pictures at a seminormal height, then comes to show them to me. I legitimately gasp when I see the last shot and grab for his arm the same way he must've latched on to the octogenarian he rode next to on the flight.

"What?" he says.

"You have portrait mode."

"I do," he agrees.

"And you *used* it," I point out.

"Yes."

"You know *how* to use portrait mode," I say, still aghast.

"Ha ha."

"*How* do you know how to use portrait mode? Did your grandson teach you that when he was home for Thanksgiving?"

"Wow," he deadpans. "I've missed this so much."

"I'm sorry, I'm sorry," I say. "I'm impressed. You've changed." I hurry to add, "Not in a bad way! I just mean, you are not a person who relishes change."

"Maybe I am now," he says.

I cross my arms. "Do you still get up at five thirty to exercise every day?"

He shrugs. "That's discipline, not fear of change."

"At the same gym?" I ask.

"Yeah."

"The one that raises its prices every six months? And plays the same New Age meditation CD on repeat at all times? The gym you were already complaining about two years ago?"

"I wasn't complaining," he says. "I just don't understand how that's supposed to motivate you on a treadmill. I was *pondering*. Contemplating."

"You take your own playlist with you—what does it matter what they play over the speakers?"

He shrugs and takes the car keys from my hands, rounding the Aspire to open its rear door. "It's a matter of principle." He tosses our bags into the back and slams it shut.

I thought we were joking, but now I'm not so sure.

"Hey." I reach for his elbow as he's walking past. He stills, eyebrows lifting. There's a knot of pride caught in my throat, stopping up the words that want to come out. But it was pride that tore our friendship up the first time, and I'm not going to make that mistake again. I'm not going to *not* say things that need to be said, just because I want him to say them first.

"What?" Alex says.

I swallow the knot down. "I'm glad you didn't change too much."

He stares at me for a beat and then—is it my imagination, or does he swallow too? "You too," he says, and touches the end of a wave that's come loose from my ponytail to fall along my cheek, touches it so lightly I can barely feel it at the scalp and the delicate motion sends a tingle down my neck. "And I like the haircut."

My cheeks warm. My belly too. Even my legs seem to heat a couple degrees.

"You learned how to use a new feature on your phone, and I got a haircut," I say. "Watch out for us now, world."

"Radical transformation," Alex agrees.

"A true glow-up."

"The question is, have you gotten any better at driving?"

I arch an eyebrow and cross my arms. "Have you?"

"IT ASPIRES TO have working air-conditioning," Alex says.

"It aspires to *not* smell like a butthole that's smoking a blunt," I say.

We've been playing this game since we got on the highway heading into the desert. Sasha the Ceramicist had mentioned in her post about the car that its air-conditioning came and went at random, but she'd left out the fact that she'd evidently been using it to hotbox for five years straight.

"It aspires to live long enough to see the end of all human suffering," I add.

"This car," Alex says, "isn't going to live long enough to see the end of the *Star Wars* franchise."

"But who among us will?" I say.

Alex wound up driving by virtue of the fact that my driving makes him carsick. And terrified. Truthfully, I don't like driving anyway, so I usually defer the position to him.

Los Angeles traffic proved challenging for someone as cautious as him: we sat at a stop sign waiting to turn right onto a busy road for, like, ten minutes, until three cars behind us were holding down their horns.

Now that we're out of the city, though, he's doing great. Not even the lack of AC seems like a big deal with the windows down and sweetly flowery wind rushing over us. The bigger issue is the lack of an aux input, which has us relying on the radio.

"Has there always been this much Billy Joel traveling over the airwaves?" Alex asks the third time we switch channels mid-commercial only to plunge back into the middle of "Piano Man."

"Since the dawn of time, I think. When the cavemen built the first radio, this was already playing."

"I didn't know you were a historian," he deadpans. "You should come talk to my class."

I snort. "You could not drag me into the halls of East Linfield High with the combined force of every tractor in a five-mile radius of that building, Alex."

"You know," he says, "your bullies have likely graduated by now."

"We really can't be sure," I say.

He looks over, face sober, mouth pressed small. "Do you want me to kick their asses?"

I sigh. "No, it's too late. Like, all of them have kids now with those cute oversized baby glasses and most have found the Lord or started one of those weird pyramid-scheme businesses selling lip gloss."

He looks at me, his face pink from the sun. "If you change your mind, just say the word."

Alex knows about my rocky years in Linfield, of course, but for the most part, I try not to revisit them. I've always preferred the version of me that Alex brings out to the one I was back in our hometown. *This* Poppy feels safe in the world, because he's in it too, and he, deep down where it matters, is like me.

Still, he had an exceptionally different experience at West Linfield High than I had at its sister school. I'm sure it helped that he played sports—basketball, both for the school and in the intramural league at his family's church—and was handsome, but he's always insisted the clincher was that he was quiet enough to pass for mysterious rather than weird.

Maybe if my parents hadn't been so completely encouraging of every facet of my brothers' and my individualism, I would've had better luck. There were kids who dealt with disapproval by adapting, making themselves more palatable, like Prince and Parker had in school, finding the overlap between their personalities and everyone else's.

And then there were people like me, who labored under the misconception that eventually, My Fellow Children would not only tolerate but ultimately respect me for being myself.

There's nothing so off-putting to some people as someone who seems not to care whether anyone else approves of them. Maybe it's resentment: *I have bent for the greater good, to follow the rules, so why haven't you? You should care.*

Of course, secretly, I did care. A lot. Probably it would've been better if I'd just openly cried at school instead of shrugging off insults and weeping under my pillow later. It would've been better if, after the first time I was mocked for the flared overalls my mom had sewn embroidered patches onto, I hadn't kept wearing them with my chin held high, like I was some kind of eleven-year-old Joan of Arc, willing to die for my denim.

The point was, Alex had known how to play the game, whereas I'd often felt like I'd read the pages of the guidebook backward, while the whole thing was on fire.

When we were together, though, the game didn't even exist. The rest of the world dissolved until I believed *this* was how things truly were. Like I'd never been that girl who'd felt entirely alone, misunderstood, and I'd always been this one: known, loved, wholly accepted by Alex Nilsen.

When we met, I hadn't wanted him to see me as Linfield Poppy— I wasn't sure how it would change the dynamic of our world for two once we let certain outside elements wriggle their way in. I still remember the night I finally told him about it. The last night of class our junior year, we'd stumbled back to his dorm from a party to find his roommate already gone for the summer. So I borrowed a T-shirt and some blankets from Alex and slept on the spare twin bed in his room.

I hadn't had a sleepover like that since I was probably eight: the sort where you keep talking, eyes long since shut, until you both drift off midsentence.

We told each other everything, the things we'd never touched. Alex told me about his mom passing away, the months his dad barely changed out of pajamas, the peanut butter sandwiches Alex made for his brothers, and the baby formula he learned to mix.

For two years, he and I'd had so much fun together, but that night it felt like a whole new compartment in my heart opened where before there had been none.

And then he asked me what happened in Linfield, why I was

dreading going back for summer, and it should've felt embarrassing to air my small grievances after everything he'd just told me, except Alex had a way of *never* making me feel small or petty.

It was so late it was almost morning, those slippery hours when it feels safest to let your secrets out. So I told him all of it, starting with seventh grade.

The unfortunate braces, the gum Kim Leedles put in my hair, and the resulting bowl cut. The insult added to injury when Kim told my whole class that anyone who talked to me wouldn't be invited to her birthday party. Which was still a solid five months off, though it promised to be worth the wait, thanks to her pool's waterslide and the movie theater in her basement.

Then, in ninth grade, once the stigma had finally worn off and my boobs had arrived practically overnight, there was the three-month stretch during which I was a Hot Commodity. Until Jason Stanley kissed me unexpectedly and responded to my disinterest by telling everyone I gave him an unprompted blow job in the janitor's closet.

The entire soccer team called me Porny Poppy for, like, a year after that. No one wanted to be my friend. Then there was tenth grade, the worst of all.

It started off better because the younger of my two brothers was a senior and willing to share his Theater Kid friend-group with me. But that only lasted until I had a sleepover for my birthday, at which point I found out how embarrassing everyone thought my parents were. I quickly realized I didn't like my friends as much as I'd thought.

I'd told Alex too about how much I loved my family, how protective I felt of them, but how even with them, I was sometimes a little lonely. Everyone else was someone else's top person. Mom and Dad. Parker and Prince. Even the huskies were paired up, while

our terrier mix and the cat spent most days curled together in a
sun patch. Before Alex, my family was the only place I belonged,
but even with them, I was something of a loose part, that baffling
extra bolt IKEA packs with your bookcase, just to make you sweat.
Everything I'd done since high school had been to escape that feeling, that *person*.

And I told him all of that, minus the part about feeling like I
belonged with him, because even after two years of friendship, that
seemed like a bit much. When I finished, I thought he'd finally
fallen asleep. But after a few seconds, he shifted onto his side to
gaze at me through the dark and said quietly, "I bet you were adorable with a bowl cut."

I really, really wasn't, but somehow, that was enough to cool the
harsh sting of all those memories. He saw me, and he loved me.

"Poppy?" Alex says, bringing me back to the hot, stinky car and
the desert. "Where are you right now?"

I stick my hand out the window, grasping at the wind. "Wandering the halls of East Linfield High to a chant of *Porny Poppy! Porny
Poppy!*"

"Fine," Alex says gently. "I won't make you visit my classroom
to teach Billy Joel Radio History. But just so you know . . ." He
looks at me, face serious, voice deadpan. "If any of my juniors
called you Porny Poppy, I'd fucking waste them."

"That has to be," I say, "the hottest thing anyone has ever said
to me."

He laughs but looks away. "I'm serious. Bullying's the one thing
I don't let them get away with." He tips his head in thought. "Except me. They bully *me* constantly."

I laugh even though I don't believe him. Alex teaches the AP
and Honors kids, and he's young, handsome, quietly hilarious, and
freakishly smart. There's no way they don't adore him.

"But do they call you Porny Alex?" I ask.

He grimaces. "God, I hope not."

"Sorry," I say, "*Mr.* Porny."

"Please. Mr. Porny is my father."

"I bet so many students have crushes on you."

"One girl told me I look like Ryan Gosling . . ."

"Oh my god."

". . . if he got stung by a bee."

"Ouch," I say.

"I know," Alex agrees. "Tough but fair."

"Maybe Ryan Gosling looks like *you* if he was left outside to dehydrate, did you ever think of that?"

"Yeah. Take that, Jessica McIntosh," he says.

"You bitch," I say, then immediately shake my head. "Nope. Did not feel good to call a child a bitch. Bad joke."

Alex grimaces again. "If it makes you feel any better, Jessica *is* . . . not my favorite. But she'll grow out of a lot of it, I think."

"Yeah, I mean, for all you know she might be working against a lifetime of postgum bowl cuts. It's nice of you to give her a chance."

"You were never a Jessica," he says confidently.

I arch an eyebrow. "How do you know?"

"Because." His eyes hold fast to the sun-bleached road. "You've always been Poppy."

THE DESERT ROSE apartment complex is a stucco building painted bubblegum pink, its name embossed in curling midcentury letters. A garden full of scrubby cacti and massive succulents winds around it, and through a white picket fence, we spot a sparkling teal pool, dotted with sun-browned bodies and ringed in palm trees and chaise lounges.

Alex turns the car off. "Looks nice," he says, sounding relieved.

I step out of the car, and the asphalt's hot even through my sandals.

I thought from summers in New York, trapped between skyscrapers with the sun pinballing back and forth ad infinitum—and all those earlier ones in the Ohio River Valley's natural humidity trap—that I knew what hot was.

I did not.

My skin tingles under the merciless desert sun, my feet burning just from standing still.

"Shit," Alex pants, sweeping his hair off his forehead.

"I guess this is why it's the off-season."

"How do David and Tham live here?" he says, sounding disgusted.

"The same way you live in Ohio," I say. "Sadly, and with heavy drinking."

I mean it as a joke, but Alex's expression flattens out, and he heads to the back of the car without acknowledging what I said.

I clear my throat. "Kidding. Plus, they mostly live in L.A., right? It was nowhere near this hot back there."

"Here." He passes me the first bag, and I take it, feeling chastened.

Note to self: no more shitting on Ohio.

By the time we get out our luggage—and the two paper bags of groceries we grabbed during a CVS pit stop—and wrestle it up three flights of stairs to our unit, we're sweat drenched.

"I feel like I'm melting," Alex says as I punch the code into the key box beside the door. "I need a shower."

The box pops open, and I stick the key into the doorknob, jiggling and twisting it per the very specific instructions the host sent me.

"As soon as we go outside, we're gonna be melting again," I

point out. "You might want to save the showering for right before bed."

The key finally catches, and I bump the door open, shuffling inside, stopping short as two simultaneous warning bells start shrieking through my body.

Alex walks into me, a solid wall of sweat-dampened heat. "What's—"

His voice drops off. I'm not sure which horrible fact he's registering. That it's disgustingly hot in here or that . . .

In the middle of this (otherwise perfect) studio apartment, there sits one bed.

"No," he says quietly, as if he didn't mean to say it aloud. I'm sure he didn't.

"It said two beds," I blurt out, frantically trying to pull up the reservation. "It definitely did."

Because there's no way I could have possibly screwed up this badly. I couldn't have.

There was a time when it might not have seemed like a huge deal for us to share a bed, but it is *not* this trip. Not when things are fragile and awkward. We have *one chance* to fix what broke between us.

"You're sure?" Alex says, and I hate that note of annoyance in his voice even more than the suspicious one riding alongside it. "You saw pictures? With two beds?"

I look up from my inbox. "Of course!"

But *did* I? This unit had been ridiculously cheap, in large part because a reservation had canceled last minute. I knew it was a studio, but I saw pictures of the sparkly turquoise pool and the happy, dancing palm trees and the reviews said it was clean, and the kitchenette looked small but chic and—

Did I actually *see* two beds?

"This guy owns a bunch of apartments here," I say, head swimming. "He probably sent us the wrong unit number."

I find the right email and click through the pictures. "Here!" I cry. "Look!"

Alex steps in close, looking over my shoulder at the pictures—a bright white and gray apartment with a couple of thriving potted fiddle-leaf figs in one corner and a vast white bed in the middle of the room, a slightly smaller one beside it.

Okay, so there might have been *some* artful angling to these photographs, because in the shot the bigger bed looks like it's king-sized when it's actually a queen, which means the other couldn't be bigger than a double, but it *definitely* should exist.

"I don't understand." Alex looks from the photo to where the second bed should be.

"Oh," he and I say in unison as it clicks.

He crosses to the wide, armless chair, in coral imitation suede, and yanks off the decorative pillows, reaching into the seam of the chair. He folds the bottom out, the back pressing down so that the whole thing flattens into a long, skinny pad with sagging seams between its three sections. "A pullout . . . chair."

"I'll take that!" I volunteer.

Alex shoots me a look. "You can't, Poppy."

"Why, because I'm a woman, and they'll take your Midwestern masculinity away if you don't fall on the sword of every gender norm presented to you?"

"No," he says. "Because if you sleep on that, you'll wake up with a migraine."

"That happened once," I say, "and we don't *know* it was from sleeping on the air mattress. It could've been the red wine." But even as I say it, I'm searching for the thermostat, because if anything's going to make my head throb, it's sleeping in this heat. I find the controls inside the kitchenette. "Oh my gosh, he has it set to eighty degrees in here."

"Seriously?" Alex scrubs a hand through his hair, catching the sweat beading on his forehead. "And to think, it doesn't feel a degree over two hundred."

I crank the thermostat down to seventy, and the fans kick on loudly, but without any instant relief. "At least we have a view of the pool," I say, crossing to the back doors. I throw the blackout curtains back and balk, the remnants of my optimism fizzling out.

The balcony is way bigger than mine at home, with a cute red café table and two matching chairs. The problem is, three-quarters of it is walled off with plastic sheeting as, somewhere overhead, a horrible melee of mechanical rattles and screeches sound off.

Alex steps out beside me. "Construction?"

"I feel like I'm inside a ziplock bag, *inside* of someone's body."

"Someone with a fever," he says.

"Who's also on fire."

He laughs a little. A miserable sound he tries to play off as lighthearted. But Alex isn't lighthearted. He's Alex. He's high-stress and he likes to be clean and have his space and he packs his own pillow in his luggage, because his "neck is used to this one"—even though it means he can't bring as many clothes as he'd like—and the last thing this trip needs is any unnecessary pushing on our pressure points.

Suddenly, the six days ahead of us seem impossibly long. We should have taken a three-day trip. Just the length of the wedding festivities, when there'd be buffers galore and free booze and time blocked out that Alex would be busy with his brother's bachelor party and whatever else.

"Should we go down to the pool?" I say, a little too loud, because by now my heart is racing and I have to yell to hear myself over it.

"Sure," Alex says, then turns back to the door and freezes. His mouth hangs open as he considers his words. "I'll change in the bathroom, and you can just shout when you're finished?"

Right. It's a studio. One open room with no doors except the one to the bathroom.

Which wouldn't have been awkward, if we weren't both being so freaking awkward.

"Mm-hm," I say. "Sure."

10

Ten Summers Ago

WE WANDER THE city of Victoria until our feet hurt, our backs ache, and all that sleep we *didn't* get on the flights makes our bodies feel heavy and our brains light and floaty. Then we stop for dumplings in a tiny nook of a place whose windows are tinted and whose red-painted walls are elaborately looped in gold mountainscapes and forests and flowing rivers that serpentine through low, rounded hills.

We're the only people inside—it's three p.m., not quite late enough for dinner, but the air-conditioning is powerful and the food is divine, and we're so exhausted we can't stop laughing about every little thing.

The hoarse, voice-cracking yelp Alex let out when the plane touched down this morning.

The suit-wearing man who sprints past the restaurant at top speed, his arms held flat to his sides.

The gallery girl in the Empress Hotel who spent thirty minutes trying to sell us a six-inch, twenty-one-thousand-dollar bear sculpture while we dragged our tattered luggage around behind us.

"We don't really . . . have money for . . . that," Alex said, sounding diplomatic.

The girl nodded enthusiastically. "Hardly anyone does. But when art speaks to you, you find a way to make it work."

Somehow, neither of us could bring ourselves to tell the girl that the twenty-one-thousand-dollar bear was *not* speaking to us, but we'd spent all day, since then, picking things up—a signed Backstreet Boys album in the used record shop, a copy of a novel called *What My G-Spot Is Telling You* in a squat little bookstore off a cobbled street, a pleather catsuit in a fetish shop I led Alex into primarily to embarrass him—and asking, *Does this speak to you?*

Yes, Poppy, it's saying, Bye-Bye-Bye.

No, Alex, tell your G-spot to speak up.

Yes, I'll take it for twenty-one thousand dollars and not a penny less!

We took turns asking and answering, and now, slumped over our black lacquered table, we can't stop half-deliriously picking up spoons and napkins, making them talk to one another.

Our server is around our age, heavily pierced with a soft lisp and a good sense of humor. "If that soy says anything saucy, let me know," she says. "It's got a reputation around here."

Alex tips her 30 percent, and the whole walk to the bus stop, I tease him for blushing whenever she looked at him, and he teases me for making eyes at the cashier in the record shop, which is fair, because I definitely did.

"I've never seen a city this flowery," I say.

"I've never seen a city this clean," he says.

"Should we move to Canada?" I ask.

"I don't know," he says. "Does Canada *speak to you?*"

With the buses, and the walking between stops, it takes two hours total to get the car I informally rented online through WWT, Women Who Travel.

I'm so relieved it actually exists—and that the keys are under the floor mat in the back seat, just like the car's owner, Esmeralda, said they would be—that I start clapping at the sight of it.

"Wow," Alex says, "this car is really speaking to you."

"Yes," I say, "it's saying, *Don't let Alex drive.*"

His mouth droops open, eyes going wide and glossy with feigned hurt.

"Stop!" I yelp, diving away from him and into the driver's seat like he's a live grenade.

"Stop what?" He bends to insert his Sad Puppy Face in front of me.

"*No!*" I screech, shoving him away and writhing sideways in the seat as if trying to escape a swarm of ants pouring off him. I fling myself into the passenger seat, and he calmly climbs into the driver's seat.

"I hate that face," I say.

"Untrue," Alex says.

He's right.

I love that ridiculous face.

Also, I hate driving.

"When you find out about reverse psychology, I'm screwed," I say.

"Hm?" he says, glancing sidelong as he starts up the car.

"Nothing."

We drive two hours north to the motel I found on the eastern side of the island. It's a misty wonderland, wide uncluttered roads lined in forests as ancient as they are dense. There's not a ton to do in town, but there *are* redwoods and hiking trails to waterfalls and a Tim Hortons just a few miles down the road from our motel, a low, lodge-like place with a gravel parking lot out front and a wall of fog-cloaked foliage behind it.

"I sort of love it here," Alex says.

"I sort of do too," I agree.

And it doesn't matter that it rains all week and we finish every hike soaked to the bone, or that we can only find two affordable restaurants and have to eat at each of them thrice, or that we slowly start to realize nearly everyone else we cross paths with is in the upper-sixties-and-older set and that we're definitely staying in a retirement village. Or that our motel room is always damp, or that there's so little to do we have time to kill one full day in a nearby Chapters bookstore (where we eat both breakfast *and* lunch in their café in silence while Alex reads Murakami and I take notes for future reference from a stack of Lonely Planet guides).

None of it matters. I spend the whole week thinking, *This speaks to me.*

This is what I want for the rest of my life. To see new places. To meet new people. To try new things. I don't feel lost or out of place here. There's no Linfield to escape or long, boring classes to dread going back to. I'm anchored only in this moment.

"Don't you wish we could always be doing this?" I ask Alex.

He looks up over his book at me, one corner of his mouth curling. "Wouldn't leave a lot of time for reading."

"What if I promise to take you to a bookstore in every city?" I ask. "Then will you quit school and live in a van with me?"

His head tilts to one side as he thinks. "Probably not," he says, which is no surprise for a variety of reasons, including the fact that Alex *loves* his classes so much he's already researching English grad programs, whereas I'm muscling through with straight Cs.

"Well, I had to try," I say with a sigh.

Alex sets his book down. "I tell you what. You can have my summer breaks. I'll keep those wide open for you, and we'll go anywhere you want, that we can afford."

"Really?" I say, dubious.

"Promise." He holds out his hand, and we shake on it, then sit there grinning for a few seconds, feeling like we've just signed some life-alteringly significant contract.

Our second-to-last day, we hike through the quiet of Cathedral Grove just as the sun is coming up, spilling golden light over the forest in little droplets, and when we leave, we drive straight to a town called Coombs, whose main attraction is a handful of cottages with grass roofs and a herd of goats grazing over them. We take pictures of them, stick our heads through photo-op cutouts that put our faces on crudely painted goat bodies, and spend a luxurious two hours wandering a market stuffed with samples of cookies, candies, and jams.

On the last full day of our trip, we drive across the island to Tofino, the peninsula we *would* have stayed on if we weren't trying to save every possible penny. I surprise Alex with (perhaps worryingly cheap) tickets for a water taxi that takes us to the island I read about, with the trail through the rain forest to the hot spring.

Our water taxi driver is named Buck, and he's not much older than us, with a tangle of sun-bleached yellow hair sticking out from under his mesh-backed hat. He's handsome in an utterly filthy way, with that specifically beachy kind of body odor mixed with patchouli. It should be repulsive, but he makes it work.

The ride itself is a violent affair, the taxi's motor so loud I have to scream into Alex's ear, my hair slapping against his face from the wind, to say, "THIS MUST BE WHAT A ROCK FEELS LIKE WHEN YOU SKIP IT OVER WATER," my voice thunking in and out with each rhythmic hit of the little vessel against the top of the dark, choppy waves.

Buck waves his hands like he's talking to us for the whole length of the (much-too-long) ride, but we can't hear him, which makes both Alex and me semihysterical with laughter after the first twenty minutes of inaudible monologue.

"WHAT IF HE'S CONFESSING TO A CRIME RIGHT NOW?" Alex yells.

"RECITING THE DICTIONARY. FROM BACK TO FRONT," I suggest.

"SOLVING COMPLEX MATH EQUATIONS," Alex says.

"COMMUNING WITH THE DEAD," I say.

"THIS IS WORSE THAN—"

Buck cuts the engine, and Alex's voice far overshoots it. He drops his voice into a whisper against my ear: "Worse than flying."

"Is he stopping to kill us?" I whisper back.

"Was that what he was saying?" Alex hisses. "Is it time to panic?"

"Look out that way," Buck says, spinning leftward in his chair and pointing ahead.

"Where he's going to kill us?" Alex murmurs, and I turn my laugh into a cough.

Buck turns back with a wide, crooked, but admittedly handsome grin. "Family of otters."

A very high-pitched and one-hundred-percent genuine squeal rockets out of me as I lurch to my feet and lean over to see the fuzzy little lumps of fur floating over the waves, paws folded together so that they drift as one, a net made of adorable sea creatures. Alex comes to stand behind me, his hands light on my arms as he leans over me to see.

"Okay," he says. "Time to panic. That's fucking adorable."

"Can we take one home?" I ask him. "They speak to me!"

After that, the hike through the lush ferns of the rain forest, and the hot, earthy waters of the spring—though amazing—can't quite compare to that spine-compressing water taxi ride.

When we strip down to our bathing suits and slip into the warm, cloudy pool within the rocks, Alex says, "We saw otters holding hands."

"The universe likes us," I say. "This has been a perfect day."

"A perfect trip."

"It's not over yet," I say. "One more night."

When Buck's water taxi delivers us safely into harbor that night, we huddle into the little time-warped shack the company uses as an office to pay.

"Where you guys staying?" Buck asks as he takes the coupons I printed out and manually punches their code into a computer.

"Other side of the island," Alex says. "Outside Nanoose Bay."

Buck's blue eyes come up, cut between Alex and me appraisingly. "My grandparents live in Nanoose Bay."

"It kind of seems like every grandparent in British Columbia might live in Nanoose Bay," I say, and Buck lets out a bark of laughter.

"What are you doing *there*?" he asks. "Not a great spot for a young couple."

"Oh, we're not . . ." Alex shifts uncomfortably from one foot to the other.

"We're like nonbiological, nonlegal siblings," I say.

"Just friends," Alex translates, seeming embarrassed for me, which is understandable because I can *feel* my cheeks go lobster red and my stomach flip when Buck's eyes settle on me.

They shift back to Alex, and he smiles. "If you don't want to drive back to the old folks' home tonight, my housemates and I have got a yard and a spare tent. You're welcome to crash there. We've always got people staying with us."

I'm fairly sure Alex does *not* want to sleep on the ground, but he takes one look at me and must see how into this idea I am—this is exactly the kind of spur-of-the-moment, out-of-nowhere surprise turn I've been hoping this trip would take—because he lets out an almost imperceptible sigh, then turns back to Buck with a fixed smile. "Yeah. That'd be great. Thanks."

"Cool, you all were my last trip, so let me close up and we can head out."

As we're walking back down the dock afterward, Alex asks for the address so we can plug it into the GPS. "Nah, man," Buck says. "You don't need to drive."

It turns out Buck's house is just up a short, steep driveway a half block from the dock. A droopy, graying two-story house with a second-floor balcony covered in drying towels and bathing suits and shitty folding furniture. There's a bonfire burning in the front yard, and even though it's only six p.m., there are dozens of grungy Buck-types gathered in sandals and hiking boots or dirt-crusted bare feet, drinking beer and doing acro-yoga in the grass while trance music plays over a pair of duct-tape-ridden speakers on the porch. The whole place smells like weed, like this is some kind of low-rent, miniature Burning Man.

"Everyone," Buck calls as he leads us up the hillside, "this is Poppy and Alex. They're from . . ." He looks over his shoulder at me, waiting.

"Chicago," I say as Alex says, "Ohio."

"Ohio and Chicago," Buck repeats. People call out greetings and tip their beers, and a lean, muscly girl in a woven crop top brings me and Alex each a bottle, and Alex tries very hard not to look at her stomach as Buck disappears into the circle of people around the fire, doing that backslapping hug with a handful of people.

"Welcome to Tofino," she says. "I'm Daisy."

"Another flower!" I say. "But at least they don't use yours to make opium."

"I haven't tried opium," Daisy says thoughtfully. "I pretty much stick to LSD and shrooms. Well, and weed, obviously."

"Have you tried those sleep gummies?" I ask. "Those things are fucking amazing."

Alex coughs. "Thanks for the beer, Daisy."

She winks. "My pleasure. I'm the welcome committee. And the tour guide."

"Oh, do you live here too?" I ask.

"Sometimes," she says.

"Who else does?" Alex says.

"Hmm." Daisy turns, scouring the crowd and vaguely pointing. "Michael, Chip, Tara, Kabir, Lou." She gathers her dark hair off her back and pulls it to one side of her neck as she continues. "Mo, Quincy sometimes; Lita's been here for a month, but I think she's leaving soon. She got a job as a rafting guide in Colorado—how far is Chicago from there? You should look her up if you're ever visiting."

"Cool," Alex says. "Maybe so."

Buck reappears between me and Alex, with a joint tucked in his mouth, and slings a casual arm around each of us. "Has Daisy given you the tour yet?"

"Was just about to," she says.

But somehow, I don't wind up on a tour of this soggy house. I wind up sitting in a cracked plastic Adirondack chair by the fire with Buck and—I think?—Chip and Lita-the-soon-to-be-rafting-guide, ranking Nicolas Cage movies by various criteria as the deep blues and purples of twilight melt into the deeper blues and blacks of night, the starry sky seeming to unfurl over us like a great, light-pricked blanket.

Lita is an easy laugher, which I've always thought was a criminally underappreciated trait, and Buck is so laid-back I start to get a secondhand high just from sharing a chair with him, and then I get my first firsthand high when I share his joint with him.

"Don't you love it?" he asks eagerly when I'm a few puffs in.

"Love it," I say. Truthfully, I think it's just okay, and moreover, if I were anywhere else, I think I might even hate it, but tonight it's perfect because *today* is perfect, this *trip* is perfect.

Alex checks back in on me after his "tour," by which point, yes, I'm sitting curled up in Buck's lap with his sweatshirt draped around my chilly shoulders.

You okay? Alex mouths from the far side of the fire.

I nod. *You?*

He nods back, and then Daisy asks him something and he turns away, falling into conversation with her. I tip my head back and stare up past Buck's unshaven jawline to the stars high above us.

I think I could stand it if this night lasted three more days, but eventually the sky is changing color again, the morning mist hissing off the damp grass as the sun peeks over a horizon somewhere in the distance. Most of the crowd has drifted off, Alex included, and the fire has burned down to embers when Buck asks me if I want to come inside, and I tell him yes, I do.

I almost tell him that *going inside speaks to me*, then remember that's not a worldwide joke, it's just one of mine and Alex's, and I don't really want to say it to Buck after all.

I'm relieved to discover that he has a room of his own, even if it is closet sized with a mattress on the floor dressed in nothing but two unzipped sleeping bags rather than bedding. When he kisses me, it's rough and scratchy and tastes like weed and beer, but I've only kissed two people before this and one of those was Jason Stanley, so this is still going great in my book. His hands are confident if a little lazy, to match the rest of him, and soon we're climbing onto the mattress, hands catching in each other's seawater-tangled hair, hips locking together.

He has a nice body, I think, the kind that's mostly taut from an active lifestyle with a little pudge from indulging in his various vices. Not like Alex's, which has been made in the gym over years with discipline and care. Not that Alex's body isn't great. It *is* great.

And not that there's any reason to compare the two, or *any two* bodies, really. It's sort of messed up that the thought even popped into my head.

But it's just because Alex's is the man-body I'm most used to being around and it's also the kind I expect I won't ever touch. People like Alex—careful, conscientious, gym-fit, reserved people—tend to go for people like Sarah Torval—Alex's careful, conscientious, yoga-bunny crush from the library.

Whereas people like me are more likely to wind up making out with people like Buck on their floor mattresses on top of their unzipped sleeping bags.

He's all tongue and hands, but even so it's *fun*, to kiss this near-stranger, to have fervent, appreciative permission to touch him. It's like practice. Perfect, fun practice with some guy I met on vacation, who holds no bearing on my real life. Who knows only Poppy Right Now, and doesn't need any more than that.

We kiss until my lips feel bruised and our shirts have come off and then I sit up in the dawn-dark, catching my breath. "I don't want to have sex, okay?"

"Oh, right on," he says lightly, sitting up against the wall. "That's cool. No pressure."

And he doesn't seem to feel any hint of awkwardness about this, but he also doesn't pull me back to him, kiss me again. He just sits there for a minute, like he's waiting for something.

"What?" I say.

"Oh." He glances toward the door then back to me. "I just thought, if you don't want to hook up . . ."

And then I understand. "You want me to leave?"

"Well . . ." He gives a sheepish (or sheepish for him, anyway) half laugh that still sounds kind of barky. "I mean, if we're not going to have sex, then I might . . ."

He trails off, and now my own laugh catches me by surprise. "Are you going to hook up with someone else?"

He seems genuinely concerned when he says, "Does that make you feel bad?"

I stare back at him for a three full seconds.

"Look, if you wanted to have sex, you'd be, like . . . I'd want to. Like, I definitely do. But since you don't . . . Are you mad?"

I burst out laughing. "No," I say, pulling my shirt back on. "I'm actually really, really not mad. I appreciate the honesty."

And I mean it. Because this is just Buck, some guy I met on vacation, and all things considered, he has been something of a gentleman.

"Okay, cool," he says, and flashes that laid-back grin of his, which almost glows in the dark. "I'm glad we're cool."

"We're cool," I agree. "But . . . you said something about a tent?"

"Oh, right." He slaps his hand to his forehead. "The red-and-black one out front's all you, girl."

"Thanks, Buck," I say, and stand. "For everything."

"Hey, hold on a second." He leans over and grabs a magazine off the floor beside his mattress, digs around for a marker, then scribbles something on the white edge of a page and tears it out. "If you're ever back on the island," he says, "don't stay in my grandparents' neighborhood, okay? Just come stay here. We've always got room."

With that, I slip out of the house, past rooms that are already— or still—playing music and doors through which soft sighs and moans emanate.

Outside, I pick my way down the dewy porch steps and head to

the red-and-black tent. I'm fairly sure I saw Alex disappear inside
the house with Daisy hours ago, but when I unzip the tent, he's fast
asleep in it. I carefully crawl inside, and when I lie down beside him,
he just barely opens his puffy-with-sleep eyes and rasps, "Hey."

"Hey," I say. "Sorry to wake you."

"'S okay," he says. "How was your night?"

"Okay," I tell him. "I made out with Buck."

His eyes widen for a second before shrinking back to sleepy
slivers of hazel. "Wow," he croaks, then tries to swallow down a
spark of sleepy laughter. "Did the curtains match the very trou-
bling drapes?"

Laughing, I give his leg a shove with my foot. "I didn't tell you
so you could mock me."

"Did he tell you what he was saying that whole time on the water
taxi?" Alex asks through another rattle of laughter. "How many
people were in the hammock with you?"

I start to laugh so hard there are tears leaking from the corners
of my eyes. "He . . . kicked . . ." It's hard to get words out between
wheezes of laughter, but eventually I manage, ". . . kicked me out
when I told him I didn't want to have sex."

"Oh my god," Alex says, sitting up on his elbow, the sleeping
bag falling down from his bare chest and his hair dancing with
static. "What a dick."

"No," I say. "It was fine. He just wanted to get some, and if not
from me, there are easily four hundred more girls on this half acre
of sinking woods."

Alex flops back down on his pillow. "Yeah, well, I still think
that's kind of shitty."

"Speaking of girls," I say, smirking.

"We . . . weren't?" Alex says.

"Did you hook up with Daisy?"

He rolls his eyes. "Do you *think* I hooked up with Daisy?"

"Until you said it like that, yes."

Alex adjusts his arm under his pillow. "Daisy isn't my type."

"True," I say. "She's nothing like Sarah Torval."

Alex rolls his eyes again then closes them entirely. "Go to sleep, weirdo."

Through a yawn, I say, "Sleep speaks to me."

11

This Summer

THERE ARE PLENTY of empty chaise lounges available at the Desert Rose complex pool—everyone's in the water—so Alex and I take our towels over to two in the corner.

He winces as he lowers himself to sitting. "The plastic's hot."

"Everything's hot." I plop down beside him and peel off my cover-up. "What percentage of that pool do you think is pee by now?" I ask, tipping my head to the gaggle of sunhat-wearing babies splashing on the steps with their parents.

Alex grimaces. "Don't say that."

"Why not?"

"Because it's so hot I'm going to get in the water anyway, and I don't want to think about it." He glances away as he draws his white T-shirt over his head, then folds it and twists to set it on the ground behind him, the muscles pulling taut along his chest and stomach in the process.

"How have you gotten more ripped?" I ask.

"I haven't." He pulls the sunblock from my beach bag and pumps some into his hand.

I look down at my own stomach, hanging over the tight high-lighter orange of my bikini bottoms. In the last few years my life-style of airplane cocktails and late-night burritos, gyros, and noodles has started to fill me out and soften me. "Fine," I say to Alex, "then you look exactly the same, while the rest of us are start-ing to droop in the eyes and the boobs and the neck, and get more and more stretch marks and pockmarks and scars."

"Do you really want to look like your eighteen-year-old self?" he asks, and starts to smear big globs of sunblock onto his arms and chest.

"Yes." I pick up the bottle of Banana Boat and work some of it onto my shoulders. "But I'd settle for twenty-five."

Alex shakes his head, then bows it as he slathers more sunblock onto his neck. "You look better than you did back then, Poppy."

"Really? Because the comments section on my Instagram would disagree," I say.

"That's all bullshit," he says. "Half the people on Instagram have never lived in a world where every picture wasn't edited. If they saw you in real life, they'd pass out. My students are all obsessed with this 'Instagram model' who's completely CGI. This animated girl. Liter-ally looks like a video game character and every time the account posts, they all freak out about how beautiful she is."

"Oh, yeah, I know that girl," I say. "I mean, I don't *know* her. She's not real. But I know the account. Sometimes I go down deep rabbit holes reading the comments. She has a rivalry with another CGI model—do you want me to get your back?"

"What?" He looks up, confused.

I lift the bottle of sunblock up. "Your back? It's facing the sun right now."

"Oh. Yeah. Thanks." He turns around and ducks his head, but he's still tall enough that I have to sit up on my knees to get the spot between his shoulder blades. "Anyway." He clears his throat. "The kids know I get seriously repulsed by the uncanny valley so they always try to trick me into looking at pictures of that fake girl, just to watch me writhe. It kind of makes me feel bad for doing that Sad Puppy Face at you all these years."

My hands go still on his warm, sun-freckled shoulders, my stomach pinching. "I'd be sad if you stopped doing that."

He looks over his shoulder at me, his profile cast in cool blue shadow as the sun beats down on him from the other side. For a millisecond, I feel fluttery from his closeness, from the feeling of his shoulder muscles under my hands and the way his cologne mixes with the coconut sweetness of the sunblock and the way his hazel eyes fix on me firmly.

It's a millisecond that belongs to that other five percent—the what-if. *If* I leaned forward and kissed him over his shoulder, slipped his bottom lip between my teeth, twisted my hands into his hair until he turned himself around and pulled me into his chest.

But there's no more room for that what-if, and I know that. I think he knows it too, because he clears his throat and glances away. "Want me to get your back too?"

"Mm-hm," I manage, and we both turn again so that now he's facing my back, and the whole time his hands are on me, I'm actively trying not to register it. Trying not to feel something hotter than the Palm Springs sun gathering behind my belly button as his palms gently scrape over me.

It doesn't matter that there are babies squealing and people laughing and preteens cannonballing into far-too-small spaces in the pool. There's not enough stimuli in this busy pool to distract me, so I move on to a hastily formed plan B.

"Do you ever talk to Sarah?" I blurt out, my voice a full octave higher than usual.

"Um." Alex's hands lift off me. "Sometimes. You're done, by the way."

"Cool. Thanks." I turn around and shift back onto my chaise, putting a good foot of space between us. "Is she still teaching at East Linfield?" With how competitive teaching jobs were these days, it seemed like a dream when they both found positions at the same school and moved back to Ohio. Then they broke up.

"Yep." He reaches into my bag and pulls out the water bottles we filled with the premade margarita slushies we got at CVS. He hands me one of them. "She's still there."

"So you must see each other a lot," I say. "Is that awkward?"

"Nah, not really," he offers.

"You don't really see each other a lot or it's not really awkward?"

He buys some time with a long chug on the water bottle. "Uhh, I guess either."

"Is . . . she seeing anyone?" I ask.

"Why?" Alex says. "I didn't think you even liked her."

"Yeah," I say, embarrassment coursing through my veins like a quick-hitting drug. "But you did, so I want to make sure you're okay."

"I'm okay," he says, but he sounds uncomfortable so I drop it.

No shitting on Ohio, no talking about Alex's ridiculously fit body, no looking him deep in the eyes from fewer than six inches away, and no bringing up Sarah Torval.

I can do that. Probably.

"Should we get in the water?" I ask.

"Sure."

But as we pick our way through the herd of babies to move down the whitewashed pool steps, it rapidly becomes clear that *this* isn't the solution to the touch-and-go awkwardness between us. For one thing, the water, with all the many bodies standing (and potentially peeing) in it, feels nearly as hot as the air and somehow even more unpleasant.

For another thing, it's so crowded that we have to stand so close that the upper two-thirds of our bodies are almost touching. When a stocky man in a camo hat pushes past me, I collide with Alex and a lightning bolt of panic sizzles through me at the feeling of his slick stomach against mine. He catches me by the hips, at once steadying me and easing me away, back to my rightful place two inches away from him.

"You okay?" he asks.

"Mm-hm," I say, because all I can really focus on is the way his hands spread over my hip bones. I expect there to be a lot of that on this trip. The *mm-hm*ing, not the gigantic Alex-hands on my hips.

He lets go of me and cranes his neck over his shoulder, looking back to our lounges. "Maybe we should just read until it's less crowded," he suggests.

"Good idea." I follow him in a zigzagging path back to the pool steps, to the burning-hot cement, to the too-short towels spread on the chaises, where we lie down to wait. He pulls out a Sarah Waters novel, which he finishes, then follows with an Augustus Everett book. I take out the latest issue of *R+R*, planning to skim everything I *didn't* write. Maybe I'll find a spark of inspiration I can take back to Swapna so she won't be mad at me.

I pretend to read for two sweaty hours and the pool never empties out.

AS SOON AS we open the door to the apartment, I know things are going to get worse.

"What the hell," Alex says, following me inside. "Did it get *hotter*?"

I hurry to the thermostat and read the numbers illuminated there. "Eighty-*two*?!"

"Maybe we're pushing it too hard?" Alex suggests, coming to

stand beside me. "Let's see if we can get it back down to eighty at least."

"I know eighty is, technically speaking, better than eighty-two, Alex," I say, "but we're still going to murder each other if we have to sleep in eighty-degree heat."

"Should we call someone?" Alex asks.

"Yes! We should definitely call someone! Good thinking!" I rifle through the beach bag for my phone and search my email for the host's phone number. I hit call, and it rings three times before a gruff, smoky voice comes over the line. "Yeah?"

"Nikolai?"

Two seconds of silence. "Who is this?"

"This is Poppy Wright. I'm staying in 4B?"

"Okay."

"We're having some trouble with the thermostat."

Three seconds of silence this time. "Did you try Googling it?"

I ignore the question and forge ahead. "It was set to eighty degrees when we got here. We tried to turn it down to seventy two hours ago and now it's eighty-two."

"Oh, yeah," Nikolai says. "You're pushing it too hard."

I guess Alex can hear what Nikolai's saying, because he nods, like, *Told you.*

"So . . . it can't handle . . . going colder than seventy-eight?" I say. "Because that wasn't in the posting, and neither was the construction outside the—"

"It can only do a degree at a time, honey," Nikolai says with a beleaguered sigh. "You can't just push a thermostat down to seventy degrees! And who keeps an apartment seventy degrees anyway?"

Alex and I exchange a look. "Sixty-seven," he whispers.

Sixty-five, I mouth, gesturing to myself. "Well—"

"Look, look, look, honey." Nikolai cuts me off again. "Turn it down to eighty-one. When it gets down to eighty-one, turn it down to eighty. Then turn it down to seventy-nine, and when it gets down to seventy-nine, you set it to seventy-eight. And once it's seventy-eight—"

"—go ahead and just cut off your own head," Alex whispers, and I pull the phone away from me before Nikolai can hear me laugh.

I drag it back to my cheek, and Nikolai's *still* explaining how to count backward from eighty-two. "Got it," I say. "Thanks."

"No prob," Nikolai says with another sigh. "Have a good stay, honey."

As I hang up, Alex crosses back to the thermostat and turns it back up to eighty-one. "Here goes literally nothing."

"If we can't get it to work . . ." I trail off as the full force of our situation hits me. I was going to say that, if we couldn't get it to work, I'd just book us a hotel room with the *R+R* card.

But of course we can't.

I could put it on my *own* credit card, but, living in New York, in a too-nice-for-me apartment, I don't *actually* have a ton of expendable income. The perks of my job are arguably the biggest form of income. I could try to score us a room through an advertising trade, but I've been slacking on my social media and blogging, and I'm not sure I still have enough clout. Besides, a lot of places won't do that with influencers. Some will even screenshot your email requests and post them online to shame you. It's not like I'm George Clooney. I'm just some girl who takes pretty pictures—I might be able to land us a discount; a free room's unlikely.

"We'll figure something out," Alex says. "Do you want to shower first, or should I?"

I can tell from the way he's holding his arms slightly away from his body that he's desperate to be clean. And if he hops in the shower now, maybe I'll even manage to get the temperature down a few degrees in the meantime.

"Go ahead," I tell him, and he slips away.

The whole time I can hear the water running, I'm pacing. From the foldout pseudo bed to the plastic-wrapped balcony to the thermostat. Finally, it drops down to eighty-one, and I reset the goal temperature to eighty and keep pacing.

After deciding to document this so I can report it to Airbnb and try to get some money back, I take pictures of the chair bed and the porch—the construction upstairs has mercifully ceased for the day so at least it's quiet, the hum of conversation and splash of water drifting up from the pool—then head back to the thermostat, down to eighty now, to take a picture of that too.

Just as I'm resetting the temperature for seventy-nine, the shower turns off, so I swing my suitcase up onto the foldout chair, unzip the bag, and start rooting through it for something lightweight to wear to dinner.

Alex steps out of the bathroom in a cloud of steam with a towel wrapped around his waist, one hand securing it at the hip as the other swipes through his wet hair, leaving it sticking up and out messily. "Your turn," he says, but it takes me a second to compute through the haze of his long, lean torso and the sharp jut of his left hip bone.

Why is it so different seeing someone in a towel than in a bathing suit? Thirty minutes ago, Alex was technically more naked than this, but now, the smooth lines of his body feel more scandalous. I feel like all the blood in my body is just bobbing to the surface, pressing against my skin so that every inch of me is more alert.

It never used to be like this.

This is all because of Croatia.

Damn you and your gorgeous islands, Croatia!

"Poppy?" Alex prompts.

"Mm-hm," I say, then remember to at least add, "Yeah." I spin back to my bag and grab a dress, bra, and underwear at random. "Okay. Bedroom's all yours."

I hurry into the steamy bathroom and shut the door as I'm stripping off my bikini top only to freeze, stunned at the sight of a huge blue-tinted glass capsule that occupies the entirety of one wall, complete with a reclined seat *on either side*, like it's some kind of group shower from *The Jetsons*.

"Oh my god." This, I'm sure, was not in the photographs. In fact, this whole room is unrecognizable from the one on the website, transformed from the subtle, beachy grays of its former self into the glowing blue and sterile whites of the hypermodern sight before me.

I snatch a towel off the rack, wrapping it around myself, and throw the door open. "Alex, why didn't you say anything about the—"

Alex grabs for his towel and pulls it around himself and I do my absolute best to pick up where my sentence stumbled off and pretend that didn't happen. "—spaceship bathroom?"

"I figured you knew," Alex says, his voice hoarse. "You booked this place."

"They must've remodeled since the photos were taken," I say. "How did you even figure out how to work that thing?"

"Honestly," Alex says, "the hardest thing was just wresting control from the *2001: A Space Odyssey*–style artificial intelligence system. After that, the biggest issue was just that I kept mixing up the controls for the sixth shower head with the ones for the foot massager."

It's enough to break the tension. I dissolve into laughter and he does too, and it stops mattering so much that we're standing here in our towels.

"This place is purgatory," I say. Everything is just nice enough to make the issues that much more glaring.

"Nikolai is a sadist," Alex agrees.

"Yes, but he's a sadist with a spaceship bathroom." I lean back into the bathroom to study the many-headed, multiseated shower again.

I burst into another fit of laughter and lean back out to find Alex standing there, grinning. He's pulled a T-shirt on over his damp upper body but hasn't risked swapping the towel out.

I turn back to the bathroom. "Okay, I'll leave you to dance naked around the apartment in privacy now. Use your time wisely."

"Is that what you do?" Alex calls. "Dance around the apartment naked whenever I'm in the other room? You do, don't you?"

I spin away as I'm pulling the door shut. "Wouldn't you like to know, Porny Alex?"

12

Nine Summers Ago

DESPITE THE FACT that Alex spent every spare moment of junior year picking up shifts at the library (and thus I spent every spare moment sitting on the floor behind the reference desk eating Twizzlers and teasing him whenever Sarah Torval bashfully drifted by), there isn't money for a big summer trip this year.

His younger brother is starting community college next year, without much financial aid, and Alex, being a saint among mere men, is funneling all his income into Bryce's tuition.

When he broke the news to me, Alex said, "I understand if you want to go to Paris without me."

My reply was instantaneous. "Paris can wait. Let's visit the Paris of America instead."

He arched a brow. "Which is?"

"Duh," I said. "Nashville."

He laughed, delighted. I loved to delight him, *lived* for it. I got such a rush from making that stoic face crack, and lately there hadn't been enough of that.

Nashville is only a four-hour drive from Linfield, and miraculously, Alex's station wagon is still kicking. So Nashville it is.

When he picks me up the morning of our trip, I'm still packing, and Dad makes him sit and answer a series of random questions while I finish. Meanwhile, Mom slips into my room with something hidden behind her back, singing, "Hiiii, sweetie."

I look up from the Muppet-vomit explosion of colorful clothing in my bag. "Hiii?"

She perches on my bed, hands still hidden.

"What are you doing?" I say. "Are you handcuffed right now? Are we being burglarized? Blink twice if you can't say anything."

She brings the box forward. I immediately yelp and slap it out of her hand onto the floor.

"Poppy!" she cries.

"Poppy?!" I demand. "Not *Poppy*! *Mom*! Why are you carrying a bulk box of condoms around behind your back?"

She bends and scoops it up. It's unopened (luckily?), so nothing spilled out. "I just figured it's time we talked about this."

"Uh-uh." I shake my head. "It's nine twenty a.m. *Not* the time to talk about this."

She sighs and sets the box atop my overfilled duffle bag. "I just want you kids to be safe. You've got a *lot* to look forward to. We want all your wildest dreams to come true, honey!"

My heart stutters. Not because my mom is implying that Alex and I are having sex—now that it's occurred to me, of course that's what she thinks—but because I know she's espousing the importance of finishing college, which I still haven't told her I don't plan to do.

I've only told Alex that I'm not going back next year. I've been waiting to tell my parents until after the trip so no big blowup keeps it from happening.

My parents are ultrasupportive, but that's partly because both of them wanted to go to college and neither of them had the support to do so. They've always assumed that any dream I could have would be aided by having a degree.

But throughout the school year, most of my dreaming and energy have been devoted to traveling: weekend trips and short stints over breaks from school—usually on my own, but sometimes with Alex (camping, because that's what we can afford), or with my roommate, Clarissa, a rich hippie type I met in an informational meeting about study-abroad programs at the end of last year (visits to each of her parents' separate lake houses). She's starting next year—*senior year*—in Vienna, and getting art history credits for it, but the longer I considered any of those programs, the less interested I found myself.

I don't *want* to go to Australia only to spend all day in a classroom, and I don't want to rack up thousands more in debt just to have an Academic Experience in Berlin. For me, traveling is about *wandering*, meeting people you don't expect, doing things you've never done. And aside from that, all those weekend trips have started to pay off. I've only been blogging for eight months, and already I have a few thousand followers on social media.

When I found out I failed my biological science general requirement, and thus it would take me an extra semester to graduate, that was the final straw.

And I'm going to tell my parents all this, and somehow, I'll find a way to make them understand that school isn't right for me the way it is for people like Alex. But *today* is not that day. Today, we're going to Nashville, and after the last semester, all I want is to let loose.

Just not in the way my mother is implying.

"Mom," I say. "I am *not* having sex with Alex."

"You don't have to tell me anything," she replies with a cool, calm, and collected nod, though that manner goes completely out the window as she goes on: "I just need to know that you're being responsible. Oh my goodness, I can't believe how grown-up you are! It's making me teary just thinking about it. But you still have to be responsible! I'm sure you are, though. You're such a smart girl! And you've always known yourself. I'm so proud of you, honey."

I'm being more responsible than she knows. While I've made out with a few different guys over the last year, and did more than that with one, I've still stayed pretty safely in the slow lane. When I tipsily admitted this to Clarissa during a trip to her mom's lake house on the far shore of Lake Michigan, her eyes widened like she was gazing into a scrying pool, and she said in that airy way of hers, "What is it you're waiting for?"

I just shrugged. The truth is, I'm not sure. I just figure I'll know when I see it.

Sometimes I think I'm being too practical, which isn't something I've ever been accused of, but with this, I feel at times like I'm waiting for the perfect circumstances for a First Time.

Other times I think it might have something to do with Porny Poppy. Like after all that, I'm incapable of losing myself in a moment, in a person.

Maybe I just need to make a decision, choose someone from a lineup of the loosely held crushes I'm harboring on some of the guys Alex and I run into regularly at parties. People in the English department with him, or communications department with me, or any of the other regularly occurring characters in our lives.

But for now, I'm holding out hope, waiting for that magical moment when it feels right with one person in particular.

That person is *not* going to be Alex.

Actually, if I were to just choose someone, it probably would be. I'd be straight-up with him, explain what I wanted to do and why, and probably insist both of us sign something in blood saying it would only happen once and we would never speak of it again.

But even if it comes to that, I make a silent and solemn vow right now, I will *not* be using a condom from the bulk box my mom just tucked into my suitcase.

"I really, really swear to you I don't need these," I say.

She stands and pats the box. "Maybe not now, but why not hold on to them? Just in case. Also, are you hungry? I've got cookies in the oven, and—shoot, I forgot to run the dishwasher."

She hurries from the room, and I finish packing, then drag my bag downstairs. Mom's at the island, chopping browned bananas for banana bread while the cookies cool, and Alex is sitting in that very rigid way beside my father. "Ready?" I say, and he springs off the stool like *I was born ready to not be sitting next to your very intimidating father.*

"Yep." He scrubs his hands down the fronts of his pants legs. "Yeah." It's right around then that he clocks the box of condoms tucked under my arm.

"This?" I say. "This is just five hundred condoms my mom gave me in case we start boning."

Alex's face flushes.

"Poppy!" Mom cries.

Dad looks over his shoulder, aghast. "Since when are you two romantically involved?"

"I don't . . . We don't . . . do that, sir," Alex tries.

"Here, will you carry these out to the car, Dad?" I toss them over the island to him. "My arm's getting tired from holding it. Hopefully our hotel has those big luggage carts."

Alex is still not-quite-looking at Dad. "We really aren't . . ."

Mom digs her hands into her hips. "That was supposed to be private. Look, you're embarrassing him. Don't embarrass him, Poppy. Don't be embarrassed, Alex."

"It was never going to be private for long," I say. "If that box doesn't fit in the trunk, we're going to have to strap it to the top of the station wagon."

Dad sets the box on the side table and starts reading the side of it with a furrow in his brow. "Are these *really* made out of lambskin? Are they reusable?"

Alex cannot hide his shudder.

Mom offers up, "I wasn't sure if either of them is allergic to latex!"

"Okay, we've got to hit the road," I say. "Come give us hugs goodbye. The next time you see us, you might just be grandpar—" I drop off, stop rubbing my tummy meaningfully when I see the look on Alex's face. "Kidding! We're just friends. Bye, Mom. Bye, Dad!"

"Oh, you're going to have an amazing time. I can't wait to hear all about it." Mom comes out from behind the counter and pulls me into a hug. "Be good," she says. "And don't forget to call your brothers when you get down there! They're desperate to hear from you!"

Over her shoulder I mouth at Alex, *desperate*, and he finally cracks a smile.

"Love you, kiddo." Dad clambers off the stool to give me a squeeze. "You take care of my little baby, okay?" he says to Alex before pulling him into the backslap hug that startles him anew every time it happens. "Don't let her get engaged to a country singer or break her neck on a mechanical bull."

"Of course," Alex says.

"We'll see," I say, and then they walk us outside—box of con-doms left safely on the island—and wave to us as we back down the driveway, and Alex grins and waves back until we're finally out of sight, at which point he looks at me and says flatly, "I am very mad at you."

"How can I make it up to you?" I bat my eyelashes like a sexy cartoon cat.

He rolls his eyes, but a smirk twists up in the corner of his mouth as his eyes return to the road. "For one thing, you are *definitely* riding a mechanical bull."

I kick my feet up onto the dashboard, proudly displaying the cowgirl boots I found at a thrift store a few weeks ago. "Way ahead of you."

His eyes slide to me, move down my legs to the bright red leather. "And those are supposed to keep you on a mechanical bull *how?*"

I click my heels together. "They're not. They're just supposed to charm the handsome country singer at the bar into scraping me off the mat and into his farm-buff arms."

"Farm buff," Alex snorts, unimpressed by the idea.

"Says Gym-Buff," I tease.

He frowns. "I exercise for my anxiety."

"Yes, I'm sure you couldn't care less about that gorgeous body. It's incidental."

His jaw pulses, and his eyes fix on the road again. "I like to look nice," he says in a voice that implies an added, *Is that a crime?*

"I do too." I slide one of my feet along the dash until my red boot is in his field of vision. "Obviously."

His gaze darts over my leg down to the middle console where his aux cable sits in a neat loop. "Here." He hands it to me. "Why don't you get us started?"

These days we always take turns running sound in the station wagon, but Alex always gives me the first shot, because he is Alex, and he is the best.

I insist on an all-country playlist for the length of the drive. Mine is populated by Shania Twain, Reba McEntire, Carrie Underwood, and Dolly Parton. His is all Patsy Cline and Willie Nelson, Glen Campbell and Johnny Cash, and a helping of Tammy Wynette and Hank Williams.

We found the hotel on Groupon months ago, and it's one of those kitschy, one-off places with a neon-pink sign (cartoon cowboy hat balanced atop the word VACANCY) that makes the nickname "Nashvegas" finally make sense to me.

We check in and take our stuff inside. Each room is vaguely themed after a famous Nashville musician. Meaning there are framed pictures of them all over the room, and then the same hideous floral comforters and dense tan fleeces on all the beds. I tried to request the Kitty Wells room, but apparently when you book through Groupon, you don't get to pick.

We are in the Billy Ray Cyrus room.

"Do you think he gets paid for this?" I ask Alex, who's pulling up the bedding to check for bedbugs along the bottom of the mattresses.

"Doubtful," he says. "Maybe they throw him the occasional frozen yogurt Groupon or something." He pushes back the drapes and gazes out at the flashing neon sign. "Do they do rooms by the hour here?" he says skeptically.

"Doesn't really matter," I say, "since I left the condom crate at home."

He shudders and drops onto one of the beds, satisfied that it's bug free. "If I hadn't had to *witness* that, it would actually be pretty sweet."

"*I* would have still had to witness it, Alex. Don't *I* matter?"

"Yeah, but you're her daughter. The closest my dad ever came to giving us a sex talk was leaving a book about purity on each of our beds around the time we turned thirteen. I thought masturbating caused cancer until I was, like, sixteen."

My chest squeezes tight. Sometimes I forget how hard Alex has had it. His mom died from complications during David's birth, and Mr. Nilsen and the four Nilsen boys have been wife- and motherless since. His dad finally dated a woman from their church last year, but they broke up after three months, and even though Mr. Nilsen was the one to end it, he was still so torn up that Alex had to drive home from school in the middle of the week to get him through it.

Alex is the one his brothers call too, when something goes wrong. The emotional rock.

Sometimes I think that's why we're so drawn to each other. Because he's used to being the steadfast big brother and I'm used to being the annoying little sister. It's a dynamic we understand: I lovingly tease him; he makes the entire world feel safer for me.

This week, though, I'm not going to need anything from him. It's my mission to help Alex let loose, to bring Silly Alex back out of Overworked, Hyperfocused Alex.

"You know," I say, sitting on the bed, "if you ever want to borrow some overbearing parents, mine are obsessed with you. I mean, clearly. My mom wants you to take my virginity."

He leans back on his hands, his head tipping. "Your mom thinks you haven't had sex?"

I balk. "I *haven't* had sex. I thought you knew that." It seems like we talk about everything, but I guess there *are* still a few places we haven't gone.

"No." Alex coughs. "I mean, I don't know. You left a few parties with people."

"Yeah, but nothing serious ever happens. It's not like I dated any of them."

"I thought that was just because you didn't, like, want to date."

"I guess I don't," I say. Or at least so far I haven't. "I don't know.

I guess I just want it to be special. Not like it has to be a full moon and we're in a rose garden or anything."

Alex winces. "Outside sex isn't what it's cracked up to be."

"You little minx!" I cry. "You've been holding out on me."

He shrugs, ears reddening. "I just don't really talk about this. With anyone. Like even just saying that made me feel guilty, like I'm wronging her somehow."

"It's not like you said her name." I lean forward and drop my voice. "Sarah Torval?"

He bumps his knee into mine, smiling faintly. "You're obsessed with Sarah Torval."

"No, dude," I say. "*You* are."

"It wasn't her," he says. "It was another girl from the library. Lydia."

"Oh . . . my . . . god," I say, giddy. "The one with the big doll eyes and the same exact haircut as Sarah Torval?"

"Stoooop," Alex groans, pink spreading over his cheeks. He grabs a pillow and hurls it at me. "Stop embarrassing me."

"But it's so fun!"

He forces his face to relax into the On-the-Verge-of-Crying Puppy Face and I scream and fling myself backward on the bed, my whole body going limp with laughter as I drag the pillow over my eyes. The bed dips under his weight as he sits beside me and tugs the pillow off my face, leaning over me, hands braced on either side of my head, insinuating his Sad Puppy Face into my line of sight.

"Oh my god," I gasp through a mix of tears and laughter. "Why does this have such a confusing effect on me?"

"I don't know, Poppy," he says, the expression deepening sorrowfully.

"It speaks to me!" I cry out through laughter, and his mouth pulls into a grin.

And right then. That.

That is the first moment I want to kiss Alex Nilsen.

I feel it all the way to my toes for two breathless seconds. Then I pack those seconds into a tight knot, tucking them deep in my chest where I promise myself they will live in secret forever.

"Come on," he says softly. "Let's go get you on a mechanical bull."

13

This Summer

WE GET THE thermostat down to seventy-nine and set it for seventy-eight before we leave for a Mexican restaurant called Casa de Sam, which has a great score on Tripadvisor and only one dollar sign signifying its cost.

The food is great, but the air-conditioning is the real MVP of the night. Alex keeps leaning back in the booth, closing his eyes, and making contented sighs.

"Do you think Sam will let us sleep here?" I ask.

"We could try just hiding in the bathroom until closing," Alex suggests.

"I'm afraid to drink too much and get heat exhaustion," I say, taking another sip of the jalapeño margarita we ordered a pitcher of.

"I'm afraid to drink too little and not be able to knock myself out for an entire night."

Even thinking about it has my neck crawling with sweat. "I'm sorry about the Airbnb," I say. "None of the reviews mentioned faulty air-conditioning." Though now I'm wondering how many people stayed there in the dead of summer.

"It's not your fault," Alex says. "I hold Nikolai fully responsible."

I nod, and the silence unfurls awkwardly until I ask, "How's your dad?"

"Yeah," Alex says. "Good. He's doing good. I told you about the bumper sticker?"

I smile. "You did."

He gives a self-conscious laugh and thrusts his hand through his hair. "God, getting old is boring. My best party story is that my dad got a new bumper sticker."

"Pretty great story," I insist.

"You're right." His head tilts. "Next do you want to hear about my dishwasher?"

I gasp and clutch my heart. "You own your own dishwasher? Like, it's in your name?"

"Um. They don't typically register dishwashers to your name, but yes, I bought it. Right after I got the house."

A nameless emotion stabs at my chest. "You . . . bought a house?"

"I didn't tell you?"

I shake my head. Of course he didn't tell me. When would he have told me? But still it hurts. Every single thing I've missed in the last two years hurts.

"My grandparents' house," he says. "After my grandma passed away. She left it to my dad, and he wanted to sell it, but it needs work he didn't have the time or money for, so I've been living in it, fixing it up."

"Betty?" I swallow the tangle of emotions rising in my throat. I only met Alex's grandmother a few times, but I loved her. She was tinier than me and fierce, a lover of murder mysteries and crocheting, spicy food and modern art. She'd fallen in love with her priest and he'd left the priesthood to marry her ("And that's how we became Protestants!") and then ("*eight* months later," she told me with a wink), Alex's mother had been born with a head of thick dark hair just like hers and a "strong" nose like Alex's grandfather, God rest his soul.

Her house was a funky quad-level from the early sixties. It had the original orange and yellow floral wallpaper in the living room, and she'd had to put ugly brown carpet over the hardwood and tile—even in the bathroom—after she slipped and broke her hip several years ago.

"Betty's gone?" I whisper.

"It was peaceful," Alex says, without looking at me. "You know, she was really, really old." He's started to fold our straw wrappers, precisely, into small squares. He shows no sign of emotion, but I know Betty was pretty much his favorite family member, maybe tied with David.

"God, I'm sorry." I fight to keep my voice from shaking, but my emotion is rising, tidal-wave style. "Flannery O'Connor and Betty. I wish you'd told me."

His hazel eyes drag up to mine. "I wasn't sure you wanted to hear from me."

I blink back tears, glance away, and pretend I'm sweeping my hair out of my face rather than wiping at my eyes. When I look back at him, his gaze is still fixed on me.

"I did," I say. Shit, the tremors have arrived.

Even the mariachi band playing in the back room seems to quiet to a hum, so that it's just us in this red booth with its colorful hand-carved table.

"Well," Alex says softly. "Now I know."

I want to ask if he *wanted* to talk to me in all that time, if he ever typed out messages that went unsent or thought about calling for so long he actually started to dial.

If he too feels like he lost two good years of his life when we stopped talking, and why he let it happen. I want him to say things can be how they were before, when there was nothing we couldn't say to each other, and being together was as easy and natural as being alone, without any of the loneliness.

But then our server comes by with the check. I instinctively reach for it before Alex can.

"That's not *R+R*'s card?" he says, like it's a question.

Without actively deciding to, I lie. "They just reimburse us now." My hands tingle, itch with discomfort over the deception, but it's too late to take it back.

When we get outside, it's dark and starry. The heat of the day has broken, and though it still must be in the upper seventies, it's nothing compared to the one hundred and six we were dealing with earlier. There's even a breeze. We're silent as we cross the parking lot to the Aspire. There's a heaviness between us now that we've brushed against what happened in Croatia.

I'd convinced myself we could leave it in the past, but now I realize that every time I learn something new from the last two years, it will press on that same raw spot in my heart.

It's got to be having some kind of effect on him too, but he's always been good at bottling up his feelings when he doesn't want to share them.

The whole ride home I want to say, *I'd take it back. If it would fix this, I'd take it back.*

When we reach the apartment, it is officially hotter inside than outside. We both beeline for the thermostat. "Eighty-one?" he says. "It went up again?"

I rub the bridge of my nose. A headache is starting behind my eyes, from heat or alcohol or stress, or all of it. "Okay. Okay. We've got to turn it back up to eighty, right? And let it drop to that before we lower it again?"

Alex stares at the thermostat like it just knocked an ice cream cone out of his hand. There are unintentional shades of Sad Puppy Face in his expression.

"One degree at a time. That's what Nikolai said."

He adjusts the temperature to eighty, and I slide open the door to the balcony.

But the wall of plastic sheeting is keeping out the fresh air. In the kitchenette, I rifle through drawers until I find a pair of scissors.

"What are you doing?" Alex asks, following me onto the balcony.

"Just the bare fucking minimum," I say, slicing the scissors into the middle of the plastic.

"Oooh, Nikolai's gonna be maaaaad at you," Alex teases.

"I'm not too happy with him either," I say, and cut a long flap in the plastic, pulling it aside and loosely knotting it, so there's a gap for air to flow through.

"He's going to sue us," he deadpans.

"Come at me, Nicky."

Alex chuckles, and after a few seconds of silence, I say, "Tomorrow I was thinking we could check out the art museum and go take the tramway. The view's supposed to be amazing."

Alex nods. "Sounds good."

Again we lapse into quiet. It's only ten thirty, but things are just awkward enough that I think calling it a day might be our best bet. "Do you need into the bathroom before . . ."

"No," Alex says. "Go ahead. I'm gonna catch up on some emails."

I haven't checked my work email since I got here, and I've also let a few messages from Rachel sit, along with the always over-flowing group text between my brothers and me. It's largely just the two of them brainstorming ideas that won't go anywhere. Last I checked in, they were concocting a board game called War on Christmas and demanding I contribute puns.

So at least I'll have something to do while lying on the chair bed, wide awake.

Headache still building, I tug my hair into my go-to stubby ponytail and cross the scuffed wooden floors to the space-age bathroom. In its strange blue light, I wash my face, but rather than applying any of the fancy moisturizers or serums that Rachel is constantly offloading on me, I splash my face with cold water when I'm done, rub some on my temples and my neck.

In the mirror, my reflection looks as wretchedly stressed as I feel. I need to turn this around and remind Alex how things used to be, and I only have five days left to do it, the last three of which will be peppered with wedding festivities.

Tomorrow has to be amazing. I need to be Fun Poppy, not Weird, Hurt Poppy. Then Alex will loosen up, and everything will smooth out. I change into a pair of silky pajama shorts and a tank top, brush my teeth, then step back into the living space to find that Alex has turned off all the lights except the lamp beside the bed, and he's lying on the chair mattress in a pair of exercise shorts and a T-shirt, his same book from earlier in hand.

I happen to know that Alex Nilsen has *always* slept shirtless, even when the temperatures are *not* this absurdly high, but that's neither here nor there because the point is, I'm supposed to take the foldout chair.

"Get out of my bed!" I say.

"You paid," he says. "You get the bed."

"*R+R* paid." Just like that, I'm deeper into the lie. It's not like it's a harmful one, but still.

"I want the chair," Alex says. "How often does a grown man get to sleep on a fuzzy foldout chair, Poppy?"

I sit beside him and make a big show of trying to push him off, but he's too solid for me to budge him. I twist around, bracing my feet against the floor, my knees against the edge of the bed thing, and my hands against his right hip, as I grit my teeth and try to push him off of it.

"Stop it, you weirdo," he says.

"I'm not the weirdo." I turn sideways, try to use my hip and side body to force him off. "You're the one who's trying to steal my one joy in life, this weird bed."

In that moment, when all my weight is pretty much focused in my hip, he stops resisting and scoots sideways a little, and somehow I tumble halfway onto the chair bed and halfway onto his chest, forcefully knocking his book onto the floor in the process. He laughs, and I laugh too, but I'm also feeling kind of tingly and heavy and, frankly, turned on, lying on him like this.

Worst of all, I can't seem to make myself move. His arm has come around my back, loose over the curve at its base, and when his laughter settles, I look up into his eyes, my chin resting on his chest. "You tricked me," I hum. "I bet you didn't even *have* emails to respond to."

"For all you know, I don't even have an email *account*," he teases. "Are you mad?"

"Furious."

His laugh shivers through me, goose bumps chasing it down my spine, and the heat of the apartment sinks into my skin, gathers between my legs.

"I'd forgive you eventually," I say. "I'm very forgiving."

"You are," he agrees. "I've always liked that about you."

His hand just barely brushes the skin between the bottom of my tank top and the top of my shorts, and I shift against him, feeling as if we could melt into each other.

What am I doing?

I sit up suddenly and take my hair down just to put it back up.

"You're sure you're cool to sleep on the chair bed?" My voice comes out too high.

"Of course. Yeah."

I stand and pad over to the bed. "Okay, cool, then . . . good night."

I turn off the light and climb onto bed. Onto, not into, because it's way too hot for blankets.

14

This Summer

WHEN I STARTLE awake, it's still dark out, and I'm sure we're being robbed.

"Shit, shit, shit," the robber is saying for some reason, and it sounds like he's in pain.

"The police are on their way!" I yelp—which is neither a true statement nor a premeditated one—and scramble to the edge of the bed to snap on the light.

"What?" Alex hisses, eyes squinting against the sudden brightness.

He's standing in the dark in the same black shorts he went to sleep in and no shirt. He's bent slightly at the waist and gripping his lower back with both hands, and as the sleep clears from my brain, I realize he's *not* just squinting against the light.

He's gasping for breath like he's in pain.

"What happened?" I cry, half tumbling off the bed toward him. "Are you okay?"

"Back spasm," he says.

"What?"

"I'm having a back spasm," he gets out.

I'm still not sure what he's talking about, but I can tell he's in horrible pain, so I don't press for more information aside from asking, "Do you need to sit down?"

He nods, and I guide him toward the bed. He slowly lowers onto it, wincing until he's finally sitting, at which point some of the pain seems to ease up.

"Do you want to lie down?" I ask.

He shakes his head. "Getting up and down is the hardest part when this happens."

When this happens? I think but don't say, and guilt stabs through my chest. Apparently this is another one of those Poppy-less developments from the last two years.

"Here," I say. "Let me prop some pillows up behind you."

He nods, which I take as confirmation that this won't make things worse. I puff up the pillows, stacking them against the headboard, and he slowly reclines, his face contorted in pain.

"Alex, what happened?" I glance at the alarm clock on the bedside table. It's five thirty in the morning.

"I was getting up to run," he says. "But I guess I sat up weird? Or too fast or something, because my back spasmed and—" He tips his head back against the pillows, eyes scrunching closed. "Shit, Poppy, I'm sorry."

"Sorry?" I say. "Why are *you* sorry?"

"It's my fault," he says. "I didn't think about how low to the ground that cot thing is. I should've known popping out of bed like that would do this."

"How could you have possibly known that?" I say, disbelieving.

He massages his forehead. "I should have," he repeats. "This has been happening for, like, a year now. I can't even bend over to pick up my shoes until I've been awake and moving around for at least half an hour. It just didn't occur to me. And I didn't want you to get a migraine from the chair, and—"

"And *that's* why you should never be a hero," I say gently, teasing, but his expression of misery doesn't so much as waver.

"I wasn't thinking," he says. "I didn't mean to mess up your trip."

"Alex, hey." I touch his arm lightly so it won't disturb the rest of his body. "You didn't mess up this trip, okay? Nikolai did."

The corners of his mouth twist into an unconvinced smile.

"What do you need?" I ask. "How can I help you?"

He sighs. If there's one thing Alex Nilsen hates, it's being helpless. Which goes hand in hand with being waited on. In college, when he had strep throat, he ghosted me for a week (the first time I was truly mad at him). When his roommate told me Alex was laid up with a fever, I made very bad chicken noodle soup in our dorm kitchen and brought it to his room.

He locked the door and wouldn't let me in for fear of passing the strep along, so I started yelling, *"I'm keeping the baby, okay?"* through the doorway and he relented.

It makes him uncomfortable to be fussed over. Thinking about that has a similar, if distilled, effect on me as looking at the formidable Sad Puppy Face. It overwhelms. The love rises less like a wave and more like an instantaneously erected steel skyscraper, shooting up through my center and knocking everything else out of its way.

"Alex," I say. *"Please* let me help."

He sighs, defeated. "There are muscle relaxants in the front pocket of my laptop bag."

"On it." I retrieve the bottle, fill a glass of water in the kitchenette, and bring him both.

"Thanks," he says apologetically, then takes the pill.

"No problem," I say. "What else?"

"You don't have to do anything," he says.

"Look." I take a deep breath. "The sooner you tell me how I can help you, the sooner you get better, and the sooner this is over, okay?"

His teeth skim over his full bottom lip, and I'm mesmerized by the sight. I startle when his gaze cuts back to me. "If there's an ice pack here, that would help," he admits. "Usually I alternate between cold compresses and heating pads, but the important thing is just sitting still."

He says this with disdain.

"Got it." I slip my sandals on and grab my purse.

"What are you doing?" he asks.

"Going to the pharmacy. That freezer doesn't even have an ice cube tray, let alone an ice pack, and I doubt Nicky has a heating pad either."

"You don't have to do that," Alex says. "Really, if I sit still, I'm fine. Go back to sleep."

"While you sit upright in the dark? No way. For one thing, that's extremely creepy, and for another, I'm up, so I might as well be of use."

"This is your vacation."

I walk toward the door, because there's nothing he can do to stop me. "No," I say. "It's our summer trip. Don't dance around naked until I get back, okay?"

He heaves a sigh. "Thanks, Poppy. Seriously."

"Stop thanking me. I'm already drafting an absurd list of ways for you to repay me."

That finally wins a faint smile. "Good. I like to be useful."

"I know," I say. "I've always liked that about you."

15

Eight Summers Ago

WE GET BACK to our downtown hotel room at two thirty in the morning, a little bit hammered. Usually, we don't drink so much, but this whole trip has been a celebration.

We are celebrating the fact that Alex has graduated from college, and that soon he'll be leaving to get his MFA in creative writing from Indiana University.

I tell myself it's not that far away. In fact, we'll be living closer to each other than we have been since I dropped out.

But the truth is, even with all the traveling I've been doing, I'm itching to get out of my parents' house in Linfield. I've started looking for apartments in other cities, flexible jobs bartending and serving where I can work myself to exhaustion, then take weeks off to travel.

Spending time with my parents has been great, but everything else about being home makes me feel claustrophobic, like the suburbs are a net pulling tighter and tighter around me as I struggle against it.

I run into my old teachers, and when they ask what I'm doing, their mouths twist judgmentally at the answer. I see classmates who used to bully me, and some that were friendly enough, and I hide. I work at an upscale bar forty minutes south, in Cincinnati, and when Jason Stanley, my first kiss, came in with his orthodontist-perfected smile and the kind of clothes full-time white-collar jobs require, I dove into the bathroom. Told my boss I had vomited.

For weeks after that, she kept asking how I was doing in a voice that made it perfectly clear she thought I was pregnant.

I was not pregnant. Julian and I are always careful about that. Or at least I am. Julian, in general, is not careful by nature. He is a person who says yes to the world, almost regardless of what it asks. When he visits me at work, he finishes drinks that get left on the bar, and he's tried most drugs (heroin excluded) once. He's always up for weekend trips to Red River Gorge or Hocking Hills—or slightly longer trips to New York, on the overnight bus that's only sixty dollars round trip but often has no bathroom. He has the same kind of flexible schedule I do—he's a college dropout too, but he left the University of Cincinnati after only one year.

He was studying architectural design, but really, he wants to be a working artist. He shows his paintings at DIY spots around the city, and he lives with three other painters in an old white house that makes me think of Buck and the transients of Tofino. Sometimes, after one too many beers, sitting on the porch while they all smoke weed or clove cigarettes and talk about their dreams, it makes me so nostalgic I could cry from some mixture of sadness and happiness whose proportions I can never quite sort out.

Julian is rake-thin with hollowed-out cheekbones and alert eyes that can feel like they're x-raying you. After our first kiss, outside his favorite bar, a grungy place downtown that has a bike repair shop in the back, he told me he didn't ever want to get married or have kids.

"That's okay," I told him. "I don't want to marry you either."

He laughed gruffly and kissed me again. He always tastes like cigarettes or beer, and when he spends his days off work—he works in a UPS warehouse at the edge of town—painting at home, he gets so lost in his work that he forgets to eat or drink. When we meet up afterward, he's usually in a foul mood but only for a few minutes, until he has a snack, at which point he melts back into a sweet, sensitive boyfriend who always kisses and touches me so sensually that I regularly find myself thinking, *I bet this would look beautiful on film.*

I consider saying it to him, asking if we should set up a camera and take some pictures, and I'm immediately embarrassed to have even considered it.

He's the second person I've ever slept with, but he doesn't know that. He didn't ask. The first still comes into my bar every once in a while and flirts a little, but we can both tell that whatever mild attraction there was when he first started coming in fizzled after those two quick hookups. They were kind of awkward but fine, and in the end, I'm glad I got them out of the way because I have a sense that Julian would've been too freaked to come near me if he'd known how inexperienced I was. He would've been afraid I'd get too attached to him, and probably I have, but I think he has too, so for now, it's okay that we spend every spare minute together.

Julian met Alex once when Alex was home for Christmas break at *my* bar, a second time during spring break at Julian's grungy bike bar, and a third time for breakfast at Waffle House before Alex and I left for this trip.

I can tell Julian has very little opinion of Alex, which is mildly disappointing, and likewise I'm aware that Alex despises Julian, which probably shouldn't have been a surprise.

He thinks Julian is reckless, careless. He doesn't like that he always shows up late, or that sometimes I don't hear from him for days, then spend weeks with him almost constantly, or that he hasn't met my parents though they live in the same city.

"It's okay," I insisted when Alex shared these opinions with me on the flight to San Francisco a few days ago. "It works for us." I don't even *want* him to meet my family.

"I can just tell he doesn't get it," Alex said.

"Get what?" I asked.

"You," he said. "He has no idea how lucky he is."

It was both a sweet and a hurtful thing for him to say. Alex's take on our relationship made me feel embarrassed, even if I wasn't sure he was right.

"I'm lucky too," I said. "He's really special, Alex."

He sighed. "Maybe I just need to get to know him better." I knew from his voice he didn't think that would fix the problem at all.

In my daydreams, I'd imagined the two of them becoming best friends, so close that it made sense for our summer trip to expand to include Julian, but after seeing how they interacted, I knew better than to even float the idea.

So Alex and I headed to San Francisco on our own. My credit card earned me enough points to get one of the round-trip plane tickets free, and Alex and I split the cost of the other.

We started with four days in wine country, staying at a new Sonoma bed-and-breakfast that comped two nights in exchange for the advertising they'd get to my twenty-five thousand followers. Alex good-naturedly agreed to take my photo doing all kinds of quaint things:

Sitting on one of the old-fashioned red bikes the B and B has for guests, wearing a giant straw sun hat, fresh flowers in the wicker basket fixed to the handlebars.

Walking on the nature trails through the scrubby meadows and their scraggly trees.

Sipping a cup of coffee on the patio, and a chilled old-fashioned in the sitting room.

We lucked out with the wine tastings too. The first winery we visited comped your tastings if you bought a bottle, and I researched the cheapest one online before we went. Alex took my picture posing in between rows of vines with a glimmering glass of rosé, one leg kicked out to the side to show off my ridiculous purple-and-yellow-striped vintage jumpsuit.

I was tipsy by then, and when he knelt, right in the dried-out dirt in his light gray pants, to take the photo, I almost fell over laughing at the bizarre angle he'd chosen for the picture. "Too many wine," I said, gasping for breath.

"Too. Many. Wine?" he repeated, delighted and disbelieving, and as I fell into a crouch in the middle of the aisle, laughing my head off, he took a few more pictures from way down low, pictures that would make me look like a sassily dressed skin triangle.

He was being a horrible photographer on purpose, not out of protest but to crack me up.

It was the flip side of the Sad Puppy coin, another performance for me and me alone.

By the time we hit the second winery, we were already sleepy from the alcohol and sunshine, and I let my head droop against his shoulder. We were inside, on a technicality: the whole back of the building was a windowed garage door that pulled up so you could move freely from the patio, with its bougainvillea-encroached lattice, to the light, airy bar with its twenty-foot ceilings, big-ass fans spinning lazily overhead, their rhythm like a lullaby.

"How long have you two been together?" the sweet, middle-aged woman running the tasting asked as she returned with our next pour, a light and crisp Chardonnay.

"Oh," Alex said.

Midyawn, I squeezed his biceps and said, "Newlyweds."

The bartender was tickled. "In that case," she said with a wink, "this one's on me."

Her name was Mathilde, and she was originally from France but moved to the United States after meeting her wife online. They lived in Sonoma but had honeymooned just outside San Francisco. "It's called the Blue Heron Inn," she told me. "It's the most idyllic place I've ever seen. Romantic and cozy, with this roaring fire and lovely patio—just a few minutes from Muir Beach. You two *must* see it. It is *perfect* for newlyweds. Tell them Mathilde sent you."

Before we left, we tipped Mathilde for the cost of the free tasting and then some.

For the next couple days, I deployed the newlyweds card regularly. Sometimes we got a discount or a free glass; sometimes we got nothing but a smile, but even those felt genuine and meaningful.

"I feel kind of bad," Alex told me as we were walking it off in one vineyard.

"If you want to go get married," I said, "we can."

"Somehow, I don't think Julian would take that too well."

"He won't care," I said. "Julian doesn't want to get married."

Alex stopped and looked down at me, and then, entirely because of the wine, I started crying. He cupped my face and angled it up to his. "Hey," he said. "It's all right, Poppy. You don't really want to marry Julian, do you? You're way too good for that guy. He doesn't deserve you."

I sniffed back my tears, but that just let more out. My voice came out as a squeak. "Only my parents are ever going to love me," I said. "I'm going to die alone." I knew how stupid and melodramatic it sounded, but with him, it was always so hard to rein myself in, to say anything but the absolute truth of how I felt. And worst of all, I hadn't even known that was how I felt until this moment. Alex's presence had a way of drawing the truth right to my surface.

He shook his head and pulled me into his chest, squeezing me, lifting me up into him like he planned to absorb me. "I love you," he said, and kissed my head. "And if you want, we can die alone together."

"I don't even know if I want to get married," I said, wiping the tears away with a little laugh. "I think I'm about to start my period or something."

He stared down at me, face inscrutable for another beat. It didn't make me feel x-rayed, like Julian's eyes. It just made me feel seen.

"Too many wine," I said, and he finally let a fraction of a smile slip over his lips and we went back to walking off the buzz.

We checked out bright and early from our B and B and called the Blue Heron Inn on speakerphone as we headed back toward San Francisco. It was the middle of the week, and they had plenty of rooms.

"Would you by chance be the Poppy my darling Mathilde said would be calling?" the lady on the phone asked.

Alex shot me a meaningful look, and I sighed heavily. "Yes, but here's the thing. We told her we were newlyweds, but it was a joke. So we don't, like, want any free stuff."

The woman on the other end of the phone gave a hacking cough, which turned out to be laughter. "Oh, honey. Mathilde wasn't born yesterday. People pull that trick all the time. She just liked you two."

"We liked her too," I said, grinning enormously over at Alex. He grinned enormously back.

"I don't have the authority to give anyone a free stay," the woman went on, "but I *do* have a couple year-round passes you can use to visit Muir Woods if you like."

"That would be amazing," I said.

And just like that we saved thirty bucks.

The place was adorable, a white Tudoresque cottage tucked down a narrow road. It had a shingled roof and warped windows lined with flower boxes and a chimney whose smoke curled romantically through the mist, windows softly aglow as we pulled into the parking lot.

For two days, we moved between the beach, the redwoods, the inn's cozy library, and the dining room with its dark wooden tables and blazing fire. We played UNO and Hearts and something called Quiddler. We drank foamy beers and had big English breakfasts.

We took pictures together, but I didn't post any of them. Maybe it was selfish, but I didn't want twenty-five thousand people descending on this place. I wanted it to stay exactly as it was.

Our last night we booked a room at a modern hotel that belonged to the father of one of my followers. When I posted about the upcoming trip and asked for tips, she DMed me to offer the room for free.

I love your blog, she said, *and I* love *reading about Particular Man Friend,* which is what I call Alex when I mention him at all. I mostly try to leave him out of it, because he, like the Blue Heron Inn, isn't something I want to share with thousands of people, but sometimes the things he says are too funny to leave out. Apparently he's bled through more than I realized.

I decided to try harder to keep him out of it, but I accepted the free room, because Money. Also the hotel has free parking for guests, which, in San Francisco, is the equivalent of a hotel giving out free kidney transplants.

We dropped our bags as soon as we got into the city, then headed back out to make the most of our only day in downtown San Francisco. We left the car and took cabs.

First we walked the Golden Gate Bridge, which was amazing, but also colder than I'd expected and so windy we couldn't hear each other. For probably ten minutes, we pretended to be having a conversation, waving our arms exaggeratedly and shouting nonsense at each other as we power walked over the crowded walkway.

It made me think about that water taxi ride in Vancouver, how Buck kept vaguely gesturing, talking at an easy clip like one of those orthodontists who can't stop asking you open-ended questions while his hands are in your mouth.

Luckily the weather had decided to be sunny; otherwise, we would have probably gotten hypothermia on the bridge. We stopped halfway across, and I pretended to climb over the railing. Alex made his trademark grimace and shook his head. He grabbed my hands and tugged me away from the railing, leaning in close so I could hear him over the wind when he said against my ear, "That makes me feel like I'm going to have diarrhea."

I broke into laughter and we kept walking, him on the inside, me closest to the railing, resisting a powerful urge to keep messing with him. Probably I'd accidentally *actually* fall over and not only die but traumatize poor Alex Nilsen, and that was the last thing I wanted.

At the far end of the bridge, there was a restaurant, the Round House Cafe, a round, windowed building. We ducked inside to drink a cup of coffee while we gave our ears a chance to stop ringing from the wind.

There were dozens of bookshops and vintage stores in San Francisco, but we decided two of each should be enough.

We took a cab to City Lights first, a bookstore and publisher in one that had been around since the height of the beatnik era. Neither of us was a big beat person, but the store was exactly the kind of old, meandering shop that Alex lived for. From there we stopped by a store called Second Chance Vintage, where I found a sequined bag from the forties for eighteen dollars.

After that, we'd planned to go to the Booksmith, over by the

Haight-Ashbury, but by then, that big English breakfast from the Blue Heron Inn had worn off and the Round House coffee had us both feeling a little jittery.

"Guess we just have to come back," I said to Alex as we left the shop in search of dinner.

"Guess so," he agreed. "Maybe for our fiftieth anniversary."

He smiled down at me, and my heart swelled until it felt so big and light my body could float away. "Just so you know," I said, "I would marry you all over again, Alex Nilsen."

His head tipped sideways. He affected the Sad Puppy Face. "Is that just because you want more free wine?"

It was hard to choose a restaurant in a city with this much to offer, but we were too hungry to pore over the list I'd compiled, so we just went classic.

Farallon is *not* a cheap place, but on the second day of wine tasting, when we were both slaphappy, Alex had ordered another drink, crying, "When in Rome!" and ever since, whenever one of us had waffled about buying something, the other had insisted, "When in Rome!"

So far, this had been limited mostly to enormous ice cream cones and used paperback books, and lots of wine.

But Farallon is gorgeous, and a San Francisco staple, and if we were going to spend too much money, it might as well happen there. As soon as we walked into the building, with its opulent, rounded ceilings and gilded light fixtures and golden-edged booths, I said, "No regrets," and forced Alex to high-five me.

"Giving high fives makes me feel like my insides have poison ivy," he murmured.

"Might as well get that out of the way in case you're about to find out you're allergic to seafood."

I was so enraptured by the over-the-top decor that I tripped three times on our way to the table. It was like being in the castle from *The Little Mermaid*, except not animated and everyone was fully clothed.

When our server left us with our menus, Alex did that old-man thing, where he opened it and reared back from the prices with widening eyes, like a startled horse.

"Really?" I said. "That bad?"

"It depends. Do you want more than one half-ounce of caviar?"

It wasn't the kind of expensive that the upper middle class of Linfield would avoid, but for us, yes, it was expensive.

We split a two-person platter of oysters, crab, and shrimp along with one cocktail.

Our server hated us.

When we left, we walked past him, and I thought I heard Alex saying under his breath, "Sorry, sir."

We went straight to a walk-up pizza place and scarfed down a whole large cheese pizza between the two of us.

"I ate way too much," Alex said as we were walking along the street afterward. "It was like some kind of Midwestern demon possessed me while I was sitting in that restaurant and that tiny platter came out. I could hear my dad in my head saying, 'Now, *that's* not economical.'"

"I know," I agreed. "Halfway through, I was just like, get me out of here, I need to get to a Costco and buy a five-dollar bag of noodles that could feed a family for weeks."

"I think I'm bad at vacation," Alex said. "All this living large makes me feel guilty."

"You're not bad at vacation," I argued. "And pretty much everything makes you feel guilty, so don't blame that on the living large."

"Touché," he agreed. "But still. You probably would've had more fun if you'd taken this trip with Julian." He didn't say it like a question, but the way his eyes darted over to me, then back to the sidewalk ahead of us, I could tell that it was one.

"I thought about inviting him," I admitted.

"Yeah?" Alex pulled one hand from his pocket and smoothed his hair. For some reason, the streetlights passing over him on the dark sidewalk made him seem taller. Even slouching, he was towering over me. I guess he always was. I just didn't always notice because he so often brought himself down to my level or pulled me up to his.

"Yeah." I looped my arm through his elbow. "But I'm glad I didn't. I'm glad it's just us."

He looked down over his shoulder at me and slowed. I slowed beside him. "Are you going to break up with him?"

The question caught me off guard. The way he was looking at me, his eyebrows pinched and mouth small, caught me off guard too. My heart tripped over its next beat.

Yes, I thought right away, without any consideration.

"I don't know," I said. "Maybe."

We kept walking. Up ahead we stumbled upon a bar that was Hemingway themed. That may seem rather ambiguous as a theme, but they pulled it off with their sleek dark wood and amber light and fishnets (not the stockings, actual nets for fish) suspended from the ceiling. The drinks were all rum cocktails, named after Hemingway books and short stories, and over the next two hours, Alex and I had three each, along with a shot. I kept saying, "We're celebrating! Come on, Alex!" but really, I felt like there was something I was trying to forget.

And now, as we're stumbling back into our hotel room, it occurs to me that I don't remember what I was trying to forget, so I guess it worked.

I kick off my shoes and collapse onto the nearest bed while Alex disappears into the bathroom and comes back with two cups of water.

"Drink this," he says. I grunt and try to swat his hand away. "Poppy," he says more firmly, and I brattily push myself upright and accept the cup of water. He sits on the bed beside me until I've drained my glass, then goes back to refill both of them.

I'm not sure how many times he does this—I'm edging closer to sleep all the while. All I know is that eventually, he sets the glasses aside and starts to stand up, and from my half-dream, full-drunk state, I reach for his arm and say, "Don't go."

He settles back down on the bed and lies beside me. I fall asleep curled up against his side and when I wake up the next morning to my alarm going off, he's already in the shower.

The humiliation at having made him sleep next to me is instantaneous and flaming hot. I know right then I can't break up with Julian when I get home. I have to wait, long enough to be sure I'm not confused. Long enough that Alex won't think the two events are connected.

They're not, I think. I'm pretty sure they're not.

16

This Summer

I FIND A TWENTY-FOUR-HOUR pharmacy in Palm Springs and drive toward it through the first soft rays of sunrise. Afterward, I get back to the apartment before most other stores have opened. By then the parking lot of the Desert Rose has started to bake again, and the cool hours of predawn shrink to a distant memory as I climb the steps, loaded with grocery bags.

"How are you doing?" I ask Alex as I shut the door behind me.

"Better." He forces a smile. "Thanks."

Liar. His pain is written all over his face. He's worse at hiding that than his emotions. I put the two ice packs I bought into the freezer, then go to the bed and plug in the heating pad. "Lean forward," I say, and Alex shifts enough for me to slide the pad down the stack of pillows where it can sit across his midback. I touch his shoulder, helping to slow his descent as he leans back. His skin is so warm. I'm sure the heating pad won't be *comfortable*, but hopefully it will do the trick, warming the muscle until it relaxes.

In half an hour, we'll switch to the ice pack to try to bring down any inflammation.

I may have read up on back spasms in the quiet, fluorescent-lit aisles of the drugstore.

"I've got some Icy Hot too," I say. "Does that ever help?"

"Maybe," he says.

"Well, it's worth a try. I guess I should've thought of that before you leaned back and got comfortable again."

"It's fine," he says, wincing. "I never really get comfortable when this happens. I just sort of wait for the medicine to knock me out, and by the time I wake up, I usually feel a lot better."

I slide off the edge of the bed and gather the rest of the bags, carrying them back to him. "How long does it last?"

"Usually just a day if I stay still," he says. "I'll have to be careful tomorrow, but I'll be able to move around. You should go do something you know I'd hate." He forces another smile.

I ignore the comment and search through the bag until I find the Icy Hot. "Need help leaning forward again?"

"No, I'm good." But the face he makes suggests otherwise, so I shift beside him, take his shoulders in my hands, and slowly help him ease upright.

"I feel like you're my nurse right now," he says bitterly.

"Like, in a hot and sexy way?" I say, trying to lighten his mood.

"In a sad-old-man-who-can't-take-care-of-himself way," he says.

"You own a house," I say. "I bet you even ripped the carpet out of the bathroom."

"I did," he agrees.

"Clearly you can take care of yourself," I say. "I can't even keep a houseplant alive."

"That's because you're never home," he says.

I twist the top off the Icy Hot and get a glob onto my fingers. "I don't think so. I got these hardy things, pothos and ZZ plants and snake plants—they're, like, the kinds of plants they stick in lightless malls for months at a time and they still don't die. Then they move into my apartment and immediately give up on life." I steady his rib cage with one hand so I don't jostle him too much and, with my other, reach around to carefully massage the cream onto his back.

"Is that the right place?" I ask.

"A little higher and to the left. My left."

"Here?" I look up at him, and he nods. I tear my gaze away and focus on his back, my fingers turning gentle circles over the spot.

"I hate that you have to do this," he says, and my eyes wander back to his, which are low and serious beneath a furrowed brow.

My heart feels like it drops through my chest and soars back up. "Alex, has it ever occurred to you that I might like taking care of you?" I say. "I mean, obviously I don't love that you're in pain, and I hate that I let you sleep in that abominable chair, but if someone's going to have to be your nurse, I'm honored it's me."

His mouth presses closed, and neither of us says anything for a few moments.

I pull my hands away from him. "Hungry?"

"I'm okay," he says.

"Well, that's too bad." I go to the kitchen and rinse the leftover Icy Hot off my hands, grab a couple of glasses, and fill them with ice, then return to the bed and arrange the remaining grocery bags in a row. "Because . . ." I pull out a box of donuts with a flourish, like a magician producing a bunny from a hat. Alex looks dubious.

He isn't a big sugar person. I think that's partly why he smells so good, like even the obsessive cleanliness aside, his breath and body odor are always just sort of good and I'm guessing it's because he does *not* eat like a ten-year-old. Or a Wright.

"And for *you*," I say, and dump out the yogurt cups, box of granola, and berry mix, along with a bottle of cold-brew. The apartment's way too hot for drip coffee.

"Wow," he says, grinning. "You're a real hero."

"I know," I say. "I mean, thank you."

We sit and feast, picnic-style, on the bed. I eat mostly donuts and a few bites of Alex's yogurt. He eats mostly yogurt but also devours half of a strawberry donut. "I never eat this stuff," he says.

"I know," I say.

"It's pretty good," he says.

"It speaks to me," I say, but if he catches the reference to that very first trip we took together, he ignores it, and my heart sinks.

It's possible that all those little moments that meant so much to me never meant quite the same thing to him. It's possible that he didn't reach out to me for two full years because, when we stopped speaking, he didn't lose something precious the way that I did.

We have five more days of this trip, counting today—though today and tomorrow are our last wedding-event-free days—and right now I dread something bigger than awkwardness.

I think about heartbreak. The full-fledged version of this thing I'm feeling right now, but sprawling out for days on end with no relief or escape. Five days of pretending to feel fine, while inside me something is tearing into smaller and smaller pieces until it's nothing but scraps.

Alex sets his cold brew on the side table and looks at me. "You really should go out."

"I don't want to," I say.

"Of course you want to," he says. "This is your trip, Poppy. And I know you haven't gotten everything you need for your article."

"The article can wait."

His head cocks uncertainly. "Please, Poppy," he says. "I'll feel terrible if you're stuck inside with me all day."

I want to tell him I'll feel terrible if I leave. I want to say, *All I wanted for this trip was to be* anywhere *with you all day* or *Who cares about seeing Palm Springs when it's one hundred degrees out* or *I love you so much it sometimes hurts.* Instead I say, "Okay."

Then I get up and go to the bathroom to get ready. Before I go, I bring Alex an ice pack and swap out the heating pad. "Are you going to be able to do this on your own?" I ask.

"I'm just gonna sleep when you leave," he says. "I'll be fine without you, Poppy."

This is the last thing I want to hear.

NO OFFENSE TO the Palm Springs Art Museum, but I just don't really care. Maybe I could under different circumstances, but under these circumstances, it is clear to me and everyone working here that I'm just killing time. I've never really known *how* to look at art without someone else there to be my guidepost.

My first boyfriend, Julian, used to say, *You either feel something or you don't,* but he was never taking me to MoMA or the Met (when we took the overnight bus to New York we skipped those entirely) or even the Cincinnati Art Museum; he was taking me to DIY galleries where artists would lie naked on the floor with their crotches tarred-and-feathered while recordings of audio from the P.F. Chang's dining room played at full volume.

It was easier to "feel something" in those contexts. Embarrassment, revulsion, anxiety, amusement. There was so much you could feel from something that over-the-top, and the smallest details could tip you one way or another.

But most visual art doesn't trigger a visceral reaction in me, and I'm never sure how long I'm supposed to stand in front of a painting, or what face I'm supposed to make, or how to know if I've chosen the dullest one from the lot and all the docents are silently judging me.

I'm fairly sure I'm not spending the appropriate amount of time gazing meaningfully at the art here, because I'm finished walking through in less than an hour. All I want to do is go back to the apartment, but *not* if Alex specifically wants me not to.

So I do a second lap. And then a third. This time I read all the placards. I pick up the literature at the front reception area and take it with me so I have something else to study intensely. A balding docent with paper-thin skin gives me the evil eye.

He probably thinks I'm casing the joint. For all the time I've spent in here, I might as well have been. Two birds, one stone, et cetera, et cetera, et cetera.

Finally, I accept that I've worn out my welcome, and I head to Palm Canyon Drive, where there's supposed to be some amazing antiques shopping.

And there is. Galleries and showrooms and antiques stores all lined up in a neat row, sprinkled with bright pops of midcentury modernist colors—robin's-egg blues, brilliant oranges, and sour greens, vibrant mustardy yellow lamps that look almost illustrated and Sputnik-patterned couches and elaborate metal light fixtures with spokes sticking out in every direction.

It's like I'm on vacation in the 1960s' image of the future.

It's enough to hold my interest for all of twenty minutes.

Then I finally bite the bullet and call Rachel.

"Helloooooooo," she cries on the second ring.

"Are you drunk?" I ask, surprised.

"No?" she says. "Are you?"

"I wish."

"Uh-oh," she says. "I thought you weren't texting me back because you were having an amazing time!"

"I'm not texting you back because we're staying in a four-foot shoebox that's a trillion degrees and I have neither the space nor mental fortitude to send you a detailed message about how bad it's going."

"Oh, darling," Rachel sighs. "Do you want to come home?"

"I can't," I say. "There's a wedding at the end of this, remember?"

"You *could*," she says. "I could have an 'emergency.'"

"No, that's okay," I say. I don't want to go home—I just want things to go better.

"Bet you're wishing you were in Santorini right now," she says.

"Mostly I just wish Alex weren't laid up back in the room with a *back spasm*."

"*What?*" Rachel says. "Young, fit, rockin'-bod Alex?"

"The very same. And he won't let me do anything to help him, really. He kicked me out and I went to the art museum, like, four times already today."

"Four . . . times?" she says.

"I mean," I say, "I didn't, like, leave and come back. I just feel like I took four full-length seventh-grade field trips in a row. Ask me anything about Edward Ruscha."

"Oh!" Rachel says. "What was his pseudonym when he was working at *Artforum* magazine in layout?"

"Okay, don't ask me anything," I say. "Turns out I did not actually read the pamphlet I was staring at that whole time."

"Eddie Russia," Art School Rachel blurts out. "Don't at all remember why. I mean, obviously it just sounds like his name, but why not use your real name in that case, you know?"

"Totally," I agree, starting back to the car. There's sweat gathering at my armpits and in the backs of my knees, and I feel like I'm getting a sunburn even standing under the awning of this coffee shop. "Should I start writing under the name Pop Right, without the *W*?"

"Or become a DJ in the nineties," Rachel says flatly. "DJ Pop-Right."

"Anyway," I say. "How are you? How's New York? How are the pooches?"

"Good," she says, "hot, and okay. Otis had a minor surgery this morning. Tumor removal—benign, thank God. I'm on my way to pick him up now."

"Give him kisses for me."

"Obviously," she says. "I'm almost to the vet, so I should go, but let me know if you need me to get injured or whatever so you can come home early."

I sigh. "Thanks. And *you* let me know if you need any expensive mod furniture."

"Um. Sure."

We hang up, and I check the time. I've successfully made it to four thirty p.m. I think that means it's appropriately late to pick up sandwiches and head back to the Desert Rose.

When I get inside, the balcony door is shut against the heat of the day, but the apartment is still nastily hot. Alex has put a gray T-shirt back on and is sitting up where I left him with his book open and two more sitting on the mattress beside him.

"Hey," he says. "Have a good time?"

"Yep," I lie. I tip my chin toward the door. "You've been up and walking around."

His mouth twists into a guilty frown. "Just a little bit. I had to pee anyway, and take another pill."

I climb onto the bed and set the bag of sandwiches between us, pulling my legs underneath me. "How do you feel?"

"A lot better," he says. "I mean, I'm still trapped here, but it hurts less."

"Good. I brought you a sandwich." I tip the plastic bag upside down and the paper-wrapped sandwich slides out of it.

He takes his and slightly smiles as he unwraps it. "A Reuben?"

"I know it's not the same thing as stealing it from Delallo," I say. "But if you want, I'll put it in the fridge and go to the bathroom long enough for you to hobble over and take it."

"That's okay," he says. "In my heart, it's stolen from Delallo, and some would say that's what really matters."

"We're learning so many important lessons on this trip," I say. "P.S., I left Nikolai a voicemail on my way home about the air situation. Pretty sure he's screening my calls."

"Oh!" Alex says, brightening. "I forgot to tell you! I got it down to seventy-eight."

"Seriously?" I spring off the bed and go check. "That's amazing, Alex!"

He laughs. "This is a pathetic thing to celebrate."

"The theme of this trip is Taking What We Can Get," I say as I sit back down beside him.

"I thought it was Aspire," Alex says.

"Aspire to reach seventy-five degrees."

"Aspire to fit inside the swimming pool at some point."

"Aspire to get away with the murder of Nikolai."

"Aspire to get out of bed."

"You poooooor thing," I moan. "Trapped in bed with a book— your personal hell!—while I rub menthol on your back and hand deliver you your ideal breakfast *and* lunch."

Alex makes the puppy face.

"Unfair!" I say. "You know I can't use self-defense against you right now!"

"Okay," he says. "I'll stop until you're comfortable causing me bodily harm again."

"When did this start happening?" I ask.

"I don't know," he says. "I guess a couple months after Croatia?"

The word lands like a firework in the middle of my chest. I try to keep my face placid but have no idea how I'm faring. He, for his part, shows no sign of discomfort. "Do you know why?" I recover.

"I hunch a lot?" he says. "Especially when I'm reading or on my computer. A massage therapist told me my hip muscles were probably shortening, pulling on my back. I don't know. My doctor just prescribed me muscle relaxants, then left before I could think of any questions."

"And it happens a lot?" I say.

"Not a lot," he says. "This is the fourth or fifth time. It happens less when I'm exercising regularly. I guess sitting on the plane and in the car and all that . . . and then the chair bed."

"Makes sense."

After a moment, he asks, "You okay?"

"I guess I just . . ." I trail off, unsure how much I want to say. "I feel like I missed a lot."

His head tilts back against the pillows, and his eyes wander down my face. "Me too."

A half-hearted laugh rises out of me. "No, you didn't. My life's exactly the same."

"That's not true," he says. "You cut your hair."

This time, the laugh is more genuine, and a contained smile curves over Alex's lips. "Yeah, well," I say, fighting a blush as I feel his gaze move over my bare shoulder, down the length of my arm to where my hand rests on the bed near his knee. "I didn't get a house or buy my own dishwasher or anything. I doubt I'll ever be able to."

His eyebrow arches, and his eyes retrain on my face. "You don't want to," he says quietly.

"Yeah, you're probably right," I say, but honestly I'm unsure. That's the problem. I haven't wanted the things I used to want, the things I wanted when I made just about every big life decision I've made. I'm still paying off student loans for a degree I didn't finish, and even if I saved myself another year-and-a-half's worth of tuition, lately I find myself wondering if *that* was the right choice.

I fled Linfield. I fled the University of Chicago, and if I'm being honest, I sort of fled Alex when everything happened. He fled me too, but I can't place all the blame on him.

I was terrified. I ran. And I left it up to him to fix it.

"Remember when we went to San Francisco, and we kept saying 'when in Rome' whenever we wanted to buy something?" I ask.

"Maybe," he says, sounding uncertain. I'm guessing my expression must be something along the lines of *crushed*, because he apologetically adds, "I don't have a great memory."

"Yeah," I say. "That makes sense."

He coughs. "Do you want to watch something, or are you going back out?"

"No," I say, "let's watch something. If I go back to the Palm Springs Art Museum, I think the FBI will be waiting for me."

"Why, did you steal something priceless?" Alex asks.

"I won't know until I have it appraised," I joke. "Hopefully this Claude Moan-ay guy turns out to be a big deal."

Alex laughs and shakes his head, and even that small gesture seems to cost him a shock of pain. "Shit," he says. "You have to stop making me laugh."

"You have to stop assuming I'm joking when I'm talking about robbing art museums."

He closes his eyes and presses his mouth into a straight line, smothering any more laughter. After a second he opens his eyes. "Okay, I'm going to go pee for—hopefully—the last time today and take another pill. You can grab my laptop from the bag and pull up

Netflix, if you want." He cautiously turns, sets his feet on the ground, and stands.

"Got it," I say. "And do you want me to leave the nudie mags in there or get those out too?"

"Poppy," he groans without looking back. "No joking."

I push off the bed and tug Alex's laptop bag onto the chair as I sort through it for the computer, then carry it back to the bed with me, opening it as I go.

He hasn't shut it down, and when I brush the mousepad, the screen flares to life, demanding that I log in. "Password?" I call toward the bathroom.

"Flannery O'Connor," he calls back, then flushes the toilet and turns on the sink.

I don't ask about spaces, capitalization, or punctuation. Alex is a purist. I type it in and the log-in screen vanishes, replaced by an open web browser. Before I've realized it, I'm inadvertently snooping.

My heart is racing.

The water turns off. The door opens. Alex steps out, and while it might be better to pretend I didn't see the job posting Alex had pulled up, something's come over me, yanked out the part of my brain that—at least *occasionally*—filters out things I shouldn't say.

"You're applying to teach at Berkeley Carroll?"

The confusion on his face quickly transforms into something akin to guilt. "Oh, that."

"That's in New York," I say.

"So the website suggested," Alex says.

"New York City," I clarify.

"Wait, *that* New York?" he deadpans.

"You're moving to New York?" I say, and I'm sure I'm talking loud, but the adrenaline has me feeling like the whole world is stuffed with cotton, deadening all sound to a muffled hum.

"Probably not," he says. "I just saw the posting."

"But you would love New York," I say. "I mean, think about the bookstores."

Now he gives a smile that seems both amused and sad. He comes back to the bed and slowly lowers himself down next to me. "I don't know," he says. "I was just looking."

"I won't bother you," I say. "If you're worried I'll, like, show up on your doorstep every time I have a crisis, I promise I won't."

His eyebrow lifts skeptically. "And if you find out I have a back spasm, will you break into my apartment with donuts and Icy Hot?"

"No?" I say, pitch lifting guiltily. His smile widens, but still, there's something vaguely sad about it. "What is it?"

He holds my eyes for a while, like we're caught in a game of chicken. Then he sighs and runs a hand over his face. "I don't know," he says. "There's some stuff I'm still trying to work out. In Linfield. Before I make a decision like that."

"The house?" I guess.

"That's part of it," he says. "I love that house. I don't know if I could bear to sell it."

"You could rent it out!" I suggest, and Alex gives me a look. "Right. You're way too high-strung to be a landlord."

"I believe you mean that everyone else is *way too lax* to be a tenant."

"You could rent it to one of your brothers," I say. "Or you can just keep it. I mean, your grandma owned it, right? Do you owe anything on it?"

"Just property taxes." He pulls the computer away from me and exits out of the job posting. "But it's not just the house. And it's not just because of my dad and brothers either," he adds when he sees my mouth opening. "I mean, obviously I'd miss my nieces and nephew a lot. But there are other things keeping me there. Or, I don't know, there might be. I'm just kind of . . . waiting to see what happens."

"Oh," I say, realization dawning. "So, like . . . a woman."

Again he holds my gaze, as if daring me to push the matter. But I don't blink, and he cracks first. "We don't have to talk about this."

"Oh." And now all that vibrating excited energy seems to be freezing over, sinking low in my stomach. "So it's Sarah. You *are* getting back together."

He bows his head, rubs at his brow. "I don't know."

"She wants to?" I say. "Or you do?"

"I don't know," he says again.

"Alex."

"Don't do that." He looks up. "Don't chastise me. It's really grim out there, dating-wise, and Sarah and I have a lot of history."

"Yeah, a sordid history," I say. "There's a reason you broke up. Twice."

"And a reason we dated," he fires back. "Not everyone can just *not look back* like you."

"What's that supposed to mean?" I demand.

"Nothing," he says quickly. "We're just different."

"I know we're different," I say, defensive. "I also know it's grim out there. I'm single too, Alex. I'm a card-carrying member of the Unsolicited Dick Pic Support Group. Doesn't mean I'm running to get back with one of my exes."

"It's different," he insists.

"How?" I snap.

"Because you don't want the same things I want," he says, half shouting, possibly the loudest I've ever heard him speak, and while his voice isn't angry, it's definitely frustrated.

When I rear back from him, I see him deflate a little, embarrassed.

He goes on, quiet and controlled once more. "I want all that stuff my brothers have," he says. "I want to get married and have kids and grandkids and get really fucking old with my wife, and to live in our house for so long that it smells like us. Like, I want to pick out fucking furniture and paint colors and do all that Linfield stuff you think is so unbearable, okay? That's what I want. And I don't want to wait. No one knows how long they get, and I don't want ten more years to go by and to find out I have fucking dick cancer or something and it's too late for me. *That* stuff is what matters to me."

Any remaining fire goes out of him, but I'm still quivering with nerves and hurt and shame, and most of all anger with myself for not understanding what was going on every time he defended our Podunk hometown, or changed the topic from Sarah, or anything else.

"Alex," I say, on the verge of tears. I shake my head, trying to clear the storm clouds of gathering emotion. "I don't think that stuff is unbearable. I don't think any of it's unbearable."

His eyes lift heavily to mine, dart away again. Careful not to knock him, I shift closer and pull his hand into mine, fold my fingers through his. "Alex?"

He looks down at me. "Sorry," he murmurs. "I'm sorry, Poppy."

I shake my head. "I love Betty's house," I say. "And I love thinking about you having it, and as much as I hated school, I love thinking about you teaching there and how lucky those kids are. And I love what a good brother and son you are, and—" My words catch in my throat, and I have to stammer tearily through the rest of them. "And I don't want you to marry Sarah, because she takes you for granted. She would never have broken up with you in the first place if she didn't. And honestly, aside from that, I don't want you to marry her, because she never liked me, and if you marry her . . ." I trail off before I can start sobbing.

If you marry her, I think, *I will lose all of you forever.*

And then, *Probably no matter who you marry, I will have to lose you forever.*

"I know that's so selfish," I say. "But it's not just that. I really think you can do better. Sarah will be great for someone, but not for you. She doesn't like karaoke, Alex."

This last part comes out pathetically teary, and as he gazes down at me, he tries his best to hide the smile that pulls at his mouth. He frees his hand from mine and wraps his arm around me, pressing me lightly to him, but I don't let myself sink into him like I want for fear of hurting him.

This injury, while miserable for him, is actually turning out to be a good buffer, because everywhere we're touching has started to buzz, like my nerves are jockeying for more of him. He presses a kiss to the top of my head, and it feels like someone cracked an egg there, something warm and sultry dripping down over me.

I shove down the hazy memories of everything that mouth did in Croatia.

"I'm not sure I actually can do better," Alex says, drawing me out of a blushworthy scene. "When I open Tinder, it just shows me a middle finger."

"Seriously?" I sit up. "You have a Tinder account?"

He rolls his eyes. "Yes, Poppy. Grandpa has a Tinder."

"Let me see it."

His ears go red. "No, thanks. I'm not in the mood to get brutally heckled."

"I can help you, Alex," I say. "I'm a straight woman. I know how

men's Tinder profiles are received. I can figure out what you're doing wrong."

"What I'm doing wrong is trying to find a meaningful connection on a dating app."

"Well, obviously," I say. "But let's see what else."

He sighs. "Fine." He pulls his phone out of his pocket and
hands it to me. "But go easy on me, Poppy. I'm fragile right now."

And then he makes the face.

17

Seven Summers Ago

NEW ORLEANS.

Alex is curious about the architecture—all those old Crayola-colored buildings with their wrought-iron balconies and the ancient trees writhing up right through the sidewalks, roots sprawling out for yards in every direction, breaking up cement like it's nothing. The trees predate it, and they'll outlast it.

I'm excited for alcohol in slushy form and kitschy supernatural shops.

Luckily there is no shortage of any of it.

I'm thrilled to find a large studio apartment not far from Bourbon Street. The floors are stained dark, and the furniture is heavy wood, and colorful paintings of jazz musicians hang on exposed brick walls. The beds are cheap looking, as is the bedding, but they're queens, and the place is clean, and the air-conditioning game is so strong we have to crank it down so that every time we come in after a day in the heat, our teeth don't chatter.

All there really is to do in New Orleans, it seems, is walk, eat, drink, look, and listen. This is basically what we do on every trip, but the fact is underscored here by the hundreds of restaurants and bars sitting shoulder to shoulder on every slender street. And the thousands of people milling through the city with tall neon novelty cups and mismatched straws. Every block or so the smells of the city switch from fried and delicious to stinking and rotten, the humidity trapping the sewage and putting it on display.

Compared to most American cities, everything looks so old that I imagine we're smelling waste from the 1700s, which miraculously makes it more bearable.

"It feels like we're walking around inside someone's mouth," Alex says more than once about the humidity, and from then on, whenever the smell hits, I think of food trapped between molars.

But the thing is, it never lasts. A breeze sweeps through to clear it out, or we wander past another restaurant with all its doors propped open, or we round the corner and stumble onto some beautiful side street where every balcony overhead is dripping with purple flowers.

Besides, I've been in New York for five months now, and during the last two months of summer, it's not like my subway stop has smelled like roses. I've seen three different people peeing on the steps inside, and watched *one* of those people do it a second time a week later.

I love New York, but, wandering New Orleans, I wonder if I could be just as happy here. If maybe I could be happier. If maybe Alex would visit me more often.

So far he's visited New York once, a few weeks after his first year of grad school ended. He brought a carload of my stuff from my parents' house to my apartment in Brooklyn, and on the last day of his trip, we compared calendars, talked about when we'd next see each other.

The Summer Trip, obviously. Possibly (but probably not) Thanksgiving. Christmas if I could get time off work at the restaurant where I'm serving. But everyone wants off for Christmas, so instead I floated the idea of New Year's Eve and we agreed to figure it out later.

So far we haven't talked about any of that on this trip. I haven't wanted to think about *missing* Alex while I'm with him. It seems like a waste.

"If nothing else," he joked, "we'll always have the Summer Trip."

I had to actively decide to see that as comforting.

From morning until hours after dark, we wander. Bourbon Street and Frenchmen, and Canal and Esplanade (Alex is particularly enamored of the stately old houses on this street, with their overflowing flower beds and sun-blanched palms rising up alongside craggy oaks).

We eat fluffy, sugar-dusted beignets in an open-air café and spend hours picking our way through the knickknacks being sold outside the French Market (alligator-head key chains and silver rings set with moonstones), the freshly baked breads and chilled local produce and dense little cakes topped with kiwi and strawberries and bourbon-soaked cherries and pralines (in every imaginable manner) being sold in the booths inside.

We drink Sazeracs and hurricanes and daiquiris everywhere we go, because "Staying on theme matters," as Alex says dramatically when I try to order a gin and tonic, and from there, we have both our mantra and our alter egos for the week.

Gladys and Keith Vivant are a Broadway power couple, we decide. True performers, to their very cores, and as their matching tattoos read, *All the world's a stage!*

They start every day with some acting exercises, stick to one prompt for a whole week at a time, letting it guide their every interaction so as to better inhabit the Character.

And theme, of course, is vital.

Or, you could say, it matters.

"Theme matters!" we scream back and forth, stomping our feet whenever we want each other to do something the other isn't thrilled about.

There are a whole lot of vintage stores that seem to have never been cleaned before, and Alex is not thrilled about trying on the suede leather pants I pick out for him in one of these, just as I am not thrilled when he wants to spend six hours in an art museum.

"Theme matters!" I shout when he refuses to enter a bar with an—no joke—all-saxophone band playing in the middle of the day.

"Theme matters!" he cries when I say I don't want to buy shirts that say *Drunk Bitch 1* and *Drunk Bitch 2* like those Thing 1 and Thing 2 shirts they sell at theme parks, and we leave the shop wearing the shirts over our clothes.

"I love when you get weird," I tell him.

He squints tipsily at me as we walk. "You make me weird. I'm not like this with anyone else."

"You make me weird too," I say; then, "Should we get *real* tattoos that say 'All the world's a stage'?"

"Gladys and Keith would," Alex says, taking a long drink from his water bottle. He passes it to me afterward, and I greedily chug half of it.

"So that's a yes?"

"Please don't make me," he says.

"But, Alex," I cry. "Theme matt—"

He pops the water bottle back into my mouth. "Once you're sober, I promise you won't think it's funny anymore."

"I will *always* think *every* joke I make is hilarious," I say, "but point taken."

We hit happy hour after happy hour, with varying results. Sometimes the drinks are weak and bad, sometimes they're stiff and good, often they're stiff and bad. We go to a hotel bar that's mounted to a

carousel and each buy one fifteen-dollar cocktail. We go to, alleg-
edly, the second-oldest continuously operating bar in Louisiana.
It's an old blacksmith shop with sticky floors that looks like a half-
assed living museum, except for the gigantic trivia machine set up
in the corner.

Alex and I sip slowly on one shared drink while we wait our
turn. We don't break the record, but we make the scoreboard.

The fifth night, we wind up at a fratty karaoke bar with an over-
the-top stage and laser-lights show. After two shots of Fireball,
Alex agrees to sing Sonny and Cher's "I Got You Babe" onstage in
character as the Vivants.

Halfway through the song, we get into a miked fight about the
fact that I *know* he's sleeping with Shelly from makeup. "It doesn't
take an hour to put on a freaking fake beard, Keith!" I shout.

The applause at the end is muted and uncomfortable. We take
another shot and head to a place Guillermo told me about that
serves a frozen coffee cocktail.

Half the places we've gone have been places Guillermo recom-
mended, and I've loved all of them, especially the hole-in-the-wall
po'boy shop. Having a chef for a boyfriend has perks.

When I told him where Alex and I were going, he got out a
piece of paper and started writing down everything he could remember from his last trip, along with notes about pricing and what
to order. He starred all his must-eats, but there's no way we'll get to
all of them.

I met Guillermo a couple months after moving to New York.
My new (first New York) friend Rachel got a request to eat at his
new restaurant for free, in exchange for posting a few pictures of it
on her social media. She does that kind of thing a lot, and since I'm
a fellow Internet Person, we do these sorts of things together.

"Less embarrassing," she insists. "Plus cross-promotion."

Every time she posts a picture with me, my subscriber count

goes up by hundreds. I'd been hanging around thirty-six thousand for six months, but have ballooned to fifty-five thousand through sheer association with Her Brand.

So I went with her to this restaurant, and after the meal, the chef came out to talk to us, and he was gorgeous and sweet, with soft brown eyes, dark hair swept back off his forehead. His laugh was soft and unassuming, and by that night, he'd messaged me on Instagram, before I could even post the pictures I'd taken to my account.

He found me through Rachel, and I liked the way he told me that right up front, without embarrassment. He works most nights, so on our first date, we went for breakfast instead, and he kissed me when he picked me up rather than waiting until he dropped me off afterward.

At first, I was seeing a few other people and he was too, but several weeks into it, we decided neither of us wanted to see anyone else. He laughed when he told me, and I laughed too, just because I'd gotten in the habit of giving encouraging laughter from being around him.

It's not like it was with Julian, not all-consuming and unpredictable. We see each other two or three times a week, and it's nice, the way this leaves space in my life for other things.

Spin classes with Rachel and long walks down the mall of Central Park with a dripping ice cream cone in hand, gallery openings and special movie nights at neighborhood bars. People in New York are friendlier than the rest of the world warned me they would be.

When I tell Rachel this, she says, "Most people here aren't assholes. They're just busy."

But when I say the same thing to Guillermo, he gently cups my jaw, laughs, and says, "You are so sweet. I hope you don't let this place change you."

It's sweet, but it also worries me. Like maybe the thing Gui loves best about me isn't some essential part, but something change-able, something that could be stripped away by a few years in the right climate.

As we wander the streets of New Orleans, I think multiple times of telling Alex about what Guillermo said, but every time I catch myself. I want Alex to like Guillermo, and I worry he'd be offended on my behalf.

So I tell him other things. Like how calm Guillermo is, that he laughs easily, how passionate he is about his job, and food in general.

"You'll like him," I say, and I really believe it.

"I'm sure I will," Alex insists. "If you like him, I'll like him."

"Good," I say.

And then he tells me about Sarah, his unrequited college crush. He ran into her when he was up in Chicago visiting friends a few weeks ago. They grabbed a drink.

"And?"

"And nothing," he says. "She lives in Chicago."

"It's not Mars," I say. "It's not even that far from Indiana Univer-sity."

"She's been texting me a little," he admits.

"Of course she is," I say. "You're a catch."

His smile is bashful and adorable. "I don't know," he says. "Maybe next time I'm in town we'll meet up again."

"You should," I press.

I'm happy with Guillermo, and Alex deserves to be happy too. Any tension that five percent of our relationship—the what-if—let in seems to have been resolved.

While staying in the French Quarter had seemed ideal when I booked our Airbnb, it turns out the nights are pretty loud. The music goes on until three or four and starts up surprisingly early in the morning. We find ourselves venturing to the rooftop pool at the Ace Hotel, which is free on weekdays, and napping on a couple of chaise lounges in the sun.

It's probably the best sleep I get all week, so by the time we take the cemetery tour on the last day of the trip, I'm slaphappy from fatigue. Alex and I expected haunting ghost stories. Instead we get information about how the Catholic Church cares for some graves—the ones for which people bought "perpetual care" generations ago—and lets the others crumble to dust.

It is decidedly boring, and we're baking in the sun, and my back hurts from walking in sandals all week, and I'm exhausted from barely sleeping, and halfway through, when Alex realizes how miserable I am, he starts raising his hand every time we stop at another grave for more bland factoids and asking, "So is *this* grave haunted?"

At first our tour guide laughs his question off, but he's less amused every time it happens. Finally, Alex asks about a big white marble pyramid at odds with the rest of the stacked, rectangular French- and Spanish-style graves, and the tour guide huffs, "I certainly hope not! That one belongs to Nicolas Cage!"

Alex and I deteriorate into cackles.

It turns out he's not joking.

This was supposed to be a big reveal, probably with a built-in joke, and we ruined it. "Sorry," Alex says, and passes him a tip as we're leaving. I'm the one who works in a bar, but he's the one who always has cash.

"Are you secretly a stripper?" I ask him. "Is that why you always have cash?"

"Exotic dancer," he says.

"You're an exotic dancer?" I say.

"No," he says. "It's just helpful to carry cash."

The sun is going down, and we're both bone-tired, but it's our last night, so we decide to get cleaned up and rally. While I'm sitting on the floor in front of the full-length mirror, putting on makeup, I peruse Guillermo's list and shout out suggestions to Alex.

"Eh," he says after each one. After a handful, he comes to stand behind me, making eye contact in the mirror. "Can we just wander?"

"I'd love to," I admit.

We hit a couple dingy pubs before we wind up at the Dungeon, a small, dark goth bar at the end of a skinny alleyway. We're told that pictures are expressly forbidden, before the bouncer lets us into the red-lit front room. It's so packed that I have to hold on to Alex's elbow as we make our way upstairs. There are plastic skeletons hanging on the wall, and a red-satin-lined coffin stands waiting for a photo op that you're not allowed to take.

Despite our mantra for this trip, and all the free personal shopping I've done for him, Alex has continued to largely loathe themed parties, events, and apparently bars too.

"This place is horrible," he says. "You love it, don't you?"

I nod, and he grins. We have to stand so close I have to tip my head all the way back to see him at all. He brushes my hair from my eyes and cups the back of my neck, as if to stabilize it. "I'm sorry for being so tall," he says over the metal music thrumming through the bar.

"I'm sorry for being so short," I say.

"I like you short," he says. "Never apologize for being short."

I lean into him, a hug minus the arms. "Hey," I say.

"Hey, what?" he asks.

"Can we go to that country-western bar we passed?"

I'm sure he doesn't want to. I'm sure he finds the whole thing humiliating. But what he says is, "We have to. Theme matters, Poppy."

So we go there next, and it's the polar opposite of the Dungeon, a big open bar with saddles for seats and Kenny Chesney blaring out to no one but us.

Alex is chagrined at the thought of sitting on the saddles, but I hop up and try to make his Sad Puppy Face at him.

"What is that?" he says. "Are you okay?"

"I'm being pathetic," I say. "So that you will please make me the happiest woman in the state of Louisiana and sit on one of these saddle seats."

"I can't decide if you're too easy to please or too hard," he says, and swings one leg over, pulling himself onto the saddle next to mine. "Excuse me," he says, to a burly bartender in a black leather vest. "Give me something that will make me forget this ever happened."

Still polishing a glass, he turns and glares. "I'm no mind reader, kid. What do you want?"

Alex's cheeks flush. He clears his throat. "Beer's fine. Whatever you've got."

"Make that two," I say. "Two of those alcohols, please."

As the bartender turns to get our drinks, I lean over to Alex and almost fall off my saddle in the process. He catches me and holds me up as I whisper, "*He's* so *on theme!*"

It's only eleven thirty when we leave, but I'm wiped out and as unthirsty as I've ever been in my life. So we just walk down the middle of the street with all the other revelers: families in matching reunion T-shirts; white-clad brides with silky pink BACHELOR-ETTE sashes and towering heels; drunk middle-aged men hitting on the girls in pink BACHELORETTE sashes, stuffing dollar bills in their dress straps as they walk past.

Overhead, people line the upstairs balconies of bars and restaurants, waving purple, gold, and green beads around, and when a man wolf-whistles and shakes a handful of necklaces at me, I hold my arms up to catch them. He shakes his head and pantomimes lifting his shirt up.

"I hate him," I say to Alex.

"Me too," Alex agrees.

"But I have to admit, he *is* on theme."

Alex laughs, and we walk onward, with no destination in mind. Gradually, the foot traffic slows as we approach a brass band (saxophone-and-other-woodwind free) that's set up shop in the middle of the street, horns blasting, drums rattling. We stop to watch, and a few couples start dancing. In the twist of the century, Alex offers me his hand, and when I take it, he twirls me in a lazy circle and pulls me in close, one hand around my back, the other folded against mine. He rocks me back and forth, and we both giggle sleepily. We're not on the beat, but it doesn't matter. It's just us.

Maybe that's why he can handle the public affection. Maybe, like me, when we're together he feels like no one else is there, like they're phantoms we dreamed up as set dressing.

Even if Jason Stanley and every other bully from my past were here, mocking me through a megaphone, I don't think I'd stop dancing clumsily with Alex in the street. He spins me out and back in, tries to dip me, almost drops me. I yelp when it happens, laugh so hard I snort when he catches me and swings me upright onto my feet, rocking me some more.

When the song ends, we break apart and join the crowd in applause. Alex crouches for a second, and when he stands up, he's holding out a strand of chipped purple Mardi Gras beads.

"Those were on the ground," I say.

"You don't want them?"

"No, I want them," I say. "But they were on the ground."

"Yes," he says.

"Where there's dirt," I say. "And spilled booze. Possibly vomit."

He winces, starts to lower the beads. I catch his wrist, stilling him. "Thank you," I say. "Thank you for touching these filthy beads for me, Alex. I love them."

He rolls his eyes, smiles, slips the beads over my neck as I duck my head.

When I look back up at him, he's beaming at me, and I think, *I love you more now than I ever have.* How is it possible that this keeps happening with him?

"Can we take a picture together?" I ask, but what I'm thinking is, *I wish I could bottle this moment and wear it as a perfume.* It would always be with me. Everywhere I went, he'd be there too, and so I'd always feel like myself.

He takes his phone out, and we huddle together as he snaps a picture. When we look at it, he makes a sound of strangled surprise. Probably in an effort not to look so sleepy, he threw his eyes wide in the last possible second.

"You look like you saw something horrible exactly when the flash went off," I say.

He tries to pull the phone out of my hands, but I spin away from him, jog out of reach as I text it to myself. He follows, fighting a smile, and when I hand it back, I say, "There, now that I have a copy, you can delete it."

"I would never delete it," Alex says. "I'm just only going to look at it when I'm alone, locked in my apartment, so that no one else ever sees my face in this picture."

"I'm going to see it," I say.

"You don't count," he says.

"I know," I agree. I love that, being the one who doesn't count. The one who's allowed to see all of Alex. The one who makes him weird.

When we get back to the apartment, I ask when he's going to let me read the short stories he's been working on.

He says he can't—if I don't like them, he'll be too embarrassed.

"You got into an amazing MFA program," I say. "You're obviously good. If I don't think they're good, I'm obviously wrong."

He says that if I don't think they're good, then U of I is wrong.

"Please," I say.

"Okay," he says, and gets out his computer. "Just wait until I'm in the shower, okay? I don't want to have to watch you reading it."

"Okay," I say. "If you have a novel, I could read that instead, since I'll have the whole length of an Alex Nilsen shower."

He tosses a pillow at me and goes into the bathroom.

The story really is short. Nine pages, about a boy who was born with a pair of wings. All his life, people tell him that this means he should try to fly. He's afraid to. When he finally does, jumps off a two-story roof, he falls. He breaks his legs and wings. He never gets them reset. As he recovers, the bone heals in its misshapen form. Finally, people stop telling him that he must've been born to fly. Finally, he's happy.

When Alex comes back out, I'm crying.

He asks me what's wrong.

I say, "I don't know. It just speaks to me."

He thinks I'm making a joke and chuckles along, but for once, I wasn't referencing the gallery girl who tried to sell us a twenty-one-thousand-dollar bear sculpture.

I was thinking about what Julian used to say about art. How it either makes you feel something or it doesn't.

When I read his story, I started crying for a reason I can't totally explain, not even to Alex.

When I was a kid, I used to have these panic attacks thinking about how I could never *be* anyone else. I couldn't be my mom or my dad, and for my whole life, I'd have to walk around inside a body that kept me from ever truly knowing anyone else.

It made me feel lonely, desolate, almost hopeless. When I told my parents about this, I expected them to know the feeling I was talking about, but they didn't.

"That doesn't mean there's anything wrong with feeling that way, though, sweetie!" Mom insisted.

"Who else do you think about being?" my dad said with his particular blunt fascination.

The fear lessened, but the feeling never went away. Every once in a while, I'd roll it back out, poke at it. Wonder how I could ever stop feeling lonely when no one could ever know me all the way. When I could never peer into someone else's brain and see it all.

And now I'm crying because reading this story makes me feel for the first time that I'm not in my body. Like there's some bubble that stretches around me and Alex and makes it so we're just two different colored globs in a lava lamp, mixing freely, dancing around each other, unhindered.

I'm crying because I'm relieved. Because I will never again feel as alone as I did during those long nights as a kid. As long as I have him, I will never be alone again.

18

This Summer

A LEX!" I SHRIEK at the sight of his Tinder profile. "No!"

"What? What?" he says. "There's no way you've read everything by now!"

"Um, first of all," I say, brandishing his phone out in front of us, "don't you think that's a problem? Your bio looks like the cover letter to a résumé. I didn't even know Tinder bios could *be* this long! Isn't there some kind of character limit? No one is going to read this whole thing."

"If they're really interested, they will," he says, slipping the phone out of my hand.

"Maybe if they're interested in harvesting your organs, they'll skim to the bottom just to make sure you don't mention your blood type—*do* you?"

"No," he says, sounding hurt, then adds, "just my weight, height, BMI, and social security number. Is what I wrote good at least?"

"Oh, we're not talking about that just yet." I pluck his phone from his hand again, angle the screen toward him, and zoom in on his profile picture. "First we have to talk about this."

He frowns. "I like that picture."

"Alex . . ." I say calmly. "There are four people in this picture."

"So?"

"So we have found the first and largest problem."

"That I have *friends*? I thought that would help."

"You poor innocent baby creature, freshly arrived to earth," I coo.

"Women don't want to date men who have friends?" he says dryly, disbelieving.

"Of course they do," I say. "They just don't want to play Dating App Roulette. How are they supposed to know which one of these guys is you? That guy on the left is, like, eighty."

"Biology teacher," he says. His frown deepens. "I don't really take pictures by myself."

"You sent me those Sad Puppy selfies," I point out.

"That's different," he says. "That was for you . . . You think I should use one of those?"

"God, no," I say. "But you could take a new picture where you're not making that face, or you could crop one that's you and three biology teachers of a certain age so that it's *just* you."

"I'm making a weird face in that picture," he says. "I'm always making a weird face in pictures."

I laugh, but really, warm affection is growing in my belly. "You have a face for movies, not photographs," I say.

"Meaning?"

"Meaning you're extremely handsome in real life, when your face is moving how it does, but when one millisecond is captured, yes, sometimes you're making a weird face."

"So basically I should delete Tinder and throw my phone into the sea."

"Wait!" I jump out of bed and snatch my phone off the counter where I left it, then climb back up beside Alex, tucking my legs underneath me. "I know what you should use."

He dubiously watches me scroll through my photos. I'm looking for a picture from our Tuscany trip, the last trip before Croatia. We'd been sitting outside on the patio, eating a late dinner, and he slipped away without a word. I figured he'd gone to the bathroom, but when I went inside to get dessert, he was in the kitchen, biting his lip and reading an email on his phone.

He looked worried, didn't seem to notice I was there until I touched his arm and said his name. When he looked up, his face went slack.

"What is it?" I asked, and the first thing that jumped into my mind was *Grandma Betty!* She was getting old. Actually, as long as I'd known her she'd been old, but the last time we'd gone to her house together, she'd barely gotten up from the chair she did her knitting in. Until then, she'd always been a *bustler.* Bustling to the kitchen to get us lemonade. Bustling over to the sofa to fluff the cushions before we sat down.

But the thought didn't have time to gestate because Alex's tiny, ever-suppressed smile appeared.

"Tin House," he said. "They're publishing one of my stories."

He gave a surprised laugh after he said it, and I threw my arms around him, let him draw me up and in against him tight. I kissed his cheek without thinking, and if it had felt any less natural to him than it did to me, he didn't show it. He turned me in half a circle, set me down grinning, went back to staring at his phone. He forgot to hide his emotions. He let them run wild over his face. I tugged my phone out of my pocket, pulled up the camera, and said, "Alex."

When he looked up, I captured my favorite picture of Alex Nilsen.

Unfiltered happiness. Naked Alex.

"Here," I say, and show him the picture. Him, standing in a warm golden kitchen in Tuscany, his hair sticking up like it always did, his phone loose in his hand, and his eyes locked onto the camera, his mouth smiling but ajar. "You should use this one."

He turns from the phone to me, our faces close though, as ever, his hangs over mine, his mouth soft with a trace of smile. "I forgot about that," he says.

"It's my favorite." For a while neither of us moves. We linger in this moment of close silence. "I'll send it to you," I say weakly, and break eye contact, pulling up our text thread and dropping the picture into it.

Alex's phone buzzes in his lap where I must've dropped it. He picks it up, does his half-cough tic. "Thanks."

"So," I say. "About that bio."

"Should we print it out and find a red pen?" he jokes.

"No way, man. This planet is dying. No way I'm wasting that much paper."

"Ha ha ha," he says. "I was trying to be thorough."

"As thorough as Dostoyevsky."

"You say that like it's a bad thing."

"Shh," I say. "Reading."

Already knowing Alex, I *do* find the bio kind of charming. Mostly in that it speaks to that lovable grandpa side of him. But if I *didn't* know him, and one of my friends read me this bio, I would suggest that perhaps this man was a serial killer.

Unfair? Probably.

But that doesn't change things. He lists where he went to school, when he graduated, talks in depth about what he studied, the last few jobs he had, his strengths at said jobs, the fact that he hopes to get married and have kids, and that he is "close with [his] three brothers and their spouses and children" and "enjoys teaching literature to gifted high school students."

I must be making a face, because he sighs and says, "It's really that bad?"

"No?" I say.

"Is that a question?" he asks.

"No!" I say. "I mean, no, it's not bad. It's kind of cute, but, Alex, what are you supposed to talk about when you go out with a girl who's already read all this?"

He shrugs. "I don't know. Probably I'd just ask them questions about themselves."

"That feels like a job interview," I say. "I mean, yes, it *is* a rare and wonderful thing when your Tinder date asks you a single question about yourself, but you can't just not talk about yourself at all."

He rubs at the line in his forehead. "God, I really hate having to do this. Why's it so hard to meet people in real life?"

"It might be easier . . . in another city," I say pointedly.

He glances askance at me and rolls his eyes, but he's smiling. "Okay, what would *you* write, if you were a guy, trying to woo yourself?"

"Well, I'm different," I say. "What you've got here would totally work on me."

He laughs. "Don't be mean."

"I'm not," I say. "You sound like a sexy, child-rearing robot. Like the maid from *The Jetsons* but with abs."

"Poppyyyyy," he groan-laughs, throwing his forearm over his face.

"Okay, okay. I'll take a crack at it." I take his phone again and erase what he wrote, committing it to memory as well as I can in case he wants to restore it. I think for a minute, then type and pass the phone back to him.

He studies the screen for a *long* time, then reads aloud, "'I have a full-time job and an actual bed frame. My house isn't full of Tarantino posters, and I text back within a couple hours. Also I hate the saxophone'?"

"Oh, did I put a question mark?" I ask, leaning over his shoulder to see. "That's supposed to be a period."

"It's a period," he says. "I just wasn't sure if you were serious."

"Of course I'm serious!"

"'I have an actual bed frame'?" he says again.

"It shows that you're responsible," I say, "and that you're funny."

"It actually shows that *you're* funny," Alex says.

"But you're funny too," I say. "You're just overthinking this."

"You really think women will want to go out with me based on a picture and the fact that I have a bed frame."

"Oh, Alex," I say. "I thought you said you knew how grim it was out there."

"All I'm saying is, I walk around all day with this face and a job and a bed frame, and none of that has gotten me very far."

"Yeah, that's because you're intimidating," I say, saving the bio and going back to the slideshow of women's accounts.

"Yeah, that's it," Alex says, and I look up at him.

"Yes, Alex," I say. "That *is* it."

"What are you talking about?"

"Remember Clarissa? My roommate at U of Chicago?"

"The trust-fund hippie?" he says.

"What about Isabel, my sophomore-year roommate? Or my friend Jaclyn from the communications department?"

"Yes, Poppy, I remember your friends. It wasn't twenty years ago."

"You know what those three people had in common?" I say. "They all had crushes on you. All of them."

He blushes. "You're full of shit."

"No," I say. "I'm not. Clarissa and Isabel were both constantly trying to flirt with you, and Jaclyn's 'communication skills' just utterly failed whenever you were in the room."

"Well, how was I supposed to know that?" he demands.

"Body language, prolonged eye contact," I say, "finding every excuse to touch you, making overt sexual innuendos, asking you for help with papers."

"We always did that over email," Alex says, like he's found a hole in my logic.

"Alex," I say calmly. "Whose idea was *that*?"

The look of victory leaches from his face. "Wait. Seriously?"

"Seriously," I say. "So with that in mind, would you like to take your new photo and bio for a spin?"

He looks aghast. "I'm not going to go on a date during our trip, Poppy."

"Damn right, you're not!" I say. "But you can at least try it out. Besides, I want to see what kinds of girls you swipe right for."

"Nuns," he says, "and aid workers."

"Wow, you're such a good person," I say in a breathy Marilyn Monroe voice. "Please allow me to show my appreciation with a—"

"Okay, okay," he says. "Don't give yourself an asthma attack. I'll swipe, just go gently on me, Poppy."

I bump my shoulder lightly against his. "Always."

"Never," he says.

I frown. "Please call me on it if I ever make you feel bad."

"You don't," he says. "It's fine."

"I know I joke rough sometimes. But I never want to hurt you. Not ever."

He doesn't smile, just gazes back steadily like he's taking the time to let the words soak in. "I know that."

"Okay, good." I nod, train my eyes on his phone screen. "Ooh, what about her?"

The girl on-screen is tanned and pretty, bending at the knee and blowing a kiss at the camera. "No kissy faces," he says, and swipes her off the screen.

"Fair enough."

A girl with a lip ring and dark eye makeup appears in her place. Her bio reads, *All metal, all the time.*

"That's a lot of metal," Alex says, and swipes her away too.

Next up, a girl in a green leprechaun hat, grinning in a green tank top, holding up a green beer. She has big boobs and a bigger smile.

"Oh, a nice Irish girl," I joke.

Alex vanishes that one without comment.

"Hey, what's wrong with her?" I ask. "She was gorgeous."

"Not my type," he says.

"Hokay. Moving on."

He rejects a rock climber, a Hooters waitress, a painter, and a hip-hop dancer with a body to rival Alex's own.

"Alex," I say. "I'm beginning to think the problem lies not with the bio but with the biographer."

"They're just not my type," he says. "And I'm definitely not theirs."

"How do you know that?"

"Look," he says. "Here. She's cute."

"Oh my *god*, you've got to be kidding me!"

"What?" he says. "You don't think she's pretty?"

The strawberry blonde smiles up at me from behind a polished mahogany desk. Her hair is clipped back into a half ponytail and she's wearing a navy blue blazer. According to her bio, she's a graphic designer who loves yoga, sunshine, and cupcakes. "Alex," I say. "She's Sarah."

He rears back. "This girl looks nothing like Sarah."

I snort. "I didn't say she looks like Sarah"—though she does—
"I said she *is* Sarah."

"Sarah's a teacher, not a graphic designer," Alex says. "She's
taller than this girl and her hair is darker and her favorite dessert is
cheesecake, not cupcakes."

"They dress exactly the same. They smile exactly the same.
Why do all guys want girls who look like they're carved out of
soap?"

"What are you *talking* about?" Alex says.

"I mean, you had no interest in all those cool, sexy girls and then
you see this wannabe kindergarten teacher and she's the first person you even consider. It's just . . . typical."

"She's not a kindergarten teacher," he says. "What do you have
against this girl?"

"Nothing!" I say, but it doesn't sound like it's true, even to me. I
sound annoyed. I open my mouth, hoping to walk my reaction back
a little, but that's not what happens at all. "It's not the girl. It's—it's
guys. You all *think* you want a sexy, independent hip-hop dancer, but
when that person appears in front of you, when she's a real person,
she's too much and you're not interested and you'll go for the cute
kindergarten teacher in the turtleneck every time."

"Why do you keep saying she's a kindergarten teacher?" Alex
cries.

"Because she's Sarah," I blurt out.

"I don't want to date Sarah, okay?" he says. "And also Sarah
teaches ninth grade, not kindergarten. And *also*," he goes on, picking up steam, "you talk a big game, Poppy, but I guarantee that
when you're on Tinder, you're swiping right for firefighters and ER
surgeons and professional fucking skateboarders, so no, I don't
feel bad for homing in on women who look like they're probably
sweet—and to *you*, yes, maybe a little bit boring—because it doesn't

seem to have occurred to you that maybe women like you think *I'm*
boring."

"*Fuck* that," I say.

"What?" he says.

"I said, fuck that!" I repeat. "I don't think you're boring, so that
whole argument fails."

"We're friends," he says. "You wouldn't swipe right on me."

"I would too," I say.

"You would not," he argues.

And here's my chance to let it go, but I'm still too fired up, too
annoyed to let him think he's right about this.

"I. Would."

"Well, I would for you too," he retorts, like somehow this is all
some sort of argument.

"Don't say something you don't mean," I warn. "I wouldn't be
wearing a blazer or sitting behind a desk, smiling."

His lips press closed. His jaw muscles bounce as he swallows.
"Okay, show me."

I open my own Tinder app and hand my phone over so he can
see the picture. I'm smiling sleepily, dressed like an alien in a silver
dress and face paint with aluminum antennae hot-glued to my
headband. Halloween, obviously. Or wait, was it Rachel's *X-Files*-
themed birthday party?

Alex considers the photo seriously, then scrolls down to read
my bio. After a minute, he hands my phone back to me and looks
me dead in the eye. "I would."

My whole body tingles with pins and needles. "Oh," I say, then
manage a small "okay."

"So," he says, "are you done being mad at me?"

I try to say something, but my tongue feels too heavy. My whole
body feels heavy, especially where my hip is touching his. So I
just nod.

Thank God for his back spasm, I think. Otherwise I'm not sure what would happen next.

Alex studies me for a few seconds, then reaches for the forgotten laptop. His voice comes out thick. "What do you want to watch?"

19

Six Summers Ago

ALEX AND I were both pretty strapped for cash when the resort in Vail, Colorado, reached out to offer me a free stay.

At that point, whether the trip would happen was up in
the air.

For one thing, when Guillermo broke up with me for a new
hostess in his restaurant (a waifish blue-eyed girl almost fresh off
the plane from Nebraska)—six weeks after I took the plunge and
moved into his apartment—I had to scramble to find a new place
to live.

Had to take an apartment on the high end of my price range.

Had to pay for a U-Haul for the second time in two months.

Had to buy new furniture to replace the stuff that had become
redundant and thus been discarded—Gui already had nicer versions of my things: sofa, mattress, Danish-look kitchen table. We'd
kept my dresser, because the leg on his was broken, and my bedside
table, because he only had the one, but other than that, pretty much
everything we'd kept was his.

The breakup came just after we'd gone to Linfield for Mom's birthday.

For weeks beforehand, I'd debated whether to warn Gui what to expect.

For example, the *Beverly Hillbillies*–style junkyard that was our front lawn. Or Mom's Museum to Our Childhood, as me and my brothers called the house itself. The baked goods my mother would pile up around the kitchen the whole time we were there, often with a frosting so thick and sweet it made non-Wrights cough as they ate, or the fact that our garage was riddled with things like once-used duct tape Dad was sure he could repurpose. Or that we'd be expected to play a days-spanning board game we'd invented as kids based on *Attack of the Killer Tomatoes.*

That my parents had recently adopted three senior cats, one of whom was incontinent to the point of having to wear a diaper.

Or that there was a decent chance he'd hear my parents having sex, because our house had thin walls, and as previously stated, the Wrights are a loud clan.

Or that there'd be a New Talent Show at the end of the weekend, where everyone was expected to perform some new feat they'd only started learning at the start of the visit.

(Last time I'd been home, Prince's talent had been having us call out the name of any movie and trying to connect it back to Keanu Reeves within six degrees.)

So I should've warned Guillermo what he was walking into, definitely, but doing so would've felt like treason. Like I was saying there was something wrong with them. And sure, they were loud and messy, but they were also amazing and kind and funny, and I hated myself for even *considering* being embarrassed by them.

Gui would love them, I told myself. Gui loved me, and these were the people who'd made me.

At the end of our first night there, we shut ourselves into my childhood bedroom and he said, "I think I understand you better now than ever before."

His voice was as tender and warm as ever, but instead of love, it sounded like sympathy.

"I get why you had to flee to New York," he said. "It must've been so hard for you here."

My stomach sunk and my heart squeezed painfully, but I didn't correct him. Again, I just hated myself for being embarrassed.

Because I *had* fled to New York, but I hadn't fled my family, and if I'd kept them separate from the rest of my life, it was only to protect them from judgment, and myself from this familiar feeling of rejection.

The rest of the trip was uncomfortable. Gui was kind to my family—he was always kind—but I saw every interaction they had through a lens of condescension and pity after that.

I tried to forget the trip had happened. We were happy together, in our *real life*, in New York. So what if he didn't understand my family? He loved me.

A few weeks later, we went to a dinner party at his friend's brownstone, someone he'd known from boarding school, a guy with a trust fund and a Damien Hirst painting hanging over the dining room table. I knew this—would never forget it—because when someone said the name, unrelated to the painting, I said, "Who?" and laughter followed.

They weren't laughing at me; they genuinely thought I was making a joke.

Four days after that, Guillermo ended our relationship. "We're just too different," he said. "We got swept up in our chemistry, but long term, we want different things."

I'm not saying he dumped me for not knowing who Damien Hirst was. But I'm not *not* saying that either.

When I moved out of the apartment, I stole one of his fancy cooking knives.

I could've taken them all, but my mild form of revenge was imagining him looking everywhere for it, trying to figure out if he took it with him to a dinner party or it fell into the gap between his enormous refrigerator and the kitchen island.

Frankly, I wanted the knife to haunt him.

Not in a My-Ex-Is-Going-to-Go-All-Glenn-Close-in-*Fatal-Attraction* way, but in a Something-About-This-Missing-Knife-Seems-to-Be-Conjuring-a-Strong-Metaphor-and-I-Can't-Figure-Out-What-It's-Saying way.

I started feeling guilty after a week in my new apartment—once the sobbing wore off—and considered mailing the knife back but thought that might send the wrong message. I imagined Gui showing up to the police department with the package, and decided I'd just let him buy a new knife.

I thought about selling the stolen one online, and worried the anonymous buyer would turn out to be him, so I just kept it and resumed my sobbing until I was done threeish weeks later.

The point is, breakups suck. Breakups between cohabitating partners in overpriced cities suck a little extra, and I wasn't sure I'd be able to afford a summer trip this year.

And then there was the matter of Sarah Torval.

Adorable, willowy yet athletic, clean-faced, brown-eyeliner-wearing Sarah Torval.

Who Alex has been seriously dating for nine months. After their first chance encounter when Alex was visiting friends in Chicago, their texting had quickly evolved into phone calls, and then another visit. After that they'd gotten serious fast, and after six months long distance, she'd taken a teaching job and moved to Indiana to be with him while he finished his MFA. She's happy to stay there while he works toward his doctorate, and will probably follow him wherever he lands afterward.

Which would make me happy if not for my increasing suspicion that she hates me.

Whenever she posts pictures of herself holding Alex's brand-new baby niece with captions like *family time*, or *this little love bug*, I like the post and comment, but she refuses to follow me back. I even unfollowed and refollowed her once, in case she hadn't noticed me the first time.

"I think she feels kind of weird about the trip," Alex admits on one of our (now fewer and farther between) calls. I'm pretty sure he only calls me from the car, when he's on his way to or from the gym. I want to tell him that calling me only when she's not around probably isn't helping.

But the truth is, I don't want to talk to him while anyone else is around, so instead this is what has become of our friendship. Fifteen-minute calls every couple weeks, no texting, no messaging, hardly any emailing except the occasional one-liner with a picture of the tiny black cat he found in the dumpster behind his apartment complex.

She looks like a kitten, but according to the vet she's fully grown, just small. He sends me pictures of her sitting in shoes and hats and bowls, always writing *for scale*, but really I know he just thinks everything she does is adorable. And sure, it's cute that cats like to sit in things . . . but it's quite possibly cuter that Alex can't stop himself from taking pictures of it.

He hasn't named her yet; he's taking his time. He says it wouldn't feel right to name a grown thing without knowing it, so for now he calls her *cat* or *tiny sweetie* or *little friend*.

Sarah wants to call her Sadie, but Alex doesn't think that fits so he's biding his time. The cat is the only thing we ever talk about these days. I'm surprised Alex would be so forthright as to tell me that Sarah feels weird about the Summer Trip.

"Of course she does," I tell him, "I would too." I don't blame her at all. If my boyfriend had a friendship with a girl like Alex's and mine, I would wind up in *The Yellow Wallpaper*.

There's no way in hell I could believe it was wholly platonic. Especially having been in this friendship long enough to accept that five (to fifteenish) percent of what-if as part of the deal.

"So what do we do?" he asks.

"I don't know," I say, trying not to sound miserable. "Do you want to invite her?"

He's quiet for a minute. "I don't think that's a good idea."

"Okay . . ." And then, after the longest pause ever, I say, "Should we just . . . cancel?"

Alex sighs. He must have me on speakerphone because I can hear his turn signal clicking. "I don't know, Poppy. I'm not sure."

"Yeah. Me neither."

We stay on the phone, but neither of us says anything else for the rest of his drive. "I just got home," he says eventually. "Let's talk about this again in a few weeks. Things could change by then."

What things? I want to ask, but don't, because once your best friend is someone else's boyfriend, the boundaries between what you can and can't say get a whole lot firmer.

I spend the whole night after our phone call thinking, *Is he going to break up with her? Is she going to break up with* him?

Is he going to try to reason with her?

Is he going to break up with me?

When I get the offer of a free stay from the resort in Vail, I send him the first text I've sent in months: Hey! Give me a call when you've got a sec!

At five thirty the next morning, my phone rings me awake. I

peer through the dark at his name on the screen and fumble the call on to hear his turn signal tapping out a rhythm. He's on his way to the gym. "What's up?" he asks.

"I'm dead," I groan.

"What else?"

"Colorado," I say. "Vail."

20

This Summer

WAKE UP NEXT to Alex. He insisted that the bed in Nikolai's Airbnb was plenty big, that neither of us should risk another night on the foldout chair, but we're right in the middle of the mattress by the time morning comes.

I'm on my right side, facing him. He's on his left, facing me. There's half a foot between us, except that my left leg is sprawled over him, my thigh hooked up against his hip, his hand resting high up on it.

The apartment is hellishly hot, and we're both drenched with sweat.

I need to extricate myself before Alex wakes up, but the ludicrous part of my brain wants to stay here, replaying the look he gave me, the way his voice sounded last night when he sized up my dating profile and said, "I would."

Like a dare.

Then again, he was on muscle relaxants at the time.

Today, if he remembers that at all, he will almost definitely be regretful and embarrassed.

Or maybe he'll remember sitting next to me for the length of an egregiously underwhelming documentary about the Kinks and feeling like a live wire, sparking every time our arms brushed.

"You usually fall asleep during these," he pointed out with a mild smile, jostling his leg against mine, but when he looked down at me, his hazel eyes seemed to be part of a different expression entirely, one with sharp edges and even some hunger.

I shrugged, said something like, "Just not tired," and tried to focus on the movie. Time moved at an oily slog, every second beside him striking me with new intensity as if we'd just started touching again and again and again for almost two hours.

It was early when the movie ended, so we started another documentary that was boring and mindless, just background noise to make it feel okay that we were riding this line.

At least I was pretty sure that was what we'd been doing.

The way his hand is spread over my thigh now sends another prickly rush of want through me. A very nonsensical part of me wants to nestle closer, until we're touching all over, and wait to see what happens when he wakes up.

All those memories from Croatia froth to the surface of my mind, sending desperate flashes out through my body.

I pull my leg off him, and his hand tightens on me reflexively, loosening when I drag myself clear from under it. I roll away and sit up just as Alex is stirring awake, his eyes slitting open sleepily, hair wild with bedhead. "Hey," he rasps.

My own voice comes out thick. "How'd you sleep?"

"Good, I think," he says. "You?"

"Good. How's your back?"

"Let me see." Slowly, he pushes himself up, turning to slide his long legs over the side of the bed. He cautiously stands. "A lot better."

He has an enormous erection and seems to notice at the same

time I do. He folds his hands in front of himself and looks around the apartment squinting. "There's no way it was this hot when we fell asleep."

He's probably right, but I have no real recollection of how hot it was last night.

I wasn't thinking clearly enough to process the heat.

Today cannot go the way of yesterday.

No more lounging around the apartment. No more sitting together on the bed. No more talking about Tinder. No more falling asleep together and half mounting him while unconscious.

Tomorrow, wedding festivities will begin for David and Tham (bachelor parties, rehearsal dinner, wedding). Today, Alex and I need to have enough uncomplicated, unconfusing fun that when we get home, he doesn't need another two-year break from me.

"I'll call Nikolai about the AC again," I say. "But we should get moving. We've got a lot to do."

Alex runs his hand up his forehead into his hair. "Do I have time to shower?"

My heart gives a sharp pulse, and just like that I'm imagining taking a shower with him.

"If you want," I manage. "But you *will* be drenched in sweat again in seconds."

He shrugs. "I don't think I can make myself leave the apartment feeling this dirty."

"You've been dirtier," I joke, because I have misplaced my already faulty filter.

"Only in front of you," he says, and rustles my hair as he walks past to the bathroom.

My legs feel like jelly under me as I stand there waiting for the shower to turn on. Only once it does do I feel capable of moving again, and my first stop is the thermostat.

Eighty-five?!

Eighty-five miserable degrees in this apartment and the thermostat's been set to seventy-nine since last night. So we can officially rule the air conditioner fully broken.

I walk onto the balcony and dial Nikolai, but he sends me to voicemail on the third ring. I leave another message, this one a little angrier, then follow up with an email and a text too before going inside to search for the lightest-weight piece of clothing I brought.

A gingham sundress that's so baggy it hangs on me like a paper bag.

The water turns off, and Alex does *not* make the mistake of coming out in his towel this time. He emerges fully dressed, hair wicked back and water droplets still clinging (sensuously, I might add) to his forehead and neck.

"So," he says. "What did you have in mind today?"

"Surprises," I say. "Lots of them." I try to dramatically fling the car keys to him. They fall to the floor two feet short. He looks down at where they lie.

"Wow," he says. "Was that . . . one of the surprises?"

"Yes," I say. "Yes, it was. But the others are better so pick those up and let's hit it."

His mouth twists. "I probably . . ."

"Oh, right! Your back!" I run over and retrieve the keys, handing them to him like a normal adult human might.

When we walk out onto the exterior hallway of the Desert Rose, Alex says, "At least it's not *just* our apartment that feels like Satan's anal glands."

"Yes, it's much better that the entire city be this ungodly hot," I say.

"You'd think with all the rich people vacationing here they'd have money to just air-condition the whole place."

"First stop: city council, to pitch that bomb-ass idea."

"Have you considered building a *dome*, Councilwoman?" he says dryly as we plod down the steps.

"Hey, that one guy did it in that one Stephen King novel," I say.

"I'll probably leave that out of the pitch."

"I have good ideas." I try again to give him the puppy face as we're crossing the parking lot, and he laughs and shoves my face away.

"You're not good at that," he says.

"Your severe reaction would suggest otherwise."

"You legitimately look like you're shitting."

"That's not my shitting face," I say. "This is." I strike a Marilyn Monroe pose, legs wide, one hand braced against my thigh, the other covering my open mouth.

"That's nice," he says. "You should put that on your blog." Quickly, stealthily, he whips his phone out and snaps a picture.

"Hey!"

"Maybe a toilet paper company will endorse you," he suggests.

"That's not bad," I say. "I like the way you think."

"I have good ideas," he parrots, and unlocks the door for me, then circles to the driver's seat as I get in and take a deep whiff of the perma-weed smell.

"Thank you for never making me drive," I say as he gets in, hissing at the feel of the hot seat, and clicks his seat belt.

"Thank you for hating driving and allowing me to have some modicum of control over my life in this vast and unpredictable universe."

I wink at him. "No prob."

He laughs.

Weirdly, he seems more relaxed than he has this whole trip. Or maybe it's just that I'm being more insistently normal and chatty, and this really was the key to a successful, old-school Poppy and Alex summer trip all along.

"So are you going to tell me where we're going, or should I just aim for the sun and go?"

"Neither," I say. "I'll navigate."

Even driving full speed with all the windows down, it feels like we're standing in front of an open furnace, its blasts racing through our hair and clothes. Today's heat makes yesterday's look like the first day of spring.

We are going to be spending a *lot* of time outdoors today, and I make a mental note to buy enormous water bottles the first chance we get.

"This next left," I say, and when the sign appears ahead, I cry, "Ta-da!"

"The Living Desert Zoo and Gardens," Alex reads.

"One of the top ten best zoos in the world," I say.

"Well, *we'll* be the judge of that," he replies.

"Yeah, and if they think we're going to go easy on them just because we're delusional from heat exhaustion, they've got another think coming."

"But if they sell milkshakes, I'm inclined to leave them a largely positive review," Alex says quickly under his breath, and turns the car off.

"Well, we're not monsters."

It's not like we're zoo people, but this place specializes in animals native to the desert, and they do a lot of rehabilitation with the goal of releasing animals back into the wild.

Also they let you feed giraffes.

I don't tell Alex this because I want him to be surprised. While he is a young, hot cat lady in his heart, he's also just a general animal lover, so I expect this to go over well.

The feeding goes until eleven thirty a.m., so I figure we have time to wander freely before I have to figure out where the giraffes are, and if we happen upon them by accident before then, all the better.

Alex still has to be careful with his back, so we move slowly, wandering from an informative reptile show to one about birds, during which Alex leans over and whispers, "I think I just decided to be afraid of birds."

"It's good to find new hobbies!" I hiss back. "It means you're not stagnant."

His laugh is quiet but unsuppressed, rattling down my arm in a way that makes me feel light-headed. Of course, that could also be the heat.

After the bird show we head to the petting zoo, where we stand among a coterie of five-year-olds and use special brushes to comb Nigerian dwarf goats.

"I misread that sign as *ghosts*, not *goats*, and now I'm just disappointed," Alex says under his breath. He punctuates it with the face.

"It is so freaking hard to find a good ghost exhibit these days," I point out.

"Too true," he agrees.

"Remember our cemetery tour guide in New Orleans? He hated us."

"Huh," Alex says in a way that suggests he *doesn't* remember, and my stomach, which has been somersaulting all day, rolls into a wall and sinks. I want him to remember. I want every moment to matter as much to him as it has to me. But if the old ones don't, then maybe at least this trip can. I'm determined that it will.

In the petting zoo, we meet some other African livestock, including a few Sicilian dwarf donkeys.

"There sure are a lot of tiny things in the desert," I say.

"Maybe you should move here," Alex teases.

"You're just trying to get me out of New York so you can swoop in and get my apartment."

"Don't be ridiculous," he says. "I could never afford that apartment."

After the petting zoo, we track down some milkshakes—Alex gets vanilla despite all my desperate pleading. "Vanilla isn't a flavor."

"It is too," Alex says. "It's the taste of the vanilla bean, Poppy."

"You might as well just be drinking frozen heavy cream."

He thinks for a second. "I would try that."

"At least get chocolate," I say.

"You get chocolate," he says.

"I can't. I'm getting strawberry."

"See?" Alex says. "Like I said last night, you think I'm boring."

"I think vanilla milkshakes are boring," I say. "I think *you* are misguided."

"Here." Alex holds his paper cup out to me. "Want a sip?"

I heave a sigh. "Fine." I lean forward and take a sip. He arches his eyebrow, waiting for a reaction. "It's *okay*."

He laughs. "Yeah, honestly it's not that good. But that's not Vanilla as a Flavor's fault."

After we've polished off our milkshakes and tossed the cups, I decide we should ride the Endangered Species Carousel.

But when we get there, we find it's closed due to heat.

"Global warming's really hitting the endangered species when they're down," Alex muses. He wipes his forearm up his head, catching the sweat gathering there.

"You need some water?" I ask. "You don't look so good."

"Yeah," he says. "Maybe."

We go buy a couple bottles and sit on a bench in the shade. A few sips in, though, Alex looks worse. "Shit," he says. "I'm pretty dizzy." He hunches over his knees and hangs his head.

"Can I get you something?" I ask. "Maybe you need real food?"

"Maybe," he agrees.

"Here. Stay here and I'll get you, like, a sandwich, okay?"

I know he must be feeling awful because he doesn't argue. I walk back to the last café we passed. There's a long line by now—it's almost lunchtime.

I check my phone. Eleven oh three. Just under thirty minutes left to feed the giraffes.

I stand in line for ten minutes to get the premade turkey club, then jog back to find Alex sitting where I left him, his head resting in his hands.

"Hey," I say, and his glass eyes rise. "Feeling any better?"

"I'm not sure," he says, and accepts the sandwich, unwrapping it. "Want some?"

He gives me half, and I take a couple bites, trying my best not to time him as he slowly munches on his half. At eleven twenty-two, I ask, "Is it helping?"

"I think so. I feel less dizzy anyway."

"Do you think you're okay to walk?"

"Are we . . . in a hurry?" he asks.

"No, of course not," I say. "There's just this thing. Your surprise. It ends pretty soon."

He nods, but he looks queasy, so I'm torn between pushing him to rally or insisting he stay put. "I'm okay," he says, climbing to his feet. "Just need to remember to drink more water."

We make it to the giraffes at eleven thirty-five.

"Sorry," a teenage employee tells me. "Giraffe feeding is over for the day."

As she walks away, Alex looks at me hazily. "Sorry, Pop. I hope you're not too disappointed."

"Of course not," I insist. I don't care about feeding giraffes (at least not much). What I care about is making this trip *good*. Proving we should keep taking them. That we can salvage our friendship.

That's why I'm disappointed. Because it's the first strike of the day.

My phone buzzes with a message, and at least it's some good news.

Nikolai writes, Got all of you [*sic*] messages. I'll see what I can do.

Okay, I write back. Just keep us updated.

"Come on," I say, "let's go somewhere air-conditioned until our next stop."

21

Six Summers Ago

DON'T KNOW HOW Alex got Sarah on board with the Vail trip, but he did.

Asking how strikes me as dangerous. There are things we talk around these days, to keep everything aboveboard, and Alex is careful not to share anything that might embarrass Sarah.

There's no talk of jealousy. Maybe there *is* no jealousy. Maybe there's some other reason she didn't initially like the idea of the trip. But she changes her mind, and the trip is on, and once Alex and I are together, I stop worrying about it. Things feel normal between us again, that fifteenish percent of what-if shrunken back to a manageable two.

We rent bikes and rumble over the cobblestone streets, take a gondola up the mountain, and pose for photos with the vast blue sky behind us, wind blowing our hair across our faces in midlaugh. We sit on patios, sipping chilled green tea or coffee in the mornings before it gets hot, take long hikes on mountain trails during the day with our sweatshirts shed and tied around our waists, only to wind up at different outdoor patios, drinking red wine and sharing three orders of fries with pressed garlic and freshly grated Parmesan. We sit outside until we're goose-bump-covered and shivering, and then pull on our sweatshirts, and I draw my knees up to my chest inside mine. Every time I do this, Alex leans over and flicks my hood up over my head, then tugs the drawstrings tight so that only the very middle of my face is visible, and most of that is blocked by tufts of wind-tangled blond hair.

"Cutie," he says, grinning, the first time he does this, but it feels almost brotherly.

One night, there's a live band playing Van Morrison hits while we're eating dinner outside under strands of globe lights that remind me of the night we met as freshmen. We follow older couples onto the dance floor, hand in hand. We move like we did back in New Orleans—clumsy and rhythmless but laughing, happy.

Now that it's behind us, I can admit that things were different that night.

In the magic of the city and its music and smells and glimmering lights, I felt something I'd never felt with him before. Scarier than that, I'd known from the way Alex looked into my eyes, smoothed his hand down my arm, eased his cheek against mine, that he felt it too.

But now, dancing to "Brown Eyed Girl," the heat has gone out of his touch. And I'm happy, because I never want to lose this.

I would rather have one tiny sliver of him forever than have all of him for just a moment and know I'd have to relinquish all of it when we were through. I could never lose Alex. I couldn't. And so this is good, this peaceful, sparkless dance. This sparkless trip.

Alex calls Sarah twice a day, morning and night, but never in front of me. In the morning, they talk while he jogs, before I'm even out of bed, and when he gets back, he wakes me up with coffee and a pastry from the café in the resort's clubhouse. At night, he steps out onto the balcony to call her and shuts the door behind him.

"I don't want you to make fun of my phone voice," he says.

"God, I'm an asshole," I say, and though he laughs, I do feel bad. Teasing has always been a big part of our dynamic, and it's felt like our thing. But there are things he won't do in front of me now, parts of him he doesn't trust with me, and I don't like how that feels.

When he comes inside after his jog and morning call the next day, I sit up sleepily to accept the proffered coffee and croissant and say, "Alex Nilsen, for whatever it's worth, I'm sure your phone voice is amazing."

He blushes, rubs the back of his head. "It's not."

"I bet you're all buttery and warm and sweet and perfect."

"Are you talking to me or the croissant?" he asks.

"I love you, croissant," I say, and tear a piece off, lowering it into my mouth. He stands there, hands in his pockets, grinning, and my heart swells, Grinch-style, just looking at him. "But I'm talking about you."

"You're sweet, Poppy," he says. "And buttery and warm and whatever. But I still would just rather talk on the phone alone."

"Heard," I say, nodding, and hold my croissant out to him. He tears off the teensiest piece and pops it between his lips.

Later that day, while we're sitting at lunch, something brilliant occurs to me. "Lita!" I cry, seemingly out of nowhere.

"Bless you?" Alex says.

"Remember Lita?" I say. "She was living in that dumpy house in Tofino. With Buck?"

Alex narrows his eyes. "Is she the one who tried to put her hand down my pants while she was giving me a 'tour'?"

"Um, one, you didn't tell me that happened, and two, no. She was hanging out with me and Buck. She was leaving soon, remember? Moving to *Vail* to be a rafting guide!"

"Oh," Alex says. "Yeah. Right."

"Do you think she's still here?"

He squints. "On this earthly plane? I'm not sure any of those people are."

"I've got Buck's number," I say.

"You do?" Alex gives me a pointed look.

"I haven't *used* it," I say. "But I have it. I'll text him and see if he has Lita's number."

Hey, Buck! I write. Not sure if you remember me, but you gave me and my friend Alex a water taxi ride to the hot springs, like, five years ago, right before your friend Lita moved to Colorado? Anyway, I'm in Vail and was gonna see if she was still here! Hope you're well and that Tofino is still the most beautiful place on this whole entire planet.

By the time we've finished eating, Buck has written back.

Damn, girl, he says. Is this sexy little Poppy? Took you long enough to use those digits. Guess I shouldn't have kicked you out of my room.

I snort-laugh, and Alex leans over the table to read the message upside down. He rolls his eyes. "Yeah, you fucking think, pal?"

No, no, no worries about that, I tell him. It was a great night. We had an amazing time.

Sweet, he says. I haven't talked to Lita in years but I'll shoot u her contact info if u want.

That would be amazing, I tell him.

If you ever make it back to the island r u gonna tell me? he asks.

Obviously, I say. I have no idea how to operate a water taxi. You'll be invaluable.

Lol, he says, ur such a freak I love it.

By that night, we've booked a rafting trip with Lita, who does *not* remember us but insists on the phone that she's sure we had a great time together.

"To be fair, I was on, like, a *ton* of drugs back then," she says. "I was *always* having a great time, and I remember almost none of it."

Alex, overhearing this, pulls a face that reads as anxiety with a side of unanswered questions. I know exactly what he wants me to find out.

"So," I say, as casually as I can, "do you still . . . use . . . drugs?"

"Three years sober, mama," she replies. "But if you're looking to buy something, I can send you my old dude's number."

"No, no," I say. "That's okay. We'll just . . . do . . . the stuff . . . we brought . . . from home."

Looking beleaguered, Alex shakes his head.

"All right, then. See you two bright and early."

When I hang up, Alex says, "Do you think Buck was on drugs when he drove our water taxi?"

I shrug. "We never *did* find out what he was ranting to no one about. Maybe he thought Jim Morrison was hovering on the water just in front of him."

"I am so glad we're still alive," Alex says.

The next morning we meet Lita at the raft rental place, and she looks almost exactly as I remember her, but with a wedding band tattoo and a small baby bump.

"Four months," she says, jogging it in her hands.

"And it's . . . safe? To do this?" Alex asks.

"Baby number one did just fine," Lita assures us. "You know, in Norway, they stick their babies outside to take naps."

"Oh . . . kay," Alex says.

"I would *love* to go to Norway," I say.

"Oh, you've *got* to!" she says. "My wife's twin sister lives there—

she married a Norwegian. Gail sometimes talks about legally divorcing me and offering to pay a couple nice Norwegians to marry us so we can both get citizenship and move there. Call me old-fashioned, but I just don't feel right about *paying* for my sham marriage."

"Well, I guess you'll just have to survive on Norwegian vacations, then," I say.

"Guess so."

Out of an abundance of caution, we opt for the beginner route, and we soon discover that this means that our "rafting trip" consists largely of sunbathing and floating with the current, sticking out our oars to shove off of rocks when we get too close, and amping up our rowing whenever a rapid crops up.

Lita, it turns out, remembers a lot more than she let on about Buck and the other people she lived with in the Tofino house, and she regales us with stories of people jumping off the roof onto a trampoline, and drunkenly giving each other stick-and-poke tattoos with red ink pens.

"Turns out some people are allergic to red ink," she says. "Who knew?"

Every story she tells is more ludicrous than the last, and by the time we drag the raft onto the riverbank at the end of our route, my abs ache from laughing.

She wipes laugh-tears away from the just-starting-to-wrinkle corners of her eyes and heaves a contented sigh. "I can laugh because I survived it. Makes me happy knowing Buck did too." She rubs her tummy. "Makes me so happy every time you find out how small the world is, you know? Like, we were in that place at the same time and now here we are. At different points in our lives but still connected. Like quantum entanglement or some shit."

"I think about that every time I'm in an airport," I tell her. "It's one reason I love traveling so much." I hesitate, searching for how to pour this long-steeping soupy thought into concrete words. "As a kid, I was a loner," I explain, "and I always figured that when I grew up, I'd leave my hometown and discover other people like me somewhere else. Which I have, you know? But everyone gets lonely sometimes, and whenever that happens, I buy a plane ticket and go to the airport and—I don't know. I don't feel lonely anymore. Because no matter what makes all those people different, they're all just trying to get somewhere, waiting to reach someone."

Alex gives me an odd look whose meaning I can't interpret.

"Ah, shit," Lita says. "You're gonna make me cry. These damn pregnancy hormones. I react worse to them than I did to ayahuasca."

Before we part ways, Lita pulls each of us into a long hug. "If you're ever in New York . . ." I say.

"If you ever feel like taking a *real* rafting trip," she answers with a wink.

Several silent minutes into our drive back to the resort, with worried creases shooting up from the insides of his eyebrows, Alex says, "I hate thinking about you being lonely."

I must look confused, because he clarifies: "The thing about how you go to the airport. When you feel like you're alone."

"I'm not really that lonely anymore," I say.

I have the group text with Parker and Prince—we've been planning out a no-budget *Jaws* musical. Then there are the weekly calls with both my parents on speakerphone. Plus there's Rachel, who's really come through for me post-Guillermo, with invites to exercise classes and wine bars and volunteering days at dog shelters.

Even though Alex and I don't talk as much as we used to, there are also the short stories he's been mailing me with brief hand-scribbled notes on Post-its. He could email them, but he doesn't, and after I've read each hard copy, I put it in a shoebox where I've started keeping the things that matter to me. (One shoebox, so I don't end up with huge plastic bins of my future children's dragon drawings like Mom and Dad have.)

I don't feel alone when I read his words. I don't feel alone when I hold those Post-its in my hand and think about the person who wrote them.

"I'm sorry if I haven't been there for you," Alex says quietly. He opens his mouth as if to go on, then shakes his head and closes it again. We've made it back to the resort, pulled into our parking space, and when I turn in my seat to face him, he angles toward me too.

"Alex . . ." It takes me a few seconds to go on: "I've never really felt alone since I met you. I don't think I'll ever feel truly alone in this world again as long as you're in it."

His gaze softens, holds steady for a beat. "Can I tell you something embarrassing?"

For once, it doesn't occur to me to joke, to be sarcastic. "Anything."

He runs his hand over the steering wheel in a slow back-and-forth. "I don't think I knew I was lonely until I met you." He shakes his head again. "At home, after my mom died and my dad fell apart, I just wanted everyone to be okay. I wanted to be exactly what Dad needed, and exactly what my little brothers needed, and at school, I wanted to be who everyone wanted, so I tried to be calm and responsible and steady, and I think I was nineteen years old the first time it occurred to me that maybe that wasn't how some people lived. That maybe I just *was* someone, beyond who I *tried* to be.

"I met you, and honestly . . . at first, I thought it was an act. The shocking clothes, the shocking jokes."

"Whatever do you mean?" I tease quietly, and a smile winks in the corner of his mouth, brief as a beat of a hummingbird's wings.

"On that first drive back to Linfield, you asked me all these questions about what I liked and what I hated, and I don't know. It just felt like you really wanted to know."

"Of course I did," I say.

He nods. "I know. You asked me who I was, and—it was like the answer came out of nowhere. Sometimes it feels like I didn't even exist before that. Like you invented me."

Heat rushes to my cheeks, and I adjust my position in my seat, pulling my knees into my chest. "I'm not smart enough to have invented you. No one's that smart."

The muscles along his jaw leap as he considers his next words, never one to blurt anything out without first weighing it. "My point is, no one really knew me before you, Poppy. And even if . . . things change between us, you'll never be alone, okay? I'll always love you."

Tears cloud my eyes, but miraculously I blink them clear. Somehow, my voice comes out steady and light, and not like someone reached into my rib cage and held my heart inside his hand just long enough to run a thumb across a secret wound.

"I know," I tell him, and, "I love you too."

It's true, but not the full truth. There aren't words vast or specific enough to capture the ecstasy and the ache and love and fear I feel just looking at him now.

So the moment sweeps past, and the trip goes on, and nothing is different between us, except that a part of me has woken up, like a bear emerging from hibernation with a hunger it has managed to sleep through for months but can't ignore one second longer.

The next day, the second to last of the trip, we take a hike up a mountain pass. Near the top, I step to the edge of the path to take a photo through an opening in the trees of the deep blue lake below and lose my footing. My ankle rolls, hard and fast. It feels like the bone jabs through my foot to hit the ground, and then I'm sprawled in mud and leaves, hissing out swear words.

"Stay still," Alex says, crouching beside me.

At first I can barely breathe, so I'm not crying, just choking, "Do I have a bone sticking out of my skin?"

Alex glances down, checks my leg. "No, I think you just sprained it."

"Fuck," I gasp from beneath a wave of pain.

"Squeeze my hand if you need to," he says, and I do, as tight as I can. In his giant, masculine palm, my own looks tiny, my knuckles knobby and bulbous.

The pain lets up enough that mania rushes in to replace it. Tears falling in great gushes, I ask, "Do I have slow loris hands?"

"What?" Alex asks, understandably confused. His worried expression judders. He turns a laugh into a cough. "Slow loris hands?" he repeats seriously.

"Don't laugh at me!" I squeak out, fully regressed into an eight-year-old little sister.

"I'm sorry," he says. "No, you don't have slow loris hands. Not that I know what a slow loris is."

"It's kind of like a lemur," I say tearfully.

"You have beautiful hands, Poppy." He tries very, very hard— perhaps his hardest ever—not to smile, but slowly it happens anyway, and I break into a teary laugh. "Do you want to try to stand?" he asks.

"Can't you just roll me down the mountain?"

"I'd rather not," he says. "There might be poison ivy once we get off the trail."

I sigh. "Okay, then." He helps me up, but I can't put any weight on my right foot without a lightning bolt of pain crackling up my leg. I stop shambling along, start to cry again, and bury my face in my hands to hide the snotty mess I'm crumbling into.

Alex rubs his hands slowly up and down my arms for a few seconds, which only makes me cry harder. People being nice to me when I'm upset always has this effect. He pulls me in against his chest and hooks his arms against my back.

"Am I going to have to, like, pay for a helicopter to get down there?" I get out.

"We're not that far," he says.

"I'm not kidding, I can't put any weight on it."

"Here's what's going to happen," he says. "I'm going to pick you up, and I'm going to carry you—very slowly—down the trail. And I'm probably going to have to stop a lot and set you down, and you're not allowed to call me Seabiscuit, or scream *Faster! Faster!* in my ear."

I laugh into his chest, nod against him, leaving wet marks behind on his T-shirt.

"And if I find out you faked this whole thing just to see if I would carry you half a mile down a mountain," he says, "I'm going to be really annoyed."

"Scale of one to ten," I say, leaning back to look into his face.

"Seven at *least*," he says.

"You are so, so nice," I say.

"You mean buttery and warm and perfect," he teases, widening his stance. "Ready?"

"Ready," I confirm, and Alex Nilsen sweeps me up into his arms and carries me down a motherfucking mountain.

No. I really could not have invented him.

22

This Summer

FULLY RECHARGED AFTER two water bottles and forty minutes in a zoo gift shop full of stuffed camels, we head to our
next destination.

The Cabazon Dinosaurs are pretty much exactly what they
sound like: two big-ass dinosaur sculptures on the side of the highway in the middle of nowhere, California.

A theme-park sculptor built the steel monsters hoping to drive
business to his roadside diner. Since he died, the property's been
sold to a group that put in a creationist museum and gift shop inside the tail of one of the dinosaurs.

It's the kind of place you stop at because you're already driving
past. It's also the kind of place you drive to, out of your way, when
you're trying to fill every second of your day.

"Well," Alex says when we get out of the car. The dusty T. rex
and brontosaurus tower over us, a few spiky palm trees and scraggly bushes dotting the sand beneath them. Time and sunlight have
drained the dinos of almost any color. They look thirsty, like they've

been shambling through this place and its harsh sunlight for millennia.

"Well, indeed," I agree.

"Guess we should get some pictures?" Alex says.

"Definitely."

He takes his phone out and waits for me to strike some poses in front of the dinosaurs. After a couple tame Instagram-appropriate pictures, I start jumping and flailing my arms, hoping to make him laugh.

He smiles but still looks a little peaked, and I decide it's best if we get into the shade. We amble through the grounds, take a couple more photos closer up and with the smaller dinosaurs that have been added within the scrubby brush surrounding the two main offerings. Then we climb the steps to poke around the gift shop.

"You can hardly tell we're inside a dinosaur," Alex jokingly complains.

"Right? Where are the giant vertebrae? Where are the blood vessels and tail muscles?"

"*This* is not getting a favorable Yelp review," Alex mutters, and I laugh, but he doesn't join in. I'm suddenly aware of how pathetic the AC is in this shop. Nothing compared to the zoo gift shop. We might as well be back in Nikolai's hellhole.

"Should we get out of here?" I ask.

"God, yes," Alex says, and sets down the dinosaur figurine he's been holding.

I check the time on my phone. It's only four p.m. and we've burned through everything I had planned for today. I open my notes app and scan the list for something else to do.

"Okay," I say, trying to mask my anxiety. "I've got it. Come on."

The Moorten Botanical Garden. It's outside, but it's sure to have a better cooling system than the gift shop inside a steel dinosaur.

Only I don't think to check the hours and we drive all the way there only to find it closed. "Closes at *one* during the summer?" I read the sign incredulously.

"Do you think it has anything to do with the dangerously high temperature?" Alex says.

"Okay," I say. "Okay."

"Maybe we should just go home," Alex says. "See if Nikolai has fixed the AC."

"Not yet," I say, desperate. "There's something else I wanted to do."

"Fine," Alex says. Back at the car, I head him off at the driver's-side door, and he asks, "What are you doing?"

"I have to drive for this part," I say.

He arches an eyebrow but gets into the passenger seat. I open my GPS and enter the first address on the list for the "self-guided architecture tour of Palm Springs."

"It's . . . a hotel," Alex says, confused, when we pull up to the funky angular building with its flagstone siding and orange-outlined sign.

"The Del Marcos Hotel," I say.

"Is there . . . a steel dinosaur inside?" he asks.

I frown. "I don't think so. But this whole neighborhood, the Tennis Club neighborhood, is supposed to be full of all these ridiculously amazing buildings."

"Ah," he says, like that's all he can muster in the way of enthusiasm.

My stomach drops as I punch in the next address. We drive around for two hours, stop for a cheap dinner (which we drag out for another hour because Cold Air), and when we return to the car,

Alex cuts me off at the driver's-side door. "Poppy," he says pleadingly.

"Alex," I say.

"You can drive if you want," he says, "but I'm getting a little carsick, and I don't know if I can take seeing any more strangers' mansions today."

"But you love architecture," I say pathetically.

His brow furrows, his eyes narrow. "I . . . what?"

"In New Orleans," I say, "you just walked around pointing at, like, windows the whole time. I thought you loved this kind of thing."

"Pointing at windows?"

I throw my arms out to my sides. "I don't know! You just, like . . . fucking *loved* looking at buildings!"

He lets out a fatigued laugh. "I believe you," he says. "Maybe I do love architecture. I don't know. I'm just . . . really tired and hot."

I scramble to get my phone out of my purse. There's still no word from Nikolai. We cannot go back to that apartment. "What about the air museum?"

When I look up, he's studying me, head tilted and eyes still narrow. He runs a hapless hand through his hair and glances away for a second, sets his hand on his hip. "It's, like, seven o'clock, Poppy," he says. "I don't think it's going to be open."

I sigh, deflating. "You're right." I cross back to the passenger seat and flop down, feeling defeated as Alex starts the car.

Fifteen miles down the road, we get a flat tire.

"Oh, god," I groan as Alex pulls off to the side of the road.

"There's probably a spare," he says.

"And you know how to put that on?" I say.

"Yes. I know how to put that on."

"Mr. Homeowner," I say, trying to sound playful. Turns out I too am deeply grumpy and that's how my voice portrays me. Alex ignores the comment and gets out of the car.

"Do you need help?" I ask.

"Might need you to shine a light," he says. "It's starting to get dark."

I follow him to the back of the car. He pops the hatch door, moves some of the mats around, and swears. "No spare."

"This car aspires to destroy our lives," I say, and kick the side of the car. "Shit, I'm going to have to buy this girl a new tire, aren't I?"

Alex sighs and rubs the bridge of his nose. "We'll split it."

"No, that's not what I was . . . I wasn't saying that."

"I know," Alex says, irritated. "But I'm not letting you pay for the whole thing."

"What do we even do?"

"We call a towing company," he says. "We Uber home, and we mess with it tomorrow."

So that's what we do: We call the towing company. Sit in silence on the tailgate while we wait for them to come. Ride back to the shop in the front of the tow truck with a man named Stan who has a naked lady tattooed on each arm. Sign some papers, call an Uber. Stand outside while we wait for the Uber to come.

Get into a car with a lady named Marla who Alex whispers under his breath "looks exactly like Delallo," and at least that's something to laugh about.

And then Marla's app messes up and she gets lost.

And our seventeen-minute drive becomes a twenty-nine-minute drive before our eyes. And neither of us is laughing. Neither of us is saying anything, making any sound.

Finally, we're almost to the Desert Rose. It's pretty much pitch-black outside, and I'm sure the stars overhead would be amazing if we weren't trapped in the back of Marla's Kia Rio inhaling lungful after lungful of the sugar cookie Bath & Body Works spray she seems to have doused the entire car in.

When traffic suddenly stops half a mile from the Desert Rose, I almost cry.

"Must be an accident blocking the road," Marla says. "No reason on heaven or earth traffic should be *this* backed up."

"Do you want to walk?" Alex asks me.

"Why the hell not," I say, and we get out of Marla's car, watch her turn the Kia around in a fifteen-point turn, and start down the dark shoulder of the road toward home.

"I'm getting in that pool tonight," Alex says.

"It's probably closed," I grunt.

"I'll climb the fence," Alex says.

A fizzy, tired chuckle moves through my chest. "Okay, I'm in."

23

Five Summers Ago

OUR LAST NIGHT on Sanibel Island, I lie awake, listening to the rain thrum against the roof, replaying the week as if watching through a sheen that's thick and hazy and ever rippling, trying to capture this one split second that seems to wink out of view every time I reach for it.

I see the stormy beaches. The *Twilight Zone* marathon Alex and I snooze through on the couch. The seafood place where he'd finally given me the grisly details of his and Sarah's breakup—that she'd told him their relationship was about as exciting as the library where they'd met, before dumping him and leaving for a three-week yoga retreat. *If she wants excitement*, I'd said, *I'm happy to key her car.* My memory skips forward, to the bar called BAR, with its sticky floors and thatched fans, where I step out of the bathroom and see him at the bar, reading a book, and feel so much love I could split open, and how after I tried to jar him from his post-Sarah sadness with an over-the-top "Hey, tiger!"

Then there comes the moment that we ran through the downpour from BAR to our car, the ones spent listening to the windshield wipers squeak across the glass as we sliced through the torrential rain back to our rain-soaked bungalow.

I'm getting closer to that moment, that one I keep reaching for and coming up empty-handed, as if it were nothing but a bit of reflected light, dancing on the floor.

I see Alex asking to take a picture together, surprising me with the flash on the count of two instead of three. The both of us choking over laughter, moaning at the heinousness of our picture, arguing whether to delete it, Alex promising I don't look anything like that, me telling him the same.

Then he says, "Next year let's go somewhere cold."

I say okay, that we will.

And here it comes, the moment that keeps slipping through my fingers, like it's the game-changing detail in an instant replay I can't seem to pause or slow down.

We are just looking at each other. There are no hard edges to grab hold of, no distinct markers on this moment's beginning or end, nothing to separate it from the millions just like it.

But this, this is the moment I first think it.

I am in love with you.

The thought is terrifying, probably not even true. A dangerous idea to entertain. I release my hold on it, watch it slip away.

But there are points in the center of my palms that burn, scorched, proof I once held it there.

24

This Summer

THE APARTMENT HAS become the seventh ring of hell, and there's no sign Nikolai has been there. In the bathroom, I change into my bikini and an oversized T-shirt, then fire off another angry text demanding an update.

Alex knocks on the door when he's finished changing in the living room, and we skulk down to the pool, towels in hand. We sneak over to check the gate first. "Locked," Alex confirms, but I've just noticed the bigger problem.

"What. The. Hell."

He looks up and sees it: the empty concrete basin of the pool.

Behind us, someone gasps. "Oh, hon, I told you it was them!"

Alex and I spin around as a middle-aged leathery-tanned couple comes bounding up. A redheaded woman in sparkly cork heels and white capris beside a thick-necked man with a shaved head and pair of sunglasses balanced on the back of his head.

"You called it, babe," the man says.

"The Newwwwwlyweds!" the woman sings, and grabs me in a hug. "Why didn't y'all tell us you were headed to the Springs?"

That's when it clicks. Hubby and Wifey from the cab ride out of LAX.

"Wow," Alex says. "Hi. How's it going?"

The woman's neon-orange fingernails release me, and she waves a hand. "Oh, you know. Was going good until this nonsense. With the pool."

Hubby grunts agreement.

"What happened?" I ask.

"Some kid went and diarrhea'd in it! A *lot*, I guess, because they had to go and drain the whole thing. They say it should be up and running again tomorrow!" She frowns. "Of course, tomorrow, *we're* off to Joshua Tree."

"Oh, cool!" I say. It's a strain to sound bright and chipper when really, my soul is quietly shriveling within the empty shell of my body.

"Won a free stay there." She winks at me. "I'm good luck."

"Sure are," Hubby says.

"I'm not just saying that!" she goes on. "We won the lottery a few years back—not one of those quadrillion-dollar ones but a nice little chunk, and I swear, ever since then it's like I win every raffle, sweepstakes, and contest I so much as look at!"

"Amazing," Alex says. His soul, it sounds like, has also shriveled.

"Anyway! We'll leave you two lovebirds to do your bidding." She winks again. Or maybe her false eyelashes are just sticking together. Hard to say. "Just couldn't believe what weird luck it was that we were staying in the same place!"

"Luck," Alex says. He sounds like he's in a bad-luck-induced trance. "Yeah."

"It's a tiny world, ain't it?" Wifey says.

"It is," I agree.

"Anyway, y'all enjoy the rest of your trip!" She squeezes one of each of our shoulders and Hubby nods, and then they're off and we're left standing in front of the empty pool.

After three silent seconds, I say, "I'll try to call Nikolai again."

Alex says nothing. We go back upstairs. It's ninety degrees. Not metaphorically. It's literally ninety degrees. We don't turn on any lights except the one in the bathroom, like even one more illuminated bulb could get us to an even hundred degrees.

Alex stands in the middle of the room, looking miserable. It's too hot to sit on anything, to touch anything. The air feels different, stiff as a board. I dial Nikolai repeatedly as I pace.

The fourth time he rejects the call, I let out a scream and stomp back to the kitchenette for the scissors.

"What are you doing?" Alex asks. I just storm past to the balcony and stab the plastic sheeting. "That's not going to help," he says. "It's as hot out there as it is in here tonight."

But I can't be reasoned with. I'm hacking away at the plastic, cutting down giant strip after giant, tattered strip and tossing them onto the ground. Finally half of the balcony is open to the night air, but Alex was right. It doesn't matter.

It is so hot I could melt. I march back inside and splash my face with cold water.

"Poppy," Alex says, "I think we should check into a hotel."

I shake my head, too frustrated to speak.

"We have to," he says.

"That's not how this is supposed to go," I bite out, a sudden throb going through my eye.

"What are you talking about?" he says.

"We're supposed to do this how we used to!" I say. "We're supposed to be keeping things cheap and—and rolling with the punches."

"We have rolled with a *lot* of punches," Alex insists.

"Hotels cost money!" I say. "And we're already going to have to drop two hundred to get that horrible car a new tire!"

"You know what costs money?" he says. "Hospitals! We're gonna *die* if we stay here."

"This isn't how it's supposed to go!" I half shout, a broken record.

"It's how it's going!" he fires back.

"I just wanted it to be how it used to be!" I say.

"It's never going to be like that!" he snaps. "We can't go back to that, okay? Things are different, and we can't change that, so just *stop*! *Stop* trying to force this friendship back to what it used to be— it's not going to happen! We're *different* now, and you have to stop pretending we aren't!"

His voice breaks off, eyes dark, jaw taut.

There are tears blurring my vision, and my chest feels like it's being sawed in half as we stand there in the half dark, facing off in silence, breathing hard.

Something disrupts the silence. A low, distant rumble, and then, a quiet *tap-tap-tap*ping.

"Do you hear that?" Alex's voice is a dim rasp.

I give one uncertain nod, and then another rumble shivers out. Our eyes find each other's, wide and desperate. We run to the edge of the balcony.

"Holy shit." I throw my arms out to catch the falling rain. I start to laugh. Alex joins in.

"Here." He grabs the remainder of the plastic sheeting and starts to tear into it. I retrieve the scissors from the café table and we hack away the rest of the plastic, tossing it over our shoulders, the rain pouring in freely, until finally, it's all out of our way. We stand back with our faces tilted up and let the rain wash over us. Another laugh bubbles up in me, and when I look over at Alex, he's watching me, his smile wide for two beats before it disintegrates into concern.

"I'm sorry," he says, voice quiet under the rain. "I just meant . . ."

"I know what you meant," I say. "You were right. We can't go back."

His teeth skim over his bottom lip. "I mean . . . would you really want to?"

"I just want . . ." I shrug.

You, I think.

You.

You.

You. Say it.

I shake my head. "I don't want to lose you again."

Alex reaches out for me, and I go to him, let him catch my hips and pull me in. I press myself against his damp T-shirt as he wraps his arms around me and lifts me up and into him. I push up onto tiptoes and he holds me there, his face buried into my neck, and my oversized T-shirt soaking through. I thread my arms around his waist and shiver as his hands slide up my back, catching on the lump where my bathing suit ties are knotted under my shirt.

Even after a full day of sweating, he smells so good, feels so good against me and underneath my hands. Combined with the intense relief of the desert rain, this has me feeling light-headed, spinny, uninhibited. My hands skim up his neck and slip into his hair, and he draws back enough to look me in the face, but neither of us lets go, and all the stress and worry has left his brow and jaw just as it's lifted from my body like steam.

"You won't lose me," he says, voice dimmed by the rain. "As long as you want me, I'm here."

I swallow down the lump in my throat, but it keeps rising. Trying to keep the words inside. It would be a mistake to say them, right? We tell each other everything, but there are some things that can't be unsaid, just like there are things that couldn't be undone.

His hand rises to sweep a damp curl out of my eyes, tucking it behind my ear. The lump seems to melt, and the truth slips out of me like a breath I've been holding all this time.

"I always want you, Alex," I whisper. "Always."

In this dim light, his eyes look almost sparkly, and his mouth goes soft. When he bends to press his forehead to mine, my whole body feels heavy, like my want is a weighted blanket pushing on me from every side, while his hands brush over my skin as softly as sunlight. His nose slides down the side of mine, the inch between our reaching, unsure mouths pulsing.

There is still a kind of plausible deniability to this, a chance we'll let this moment pass without ever closing that final distance. But, as I listen to his unsteady breath, feel the way it tugs against me as his lips part, come closer, hesitate, I forget every reason I was trying to put this off.

We're magnets, trying to draw together even as we cradle the careful distance between us. His hand skims over my jaw, gingerly angles it so that our noses graze against each other, testing this small gap between us, our open mouths tasting the air between us.

Every breath he takes now whispers against my bottom lip. Each of my shaky inhalations tries to draw him closer. *This wasn't supposed to happen*, I think foggily.

Then, and more loudly, *This* had *to happen.*

This has *to happen.*

This is *happening.*

25

Four Summers Ago

T HIS YEAR IS going to be different. I've been working for *Rest +
Relaxation* magazine for six months. In that time, I've already
been to:

Marrakech and Casablanca.

Martinborough and Queenstown.

Santiago and Easter Island.

Not to mention all the cities in the United States they've sent
me to.

These trips are nothing like the ones Alex and I used to take,
but I may have downplayed that when I pitched combining our
summer trip with a work trip, because I want to see his reaction
when we show up to our first resort with our ratty T.J. Maxx luggage only to be greeted with champagne.

Four days in Sweden. Four in Norway.

Not cold, exactly, but *cool* at least, and since I reached out to Lita
the River Raft Guide's expatriate sister-in-law, she's been emailing
me weekly with suggestions for things to do in Oslo. Unlike Lita,

Dani has a steel-trap memory: she seems to recall every amazing restaurant she's eaten at and knows precisely what to tell us to order. In one email, she ranks various fjords by a slew of criteria (beauty, crowdedness, size, convenience of location, beauty of the drive *to* the convenient/inconvenient location).

When Lita passed along her contact information, I was expecting to get a list with a specific national park and a couple of bars, maybe. And Dani *did* do that—in her first email. But the messages kept coming whenever she thought of something else we "absolutely could not leave without experiencing!"

She uses a lot of exclamation points, and while usually I think people fall back on this in an attempt to seem friendly and definitely-not-at-all-angry, each one of her sentences reads as a command.

"You must drink aquavit!"

"Be sure to drink it at room temperature, perhaps alongside a beer!"

"Have your room-temperature aquavit on the way to the Viking Ship Museum! DO NOT MISS THIS!"

Each new email burns its exclamation points into my mind, and I *would* be afraid to meet Dani, if not for the fact that she signs every email with *xoxo*, which I find so endearing that I'm confident we'll like her a lot. Or I'll like her a lot and Alex will be terrified.

Either way, I've never been more excited for a trip in my life.

In Sweden, there's a hotel made entirely of ice, called (for some mysterious reason) Icehotel. It's the kind of place Alex and I could never have afforded on our own, and all morning leading up to the pitch meeting with Swapna, I was sweating profusely at my desk—not normal sweat, but the horrible reeking kind that comes with anxiety. It's not like Alex wouldn't have gone along with another hot beachside vacation, but ever since I found out about Icehotel, I knew it would be the absolute perfect surprise for him.

I pitch the article as a "Cool Down for Summer" feature, and Swapna's eyes light up approvingly.

"Inspired," she says, and I see a few of the other, more established writers mouthing the word to one another. I haven't been there long enough to notice her using that word, but I know how she is about *trends*, so I figure *inspired* is diametrically opposed to *trendy* in her mind.

She is fully on board. Just like that, I am cleared to spend way too much money. I can't technically buy Alex meals or plane tickets or even admission to the Viking museum, but when you're traveling with *R+R*, doors open for you, bottles of champagne you didn't order float out to your table, chefs drop by with something "a little extra," and life gets a bit shinier.

There's also the matter of the photographer who will be traveling with us, but so far everyone I've worked with has been pleasant, if not fun, and every bit as independent as I am. We meet up, we plan shots, we part ways, and though I haven't worked with the new photographer I'm paired with—we've been caught on opposite schedules of in-office days—Garrett, the other new staff writer, says Photographer Trey's great, so I'm not worried.

Alex and I text incessantly in the weeks leading up to the trip, but never about the trip itself. I tell him I'm taking care of everything, that it's all a surprise, and even if the lack of control is killing him, he doesn't complain.

Instead he texts about his little black cat, Flannery O'Connor. Shots of her in shoes and cupboards and sprawled on the top of bookshelves.

She reminds me of you, he says sometimes.

Because of the claws? I ask. Or because of the teeth or because of the fleas, and every time, no matter what comparison I try to draw, he just writes back tiny fighter.

It makes me feel fluttery and warm. It makes me think about him pulling the hood of my sweatshirt tight around my face and grinning at me through the chilly dark, murmuring under his breath: *cutie*.

In the last week before we leave, I get either a horrible cold or the worst bout of summer allergies I can remember. My nose is constantly stuffed up and/or dripping; my throat feels scratchy and tastes sour; my whole head feels clogged with pressure; and every morning, I'm wiped out before the day even begins. But I have no fever, and a quick trip to urgent care informs me that I don't have strep throat, so I do my best not to slow down. There is a lot to get done before the trip, and I do it all while coughing profusely.

Three days before we leave, I have a dream that Alex tells me he got back together with Sarah, that he can't take the trip anymore.

I wake up feeling sick to my stomach. All day I try to get the dream out of my head. At two thirty, he sends me a picture of Flannery.

Do you ever miss Sarah? I write back.

Sometimes, he says. But not too much.

Please don't cancel our trip, I say, because this dream is really, really messing with me.

Why would I cancel our trip? he asks.

I don't know, I say. I just keep getting nervous that you're going to.

The Summer Trip is the highlight of my year, he says.

Mine too, I tell him.

Even now that you get to travel all the time? You're not sick of it?

I could never get sick of it, I say. Don't cancel.

He sends me another picture of Flannery O'Connor sitting in his already packed suitcase.

Tiny fighter, I write.

I love her, he says, and I know he's talking about the cat, obviously, but even that makes that fluttery, warm feeling come alive under my skin.

I can't wait to see you, I say, feeling suddenly like saying this very normal thing is bold, risky even.

I know, he writes back, it's all I can think about.

It takes me hours to fall asleep that night. I just lie in bed with those words running through my mind on repeat, making me feel like I have a fever.

When I wake up, I realize that I actually did. That I still do. That my throat feels more swollen and raw than before, and my head is pounding, and my chest is heavy, and my legs ache, and I can't get warm no matter how many blankets I'm under.

I call in sick hoping to sleep it off before my flight the next afternoon, but by late that night, I know there's no way I'm getting on that airplane. I have a fever of one hundred and two.

Most of the things we have booked are now close enough that they're nonrefundable. Wrapped in blankets and shivering in my bed, I draft an email on my phone to Swapna, explaining the situation.

I'm unsure what to do. Unsure if this will somehow get me fired.

If I didn't feel so horrible, I'd probably be crying.

Go back to the doctor first thing in the morning, Alex tells me.

Maybe it's just peaking, I write. Maybe you can fly out on time and I can meet you in a couple days.

You shouldn't be feeling worse this late into a cold, he says. Please go to the doctor, Poppy.

I will, I write. I'm so sorry.

Then I do cry. Because if I don't make it on this trip, there's a good chance I won't see Alex for a year. He's so busy with his MFA and teaching, and I'm rarely home now that I'm working for *R+R*, and in Linfield even less. This Christmas, Mom was excited to tell me, she convinced Dad to come to the city. My brothers even agreed to come for a day or two, something they insisted they would never do once they moved to California (Parker to pursue writing for TV in L.A. and Prince to work for a video game developer in San Francisco), as if upon signing their leases they'd also committed to a die-hard rivalry between the two states.

Whenever I'm sick, I just wish I were in Linfield. Lying in my childhood bedroom, its walls papered in vintage travel posters, the pale pink quilt Mom made while she was pregnant with me pulled up tight around my chin. I wish she were bringing me soup and a thermometer, and checking that I was drinking water, keeping up on ibuprofen to lower my fever.

For once, I hate my minimalist apartment. I hate the city sounds bouncing off my windows at all hours. I hate the soft gray linen bedding I picked out and the streamlined imitation Danish furniture I've started to accumulate since landing my Big-Girl Job, as Dad calls it.

I want to be surrounded in knickknacks. I want floral-patterned lampshades and mismatched throw pillows on a plaid couch, its back draped in a scratchy afghan blanket. I want to shuffle up to an old off-white fridge covered in hideous magnets from Gatlinburg and Kings Island and the Beach Waterpark, with drawings I made as a kid and flash-blanched family photos, and to see a cat in a diaper stalk past only to bump into a wall it did not see.

I want not to be alone, and for every breath not to take an immense effort.

At five in the morning, Swapna replies to my email.

This sort of thing happens. Don't beat yourself up about it. You're right about the refunds, though—if you'd like to let your friend use the accommodations you've booked, feel free. Forward me what you had in the way of itinerary again, and we'll go ahead and send Trey to shoot. You can follow when you're well again.

And, Poppy, when this happens again (which it will), do not go in so hard on the apology. You are not the master of your immune system and I can assure you that when your male colleagues have to cancel a trip, they show no indication that they feel they have personally wronged me. Don't encourage people to blame you for something beyond your control. You are a fantastic writer, and we are lucky to have you.

Now get yourself to a doctor and enjoy some true R&R. We'll speak about next steps when you're on the mend.

I'd probably be more relieved if not for the haze superimposed over my entire apartment and the extreme discomfort of simply existing.

I screenshot the email and text it to Alex. **Go have fun!!!** I write. **I'll try to meet you for the second half!**

By then, the very thought of getting out of bed makes me feel dizzy. I set my phone aside and close my eyes, letting sleep rush up to swallow me like a well reaching up, up, up around me as I drop through it.

It's not a peaceful sleep, but a cold, glitching kind, where dreams and sentences start over, again and again, interrupting themselves before they can get off the ground. I toss in bed, waking long enough to register how cold I am, how uncomfortable both the bed and my body have become, only to tumble back into restless dreams.

I dream about a giant black cat with hungry eyes. It chases me in circles until it's too hard to breathe, too hard to keep going, and then it pounces, jolting me awake for a few fitful seconds, only to start again the moment I shut my eyes.

I should go to the doctor, I think on occasion, but I'm sure I'm unable to sit up.

I don't eat. I don't drink. I don't even get up to pee.

The day spins past until I open my eyes to the yellowy-gold light of sunset glaring off my bedroom window, and when I blink, it's changed to a deep periwinkle, and there's a pounding in my head so real it makes a thumping sound that sends shock waves through my body.

I roll over, pull a pillow over my face, but that doesn't stop it.

It's getting louder. It starts to sound like my name, the way that sounds sometimes transform into music when you're so tired you're half dreaming.

Poppy! Poppy! Poppy, are you home?

My phone clatters on the bedside table, vibrating. I ignore it, let it ring out. It starts again, and after that, a third time, so I roll over and try to read the screen despite the way the world seems to be melting, like a swirl of duo-toned ice creams twirling around each other.

There are dozens of messages from **ALEXANDER THE GREATEST**, but the last one reads, I'm here! Let me in!

The words have no meaning. I'm too confused to build a context for them, too cold to care. He's calling me again, but I'm not sure I can speak. My throat feels too tight.

The pounding starts again, the voice calling my name, and the fog lifts just enough for all the pieces to snap together into perfect clarity.

"Alex," I mumble.

"Poppy! Are you in there?" he's shouting on the other side of the door.

I'm dreaming again, which is the only reason I think I can make it to the door. I'm dreaming again, which means that probably, when I do get to the door and pull it open, that huge black cat will be there waiting, Sarah Torval riding it like a horse.

But maybe not. Maybe it will just be Alex, and I can pull him inside and—

"Poppy, please let me know you're okay!" he says on the other side of the door, and I slide off the bed, taking the linen-covered duvet with me. I sweep it around my shoulders and drag myself to the door on legs that feel weak and watery.

I fumble over the lock, finally get it switched, and the door swings open as if by magic, because that's how dreams work.

Only when I see him standing on the other side of the door, hand still resting on its knob, beat-up suitcase behind him, I'm not so sure it's a dream anymore.

"Oh, god, Poppy," he says, stepping in and examining me, the cool back of his hand pressing to my clammy forehead. "You're burning up."

"You're in Norway," I manage in a raspy whisper.

"I'm definitely not." He drags his bag inside and closes the door. "When was the last time you took ibuprofen?"

I shake my head.

"Nothing?" he says. "Shit, Poppy, you were supposed to go to the doctor."

"I didn't know how to." It sounds so pathetic. I'm twenty-six years old with a full-time job and health insurance, and an apartment and student loan bills, and I live alone in New York City, but there are just some things you don't want to have to do on your own.

"It's okay," Alex says, pulling me gently into him. "Let's get you back in bed and see if we can get rid of the fever."

"I have to pee," I say tearfully, then admit, "I may have already peed myself."

"Okay," he says. "Go pee. I'll find you some clean clothes."

"Should I shower?" I ask, because apparently I'm helpless. I need someone to tell me exactly what to do like my mom used to do when I stayed home from middle school watching Cartoon Network all day long, doing nothing for myself until she told me to.

"I'm not sure," he says. "I'll Google it. For now just pee."

It takes way too much effort to get into the bathroom. I drop the blankets just outside it and pee with the door open, shivering the whole time but comforted by the sound of Alex moving around in my apartment. Quietly opening drawers. Clicking on the gas stove top, moving the teakettle onto it.

He comes to check on me when he's finished with whatever he's doing, and I'm still sitting on the toilet with my sleep shorts around my ankles.

"I think you're okay to shower if you want to," he says, and starts the water up. "Maybe don't wash your hair. I don't know if that's a real thing, but Grandma Betty swears that wet hair makes you sick. Are you sure you won't fall down or anything?"

"If it's fast I'll be okay," I say, suddenly aware of how sticky I feel. I am almost positive I wet myself. Later this will probably be humiliating, but right now I don't think *anything* could embarrass me. I'm just so relieved to have him here.

He looks uncertain for a second. "Just go ahead and get in. I'll stay close by, and if you feel like it's getting to be too much, just tell me, okay?" He turns away from me while I force myself onto my feet and strip out of my pajamas. I climb into the hot water and pull the curtain closed, shuddering as the water hits me.

"You okay?" he asks immediately.

"Mm-hm."

"I'm going to stay here, okay?" he says. "If you need anything, just tell me."

"Mm-hm."

After only a couple minutes, I've had enough. I turn off the water and Alex passes me a towel. I'm colder than ever now that I'm all wet, and I step out with teeth chattering.

"Here." He wraps another towel around my shoulders like a cape, tries to rub heat into them. "Come sit in the room while I change your bedding, okay?"

I nod, and he leads me to the antique rattan peacock chair in the corner of my bedroom. "Spare bedding?" he asks.

I point to the closet. "Top shelf."

He gets it out, and hands me a folded pair of sweatpants and a T-shirt. Since I don't have a habit of folding my clothes, he must've instinctively folded them when he got them out of the dresser. When I take them from him, he turns pointedly away from me to work on making the bed and I drop the towels onto the floor and dress.

When he's finished making the bed, Alex pulls back a corner of the bedding and I slide in, letting him tuck me in. In the kitchen, the kettle starts whistling. He turns to go for it, but I grab on to his arm, half-drunk on the feeling of being warm and clean. "I don't want you to go."

"I'll be right back, Poppy," he says. "I need to get you some medicine."

I nod, release him. When he comes back, he's carrying a glass of water and his laptop bag. He sits on the edge of the bed and pulls out pill bottles and boxes of Mucinex, lining them up on the side table. "I wasn't sure what your symptoms were," he says.

I touch my chest, trying to explain how tight and awful it feels. "Got it," he says, and he chooses a box, peels two pills out, and hands them to me with the glass of water.

"Have you eaten?" he asks when I've taken them.

"I don't think so."

He gives a faint smile. "I grabbed some stuff on the way here so I wouldn't have to go back out. Does soup sound okay?"

"Why are you so nice?" I whisper.

He studies me for a moment, then bends and presses a kiss to my forehead. "Think the tea will be ready by now."

Alex brings me chicken noodle soup and water and tea. He sets timers for when I'm able to take more medicine, checks my temperature every couple hours throughout the night.

When I sleep, it's dreamless, and every time I stir awake, he's there, half snoozing on the bed beside me. He yawns himself awake, looks over at me. "How you doing?"

"Better," I answer, and I'm not sure if it's true in a physical sense, but at least mentally, emotionally, I do feel better having him here, and I can only manage a word or two at a time, so there's no use explaining that.

In the morning, he helps me down the stairs to a cab and we go to the doctor.

Pneumonia. I have pneumonia. Not the kind, though, that's so bad I need to be in the hospital.

"As long as you keep an eye on her and she sticks to the antibiotics, she should be fine," the doctor tells Alex, more than me, I guess because I don't really look like the kind of person who can make sense of words right now.

When Alex gets me home afterward, he tells me he has to go back out, and I want so badly to beg him to stay, but I'm just too tired. Besides, I'm sure he needs a break from my apartment and me after a whole night of playing nurse.

He comes back half an hour later with Jell-O and ice cream and eggs and more soup, and all kinds of vitamins and spices I've never even considered keeping in my apartment before now.

"Betty swears by zinc," he tells me when he brings me a handful of vitamins with a cup of red Jell-O and another glass of water. "She also told me to put cinnamon in your soup, so if it tasted bad, blame her."

"How are you here?" I struggle to get out.

"The first leg of my flight to Norway was through New York," he says.

"So, what," I say. "You panicked and left the airport instead of boarding the next plane?"

"No, Poppy," he says. "I came here to be with you."

Immediately, tears spring into my eyes. "I was going to take you to a hotel made of ice."

A quick smile flits across his mouth. "I honestly don't know if that's the fever talking."

"No." I scrunch my eyes shut, feeling the tears cutting trails down my cheeks. "It's real. I'm so sorry."

"Hey." He brushes the hair out of my face. "You know I don't care about that, right? I only care about getting to spend time with you." His thumb lightly traces the wet streak making its way down the side of my nose, heading it off just before it reaches my top lip. "I'm sorry you don't feel well, and that you're missing the ice hotel, but I'm okay right here."

Every ounce of dignity obliterated by having had this man change my pee-drenched bedding, I reach up for his neck and pull him toward me, and he shifts onto the bed beside me, maneuvering close at the beckoning of my hands. He wraps an arm around my back and draws me into his chest and I slip an arm around his waist too, and we lie there tangled together.

"I can feel your heartbeat," I tell him.

"I can feel yours," he says.

"I'm sorry I peed the bed."

He laughs, squeezes me to him, and right then, my chest aches with how much I love him. I guess I must say something like this aloud, because he murmurs, "That's probably the fever talking."

I shake my head, nestle closer, until there are no spaces left between us. His hand moves lightly up into my hair, and a shiver runs down my spine from where his fingers trail along my neck. It feels so good, in a sea of bad feelings, that it makes me arch a little, my hand tightening on his back, and I feel the way his heartbeat speeds, which only makes mine skyrocket to match it. His hand moves to my thigh, wrapping it around his hip, and my fingers twist against him as I bury my mouth against the side of his neck where I feel his pulse thudding urgently beneath it.

"Are you comfortable?" he asks thickly, like our lying like this could just be a matter of alignment, like we're building up a narrative that protects us from the truth of what's happening. That even through the fog of being sick, I can feel him wanting me like I want him.

"Mm-hm," I murmur. "Are you?"

His hand tightens on my thigh, and he nods.

"Yeah," he says, and we both go very still.

I don't know how long we lie there, but eventually, the cold medicine wins out over the sparking, alert nerve endings in my body and I fall asleep, only to find him safely on the other side of the bed the next time I wake up.

"You were asking for your mom," he tells me.

"Whenever I'm sick, I miss her," I say.

He nods, tucks a strand of hair behind my ear. "Sometimes I do too."

"Tell me about her?" I ask.

He shifts, lifting himself higher against the headboard. "What do you want to know?"

"Anything," I whisper. "What you think about when you think about her."

"Well, I was only six when she died," he says, smoothing my hair again. I don't argue or press for more, but eventually, he goes on. "She used to sing to us when she tucked us in at night. And I thought she had a beautiful voice. I mean, like, I would tell kids in my class that she was a singer. Or she would've been if she wasn't a stay-at-home mom or whatever. And you know . . ." His hand stills in my hair. "My dad couldn't talk about her. Like, at all. I mean, he still can't really without breaking down. So growing up my brothers and I didn't talk about her either. And when I was probably fourteen, fifteen, I went over to Grandma Betty's house to clean her gutters and mow her lawn and stuff, and she was watching these old home movies of my mom."

I study his face, the way his full lips curl and his eyes catch the streaks of streetlight coming through my window so that he almost looks lit from within. "We never did that at my house," he says. "I couldn't even remember what she sounded like. But we watched this video of her holding me as a baby. Singing this old Amy Grant song." His eyes cut to me, his smile deepening in one corner. "And her voice was horrible."

"How horrible are we talking here?" I ask.

"Bad enough that Betty had to turn it off so she didn't have a heart attack from laughing," he says. "And you could tell Mom knew she was bad. I mean, you could hear Betty laughing while she filmed, and my mom kept looking over her shoulder with this grin, but she didn't stop singing. I guess I think about that a lot."

"She sounds like my kind of lady," I say.

"For most of my life," he says, "she's kind of felt like this boogeyman, you know? Like the biggest part she's played in my life is just how wrecked my dad was from losing her. How scared he was to have to raise us on his own?"

I nod; makes sense.

"A lot of times, when I think about her, it's like . . ." He pauses. "She's more a cautionary tale than a person. But when I think about that video, I think about why my dad loved her so much. And that feels better. To think about her as a person."

For a while, we're quiet. I reach over and fold Alex's hand in mine. "She must've been pretty amazing," I say, "to make a person like you."

He squeezes my hand but doesn't say another word, and eventually I drift back to sleep.

The next two days are a blur, and then I'm on the rise. Not healthy but more awake, lighter, clearer headed.

There's no more intense cuddling, just a lot of watching old cartoons together on the bed, sitting out on the fire escape in the morning while we eat breakfast, taking pills whenever the alarms go off on Alex's phone, drinking tea on the sofa at night with a playlist of "traditional Norwegian folk music" playing in the background.

Four days pass. Then five. And then I'm doing well enough that I could theoretically leave the country, but it's too late, and there's no more talk of it. There's no more touching either, except the occasional bump of the arm or leg, or the compulsive reach across the table to stop me from spilling on my chin. At night, though, when Alex is lying on the far side of my bed, I stay awake for hours listening to his uneven breath, feeling like we're two magnets trying desperately to draw together.

I know deep down that it's not a good idea. The fever lowered my defenses, and his too, but when it comes down to it, Alex and I are not for each other. There might be love and attraction and history, but that just means there's more to lose if we try to take this friendship into a place it doesn't belong.

Alex wants marriage and kids and a home in one place, and he wants it all with someone like Sarah. Someone who can help him build the life that he lost when he was six years old.

And I want a tetherless life of spontaneous trips and exciting new relationships, different seasons with different people, and quite possibly to never settle down. Our only hope of maintaining this relationship is through the platonic friendship we've always had. That five percent has been creeping up for years, but it's time to tamp it back down. To squash the what-if.

At the end of the week, when I drop him off at the airport, I give him the most chaste hug I can muster, despite the way that his lifting me against him sends that same spine-arching shiver down my back and heat pooling in all the places he's never touched me.

"I'll miss you," he says in a low growl against the side of my ear, and I force myself to step back a sensible distance.

"You too."

I think about him all night, and when I dream, he's pulling my thigh over his leg, rolling his hips against mine. Every time he's about to kiss me, I wake up.

We don't talk for four days, and when he finally texts me it's just a picture of his tiny black cat sitting on an open copy of *Wise Blood* by Flannery O'Connor.

Fate, he writes.

26

This Summer

S TANDING ON THE balcony, our rain-drenched bodies flush, his gaze soft, I feel my last vestige of self-control washing off me, rinsed clear along with the desert heat and grime of the day. There's nothing left but Alex and me.

His lips press closed then part, and mine mirror them, his breath warm against my mouth. Every shallow inhale I take draws us a little closer until my tongue just barely grazes his rain-dampened bottom lip, and then he adjusts to catch my mouth just a little more with his.

A fraction of a kiss. And then another one, a bit fuller. A twist of my hands in his hair, the hiss of breath between his teeth, and then another brush of his lips, deeper, slower, careful and intent, and I'm melting against him. Shivering and terrified and exhilarated and every shade between as our mouths sink together and pull apart, his tongue sliding over mine for a second, then a little deeper, my teeth catching on the fullest part of his bottom lip, his hands moving down over my hips, my chest arching up into his as my hands glide down his wet neck.

We come together and apart, the little gaps and short breathless inhalations nearly as intoxicating as each taste, test, scrape of his rain-slicked mouth moving over mine. He draws back, leaves his mouth just hovering over mine, where I can still feel his breath. "Is this okay?" he asks me in a hush.

If I could speak, I'd tell him this is the best kiss I've had in my entire life. That I didn't know just kissing could feel this good. That I could *just* make out with him for hours and it would be better than the best sex I've ever had.

But I can't think clearly enough to say any of this. My mind is too busy with the grip of his hands on my ass and the feel of his chest flattening mine out, his wet skin and the thin, drenched clothes between us, so I just nod and catch his bottom lip between my teeth again, and he turns me against the stucco wall, presses me back into it as he kisses me more urgently.

One of his hands twists into the hem of my T-shirt where it hangs against my thigh, and the other grazes up my stomach beneath it. "What about this?" he asks.

"Yes," I breathe.

His hand lifts higher, slips under my bathing suit top, making me shiver. "This?" he says.

My breath catches, heart stumbles over a beat as his fingers lightly circle. I nod, pull his hips back to mine. He's hard between my legs, and instantly I feel a little light-headed. "I think about you all the time," he says, and kisses me slowly, drags his mouth down my neck, goose bumps fluttering out in his wake. "I think about this."

"I do too," I admit in a whisper. His mouth moves over my chest, kissing me through my wet T-shirt even as his hands work the fabric up over my hips, my ribs, and then my shoulders. He pulls away long enough to peel it over my head and discard it among the plastic sheeting.

"Yours too," I say, heart leaping. I reach for the hem of his shirt, pull it over his head. When I toss it aside, he tries to move toward me, but I hold him back for a second.

"Do you want to stop?" he asks, his eyes dark.

I shake my head. "I just . . . never get to look at you like this."

The corner of his mouth twitches into a smile. "You could have always looked," he says in a low voice. "Just so you know."

"Well, you could've too," I say.

"Trust me," he says. "I did."

And then I'm dragging him in against me, and he's roughly lifting my thigh against his hip, and I'm sinking my fingers into his wide back, my teeth into his neck, and his hands are massaging my chest, my ass. His mouth moves down my collarbones, sliding under my bikini, teeth careful on my nipple, and I'm feeling him through his shorts, then reaching into them, loving how he tenses and shifts. I push his shorts down over his hip bones, my mouth going dry at the feeling of him against me.

"Shit," I say, a realization hitting me like a bucket of ice water, "I went off birth control."

"If it helps," he says, "I had a vasectomy."

I draw back, shocked out of the moment. "You *what*?"

"They're reversible," he says, blushing for the first time since we started this. "And I took . . . precautions, in case I want kids and the reversal doesn't work. They usually do, but . . . anyway, I just . . . didn't want to accidentally get someone pregnant. I'm still always safe—it's not like . . . Why are you looking at me like that?"

I knew Alex was a black-and-white thinker. I knew he was ultra-cautious, and I knew he was the most thoughtful, courteous person on the planet. But somehow I'm still surprised all of that added up to *this* big decision. It makes my heart feel like a sore muscle, all heat and achy tenderness, because it is just so *him*. I tighten my arms around his waist, squeeze him to me. "It's just that of course you did that," I say. "Above and beyond caution and consideration. You're a prince, Alex Nilsen."

"Uh-huh," he says, his expression both amused and unconvinced.

"I'm serious," I say, pressing closer. "You're incredible."

"We can find a condom if you want," he says. "But I'm not—there's no one else."

I'm sure I'm blushing now and probably smiling ridiculously. "That's okay," I say. "It's just us."

What I mean to say is, if there's anyone I would do this with, it would be him. If there's one person I truly trust, want all of in this way, it's him.

But that's how I say it: *It's just us.* And he says it back to me, like he knows exactly what I mean, and then we're on the ground, in a sea of discarded plastic, and he's tearing my top off, pulling my bottoms off too, pressing his mouth between my legs, clutching my ass in his hands, making me gasp and rise against him as his tongue moves over me. "Alex," I plead, knotting my hands into his hair, "stop making me wait for you."

"Stop being impatient," he teases. "I've waited twelve years. I want this to last."

A shiver races down my spine, and I arch into him. Finally, he crawls up the length of me, hands tangling in my hair, roaming over my skin, and he slowly pushes into me. We find our rhythm together, and it all feels so good, so electric, so right that I can't believe all the time we wasted not doing this. Twelve years of subpar lovemaking when all along, this was how it was supposed to be.

"God, how are you so good at this," I say, and his laugh grates against my ear as he kisses behind it.

"Because I know you," he says tenderly, "and I remember what you sound like when you like something."

Everything in me pulls taut in waves. Every move of his hands, every thrust threatens to unravel me.

"I could have sex with you until I die," I pant.

"Good," he says, and he moves a little faster, harder, the intense pleasure of it making me buck and swear and move to match him.

"I love you," I hiss, by accident. I think I meant to say *I love having sex with you* or *I love your amazing body*, or maybe I did mean to say *I love you*, the same way I always say it to him when he does something thoughtful, but this is a little bit different because we're having sex, and my face goes hot and I'm not sure how to fix it, but then Alex just sits up and draws me into his lap, holding me close as he pushes into me again slow, deep, hard, and says, "I love you too."

And all at once, my chest loosens, my stomach unwinds, and any embarrassment and fear evaporates. There's nothing left but Alex.

Alex's rough hands moving gently through my hair.

Alex's wide back rippling under my fingers.

Alex's sharp hips working slowly, purposefully against mine.

Alex's sweat and skin and raindrops on my tongue.

His perfect arms holding on to me, keeping me there, against him, as we rock and clutch.

His sensual lips tugging at my mouth, coaxing it open to taste me as we draw together and apart, finding new ways to touch and kiss each other every time we reunite.

He kisses my jaw, my throat, my shoulder, his tongue hot and careful against my skin. I touch and taste every hard line and soft curve of him I can get to and he shivers under my hands, my mouth.

He lies back and draws me on top of him, and this is the best yet, because I can see so much of him, get to every place I want.

"Alex Nilsen," I say breathlessly. "You are the hottest man alive."

He laughs, just as breathlessly, and kisses the side of my neck. "And you love me."

My stomach flutters. "I love you," I murmur, this time on purpose.

"I love you so much, Poppy," he says, and somehow, just the sound of his voice tips me over the edge and I'm coming undone. We are, together.

And I don't know what we've done, what chain reaction we might have just triggered, how this will all pan out, but right then I can't think about anything else but the crush of love looping between us.

27

This Summer

FTERWARD, WE LIE on the plastic-strewn balcony, curled together and soaked to the bone, though already the storm is breaking up, the heat pushing in to burn the moisture off our skin.

"A long time ago you told me that outdoor sex wasn't all it was cracked up to be," I say, and Alex gives a hoarse laugh, his hand smoothing my hair.

"I hadn't had outdoor sex with you," he says.

"That was amazing," I say. "I mean, for me. It's never been like that for me before."

He props himself up and looks down at me. "It's never been like that for me either."

I turn my face into his skin and kiss his rib cage. "Just making sure."

After a few seconds, he says, "I want to do it again."

"Me too," I say. "I think we should."

"Just making sure," he parrots. I draw lazy patterns over his chest, and the arm he has slung low across my back squeezes tight. "We really can't stay here tonight."

I sigh. "I know. I just don't want to move. Ever again."

He flips my hair behind my shoulder, then kisses the skin left exposed there.

"Do you think that would've happened if Nikolai's AC hadn't gone out?" I ask.

Now Alex leans to kiss me right over the heart, sending chills down my stomach and up my legs that his fingers trace over. "That would've happened if Nikolai had never been born. It just might not have happened on this balcony."

I sit up and swing one knee over his waist, settling onto his lap. "I'm glad it did."

His hands run up my thighs, and heat gathers anew between my legs.

That's when we hear the pounding on the door.

"ANYONE HOME?" a man shouts. "IT'S NIKOLAI. I'M GONNA LET MYSELF—"

"Hold on a sec!" I yell, and scramble off Alex, snatching the wet T-shirt up.

"Shit," Alex says, searching for his swim trunks in the jumble of plastic sheeting.

I find the wad of black fabric and shove it toward him, then pull the hem of my shirt down over my thighs just as the door's starting to unlock. "Heyyyyy, Nikolai!" I call way too loudly, heading him off before he can see either Literally Naked Alex or the shredded plastic.

Nikolai is short and balding, dressed in an entirely maroon outfit—seventies-style golf shirt, pleated pants, loafers. He sticks one meaty hand out. "You must be Poppy."

"Yes, hi." I shake his hand and hold intense eye contact, hoping to give Alex a chance to discreetly get dressed out on the mostly dark balcony.

"Look, I'm afraid it's bad news," he says. "The AC's out."

No shit, I just barely keep myself from saying.

"Not just for this unit, but this whole wing," he says. "We've got someone coming out first thing in the morning, but I feel real bad about the delay."

Alex appears at my shoulder. At this point, Nikolai seems to clock that we're both soaking wet and rumpled, but luckily, he says nothing about it. "Anyway, I feel *real*, real bad," he repeats. "I thought you two were just being difficult, to be quite frank, but when I got here . . ." He tugs on the collar of his shirt and shudders.

"Anyway, I'm refunding you for the last three days, and . . . well, I hesitate to tell you to come back tomorrow, in case things don't get sorted out."

"That's fine!" I say. "If you refund the whole trip, we'll find someplace else to stay."

"You sure?" he says. "Things can get pretty pricey when you book last minute like that."

"We'll figure something out," I insist.

Alex bumps an arm against my back. "Poppy's an expert on traveling on the cheap."

"That so?" Nikolai couldn't sound less interested. He pulls out his phone and types with one finger. "Refund's issued. Not sure how long it'll take, so lemme know if there's a problem."

Nikolai turns to go but swivels back. "Almost forgot—found this on the welcome mat outside." He hands us a piece of paper folded in half. In looping cursive, it says on the front *THE NEWLY-WEDS* with, like, twenty-five little hearts drawn around it.

"Congrats on the nuptials," Nikolai says, and lets himself out.

"What is it?" Alex asks.

I unfold the piece of paper. It's a Groupon printed in shoddy black ink. At the top, scrawled in the margin in the same hand-writing as on the front, is a note.

> Hope y'all don't think it's creepy we figured out what apartment you were in! We thought we might've heard the sounds of passion coming from this one. ;) Also Bob said he saw you leaving this morning (we are three doors down). Anyway! We have to take off bright and early for the next stage of our vacation (Joshua Tree!!! Yay! I feel like a celebrity just writing that!) and unfortunately we never got a chance to use this. (Barely made it out of our bedroom—you two will know how it is, LOL.) Hope y'all have a great rest of your trip!
>
> Xoxo, your fairy godparents, Stacey & Bob

I blink at the voucher, stunned. "It's a one-hundred-dollar gift certificate," I say. "For a spa. I think I read about this place. It's supposed to be amazing."

"Wow," Alex says. "Feeling kind of bad that I didn't even remember their names."

"They didn't address it to us directly," I point out. "I doubt they know ours either."

"And yet they gave us this anyway," Alex says.

"I wonder if there's a way we could create a long-lasting friendship with them, get super close, take trips together, all of it, and keep them from ever finding out our names. Just for fun."

"We absolutely could," Alex says. "You just have to make it long enough that it's too awkward to ask. I had so many 'friends' like that in college."

"Oh, god, yeah, and then you have to use that trick where you ask two people if they've been introduced, and wait for them to say their names."

"Except sometimes, they just say yes," Alex points out. "Or they say no, but just keep waiting for *you* to introduce them."

"Maybe they're doing the exact same thing," I say. "Maybe those people don't even remember their names."

"Well, I doubt I'll ever forget Stacey and Bob now," Alex says.

"I doubt I'll forget much about this trip," I say. "Except the gift shop in the dinosaur. That can go, if I need to make room for more important things."

Alex smiles down at me. "Agreed."

After an awkward beat of silence, I say, "So. Should we find a hotel?"

28

This Summer

THE LARREA PALM Springs Hotel is seventy dollars a night in the summer, and even in the dark, it looks like a kid's Magic Marker drawing. In a good way.

The outside is an explosion of colors—banana-yellow pool cabanas, hot-sauce-red chaises lined up around the water, each block of the three-story building painted a different shade of pink, red, purple, yellow, green.

The room we check into is every bit as lively: orange walls and drapes and furniture, green carpet, striped bedding matched to the building's exterior. Most important, it's very cold.

"You want to shower first?" Alex asks as soon as we're inside. I realize then that the whole drive over—and before that, when we were packing our stuff up, tidying Nikolai's apartment—he's been waiting to be clean, suppressing a desire to say over and over again, *God, I need a shower*, while all I was doing was thinking about what happened on the balcony and going hot all over.

I don't want Alex to go take a shower right now. I want to get in the shower together and make out some more.

But I also remember him confiding once that he hated shower sex (worse than outdoor sex) because when he was in the shower, he just wanted to be clean, and that was hard to do with someone else's hair and dirt pouring down you, while the sex part was just as challenging because there was constantly soap in your eyes or you were brushing up against the wall and thinking about the last time the tiles were cleaned, et cetera, et cetera, et cetera.

So I just say, "Go for it!" and Alex nods but hesitates, like maybe he's going to say something, but ultimately decides not to and disappears into the bathroom for a long, hot shower.

My T-shirt and hair have both dried out, and when I go to sit out on the (non-plastic-wrapped) balcony of our new room, I realize that's already mostly dry too.

Any sign of the rain that broke the heat has burned off, like it never happened.

Except that my lips feel bruised and my body is more relaxed than I've been all week. And the air is lighter too, breezy even.

"All yours," Alex says behind me.

When I turn, he's standing there in his towel looking shiny-clean and perfect. My pulse quickens at the sight of him, but I'm aware of how filthy I am, so I swallow my want, stand up, and say, "Cool!" too loudly.

To put it lightly, I don't enjoy showering.

Being clean, yes. The act of being in the shower, also yes. But everything about having to brush out my tangled hair before-hand, stepping out onto a ratty bath mat or tile floors, getting dry, combing my hair out again—I hate all of that, which means I'm a three-shower-a-week person to Alex's one to two showers a day.

But taking this shower, after the week we've had so far, is abso-lutely luxurious.

Standing in hot, hot water within a cold, cold bathroom, watch-ing legitimate dirt and grime drip off me and swirl around the drain in shimmery gray spirals, is life giving. Massaging coconut-scented shampoo into my scalp and green-tea-scented cleanser onto my face, and running a cheapo razor up my legs, feels *divine*.

It's the longest shower I've taken in months, and when I finally emerge from the bathroom feeling like a new woman, Alex is fast asleep in one of the beds, on top of the bedding with all the lights still on.

For a second, I debate which bed to climb into. In general, I love being able to sprawl out in a queen bed on these trips, but there's a big portion of me that wants to curl up next to Alex, fall asleep with my head in the crook of his shoulder where I can smell his clean, bergamot smell, maybe conjure up a dream about him.

In the end, though, I decide it's too creepy to assume he wants to share a bed with me just because we hooked up.

The last time anything happened between us, there certainly wasn't any bed sharing afterward. There was just chaos.

I'm determined that this won't end up like that. No matter what happened or happens between us on this trip, I won't let it ruin our friendship. I won't make assumptions about what any of this means or foist any expectations onto Alex.

I pull the striped comforter up over him, flick off the lights, and climb into the empty bed across from his.

29

Three Summers Ago

H EY, ALEX TEXTS me the night before we leave for Tuscany.
Hey yourself, I write back.

Can you talk for a sec? Just want to finalize some stuff.

Immediately, I think he's calling to cancel. Which doesn't make sense.

For the first time in years we're set to have a tension-free trip. We're both in committed relationships, our friendship is better than ever, and I have never been so happy in my life.

Three weeks after my pneumonia debacle, I met Trey. A month after that, Alex and Sarah were back together—he says it's better this time, that they're on the same page. Nearly as important, this time around she seems to have finally started warming to me, and the few times that Alex and Trey have met, they've gotten along too. So once again, as always, I've come to the place of being *so, so* ecstatically happy that Alex and I never let anything happen between us.

I start to text him back, then decide to just call him from the folding chair on my balcony instead since I'm home alone. Trey's still at Good Boy Bar, up the street from my new apartment, but I came home early after a bout of nausea, a warning sign of an oncoming migraine I need to fight off before our flight.

Alex answers on the second ring, and I say, "Everything okay?"

I can hear his turn signal going. Okay, so maybe we're back to him calling me from the car, on his way home from the gym, but things really do seem better. For one thing, they sent me a joint birthday card. And Christmas card. She not only followed me back on Instagram but she likes my photos—even comments little hearts and smiley faces on some of them.

So I thought things were good, but now Alex skips right over *hello* and goes straight to, "We're not making a mistake, are we?"

"Um," I say, "what?"

"I mean, a couples' trip. That's sort of intense."

I sigh. "How so?"

"I don't know." I can hear the anxiety in his voice, imagine him grimacing, tugging at his hair. "Trey and Sarah have only met once."

In the spring, Trey and I flew to Linfield so he could meet my parents. Dad wasn't impressed by the tattoos or the holes in Trey's ears from the gauges he got when he was seventeen, or that he turns Dad's questions around on him, or that he doesn't have a degree.

But Mom was impressed by his manners, which really are topnotch. Although I think for her, it had more to do with the juxtaposition of his appearance with his easy, warm way of saying things like, "Excellent s'mores cake, Ms. Wright!" and "Can I help you with the dishes?"

By the end of the weekend, she'd decided he was a very nice young man, and when I sneaked out onto the deck to get Dad's opinion while Trey and Mom were inside dishing up homemade

Funfetti cake, Dad looked me in the eye with a solemn nod and said, "I suppose he seems right for you. And he obviously makes you happy, Pop. That's all that matters to me."

He does make me happy. So happy. And he *is* right for me. Freakily so. I mean, we work together. We get to spend pretty much every day together, either in the office or halfway around the world, but we're also both independent, like having our own apartments, our own friends. He and Rachel get along, but when Trey and I are in the city, he's mostly hanging with his skateboarding friends while Rachel and I are trying a new brunch place or reading in the park or having our whole bodies scrubbed raw in our favorite Korean spa.

Two days home in Linfield and both of us were already a little restless, but he didn't mind the mess and he *liked* the menagerie of dying animals and he joined right in when we did a New Talent Show over Skype with Parker and Prince.

Still, after how everything went down with Guillermo—and pretty much everyone else in the entire world—I was restless, eager to get out of Linfield before something scared Trey off, so we probably would've headed back early if not for the fact that it was Mr. Nilsen's sixtieth birthday, and Alex and Sarah were coming down to surprise him with a visit. We'd decided the four of us should grab dinner before the party.

"I'm so excited to meet this guy," Trey kept saying whenever a new text came in from Alex, and every time, it made my nerves inch closer to the surface. I felt fiercely protective—I just wasn't sure over whom.

"Just give him a chance," I kept saying. "He takes a while to open up."

"I know, I know," Trey insisted. "But I know how much he means to you, so I'm going to like him, P. I promise."

Dinner was okay. I mean, the food was great (Mediterranean), but the conversation could've been better. Trey, I couldn't help but think, came off a little show-offy when Alex asked him what he'd studied, but I knew his lack of formal education was something of a chip on his shoulder, and I wished there was some easy way for me to signal that to Alex as Trey launched into the story of how it all happened.

How he'd been in a metal band all through high school back in Pittsburgh. How they'd taken off when he was eighteen, gotten offered an opening slot on the tour of a *much* bigger band. Trey was an amazing drummer, but what he really loved was photography. When his band broke up after four years of near-constant touring, he took a job taking pictures on another band's tour. He loved traveling, meeting people, seeing new cities. And as those connections built up, other job offers rolled in. He went freelance, eventually started working with *R+R*, and then came on as a staff photographer.

He finished his monologue by putting an arm around my shoulders and saying, "And then I met P."

The flicker on Alex's expression was so subtle I was sure Trey didn't notice it. Maybe Sarah hadn't either, but to me, it felt like a pocketknife plunging into my belly button and dragging upward five or six inches.

"Sooo sweet," Sarah said in her saccharine voice, and probably my face made a *much* bigger twitch.

"The funny thing is," Trey said then, "we were supposed to meet sooner. I was scheduled to go on that Norway trip with you two. Before she got sick."

"Wow." Alex's eyes flicked to mine, then dipped to the glass of water in front of him. It was sweating as badly as I was. He picked it up, slowly sipped, set it down. "That *is* funny."

"Anyway," Trey said awkwardly. "What about you? What did you study?"

Trey knew exactly what Alex had gone to school for (was still going to school for), but I figured that by phrasing it as a question, he was giving Alex a chance to talk more about himself.

Instead, Alex took another sip and said only, "Creative writing, then literature."

I had to sit and watch my boyfriend struggle to find an appropriate follow-up question, give up, and go back to studying the menu.

"He's an amazing writer," I said awkwardly, and Sarah shifted in her seat.

"He is," she said, her tone so acidic you'd think I'd just said *Alex Nilsen has an incredibly sexy body!*

After dinner, we went to the party at Grandma Betty's house and things improved a bit. Alex's goofy brothers were all clamoring to meet Trey, bombarding him with all kinds of questions about the band and *R+R* and whether I snored.

"Alex would never tell us," the youngest, David, said, "but I assume Poppy sounds like a machine gun when she sleeps."

Trey laughed, took it all in stride. He's never jealous. Neither of us can afford to be: we are both relentless flirts. It sounds strange, but I love that about him. I love watching him go up to the bar to order me a drink and seeing how the bartenders smile and laugh, lean across the bar to bat their eyelashes at him. I love watching him charm his way through every city we go to, and that whenever he's next to me, he's touching me: an arm around the shoulders, a hand on my low back, or pulling me into his lap like we're home alone rather than dining at a five-star restaurant.

I've never felt so secure, so sure that I'm on the same page as someone.

At the party, he kept his hands on me at all times, and David teased us about it.

"You don't think she's going to make a run for it if you let go, do you?" he joked.

"Oh, she'll definitely make a run for it," Trey said. "This girl can't sit still for longer than five minutes. That's one thing I love about her."

The party was the first time all of Alex's brothers had been in the same place in a long time, and they were as rowdy and sweet as I remembered them being when Alex and I were nineteen, home from college and charged with driving them around in Alex's car, since none of them had their own yet and their dad was a sweet man but also a forgetful, flaky one who was incapable of keeping track of who needed to be where and when.

While Alex had always been calm and still by default, his brothers were the kind of boys who never stopped wrestling or giving one another wet willies. Even though some of them have kids now, they were still like that at the party.

Mr. and Mrs. Nilsen had named them in alphabetical order. Alex first, then Bryce, then Cameron, then David, and weirdly they're mostly sized like that too. With Alex the tallest and broadest, Bryce just as tall but lanky and narrow shouldered, Cameron a few inches shorter and thick. Then there's David, who's an inch taller than Alex with the build of a professional athlete.

They're all handsome, with varying shades of blond hair and matching hazel eyes, but David looks like a movie star (which lately, Alex said at dinner, he's been talking about moving to L.A. to *become*), with his thick, wavy hair and wide, thoughtful eyes, and his excitability, the way he lights up whenever he starts talking. He starts fifty percent of his sentences with the name of whoever he's addressing, or whoever he thinks will be most interested.

"Poppy, Alex brought a bunch of issues of *R+R* home so I could read your articles," he said at one point at Betty's house, and that was the first time I found out Alex even *read* my articles. "They're really good. They make me feel like I'm there."

"I wish you were," I told him. "Sometime we should all take a trip together."

"Hell yeah," David said, then looked over his shoulder, grinning as he checked whether his dad had heard him swear. He's a twenty-one-year-old baby, and I love him.

At some point, Betty asked for my help in the kitchen, and I followed her in to put candles in the German chocolate cake she had baked for her son-in-law. "Your young man Trey seems like a nice one," she told me without looking up from what she was doing.

"He's great," I said.

"And I like his tattoos," she added. "They're just beautiful!"

She wasn't being an asshole. Betty could be sarcastic, but she could also catch you off guard with her opinions on certain things. She was changeable. I liked that about her. Even at her age, she asked questions in conversation like she didn't already have all the answers.

"I like them too," I said.

I was attracted to Trey's energy more than his appearance during our first work trip together (Hong Kong), and I liked that he waited to ask me out until we were home because he didn't want to make anything weird for me if I said no.

I'd be lying, though, if I said Alex played no part in my saying yes.

He'd just told me that he and Sarah had been talking a lot more at work, that things seemed okay between them. At that point, I was still regularly waking up from dreams about him showing up at my door, looking sleepy and worried and too comforting, while I was in the throes of a fever.

It didn't matter that he'd said nothing about getting back together with Sarah.

He would or he wouldn't, but in the end, there would be *someone*, and I didn't think my heart could take it. So I said yes to Trey that night and we went to a bar with free Skee-Ball and hot dogs, and by the end of that night, I *knew* I could fall in love with him.

Trey was to me what Sarah Torval was to Alex. Someone who fit.

So I kept saying yes.

"Do you love him?" Betty asked me, still not looking up from the task at hand.

I had the sense that she was giving me a level of privacy. The option to lie, without her looking straight into my eyes, if that was what I needed. But I didn't need to lie. "I do."

"Good, honey. That's great." Her hands stilled, holding two thin silver candles into the frosting like they might try to jump out. "Do you love him like you love Alex?"

I remember with vivid clarity the feeling of my heart stumbling over its next several beats. That question was more complicated, but I couldn't lie to her.

"I don't think I'll ever love anyone the way I love Alex," I said, and then I thought, *But maybe I won't ever love anyone like I love Trey either.*

I should've said it, but I didn't. Betty shook her head and looked me in the eye. "Wish he knew that."

Then she walked out of the kitchen, leaving me to follow. Alex and Sarah had brought Flannery O'Connor with them, and she chose that moment to make her dramatic entrance, walking up to me with her spine arched up and eyes wide, staring into my face and meowing loudly, in a full-body expression that Alex and I call *Halloween Kitty*.

"Hi," I said, and she rubbed against my legs, so I reached to pick her up, and she hissed and swung a handful of claws toward me just as Sarah walked into the kitchen with a stack of dirty dishes. She laughed and said in that sweet voice of hers, "Wow! She does *not* like you!"

So yes, I see where Alex is coming from with his nerves about this couples trip, but we're making progress. With the Instagram likes and the perfectly pleasant time Trey, Alex, and I had at an arcade bar the last time Alex visited. And besides, being in the Tuscan countryside with an IV drip of incredible wine is *not* going to be the same as one awkward dinner in Ohio followed by a sixty-year-old teetotaler's birthday party.

"They're going to get along great," I tell him now, propping my legs up on the balcony railing and adjusting the phone between my face and shoulder.

I hear his turn signal click off, and he sighs. "How can you be sure?"

"Because we love them," I reason. "And we love each other. So they'll love each other. And we'll just all love each other. You and Trey. Me and Sarah."

He laughs. "I wish you could hear how much your voice changed for that last part. It sounded like you were inhaling helium."

"Look, I'm still working on forgiving her for dumping you the last time," I say. "It seems like she's figured out that was the biggest mistake of her life, though, so I'm giving her a chance."

"Poppy," he says. "It wasn't like that. Things were complicated, but they're better now."

"I know, I know," I say, even though, really, I don't. He insists there are no hard feelings between them about their last breakup, but whenever I think about what she said—that their relationship was about as exciting as the school library where they'd met—I still see red for a second.

Another wave of nausea hits me, and I groan. "I'm sorry," I say. "I really need to go to bed so I can be flight-ready tomorrow, but I'm telling you. This trip is going to be amazing."

"Yeah," he says stiffly. "I'm sure I'm worrying for nothing."

Mostly, it turns out that's true.

We're staying in a villa. It's hard to be in a bad mood when you're staying in a villa, with a gleaming pool and old stone patio, an outdoor kitchen with bougainvillea dripping all over everything in soft pinks and purples.

"Wow, okay," Sarah says when we walk in. "I'm never missing one of these trips again."

I flash Alex a look that's the facial equivalent of a thumbs-up, and he smiles faintly back.

"I know, right?" Trey says. "We should've thought to take a group trip sooner."

"Definitely," Sarah says, though obviously with her schedule at a high school and Alex's teaching course load at the university, it's not like they've got much time to jet-set around, even for steeply discounted Tuscan villas.

"There are, like, ten Michelin-starred restaurants within twenty miles of here—and I figured Alex would want to cook one night at least."

"That'd be amazing," Alex agrees.

Sure, it's a little stiff and awkward that first day at the villa, as the four of us meander around between jet-lagged naps in our rooms and quick dips in the pool. Trey shoots some test photos, and I go into town to grab snacks: aged cheeses and meats, fresh bread, and a variety of jams in tiny jars. And wine, plenty of wine.

By the end of the first night sitting outside on the terrace, and drinking the first two bottles of wine, everyone has softened, loosened. Sarah's become downright chatty, telling stories about her students, about Flannery O'Connor and life in Indiana, and Alex offers quiet, dry asides that make me laugh so hard wine spews out of my nose, twice.

It feels like the four of us are friends, real friends.

When Trey pulls me into his lap and rests his chin on my shoulder, Sarah touches her chest and *aww*s. "You two are so sweet," she says, looking to Alex. "Aren't they sweet?"

"And buttery," Alex says, just barely glancing my way.

"What?" Sarah says. "What's that supposed to mean?" He shrugs, and she goes on: "I wish Alex liked PDA. We barely even *hug* in public."

"I'm not a big hugger," Alex says, embarrassed. "I didn't grow up hugging."

"Yeah, but it's *me*," Sarah says. "I'm not some girl you met at a bar, babe."

Now that I think of it, I'm not sure I've seen him and Sarah touch. But it's not like he's touched me all that much in public either, unless you count dancing in the streets of New Orleans, or that time in Vail (and there was a fair amount of alcohol involved in both).

"It just feels . . . rude or something," Alex tries to explain.

"Rude?" Trey lights a cigarette. "We're all adults, man. Hold on to your girl if you want."

Sarah snorts. "Don't bother. This has been a years-long conversation. I've accepted my lot. I'm going to marry a man who hates holding hands."

My chest jolts at the word *marry*. Is it really that serious between them? I mean, obviously it's serious, but they haven't been back together that long. Trey and I talk about marriage occasionally, but in a lofty, far-off, *maybe-who-knows-let's-not-put-pressure-on-this* way.

"Now, *that* I can understand," Trey says, blowing his cigarette smoke away from us. "Hand-holding sucks. It's not comfortable, and it limits movement, and in a crowd it's inconvenient. Like, you might as well just handcuff your ankles together."

"Not to mention your hands get all sweaty," Alex says. "It's all-around uncomfortable."

"I love holding hands!" I chime in, tucking the word *marry* deep inside my brain to puzzle over later. "*Especially* in a crowd. It makes me feel safe."

"Well, it looks like if we go into Florence before this trip is over," Sarah says, "it's gonna be me and Poppy holding hands, and you two lone wolves getting utterly lost in the masses."

Sarah holds her wineglass out to me and I clink mine to hers, and we both laugh, and that might be the first moment that I like her. That I realize maybe I could've liked her all along, if I hadn't been holding so tight to Alex that there was no room for her.

I have to stop doing that. I decide I will, and from then on, the wine takes over, and all four of us are talking, joking, laughing, and this night sets the tone for the rest of the trip.

Long, sunny days wandering every old town spread out around us. Driving to vineyards and swirling glasses of wine with our mouths held ajar to inhale their deep, fruity scent. Late lunches in ancient stone buildings with world-renowned chefs. Alex leaving bright and early each morning to run, Trey dipping out not much later to scout locations or capture photos he's already planned. Sarah and I sleeping in most days, then meeting for a long swim (or to float on rafts with plastic cups full of limoncello and vodka), talking about nothing too important but with far more ease than that day at Linfield's lone Mediterranean restaurant.

At night, we go out for late dinners—and wine—then come back to our villa's patio and talk and drink until it's nearly morning.

We play every game we recognize from the closet full of them. Lawn games like bocce and badminton, and board games like Clue and Scrabble and Monopoly (which I happen to know Alex hates, though he doesn't admit that when Trey suggests we play).

We stay up later and later each night. We scribble celebrities' names onto pieces of paper, mix them up, and stick them to our foreheads for a game of twenty questions in which we guess who's on our heads, with the added obstacle of every question asked requiring another drink.

It quickly becomes obvious that none of us has the same celebrity references, which makes the game two hundred times harder, but also funnier. When I ask if my celebrity is a reality TV star, Sarah pretends to gag.

"Really?" I say. "I love reality TV."

It's not like I'm unused to this reaction. But part of me feels like her disapproval equals Alex's disapproval, and a sore spot appears along with an urge to press on it.

"I don't know how you can watch that stuff," Sarah says.

"I know," Trey says lightly. "I've never understood her interest either. It's at odds with every other thing about her, but P's all about *The Bachelor*."

"Not *all about it*," I say, defensive. I started watching a couple seasons ago with Rachel when a girl from her art program was a contestant, and within three or four episodes, I was hooked. "I just think it's, like, this incredible experiment," I explain. "And you get to watch *hours* of the footage compiled in it. You learn so much about people."

Sarah's eyebrows flick up. "Like what narcissists are willing to do for fame?"

Trey laughs. "Dead-on."

I force out a laugh, take another sip of my wine. "Not what I was talking about." I shift uncomfortably, trying to figure out how to explain myself. "I mean, there's a lot that I like. But one thing . . . I like how in the end, it seems like it's actually a hard decision for some people. There will be two or three contestants they feel a strong connection with, and it doesn't just come down to choosing the strongest one. Instead, it's like . . . you're watching them choose a life."

And that's how it is in real life too. You can love someone and still know the future you'd have with them wouldn't work for you, or for them, or maybe even for both of you.

"But do any of those relationships really work out?" Sarah asks.

"Most don't," I admit. "But that's not the point. You watch someone date all these people, and you see how different they are with each of them, and then you watch them choose. Some people choose the person they have the best chemistry with, or that they have the most fun with, and some choose the one they think will make an amazing father, or who they've felt the safest opening up to. It's fascinating. How so much of love is about who *you* are with someone."

I love who I am with Trey. I'm confident and independent, flexible and coolheaded. I'm at ease. I'm the person I always dreamed I would be.

"Fair," Sarah allows. "It's the part about making out with, like, thirty guys then getting engaged to someone you've met five times that's harder for me to swallow."

Trey tips his head back, laughing. "You'd totally sign up for that show if we broke up. Wouldn't you, P?"

"Now, *that* I would watch," Sarah says, giggling.

I know he's joking around, but it irks me, feeling like they're united against me.

I think about saying, *Why do you think that? Because I'm a narcissist who's willing to do anything to get famous?*

Alex bumps his leg into mine under the table, and when I glance at him, he's not even looking my way. He's just reminding me that he's here, that nothing can really hurt me.

I bite down on my words and let it go. "More wine?"

The next night, we eat a long, late dinner out on the terrace. When I go inside to dish up gelato for dessert, I find Alex standing in the kitchen, reading an email.

He has just gotten word that Tin House accepted one of his

stories. He looks so happy, so brilliantly himself, that I sneak a picture of him. I love it so much I would probably set it as my background if both of us were single and that wasn't extremely weird for both Sarah and Trey.

We decide we have to celebrate (as if that isn't what this whole trip has been), and Trey makes us mojitos and we sit out on the chaise lounges overlooking the valley, listening to the soft, twinkly sounds of nighttime in the countryside.

I barely sip on my drink. I've been nauseated all night, and for the first time, I excuse myself to go to sleep long before the others. Trey climbs into bed hours later, tipsy and kissing on my neck, pulling on me, and after we have sex, he falls asleep immediately, and my nausea comes back.

That's when it occurs to me.

I was supposed to start my period at some point on this trip.

Probably it's a fluke. There are a lot of reasons to wind up nauseated while traveling internationally. And Trey and I are fairly careful.

Still, I get out of bed, stomach roiling, and tiptoe downstairs, opening my notes app to see when I was expecting my period. Rachel's constantly telling me to get this period tracker app, but until now I haven't really seen the point.

My ears are pounding. My heart is racing. My tongue feels too big for my mouth.

I was supposed to start yesterday. A two-day delay isn't unheard-of. Nausea after drinking buckets of red wine isn't either. Especially for a migraineur. But still, I'm freaking out.

I grab my jacket off the coatrack, stuff my feet into sandals, and take the rental car keys. The nearest twenty-four-hour grocery store is thirty-eight minutes away. I make it back to the villa with three different pregnancy tests before the sun has even started to rise.

By then I'm in a full-blown panic. All I can do is pace back and forth on the terrace, gripping the most expensive pregnancy test in one hand and reminding myself to inhale, exhale, inhale. My lungs feel worse than they did when I had pneumonia.

"Couldn't sleep?" A quiet voice startles me. Alex is leaned against the open door in a pair of black shorts and running shoes, his pale body cast blue by the predawn.

A laugh dies in my throat. I'm not sure why. "Are you getting up to run?"

"It's cooler before the sun's up."

I nod, wrap my arms around myself, and turn back to gaze over the valley. Alex comes to stand beside me, and without looking over at him, I start to cry. He reaches out for my hand and unfurls it to see the pregnancy test clenched there.

For ten seconds, he is silent. We are both silent.

"Have you taken one yet?" he asks softly.

I shake my head and start to cry harder. He pulls me in, wraps his arms around my back as I let my breath out in a few rushes of quiet sobs. It eases some of the pressure, and I draw back from him, wiping my eyes with the heels of my hands.

"What am I going to do, Alex?" I ask him. "If I'm . . . What the hell am I supposed to do?"

He studies my face for a long time. "What do you want to do?"

I wipe at my eyes again. "I don't think Trey wants to have kids."

"That's not what I asked," Alex murmurs.

"I have no idea what I want," I admit. "I mean, I want to be with him. And maybe someday . . . I don't know. I don't know." I bury my face in my hands as a few more ugly, soundless sobs work out of me. "I'm not strong enough to do that on my own. I can't. I couldn't even handle being sick by myself, Alex. How am I supposed to . . ."

He takes my wrists gently and pulls them away from my face,

ducking his head to peer into my eyes. "Poppy," he says. "You won't be alone, okay? I'm here."

"So, what?" I say. "I'd, like, move to Indiana? Get an apartment next door to you and Sarah? How's *that* going to work, Alex?"

"I don't know," he admits. "It doesn't matter how. I'm here. Just go take the test, and then we'll figure it out, okay? You'll figure out what you want to do, and we'll do it."

I take a deep breath, nod, go inside with the bag of tests I've set down on the ground and the one I'm still gripping like a life raft.

I pee on three at once, then take them all back outside to wait. We line them up on the low stone wall surrounding the terrace. Alex sets a timer on his watch, and we stand there together, saying nothing until it beeps.

One by one the results come in.

Negative.

Negative.

Negative.

I start to cry again. I'm not sure if it's relief or something more complicated than that. Alex pulls me into his chest, rocks me soothingly side to side as I regain composure.

"I can't keep doing this to you," I say when I'm finally out of tears.

"Doing what?" he asks in a whisper.

"I don't know. *Needing* you."

He shakes his head against the side of mine. "I need you too, Poppy." It's then that I realize how thick and wet and trembling his voice is. When I pull back from him, I realize that he's crying. I touch the side of his face. "Sorry," he says, closing his eyes. "I just . . . I don't know what I'd do if something happened to you."

And then I understand.

To someone like Alex, who lost his mother how he did, pregnancy isn't just a life-changing possibility. It's a potential death sentence.

"I'm sorry," he says again. "God, I don't know why I'm crying."

I pull his face down into my shoulder, and he cries some more, his huge shoulders heaving with it. In all the years we've been friends, he has probably seen me cry hundreds of times, but this is the first time he's ever cried in front of me.

"It's okay," I whisper to him, and then, as many times as it takes, "It's okay. You're okay. We're okay, Alex."

He buries his damp face in the side of my neck, his hands curling in tight against the small of my back as I run my fingers through his hair, his damp lips warm against my skin.

I know the feeling will pass, but right then I wish so badly that we were here alone. That we had yet to even meet Sarah and Trey. That we could hold on to each other as long and tight as I think we might need to.

We've always existed in a kind of world for two, but that's not the case anymore.

"I'm sorry," he says one last time as he unwinds himself from me, straightening up, looking out over the valley as the first rays of light splash across it. "I shouldn't have . . ."

I touch his arm. "Please don't say that."

He nods, steps back, putting more distance between us, and I know, with every fiber of my being, that it's the right thing to do, but it still hurts.

"Trey seems like a great guy," he says.

"He is," I promise.

Alex nods a few more times. "Good." And that's it. He leaves for his morning run, and I'm alone again on the still terrace, watching morning chase the shadows across the valley.

My period arrives twenty-five minutes later, while I'm scrambling eggs for breakfast, and the rest of our trip is a fantastically normal couples' trip.

Except that, deep down, I am completely heartbroken.

It hurts to want it all, so many things that can't coexist within the same life.

More than anything, though, I want Alex to be happy. To have everything he's always wanted. I have to stop getting in the way, to give him the chance to have all of that.

We don't so much as brush against each other until we hug goodbye. We never speak about what happened again.

I go on loving him.

30

This Summer

So I GUESS we're not talking about what happened on Nikolai's balcony, and that needs to be fine. When I wake up in our Technicolor hotel room of the Larrea Palm Springs, Alex's bed is empty and made, and a handwritten note on the desk reads, *RUNNING—BE BACK SOON. P.S. ALREADY PICKED UP THE CAR FROM THE SHOP.*

It's not like I expected a bunch of hugs and kisses and pledges of love, but he could've spared a *Last night was great*. Or maybe a cheery exclamation point.

Also, how is he running in this heat? There's just a lot going on in that very short note and my paranoia helpfully suggests that he's running to clear his head after what happened.

In Croatia, he'd freaked out. We both had. But that had happened at the tail end of the trip, when we could retreat to our separate corners of the country afterward. This time, we've got a bachelor party, rehearsal dinner, and wedding to get through.

Still, I promised I wasn't going to let this mess us up, and I meant it.

I need to keep things light, to do my part in preventing a post-coital freak-out.

I think about texting Rachel for advice, or just to have someone to squeal with, but the truth is, I don't want to tell anyone about this. I *want* it to be something only between Alex and me, like so much of the world is when we're together. I toss my phone back onto the bed, grab a pen from my purse, and add to the bottom of Alex's note, *At pool—meet me there?*

When he shows up, he's still dressed in his running clothes and carrying a small brown bag and a paper coffee cup, and the sight of all this combined makes me feel tingly and eager.

"Cinnamon roll," he says, passing me the bag, then the cup. "Latte. And the Aspire's out in the lot with its flashy new tire."

I wave my coffee cup in a vague circle in front of him. "Angel. How much was the tire?"

"Don't remember," he says. "I'm gonna go shower."

"Before you . . . come sweat by the pool?"

"Before I come sit in that pool for the entire day."

It's not much of an exaggeration. We lounge to our hearts' content. We relax. We alternate between sun and shade. We order drinks and nachos from the poolside bar and reapply sunblock every hour, and still make it back to the room with plenty of time to get ready for David's bachelor party. He and Tham decided to do separate ones (though both are coed), and Alex jokes that David chose this plan to force a popularity contest.

"No one is more popular than your brother," I say.

"You haven't met Tham yet," he says, then walks into the bathroom and starts the water.

"Are you seriously showering again?"

"Rinsing," he says.

"Remember in elementary school how kids used to stand behind you in line for the water fountain and say 'Save some for the whales'?"

"Yes," he says.

"Well, save some for the whales, buddy!"

"You have to be nice to me," he says. "I brought you a cinnamon roll."

"Buttery and warm and perfect," I say, and he blushes as he shuts the bathroom door.

I really have no idea what's going on. For example: why didn't we just stay in the room and make out all day?

I slip into a seventies lime-green halter jumpsuit and start working on my hair at the mirror outside the bathroom, and a few minutes later, Alex emerges already dressed and almost ready to go.

"How long do you need?" he asks, looking over my shoulder to meet my eyes in the mirror, his wet hair sticking up in every direction.

I shrug. "Just long enough to spray myself with adhesive and roll in a vat of glitter."

"So ten minutes?" he guesses.

I nod, set my curling wand down. "Are you sure you want me to come?"

"Why wouldn't I?"

"Because it's your brother's bachelor party," I say.

"And?"

"And you haven't seen him in months, and maybe you don't want me tagging along."

"You're not tagging along," he says. "You're invited. Also there will probably be male strippers and I know how you love a man in uniform."

"I was invited by *David*," I say. "If *you* wanted alone time with him . . ."

"There are, like, fifty people coming tonight," he says. "I'll be lucky if I make *eye contact* with David."

"But your other brothers will be there too, right?"

"They're not coming," he says. "They're not even flying out until tomorrow."

"Okay, but what about all the hot desert broads?" I say.

"Hot desert broads," he repeats.

"You're going to be the straight-man belle of the ball."

His head tilts. "So you want me to go make out with some hot desert broads."

"Not particularly, but I figure you should know that you still have that option. I mean, just because we . . ."

His brow crinkles. "What are you doing, Poppy?"

I absently touch my hair. "I was trying for a beehive, but I think I'm going to have to settle for a bouffant."

"No, I mean . . ." He trails off. "Do you regret last night?"

"No!" I say, my face going red-hot. "Do you?"

"Not at all," he says.

I turn to face him head-on instead of through the mirror. "Are you sure? Because you've barely looked at me today."

He laughs, touches my waist. "Because looking at you makes me think about last night, and call me old-fashioned, but I didn't want to lie by the hotel pool with a raging hard-on all day."

"Really?" You'd think he just recited a love poem to me by the sound of my voice.

He presses me back onto the edge of the sink as he kisses me once, slow and heavy, his hands circling my neck to find the clasp of the jumpsuit's halter. It falls loose, and I arch back as he slides the fabric down to my waist. He cups my jaw and draws my mouth back to his, and I wrap my legs around him as our kisses deepen, his free hand moving down my bare chest.

"Do you remember when I was sick?" I whisper against his ear.

His hips grind against mine, and his voice comes out low and husky: "Of course."

"I wanted you so badly that night," I admit, untucking his shirt.

"That whole week," he says, "I kept waking up on the verge of coming. If you hadn't been sick . . ."

I lift myself against him, and his mouth sinks into the side of my neck as I work at the buttons on his shirt. "In Vail when you carried me down that mountain . . ."

"God, Poppy," he says. "I spent so much time trying not to want you." He lifts me off the sink and carries me to the bed.

"And not nearly enough time kissing me," I say, his laugh rattling against my ear as he lays us down. "How long do we have?"

He kisses the very center of my chest. "We can be late."

"How late?"

"As late as it takes."

"OH. MY. GOD," I say as we step out onto the driveway of the mid-century mansion, with its Googie-style swooped roof. "This is amazing. He has this whole place rented out?"

"Did I forget to mention that Tham is Very Fancy?"

"May have," I say. "Is it too late for *me* to marry him?"

"Well, there are two days until the wedding and he's gay," he says. "So I really don't see why not."

I laugh, and he catches my hand, slips it into his own. Somehow walking into a bachelor party holding Alex Nilsen's hand is more surreal than every surreal thing that just happened at the hotel. It makes me feel buzzy and giddy and intoxicated in the best possible way.

We follow the music up the driveway, each holding one of the bottles of wine we picked out on the way here, and step into the cool dark of the foyer.

Alex said there'd be fifty people. Making our way through the house, I'd guess there are at least a hundred, leaning on walls and sitting on the backs of fabulously gilded furniture. The back wall of the house is entirely glass and overlooks a massive pool, lit up purple and green, with a waterfall flowing into it on one side. People lounge on inflatable flamingos and swans in various states of undress: women and drag queens in full-length, sparkly gowns; men in swim trunks and thongs; people in angel wings and mermaid costumes alongside Assumed Linfield People in suits and peplum dresses.

"Wow," Alex says. "I haven't been to a party this out of control since, like, high school."

"You and I had *very* different high school experiences," I say.

Just then an Adonis of a man with a charmingly boyish grin and a mop of golden waves spots us and springs out of the egg-shaped hanging chair where he was sitting.

"Alex! Poppy!" David comes toward us with arms open and a lightly drunk sheen in his hazel eyes. He hugs Alex first, then grabs the sides of my face and plants sloppy kisses on both my cheeks. "I'm so happy you're—" His eyes fall to our clasped hands and he claps his together. "Holding hands!"

"You're welcome," I say, and he chortles, clamps a hand on each of our shoulders.

"You need some water?" Alex asks him, big-brother mode activated.

"No, Dad," he says. "You need some booze?"

"Yes!" I say, and David waves his hand to a server I *had not* noticed in the corner largely because she's spray-painted gold.

"Wow," Alex says, accepting two flutes of champagne from the faux statue's tray. "Thanks for . . . Wow."

She retreats, goes stone-still again.

"So what's Tham doing tonight?" I ask. "A bonfire of dollar bills on a solid-gold yacht?"

"I really hate to tell you this, Pop," David says, "but a golden yacht would sink. Trust me. We tried. Do you two want shots?"

"Yes," I say at the same time Alex says, "No."

As if by magic, shots are already being handed to us, vodka and Goldschläger, with its little gold shavings floating in the glasses. The three of us clink them together and down the spicy-sweet liquid in one gulp.

Alex coughs. "I hate that."

David slaps him on the back. "I'm so glad you're here, dude."

"Of course I am. Your little brothers only get married . . . three times."

"And your *favorite* one only gets married once," David says. "Fingers crossed."

"I hear you and Tham are amazing together," I say. "And that he is Very Fancy."

"The fanciest," David agrees. "He's a director. We met on set."

"On set!" I cry. "Listen to you!"

"I know," he says. "I'm an insufferable L.A. person."

"No, no, definitely not."

Someone shouts for David then from the pool, and he gives her a *one minute* signal, then faces us again. "Make yourselves at home— not *our* home, obviously," he adds to Alex, "but, like, a super-loud, super-fun, super-gay home with a dance floor out back—which I expect to see you both on shortly."

"Stop trying to make Poppy fall in love with you," Alex says.

"Yeah, you really don't need to waste your time," I say. "I'm already sold."

David grabs my head and smooches the side of it again, then does the same thing to Alex and dances over to the girl in the pool pretending to reel him in with an invisible fishing rod.

"Sometimes I worry he takes himself too seriously," Alex says flatly, and when a laugh rockets out of me, the corner of his mouth twitches in and out of a smile. We stand there grinning for a few more seconds, our locked hands swinging back and forth between us.

"I thought you didn't like holding hands," I say.

"And you said you did," he says.

"So, what? I just get whatever I want now?" I tease.

His smile flickers back into place, calm and restrained. "Yes, Poppy," he says. "You get whatever you want now. Is that a problem?"

"What if I want *you* to have what *you* want?"

He arches an eyebrow. "Are you just saying that because you know what I'm going to say, and you want to make fun of me for it?"

"No?" I say. "Why? What are you going to say?"

Our hands go still between us. "I have what I want, Poppy."

My heart flutters, and I pull my hand from his, coil it around his waist, and tip my head back to peer into his face. "I am resisting the urge to PDA all over you right now, Alex Nilsen."

He bends his neck and kisses me so long that a few people start cheering. When we pull apart, he's pink cheeked and bashful. "Damn," he says. "I feel like a horny teenager."

"Maybe if we utilize the Jäger Bomb station in the backyard," I say, "we'll go back to feeling like demure, mature thirty-year-olds."

"That sounds realistic," Alex says, tugging me toward the back patio. "I'm in."

There's a bar out back and a food truck serving fish tacos parked on the grass. Behind that, a garden stretches out like something from a Jane Austen novel, right here in the middle of the desert.

"Probably not great for conservation," Alex remarks in true grandpa form.

"Probably not," I agree. "But possibly *great* for conversation."

"True," he says. "When all else fails, you can always engage a stranger in thoughtful small talk about the dying earth."

At some point we find ourselves sitting on the edge of the pool, pants and jumpsuit legs rolled up and legs dangling in the warm water, and that's when we hear David shouting excitedly from within a crowd, "Where's my brother? He's got to be part of this."

"Sounds like you're needed."

Alex sighs. David spots him and jogs over. "I need you to do this game."

"Drinking game?" I guess.

"Not for Alex," David says. "I bet he won't have to drink one single time. It's a David Trivia game. You in?"

Alex winces. "Do you want me to be?"

David crosses his arms. "As the groom, I demand it."

"You really are never allowed to divorce Tham," Alex says, lumbering to his feet.

"For a multitude of reasons," David says, "I agree."

Alex walks over to the long, candlelit table where the game is starting up, but David lingers by me, watching him go. "He seems good," he says.

"Yeah," I agree. "I think he is."

David's gaze drops to me, and he lowers himself onto the slick side of the pool, slipping his legs into the water. "So," he says. "How did this happen?"

"This?"

He lifts his brow skeptically. *"This."*

"Um." I try to think of how to explain it. Years of undying love, occasional jealousy, missed opportunities, bad timing, other relationships, building sexual tension, a fight and the silence afterward, and the pain of living life without him. "Our Airbnb's air-conditioning broke."

David stares at me for a few seconds, then drops his face into his hands, chuckling. "Damn," he says, straightening up. "I have to say I'm relieved."

"Relieved?"

"Yeah." David shrugs. "You know. It's like . . . now that I'm getting married—now that I know I'm staying in L.A.—I guess I've just been worried about him. Back in Ohio. On his own."

"I think he likes Linfield," I say. "I don't think he's there out of necessity. Besides, I wouldn't say he's on his own. Your whole family's there. All the nieces and nephew."

"That's my point." David looks toward the trivia game at the table, watches as the three other contestants down shots of something caramel colored and Alex sips on a cup of water victoriously. "He's kind of an empty nester now." His mouth twists into a frown that's so like his brother's that I feel a quick, painful impulse to kiss it away.

When I think about what David's actually saying, the pain gets worse, harboring itself behind my rib cage like a little red knot. "You think he feels like that?"

"Like he raised us? Put all his emotional energy into making sure the three of us were okay? Driving Betty around to doctor appointments, packing our fucking school lunches and getting Dad out of bed when he had one of his episodes, and then, all of a sudden, we all went off and got married and started having kids of our own, while he's left to make sure Dad's all right?" Stony serious, David looks back at me. "No. Alex would never think like that. But I think he's been lonely. I mean . . . we all thought he was going to marry Sarah, and then . . ."

"Yeah." I lift my legs out of the pool and cross them in front of me.

"I mean, he had the ring and everything," David goes on, and my stomach drops. "He was supposed to propose, and then—she was just gone, and . . ." He trails off when he sees the look on my face.

"Don't get me wrong, Poppy." He sets his hand on mine. "I always thought it should be you two. But Sarah was great, and they loved each other, and—I just want him to be happy. I want him to stop worrying about other people and have something that's just his, you know?"

"Yeah." I can barely get the word out. I'm still sweating, but my insides have swiftly gone cold, because all I can think is, *He was going to marry her.*

She said it in Tuscany, and after a few weeks, I brushed it off as an offhand comment, but now I can't help but see everything that happened on that trip in a different light.

It was three years ago, but I still see it so vividly: Alex and me out on the terrace minutes before the sun rose, my arms crossed tight, nails bitten to the quick. Pregnancy tests lined up on the stone wall and Alex's watch chirping at us that it was time to find out what the future held.

The way he'd broken down once I finally gathered myself, hunched his head, and cried against me.

I can't keep doing this to you, I'd said. *Needing you.*

He'd told me he needed me too, but with Trey and Sarah there, the bubble that always seemed to envelop us, separate us from the world, had popped, and I'd felt so deeply ashamed for wanting so much of him, and I could tell he had too.

Trey seems like a great guy, he'd said, and that was as close to saying *We have to stop this* as we could get. Saying that would've been an admission of guilt. Even if we never kissed, never said the words outright, we were keeping whole parts of our hearts for each other only.

Alex had wanted to marry Sarah, and I know now that I'd kept him from being able to. She'd broken up with him a second time after Tuscany, and even if she never knew exactly what had transpired, I was sure it had left a mark on him, shifted things between them for the worse.

If I had been pregnant, if I'd decided to have the baby, I know beyond any doubt Alex would have been there for me, given up anything he had just to help.

Sarah, like always, would've had to deal with the reality of me or move on. I can't help but wonder if I'd forced her to that point. If our friendship had cost him the woman he wanted to marry. I feel sick, ashamed by the thought. Guilty over how I ignored my more complicated feelings for him so I could justify staying in his life.

It's one thing when your boyfriend's rowdy brothers, or his widower father, need him.

But I was just some other woman, whose needs he'd always put first to the detriment of his own wants and happiness. And this week, I'd stumbled into this selfishly, because that was my default with him. To ask for what I wanted, to let him give it to me even if it wasn't necessarily the best thing for him.

I'm no longer giddy or buzzy or anything but sick to my stomach.

David sets his hand on my shoulder and smiles at me, jarring me out of the kaleidoscope of complicated, painful feelings pinwheeling through me. "I'm glad he has you now."

"Yeah," I whisper, but a vicious little voice inside me says, *No, you* have *him.*

31

This Summer

AS I'M DIGGING through my purse for the hotel key, Alex leans into me, his hands heavy on my waist, his lips soft against the side of my neck, and it would be unwinding me if not for the buzzing in my skull, the steady throbs of alternating guilt and panic low in my stomach.

I press the keycard to the lock, then nudge the door open, and Alex releases me, stepping into the room after me. I beeline for the sink, slipping the backs off my oversized plastic earrings and setting them on the counter. Alex goes still and anxious just inside the door.

"Did I do something?" he asks.

I shake my head, grab a cotton swab and the blue bottle of eye makeup remover. I know I need to say something, but I don't want to cry, because if I cry, this becomes about me, and the whole point of it is lost. Alex will bend over backward to make me feel safe, when really what I need is for him to be honest. I swipe the cotton over my lids, loosening the black liquid eyeliner until I look like

Charlize Theron in *Mad Max: Fury Road*, gunpowder smeared across my face like war paint.

"Poppy," Alex says. "Just tell me what I did."

I spin toward him, and he doesn't even crack a smile about my makeup. That's how worried he is, and I hate myself for making him feel like that. "You didn't do anything," I say. "You're perfect."

His two expressions now are surprised and offended. "I'm not perfect."

I need to do this quick, rip it off like a Band-Aid. "Were you going to propose to Sarah?"

His lips part. But his shock quickly melts into hurt. "What are you talking about?"

"I just . . ." I close my eyes, press the back of my hand to my head as if that can stop the buzzing. I open my eyes again and his expression has barely shrunk. He's not reeling in his emotions: I'm going to get Naked Alex for this conversation. "David said you had a ring."

He jams his mouth shut and swallows hard, looks toward the sliding balcony doors, then back to me. "I'm sorry I didn't tell you."

"It's not that." I force the rising tears back down. "I just . . . I didn't realize how much you loved her."

He half laughs, but there's no humor in his tense face. "Of course I loved her. I was with her on and off for years, Poppy. You loved the guys you were with too."

"I know. I'm not accusing you of anything. Just . . ." I shake my head, trying to organize my thoughts into something shorter than an hour-long monologue. "I mean, you bought a *ring*."

"I know that," he says, "but why are you mad at me for that, Poppy? You were with Trey, fucking jet-setting around the world, sitting in his lap in all four corners of the world—was I supposed to think you weren't happy? To just wait for you?"

"I'm not mad at you, Alex!" I cry. "I'm mad at myself! For not caring that I was getting in the way. For asking so much of you and—and keeping you from what you want."

He scoffs. "What is it I want?"

"Why did she break up with you?" I bite back. "Tell me it had nothing to do with me. That Sarah didn't end things because of this—this thing between us. That since I've been out of your life, she hasn't been reconsidering everything. Just tell me that, if that's the truth, Alex. Tell me I'm not the reason you're not married with kids right now, and everything else you wanted."

He stares at me, face terse, eyes dark and cloudy.

"Tell me," I beg, and he just stares at me, the silence of the room adding to the buzz inside my skull.

Finally, he shakes his head. "Of course it's because of you."

I take a step back, like his words might burn me.

"She broke up with me before we went to Sanibel, and I felt so guilty that whole trip because all I could think was, *I hope Poppy doesn't think I'm boring too.* I didn't even remember to miss her until I got home. That's how it always is when I'm with you. No one else matters. And then you're gone again, and life goes back to normal and . . . when Sarah and I got back together, I thought things were so different, so much better, but the truth is, she didn't want to go to Tuscany and I told her I needed her to, so she agreed. Because I wasn't willing to give you up and I thought if you two were friends, it would be easier," he says, so intensely still now he rivals the faux-statue servers at the party.

"Then you thought you were pregnant and it scared me so much I got a fucking vasectomy. And it didn't even occur to me to ask Sarah what she thought. I just made the appointment, and a few days after, I was walking past this antique store and I saw this ring. An old, yellow-gold art deco thing with a pearl. I saw it and thought, *That would be a perfect engagement ring. Maybe I should buy it.* And my very next thought after that was, *What the fuck am I doing?* Not just the ring—which Sarah would've hated, by the way—but the vasectomy, all of it. I was doing it all for you, and I know that's not normal, and it definitely wasn't fair to her, so I ended things. That day."

He shakes his head. "I scared myself so much that I couldn't tell you what had happened. It was terrifying to realize how much I loved you. And then you and Trey broke up, and—God, Poppy, of course all of it was because of you. Everything is because of you. Everything."

His eyes are wet now, shimmering in the dim light over the sink, and his shoulders are rigid, and my gut feels like there's a knife twisting into it.

Alex shakes his head, a small, restrained gesture, little more than a twitch. "It's not something you've done to me," he says. "I kept hoping things would change for me, but they never have."

He takes a step toward me, and I fight to maintain my composure.

A breath slips out of me, my shoulders relaxing, and Alex takes another step toward me, his eyes heavy, mouth twisted. "And I doubted myself for a long time before I ended things, because I *did* love her," he says, "and I wanted to make it work because she's amazing, and we're good together, and we want all the same things, and I loved her in this way that feels . . . so clear and easy to understand, and manageable."

He breaks off, shaking his head again. The tears in his eyes make them look like the surface of some river, dangerous and wild and gorgeous. "I don't know how to love someone as much as I love you," he says. "It's terrifying. And I get these bursts of thinking I can handle it and then I think about what it will do to me if I lose you, and I panic and pull away, and—I've never known if I'll be able to make you happy. But the other night—it sounds so ridiculous, but we were looking at Tinder, and you said you'd swipe right on me—and that's the kind of *tiny* thing that feels so huge when it's you. I lay awake trying to figure out what you meant for *hours* that night. I'm broken, and, yeah, probably repressed, and I *know* I'm not who you've ever pictured yourself with. I know it doesn't seem like we make any sense, and we probably don't, and maybe I could never make you happy—"

"Alex." I reach out for him with both hands, pull him in against me. His arms come around me, and his head bows until he's a giant question mark, hanging over me. "It's not your job to make me happy, okay? You can't make anyone happy. I'm happy just because you exist, and that's as much of my happiness as you have control over."

His hands curve in against my spine, and I twine my fingers into his shirt.

"I don't know exactly what it all means, but I know I love you the same way you love me, and you're not the only one that scares." I scrunch my eyes shut, gathering the courage to go on.

"I feel broken too," I tell him, my voice cracking into something thin and hoarse. "I've always felt like once someone sees me deep down, that's it. There's something ugly in there, or unlovable, and you're the only person who's ever made me feel like I'm okay." His hand sweeps gently across my face, and I open my eyes, meet his head-on. "There's nothing scarier than the chance that, once you *really* have all of me, that changes. But I want all of you, so I'm trying to be brave."

"Nothing will change how I feel about you," he murmurs. "I've been trying to stop loving you since that night you went inside to make out with the pothead water taxi driver."

I laugh, and he smiles just a little. I take his jaw in my hands and kiss him softly on the mouth, and after a second, he starts to kiss me back, and it's damp from tears and urgent and powerful, sending shock waves through me.

"Can you just do me one favor?" I ask.

He knots his hands against my spine. "Hm?"

"Only hold my hand when you want to."

"Poppy," he says, "there may come a day when I no longer need to be touching you at all times, but that day is not today."

THE REHEARSAL DINNER is at a bistro that Tham invested in during its early days, a place ablaze in candlelight and dripping with bespoke crystal chandeliers. There's no wedding party, just the grooms and their officiant, thus the lack of a true rehearsal, but Tham's whole extended family lives in northern California and have shown up, along with a lot of David's friends who were at the party last night.

"Woooow," I say as we walk inside. "This is the sexiest place I've ever been."

"Nikolai's fumigation-tent balcony is deeply offended," Alex says.

"That fumigation tent will always be in my heart," I promise, and squeeze his hand, which emphasizes our size difference in a way that makes my spine tingle. "Hey, do you remember when I melted down about having slow loris hands? In Colorado? After I rolled my ankle?"

"Poppy," he says pointedly, "I remember everything."

I narrow my eyes at him. "But you said—"

He sighs. "I know what I said. But I'm telling you now, I remember it all."

"Some would say that makes you a liar."

"No," he says, "what it makes me is someone who was embarrassed to still remember exactly what you were wearing the first time I saw you, and what you ordered once at McDonald's in Tennessee, and who needed to preserve some small measure of dignity."

"Aw, Alex," I coo, teasing even as my heart flutters happily. "You forfeited your dignity when you showed up to O-Week in khakis."

"Hey!" he says, tone chiding. "Don't forget that you love me."

My cheeks flush warm without any hint of embarrassment. "I could never forget that."

I love him, and he remembers everything, because he loves me too. My insides feel like an explosion of gold confetti.

Someone calls from the far side of the restaurant then. "Is that Miss Poppy Wright?"

Mr. Nilsen strides toward us in a baggy gray suit, his blond mustache the exact size and shape as the day I met him. Alex's hand frees itself from mine. For whatever reason, he obviously does *not* want to hold my hand in front of his father, and I feel a rush of happiness that he felt comfortable doing what he needed to.

"Hi, Mr. Nilsen!" I say, and he stops abruptly a few feet in front of me, kindly smiling and definitely not planning to hug me. He's wearing a comically large rainbow pin on his lapel. It looks like, with one wrong move, it could tip him over.

"Oh, please," he says. "You're not a kid anymore. You can call me Ed."

"What the hell, you can call me Ed too," I say.

"Uh," he says.

"She's joking," Alex supplies.

"Oh," Ed Nilsen says uncertainly. Alex goes red. I go red.

Now is not the time to embarrass him. "I was so sorry to hear about Betty," I recover. "She was an amazing woman."

His shoulders slump. "She was a rock to our family," he says. "Just like her daughter." At that, he starts to tear up, pulls off his wire-frame glasses, and blows a breath out as he wipes at his eyes. "Not sure how we're going to get by without her this weekend."

And I feel sympathy for him, of course. He's lost someone he loved. Again.

But so have his sons, and standing here with him, while he tears up freely, grieves like every person deserves to, there's also something like anger building up in me.

Because next to me, Alex ironed out all his own emotion as soon as he saw his father approaching, and I know that's no coincidence.

I don't *mean* to say it aloud, but that's how it comes out, with the subtlety of a battering ram: "But you will get through it. Because your son's getting married, and he needs you."

Ed Nilsen gives me an unironic Sad Puppy Face. "Well, of course," he says, sounding mildly stunned. "If you'll excuse me, I have to . . ." He never finishes the sentence, just looks at Alex with a rather blank confusion and squeezes his son's shoulder before drifting away.

Beside me, Alex lets out an anxious breath, and I wheel toward him. "I'm sorry! I just made that weird. Sorry."

"No." He slips his hand back into mine. "Actually, I think I just developed a fetish that's specifically you delivering hard truths to my father."

"In that case," I say, "let's go have some words with him about that mustache."

I start to walk away, and Alex pulls me back to him, his hands light on my waist, voice low beside my ear. "In case I don't kiss you as pornographically as I want to for the rest of the night, please know that after this trip, I'll be investing in therapy to understand why I feel incapable of expressing happiness in front of my family."

"And thus *my* fetish of Alex Nilsen Exhibiting Self-Care was born," I say, and he sneaks a quick kiss on the side of my head.

Just then, a wash of squeals and shrieks floats through the front doors of the bistro, and Alex steps back from me. "And that will be the nieces and nephew."

32

This Summer

BRYCE'S KIDS ARE six and four years old, both girls, and Cameron's son is just over two. Tham's sister has a six-year-old daughter too, and together, the four of them run wild through the restaurant, giggles ricocheting off the chandeliers.

Alex is happy to chase after them, to fling himself onto the floor when they try to knock him over, and to hoist them, happily shrieking, into the air when he catches them.

He is the Alex I know with them, funny and open and playful, and even if I'm not sure how to interact with kids, when he pulls me into the game, I try my best.

"We're princesses," Tham's niece, Kat, tells me, taking my hand. "But we're also *warriors* so we have to kill the dragon!"

"And Uncle Alex is the dragon?" I confirm, and she nods, wide-eyed and solemn.

"But we don't *have* to kill him," she explains breathlessly. "If we can tame him, he can be our pet."

From halfway under a table where he's fending off the Nilsen brood one at a time, he shoots me an abbreviated Sad Puppy look.

"Okay," I say to Kat. "What's the plan?"

The night moves in ebbs and flows. Cocktail hour first, then dinner, a myriad of tiny gourmet pizzas all decked out in goat cheese and arugula, summer squash and balsamic drizzle, pickled red onion and grilled brussels sprouts, and all kinds of things that would make pizza purists like Rachel Krohn scoff.

We take seats at the kids' table, which Bryce's wife, Angela, thanks me tipsily for about a hundred times after the meal is over. "I love my kids, but sometimes I just want to sit down to dinner and talk about something other than Peppa Pig."

"Huh," I say, "we mostly talked about Russian literature."

She slaps my arm harder than she means to when she laughs, then grabs Bryce by the arm and pulls him over. "Honey, you have to hear what Poppy just said."

She hangs on him, and he's a little stiff—a Nilsen deep down—but he also keeps a hand on her low back. He doesn't laugh when Angela makes me repeat myself, but says in his flat, sincere, Nilsen way, "That's funny. Russian literature."

Before dessert and coffee are served, Tham's sister (hugely pregnant, with twins) stands and clinks a fork to her water glass, calling attention at the head of the arrangement of tables. "Our parents aren't much for public speaking, so I agreed to give a little toast tonight."

Already teary-eyed, she takes a deep breath. "Who would've thought my annoying little brother would turn out to be my best friend?" She talks about her and Tham's childhood in northern California, their screaming fights, the time he took her car without asking and crashed it into a telephone pole. And then the turning point, when she and her first husband divorced, and Tham asked her to move in with him. When she caught him crying while watching *Sweet Home Alabama* and, after teasing him appropriately, sunk down onto the couch to watch the rest with him, until they were both crying while laughing at themselves and decided they needed to go out in the middle of the night to get ice cream.

"When I got married again," she says, "the hardest thing was knowing I'd probably never get to live with you again. And when *you* started talking about David, I could tell how smitten you were, and I was scared I was going to lose even more of you. Then I *met* David."

She makes a face that elicits laughter, relaxed on Tham's side of the family and restrained on David's. "Right away I knew I was getting another best friend. There's no such thing as a perfect marriage, but everything you two touch becomes beautiful and this will be no different."

There's applause and hugging and kissing of cheeks, and servers have started to come out of the kitchen with dessert when suddenly Mr. (Ed) Nilsen is on his feet, swaying awkwardly, tapping a knife to his water glass so lightly he might as well be pantomiming it.

David shifts in his seat, and Alex's shoulders rise protectively as attention settles on his father.

"Yes," Ed says.

"Starting off strong," Alex whispers tightly. I squeeze his knee beneath the table and fold my hand into his.

Ed takes off his glasses, holds them at his side, and clears his throat. "David," he says, turning toward the grooms. "My sweet boy. I know we haven't always had it easy. I know *you* haven't," he adds more quietly. "But you've always been a ball of sunshine, and . . ." He blows out a breath. He swallows some rising emotion and continues. "I can't take credit for how you've turned out. I wasn't always there how I should've been. But your brothers did an amazing job raising you, and I'm proud to be your father." He looks down at the floor, gathering himself. "I'm proud to see you marrying the man of your dreams. Tham, welcome to the family."

As the applause lifts around the room, David crosses to his father. He shakes his hand, then thinks better of it and pulls Ed into a hug. It's brief and awkward, but it happens, and beside me Alex relaxes. Maybe when this wedding is over, everything will go back to how it was before, but maybe they'll change too.

After all, Mr. Nilsen is wearing a big-ass gay-pride pin. Maybe things can always get better between people who want to do a good job loving each other. Maybe that's all it takes.

That night, when we get back to the hotel, Alex takes a quick shower while I flip through channels on the TV, pausing on a rerun of *Bachelor in Paradise*. When Alex gets out of the bathroom, he climbs onto the bed and draws me into him, and I lift my arms over my head so he can take my baggy T-shirt off, his hands spanning wide across my ribs, his mouth dropping kisses down my stomach. "Tiny fighter," he whispers against my skin.

This time everything is different between us. Softer, gentler, slower. We take our time, say nothing that can't be said with our hands and mouths and limbs.

I love you, he tells me in a dozen different ways, and I say it back every time.

When we're finished, we lie together, tangled up and sheened in sweat, breathing deep and calm. If we talked, one of us would have to say *Tomorrow is the last day of this trip*. We'd have to say *What next*, and there's no answer for that yet.

So we don't talk. We just fall asleep together, and in the morning, when Alex gets back from his run with two cups of coffee and a piece of coffee cake, we just kiss some more, furiously this time, like the room's on fire and this is the best way to put it out. Then, when we have to, when we're out of time, we unwind from each other to get ready for the wedding.

The venue is a Spanish-style house with wrought-iron gates and a lush garden. Palm trees and columns and long, dark wooden tables with high-backed, hand-carved chairs. Their floral arrangements are all vibrant yellow, sunflowers and daisies and delicate sprigs of tiny wildflowers, and a white-clad string quartet plays something dreamy and romantic as guests are entering the grounds.

More high-backed chairs are lined up on a stretch of uninterrupted lawn, a burst of yellow flowers lining the aisle between them. The ceremony is short and sweet because—in David's words, as they're walking back down the aisle to an upbeat, strings version of "Here Comes the Sun"—*it's time to party!*

The day is whooshing past, and an ache takes up residence beneath my clavicles that seems to deepen with the twilight. It's like I'm experiencing the whole night twice over, two versions of the same film reel playing slightly overlapped.

There's the me who's here now, eating an incredible seven-course Vietnamese meal. The same one who's chasing kids around the legs of oblivious adults, playing hide-and-seek with them and Alex under tables. The same one who's chugging margaritas on the dance floor with Alex while "Pour Some Sugar on Me" plays at top volume and drops of sweat and champagne sprinkle over the crowd. The same one who's pulling him close when the Flamingos come on, playing "I Only Have Eyes for You," and who buries my face in his neck, trying to memorize his smell more thoroughly than the last twelve years have allowed, so I can summon it at will, and everything about this night will come rushing back: his hand tight on my waist, his mouth ajar against my temple, his hips just barely swaying as we hold on to each other.

There's that Poppy, who's experiencing it all and having the most magical night of her life. And then there's the one who's already missing it, who's watching this all happen from some point in the distance, knowing I can never go back and do it all over again.

I'm too afraid to ask Alex what comes next. I'm too afraid to ask myself that. We love each other. We want each other.

But that hasn't changed the rest of our situation.

So I just keep holding on to him and tell myself that, for now, I should enjoy this moment. I'm on vacation. Vacations always end.

It's the very fact that it's finite that makes traveling special. You could move to any one of those destinations you loved in small doses, and it wouldn't be the spellbinding, life-altering seven days you spent there as a guest, letting a place into your heart fully, letting it change you.

The song ends.

The dance ends.

Not long after that, there are sparklers being lit in a long tunnel of people who love David and Tham, and then they're running through it, their faces awash in warm light and deep love, and then, as if it's a person drifting off to sleep, the night ends.

Alex and I say our goodbyes, loose enough from a night of drinking and dancing to hug dozens of people who were perfect strangers hours ago. We drive home in silence, and when we get there, Alex doesn't shower, doesn't even undress. We just get into bed and hold on to each other until we fall asleep.

THE MORNING IS better.

For one thing, we both forgot to set alarms, and we were up late enough that even Alex's internal alarm clock doesn't wake us in time to laze around the hotel. We're running late from the moment we open our eyes, and there's nothing to do but throw clothes into bags, check under the beds for dropped socks and bras and whatever else.

"We still have to take the Aspire back!" Alex realizes aloud as he's zipping his luggage closed.

"On it!" I say. "If I can get ahold of the girl who owns it, maybe she'll let us leave it at the airport and pay her an extra fifty bucks or something."

But we don't get ahold of her, so instead we're screaming down the highway, crossing our fingers we make it to the airport in time.

"Really regretting not showering now," Alex says as he rolls his window down and rakes a hand through his dirty hair.

"Showering?" I say. "When I was falling asleep, I had the thought, *I have to pee, but I'll hold it until morning.*"

Alex glances over his shoulder. "I'm sure you left an empty cup in here at some point this week, if things get desperate."

"Rude!" I say, but he's right. There's one under my foot and another in the back seat's cup holder. "Let's hope it doesn't come to that. I'm not a *famously* good shot."

He laughs, but it's wooden. "This is not how I imagined this day going."

"Me neither," I say. "But then again, the whole trip was sort of surprising."

At that, he smiles, grips my hand against the gearshift, and lifts it to his lips a few seconds later, holding it there but not quite kissing it.

"What, am I sticky?" I ask.

He shakes his head. "Just want to remember what your skin feels like."

"That's really sweet, Alex," I say, "and not at all something a serial killer would say."

I'm deflecting, but I'm not sure how else to handle this. A mad dash, together, to the airport. A hasty goodbye at our gates—or maybe just splitting off and running in opposite directions. It's the exact antithesis of every rom-com movie I've ever loved, and if I let myself think about it, I think I might have a full-blown panic attack.

By a miracle and a fair amount of speeding (and yes, bribing an Uber driver to skim through a few late-yellow lights after dropping off the Aspire), we make it to the airport and get checked into our flights. Mine leaves fifteen minutes after Alex's, so we head to his gate first, detouring to buy a couple granola bars and the latest issue of *R+R* from a bookstore in the terminal.

We get to his gate just as boarding begins, but we have a few minutes until his group is called, so we stand there, panting, sweaty, shoulders sore from carrying our bags, my ankle scuffed from accidentally whacking it into my hard-shell carry-on bag every few steps.

"Why are airports so hot?" Alex says.

"Is this the set-up for a joke?" I ask.

"No, I genuinely want to know."

"Compared to Nikolai's apartment, this is arctic, Alex."

His smile is tense. Neither one of us is handling this well.

"So," he says.

"So."

"How do you think this article is going to go over with Swapna? Gardens that close in the middle of the day, and carousels so hot they're unsafe to ride?"

"Oh. Right." I cough. I'm less embarrassed that I lied to Alex about this trip than at the fact that I forgot to mention it until now, and am forced to use several of our last precious moments together explaining it. "So *R+R* might not have technically approved this trip."

He arches an eyebrow. "Might not have?"

"Or might have outright rejected it."

"What, seriously? Then why were they paying for—" He cuts

himself short as he reads the answer on my face. "Poppy. You shouldn't have done that. Or you should have told me."

"Would you have taken this trip if you knew I was paying for it?"

"Of course not," he says.

"Exactly," I say. "And I needed to talk to you. I mean, *obviously* we needed to talk."

"You could have called me," he reasons. "We were texting again. We were . . . I don't know, *working* on it."

"I know," I say. "But it wasn't that simple. I was having a hard time at work, just feeling over the whole thing, and lost and *bored*, and like—like I don't even know what I want next in my life, and then I talked to Rachel, and she pointed out that I'd sort of . . . *gotten* everything I wanted professionally, and maybe I just needed to find something *new* to want, and then I thought back to when I was last happy and—"

"What are you talking about?" Alex says, shaking his head. "Rachel told you to . . . trick me into going on a trip with you?"

"No!" I say, panic wriggling in my gut. How is this going off the rails so quickly? "Not that! Her mom's a therapist, and according to her, it's common to be depressed when you've met all your long-term goals. Because we need purpose. And then Rachel suggested maybe I just needed to take a break from life and let myself figure out what I want."

"A break from life," Alex says quietly, his mouth going slack, his eyes dark and stormy.

It's immediately obvious that I've said the wrong thing. This is all coming out so wrong. I have to fix it. "I just mean, I hadn't really been happy since our last trip."

"So you lied to me so I'd take a trip with you, and then you had sex with me, and you told me you loved me and came to my brother's wedding, because you needed a break from your real life."

"Alex, *of course not*," I say, reaching for him.

He steps back from me, eyes low. "Please don't touch me right now, Poppy. I'm trying to think, okay?"

"Think about *what*?" I ask, emotion thickening my voice. I don't understand what's happening, how I've hurt him or how to fix it. "Why are you so upset right now?"

"Because I meant it!" he says, finally meeting my eyes.

A pulse of pain shoots through my stomach. "So did I!" I cry.

"I meant it, and I knew I meant it," he says. "It wasn't an impulse. I knew for years that I loved you, and I thought about it from every single angle and knew what I wanted before I ever kissed you. We went two years without talking, and I thought about you every day and I gave you the space I thought you wanted, and that whole time I asked myself what I'd be willing to do, to give up, if you decided you wanted to be with me too. I spent that whole time alternating between trying to move on and let you go, so you could be happy, and looking at job postings and apartments near you, *just in case*."

"Alex." I shake my head, force the words past the knot in my throat. "I had no idea."

"I know." He rubs at his forehead as he closes his eyes. "I know that. And maybe I should have told you. But, fuck, Poppy, I'm not some water taxi driver you met on vacation."

"What's *that* supposed to mean?" I demand. When he opens his eyes, they're so teary I start to reach for him again until I remember what he said: *please don't touch me right now.*

"I'm not a vacation from your real life," he says. "I'm not a novelty experience. I'm someone who's been in love with you for a decade, and you should never have kissed me if you didn't *know* that you wanted this, all the way. It wasn't fair."

"I *want* this," I say, but even as I say it, a part of me has no idea what that means.

Do I want marriage?

Do I want to have kids?

Do I want to live in a seventies quad-level in Linfield, Ohio?

Do I want any of the things that Alex craves for his life?

I haven't thought any of that through, and Alex can tell.

"You don't know that," Alex says. "You just said you don't know, Poppy. I can't leave my job and my house and my family just to see if that cures your boredom."

"I didn't ask you to do that, Alex," I say, feeling desperate, like I'm grappling for purchase and realizing everything under me is made of sand. He's slipping through my grip for the last time, and there will be no packing this all back into form.

"I know," he says, rubbing the lines in his forehead, wincing. "God, I know that. It's my fault. I should've known this was a bad idea."

"Stop," I say, wanting so badly to touch him, aching at having to settle for clenching my hands into fists. "Don't say that. I'm figuring things out, okay? I just . . . I need to figure some things out."

The gate agent calls for group six to start boarding and the last few stragglers line up.

"I have to go," he says, without looking at me.

My eyes cloud up with tears, my skin hot and itchy like my body's shrinking around my bones, becoming too tight to bear. "I love you, Alex," I get out. "Doesn't that matter?"

His eyes cut toward me, dark, fathomless, full of hurt and want. "I love you too, Poppy," he says. "That's never been our problem." He glances over his shoulder. The line has almost disappeared.

"We can talk about this when we're home," I say. "We can figure it out."

When Alex looks back at me, his face is anguished, his eyes red ringed. "Look," he says gently. "I don't think we should talk for a while."

I shake my head. "That's the last thing we should do, Alex. We have to figure this out."

"Poppy." He reaches for my hand, takes it lightly in his. "I know what I want. *You* need to figure this out. I'd do anything for you, but—please don't ask me to if you're not sure. I really—" He swallows hard. The line is gone. It's time for him to go. He forces out the rest in a hoarse murmur. "I can't be a break from your real life, and I won't be the thing that keeps you from having what you want."

His name catches in my throat. He bends a little, resting his forehead against mine, and I close my eyes. When I open them, he's walking onto the jet bridge without looking back.

I take a deep breath, gather up my things, and head to my gate.

When I sit down to wait and pull my knees into my chest, hiding my face against them, I finally let myself cry freely.

For the first time in my life, the airport strikes me as the loneliest place in the world.

All those people, parting ways, going off in their own directions, crossing paths with hundreds of people but never connecting.

33

Two Summers Ago

AN OLDER GENTLEMAN travels with us to Croatia as the of-
ficial *R+R* photographer.

Bernard. He's a loud talker, always wearing a fleece vest, often
standing between Alex and me without noticing the funny looks we
exchange over Bernard's bald head. (He's shorter than me, though
throughout the trip, he often tells us he was five six back in his prime.)

Together, the three of us see the ancient city of Dubrovnik,
Old Town, with its high stone walls and winding streets, and further
out, the rocky beaches and pristine turquoise water of the Adriatic.

The other photographers I've traveled with have all been fairly
independent, but Bernard's a recent widower, unused to living
alone. He's a nice guy, but endlessly social and talkative, and
throughout our time in the city, I watch him wear Alex down, until
all Bernard's questions are answered in monosyllables. Bernard
doesn't notice; usually his questions are mere springboards for stories he'd like to share.

The stories involve a lot of names and dates, and he takes plenty
of time ensuring he's getting each right, sometimes going back and

forth four or five times until he's *positive* this event happened on a Wednesday and not, as he first thought, a Thursday.

From the city, we take a crammed ferry to Korčula, an island off the coast. *R+R* has booked us two apartment-style hotel rooms overlooking the water. Somehow Bernard gets it in his head that he and Alex will be sharing one of these, which makes no sense since *he* is an *R+R* employee, who should obviously get his own accommodations, while Alex is my guest.

We try to tell him this.

"Oh, I don't mind," he says. "Besides, I got two bedrooms by accident."

It's a lost cause trying to convince him that *that* room was supposed to be *Alex's and mine*, thus the two bedrooms, and honestly, I think we both feel too much sympathy for Bernard to push the matter. The apartments themselves are sleek and modern, all whites and stainless steels with balconies overlooking the glittering water, but the walls are paper-thin, and I wake every morning to the sounds of three tiny children running around and screaming in the apartment above mine. Furthermore, something has died in the wall behind the dryer in the laundry closet, and every day that I call down to the desk to tell them this, they send up a teenage boy to do something about the smell while I'm out. I'm fairly sure he just opens all the windows and sprays Lysol all over the place, because the sweet lemony scent I return to fades each night as the dead animal smell swells back to replace it.

I expected this to be the best vacation of any we've ever taken.

But even aside from the death smell and the shrieking-at-dawn babies, there's the fact of Bernard. After Tuscany, without talking about it, Alex and I both took a step back from our friendship. Instead of daily texts, we started catching up every couple weeks. It would've been too easy to go back to how things were then, but I couldn't do that, to him or to Trey.

Instead I threw myself into work, taking every trip that came up, sometimes back to back. At first Trey and I were happier than ever—this was where we thrived: on horseback and camelback, hiking volcanoes and cliff-jumping off waterfalls. But eventually our never-ending vacation started to feel like running, like we were two bank robbers making the best of a bad situation while we waited for the FBI to close in.

We started arguing. He'd want to get up early, and I'd oversleep. I was walking too slowly, and he was laughing too loud. I was annoyed by how he flirted with our waitress, and he couldn't stand how I had to browse every aisle of every identical shop we passed.

We had a week left of a trip to New Zealand when we realized we'd run our course.

"We're just not having fun anymore," Trey said.

I started laughing from relief. We parted ways as friends. I didn't cry. The last six months had been a slow unbraiding of our lives. The breakup was just the snip of one last string.

When I texted Alex to tell him, he said, What happened? Are you okay?

It'll be easier to explain in person, I wrote, heart trilling.

Fair enough, he said.

A few weeks later, also over text, he told me that he and Sarah had broken up again.

I hadn't seen that coming: They'd moved to Linfield together when he'd finished his doctorate, were even working at the same school—a miracle so profound it seemed like the universe's express approval of their relationship—and from everything Alex had told me, they'd been better than ever. Happier. It was all so natural for them. Unless he was keeping their issues private, which would make perfect sense.

You want to talk? I asked, feeling at once terrified and full of adrenaline.

Like you said, he wrote back, *probably easier to explain in person.*

I'd been waiting two and a half months to have that conversation. I missed Alex so badly, and finally there was nothing in the way of us speaking plainly, no reason to hold back or tiptoe around each other or try not to touch.

Except for Bernard.

He kayaks at sunset with us. Rides along on our tour of the family wineries gathered together a ways inland. Joins us for seafood dinners every night. Suggests a nightcap afterward. He never tires. *Bernard,* Alex whispers one night, *might be God,* and I snort into my white wine.

"Allergies?" Bernard says. "You can use my hankie."

Then he passes me an honest-to-god embroidered hankie.

I wish Bernard would do something awful, like floss at the table, or just anything that would give me the courage to demand an hour of space and privacy.

This is the most beautiful and worst trip Alex and I have ever taken.

On our last night, the three of us get roaring drunk at a restaurant overlooking the sea, watching the pinks and golds of the sun melt across everything until the water is a sheet of light, replaced gradually by a blanket of deep purple. Back at the resort, the sky gone dark, we part ways, exhausted in more ways than one and heavy with wine.

Fifteen minutes later, I hear a light knock on my door. I answer in my pajamas and find Alex standing there, grinning and flushed. "Well, *this* is a surprise!" I say, slurring a little.

"Really?" Alex says. "With how you were plying Bernard with alcohol, I thought this was part of some evil plan."

"Is he passed out?" I ask.

"Snoring so fucking loud," Alex says, and as we both start to laugh, he presses his forefinger to my lips. "Shhh," he warns, "I've tried to sneak over here the last two nights and he woke up—and *came out of his bedroom*—before I even made it to the door. I thought about taking up smoking just so I could have an ironclad excuse."

More laughter bubbles through me, warming my insides, fizzing through them. "Do you really think he would've followed you over?" I whisper, his finger still pressed to my lips.

"I wasn't willing to take that chance." On the other side of the wall, we hear a wretched snore, and I start giggling so hard my legs go watery and I sink to the floor. Alex does too.

We fall into a heap, a tangle of limbs and silent, quaking laughter. I smack futilely at his arm as another horrible thunder-roll snore roars through the wall.

"I've missed you," Alex says through a grin as the laughter's subsiding.

"Me too," I say, cheeks aching. He brushes the hair out of my face, static making a few strands dance around his hand. "But at least now I have three of you." I grip his wrist to steady myself and close one eye to see him better.

"Too many wine?" he teases, slipping his hand around my neck.

"Nah," I say, "just enough to knock out Bernard. The perfect amount." My head is pleasantly swimming and my skin feels warm beneath Alex's hand, rings of satisfying heat reverberating out from it all the way to my toes. "This must be how it feels to be a cat," I hum.

He laughs. "How so?"

"You know." I rock my head side to side, nestling my neck against his palm. "Just . . ." I trail off, too contented to go on. His fingers scratch in and out against my skin, tugging lightly on my hair, and I sigh with pleasure as I sink against him, my hand settling on his chest as my forehead rests against his.

He sets his hand on mine, and I lace my fingers into it as I tip my face up to his, our noses grazing. His chin lifts, fingers graze my jaw. Next thing I know, he's kissing me.

I'm *kissing Alex Nilsen.*

A warm, slow drink of a kiss. Both of us are almost laughing at first, like this whole thing is a very funny joke. Then, his tongue sweeps over my bottom lip, a brush of fiery heat. His teeth catch it briefly next, and there's no more laughing.

My hands slip into his hair and he pulls me across his lap, his hands running up my back and down again to squeeze my hips. My breaths are shuddering and quick as his mouth teases mine open again, his tongue sweeping deeper, his taste sweet and clean and intoxicating.

We're frantic hands and sharp teeth, fabric peeled away from skin, and fingernails digging into muscles. Probably Bernard is still snoring, but I can't hear him over Alex's deliciously shallow breath or his voice in my ear, saying my name like a swear word, or my heartbeat raging through my eardrums as I rock my hips against his.

All those things we didn't get to say no longer matter because, really, this is what we needed. I need more of him. I reach for his belt—because he's wearing a belt, of course he's wearing a belt—but he catches my wrist and draws back, his lips bee-stung and hair mussed, all of him rumpled in a completely unfamiliar and extremely appealing way.

"We can't do this," he says, voice thick.

"We can't?" Stopping feels like running into a wall. Like there are little cartoon birds twirling dazedly around my head as I try to make sense of what he's saying.

"We shouldn't," Alex amends. "We're drunk."

"Not too drunk to make out but too drunk to sleep together?" I say, almost laughing from the absurdity, or from the disappointment.

Alex's mouth twists. "No," he says, "I mean, it shouldn't have happened at all. We've both been drinking, and we're not thinking clearly—"

"Mm-hm." I scoot away from him, smoothing my pajama shirt back down. My embarrassment is the total-body kind, a gut punch that makes my eyes water. I shove myself off the floor, Alex following my lead. "You're right," I say. "It was a bad idea."

Alex looks miserable. "I just mean . . ."

"I get it," I say quickly, trying to patch the hole before the boat can take on more water. It was a mistake to go there, to risk this. But I need to convince him everything's fine, that we didn't just pour gasoline onto our friendship and light a match. "Let's not make this a big deal—it's not," I go on, my conviction building. "It's like you said: we each had, like, three bottles of wine. We weren't thinking clearly. We'll pretend it never happened, okay?"

He stares at me hard, a tense expression I can't quite read. "You think you can do that?"

"Alex, of course," I say. "We've got way more history than just one drunken night."

"Okay." He nods. "Okay." After a beat of silence, he says, "I should get to bed." He studies me for another beat, then mumbles, "Good night," and slips out the door.

After a few minutes of mortified pacing, I drag myself to bed, where every time I start drifting off, the whole encounter plays over in my mind: the unbearable excitement of kissing him and the even more unbearable humiliation of our conversation.

In the morning, when I wake, there's one blissful moment when I think I dreamed the whole thing. Then I stumble to the bathroom mirror and see a good old-fashioned hickey on my neck, and the cycle of memories starts anew.

I decide not to bring it up when I see him. The best thing I can do is pretend to truly have forgotten what happened. To prove I'm okay and nothing has to change between us.

When we get to the airport—Bernard, Alex, and I—and Bernard wanders off to use the bathroom, we have our first minute alone of the day.

Alex coughs. "I'm sorry about last night. I know I started it all and—it shouldn't have happened like that."

"Seriously," I say. "It's not a big deal."

"I know you're not over Trey," he murmurs, looking away. "I shouldn't have . . ."

Would it make things better or worse to admit how little Trey crossed my mind for weeks before this trip? That last night I hadn't been thinking about anyone but Alex?

"It's not your fault," I promise. "We both let it happen, and it doesn't have to mean anything, Alex. We're just two friends who kissed once while drunk."

He studies me for a few seconds. "All right." He doesn't look like he's all right. He looks like he'd rather be at a saxophone convention with any number of serial killers right now.

My heart squeezes painfully. "So we're good?" I say, willing it to be so.

Bernard reappears then with a story about a heavily toilet-papered airport bathroom he once visited—on the Sunday of Mother's Day, for those who want the *exact* date—and Alex and I barely look at each other.

When I get home, something keeps me from texting him.

He'll text me, I think. *Then I'll know we're okay.*

After a week of silence, I send him a casual text about a funny T-shirt I see on the subway, and he writes back ha but nothing else. Two weeks later, when I ask, Are you okay? he just replies, Sorry. Been really busy. You okay?

For sure, I say.

Alex stays busy. I get busy too, and that's it.

I always knew there was a reason we kept a boundary up. We'd let our libidos get the best of us and now he couldn't even look at me, text me back.

Ten years of friendship flushed down the drain just so I could know what Alex Nilsen tastes like.

34

This Summer

CAN'T STOP THINKING about that first kiss. Not our first kiss on Nikolai's balcony but the one two years ago, in Croatia. All this time, that memory has looked one way in my mind, but now it looks entirely different.

I'd thought he regretted what happened. Now I understood he regretted *how* it happened. On a drunk whim, when he couldn't be sure of my intentions. When *I* wasn't sure of my intentions. He'd been afraid it hadn't meant anything, and then I'd pretended it hadn't.

All this time I'd thought he'd rejected me. And he'd thought I'd been cavalier with him and his heart. It made me ache to think of how I'd hurt him, and worst of all, maybe he was right.

Because even if that kiss hadn't meant nothing to me, I also hadn't thought it through. Not the first time, and not this time either. Not like Alex had.

"Poppy?" Swapna says, leaning around my cubicle. "Do you have a moment?"

I've been at my desk, staring at this website for tourism in Siberia, for upwards of forty-five minutes. Turns out Siberia is actually sort of beautiful. Perfect for a self-imposed exile if one should have need of such a thing. I minimize the site. "Um, sure."

Swapna glances over her shoulder, checking who else is in today, parked at their desks. "Actually, are you up for a walk?"

It's been two weeks since I got back from Palm Springs, and it's technically too early for fall weather, but we've got a random pop of it today in New York. Swapna grabs her Burberry trench and I grab my vintage herringbone one and we set off toward the coffee shop on the corner.

"So," she says. "I can't help but notice you've been in a funk."

"Oh." I thought I'd been doing an okay job hiding how I was feeling. For one thing, I've been exercising for, like, four hours a night, which means I sleep like a baby, wake up still exhausted, and trudge through my days without too much brainpower left for wondering when Alex might answer one of my phone calls or call me back.

Or why this job feels as tiring as bartending back in Ohio did. I can't make anything add up how it should anymore. All day long, I hear myself saying this same phrase, like I'm desperate to get it out of my body even as I feel incapable: *I am having a hard time.*

As mild as that statement is—every bit as mild as *I can't help but notice you've been in a funk*—it sears to my center every time I hear it.

I am having a hard time, I think desperately a thousand times a day, and when I try to probe for more information—*A hard time with what?*—the voice replies, *Everything.*

I feel insufficient as an adult. I look around at the office and see everyone typing, taking calls, making bookings, editing documents, and I know they're all dealing with at least as much as I am, which only makes me feel worse about how hard everything feels to me.

Living, being responsible for myself, seems like an insurmountable challenge lately.

Sometimes I scrape myself off my sofa, stuff a frozen meal in the microwave, and as I wait for the timer to go off, I just think, *I will have to do this again tomorrow and the next day and the next day.* Every day for the rest of my life, I'm going to have to figure out what to eat, and make it for myself, no matter how bad I feel or tired I am, or how horrible the pounding in my head is. Even if I have a one-hundred-and-two-degree fever, I will have to pull myself up and make a very mediocre meal to go on living.

I don't say any of this to Swapna, because (*a*) she's my boss, (*b*) I don't know if I could translate any of these thoughts into spoken words, and (*c*) even if I could, it would be humiliating to admit that I feel exactly like that incapable, lost, melancholy stereotype of a millennial that the world is so fond of raging against.

"I guess I have been in a little bit of a funk," is what I say. "I didn't realize it was affecting my work. I'll do better."

Swapna stops walking, turns on her towering Louboutins, and frowns. "It's not only about the work, Poppy. I have personally invested in mentoring you."

"I know," I say. "You're an amazing boss, and I feel so lucky."

"It's not about that either," Swapna says, the slightest bit impatient. "What I'm saying is that of course you're not obligated to talk to me about what's going on, but I do think it would help if you spoke with *someone*. Working toward your goals can be very lonely, and professional burnout is always a challenge. I've been there, trust me."

I shift anxiously on my feet. While Swapna *has* been a mentor to me, we've never veered toward anything personal, and I'm unsure how much to say.

"I don't know what's going on with me," I admit.

I know my heart is broken at the thought of not having Alex in my life.

I know that I wish I could see him every single day, and there's no part of me that's imagining what else could be out there, who I might miss out on knowing and loving if we were to really be together.

I know that the thought of a life in Linfield terrifies the hell out of me.

I know I worked so hard to be *this* person—independent, well traveled, successful—and I don't know who I am if I let that go.

I know that there's still no other job out there calling to me, the obvious answer to my unhappiness, and that this one, which has been amazing for a good portion of the last four and a half years, lately has only left me tired.

And all of that adds up to having no fucking clue where I go next, and thus no real right to call Alex, which is why I've finally stopped trying for the time being.

"Professional burnout," I say aloud. "That's a thing that passes, right?"

Swapna smiles. "For me, so far, it always has." She reaches into her pocket and pulls out a little white business card. "But like I said, it helps to speak with someone." I accept the card, and she tips her chin toward the coffee shop. "Why don't you take a few minutes to yourself? Sometimes a change of scenery is all that's needed to get a little perspective."

A change of scenery, I think as she starts back the way we came. *That used to work.*

I look down at the business card in my hand and can't help but laugh.

Dr. Sandra Krohn, psychologist.

I pull out my phone and text Rachel. Is Dr. Mom accepting new patients?

Is the current Pope wildly transgressive? she texts back.

RACHEL'S MOTHER HAS a home office in her brownstone in Brooklyn. While Rachel's own design aesthetic is airy and light, her mother's decor is warm and cozy, all dark wood and stained glass, hanging leafy plants and books piled high on every surface, wind chimes twinkling outside almost every window.

In a way, it reminds me of being at home, although Dr. Krohn's artsy, cultivated version of maximalism is a far cry from Mom and Dad's Museum to Our Childhood.

During our first session I tell her I need help figuring out what comes next for me, but she recommends we start with the past instead.

"There's not much to say," I tell her, then proceed to talk for fifty-six minutes straight. About my parents, about school, about the first trip home with Guillermo.

She's the only person I've shared any of this with aside from Alex, and while it feels good to get it out, I'm not sure how it's helping with my life-exploding crisis. Rachel makes me promise to stick with it for at least a couple months. "Don't run from this," she says. "You won't be doing yourself any favors."

I know she's right. I've have to run *through*, not away. My only hope for figuring this out is to stay, sit in the discomfort.

In my weekly therapy sessions. In my job at *R+R*. In my mostly empty apartment.

My blog sits unused, but I start to journal. My work trips are limited to regional weekend getaways, and during my downtime, I scour the internet for self-help books and articles, looking for something that speaks to me like that twenty-one-thousand-dollar bear statue definitely did not.

Sometimes, I look for jobs in New York; other times, I check listings near Linfield.

I buy myself a plant, a book about plants, and a small loom. I try to teach myself how to weave with YouTube videos and realize within three hours that I'm as bored by it as I am bad at it.

Still, I let the half-finished weaving sit out on my table for days, and it feels like proof that I live here. I have a life, here, a place that's mine.

On the last day of September, I'm on my way to meet Rachel at the wine bar when my bag gets caught in the subway doors of a crowded train car.

"Shit, shit, shit!" I hiss, while on the other side, a few people work to pry them open. A balding but youngish man in a blue suit manages to get the doors apart, and when I look up to thank him, recognition flashes clear and sharp across his blue eyes.

"Poppy?" he says, pushing the doors a little further apart. "Poppy Wright?"

I'm too stunned to reply. He steps out of the train car, despite having made no effort to get out the first time the doors opened. This isn't his stop, but he's getting out and I have to step back to make room for him as the doors snap closed again.

And then we're standing there on the platform, and I should say something, I know I have to—he got off the freaking train. I manage only, "Wow. Jason."

He nods, grinning, touching his chest where a light pink tie hangs from the pressed collar of his white shirt. "Jason Stanley. East Linfield High School."

My brain is still trying to process this. It can't reconcile him against this backdrop. In *my* city, in the life I built to never touch my old one. I stammer, "Right."

Jason Stanley has lost most of his hair. He's put on some weight around the middle, but there's still something of the cute boy I once had a crush on, who then ruined my life.

He laughs, elbows me. "You were my first girlfriend."

"Well," I say, because that doesn't seem quite right. I've never thought of Jason Stanley as my first boyfriend. First-crush-turned-bully maybe.

"Are you busy right now?" He glances at his watch. "I've got a few minutes if you want to catch up."

I do not want to catch up.

"I'm actually on my way to therapy," I say, for some fucking reason. It was the first excuse that came to mind. I'd prefer to have blurted out that I was taking a metal detector to the nearest beach to look for quarters. I stride toward the steps, and Jason follows along.

"Therapy?" he says, still grinning. "Not because of that shit I pulled when I was a jealous little prick, I hope." He winks. "I mean, you hope to make an impression, just not that sort."

"I don't know what you're talking about," I lie as we climb the steps.

"Really?" Jason says. "God, that's a relief. I think about it all the time. Even tried to look you up on Facebook once so I could apologize. You don't have Facebook, do you?"

"Not really, no," I say.

I do have Facebook. I do not have my last name on Facebook specifically because I didn't want people like Jason Stanley finding me. Or anyone from Linfield. I wanted to vanish that part of me and reappear fully formed in a new city, and that's what I did.

We emerge from the subway onto the tree-lined streets. That

same nip is back in the air. Fall has finally swallowed up the last bites of summer.

"Anyway," Jason says, the first signs of embarrassment kicking in. He stops, rubbing the back of his head. "I'll leave you alone. I saw you and I couldn't believe it. I just wanted to say hi. And sorry, I guess."

But I stop too, because haven't I been saying for a month that I'm done running from problems, damn it? I left Linfield, and somehow that wasn't enough. He's here. Like the universe is giving me a hard shove in the right direction.

I take a breath and wheel toward him, crossing my arms. "Sorry for *what*, Jason?"

He must see it in my face, that I was lying about not remembering, because he looks hugely embarrassed now.

He takes a stiff, stuttering breath, studies his brown dress shoes guiltily. "You remember how awful middle school was, right?" he says. "You feel so out of place—like something's wrong with you and any second everyone else is gonna figure it out. You see it happen to other people. Kids you used to play four square with suddenly getting mean nicknames, not getting invited to birthday parties. And you know you could be next, so *you* turn into a little asshole. If you point at other people, no one will look too closely at you, right? I was your asshole—I mean, I was the asshole in your life, for a while."

The sidewalk sways in front of me, a wave of dizziness crashing over me. Whatever I was expecting, that wasn't it.

"I honestly can't believe I'm even saying this," he says. "I just saw you on that train platform and—I had to say something."

Jason takes a deep breath, his frown drawing tired wrinkles at the corners of his mouth and eyes.

We're so old, I think. *When did we get so old?*

Suddenly we're not kids anymore, and it feels like it happened overnight, so fast I didn't have time to notice, to let go of everything that used to matter so much, to see that the old wounds that once felt like gut-level lacerations have faded to small white scars, mixed in among the stretch marks and sunspots and little divots where time has grazed against my body.

I've put so much time and distance between myself and that lonely girl, and what does it matter? Here is a piece of my past, right in front of me, miles away from home. You can't outrun yourself. Not your history, not your fears, not the parts of yourself you're worried are wrong.

Jason darts another glance at his feet. "At the reunion," he says, "someone told me you were doing great. Working at *R+R*. That's amazing. I actually, um, grabbed an issue a while back and read your articles. It's so cool, seems like you've seen the whole world."

Finally, I manage to speak. "Yeah. It's . . . it's really cool."

His smile widens. "And you live here?"

"Mm-hm." I cough to clear my throat. "What about you?"

"Nah," he says. "I'm on business. Sales stuff. I'm still back in Linfield."

This, I realize, is what I've been waiting for for years. The moment when I finally know I've won: I got out. I made something of myself. I found a place I belonged. I proved I wasn't broken while the person who was cruelest to me stayed stuck in crappy little Linfield.

Except that's not how I feel. Because Jason doesn't seem stuck, and he certainly isn't being cruel. He's here, in this city, in a nice white shirt, being genuinely kind.

There's a stinging in my eyes, a hot feeling in the back of my throat.

"If you're ever back there," Jason says uncertainly, "and you wanna meet up . . ."

I try to make some kind of noise of assent, but nothing happens. It's like the tiny person who sits at the control panel in my brain has just passed out. "So," Jason goes on. "Sorry again. I hope you know it was always about me. Not you."

The sidewalk swings again, a pendulum. Like the world as I've always seen it has been jostled so hard it's rocking, might come crashing down entirely.

Obviously people grow up, a voice says in my head. *You think all those people were just frozen in time, just because they stayed in Linfield?*

But like he said, it's not about them, it's about me.

That's exactly what I thought.

That if I didn't get out, I'd always be that lonely girl. I would never belong anywhere.

"So if you're in Linfield . . ." he says again.

"But you're not hitting on me, right?" I say.

"Oh! God no!" Now he holds up his hand, showing off one of those thick black bands on his ring finger. "Married. Happily. Monogamously."

"Cool," I say, because it's really the only English word I remember at present. Which is saying something since I don't speak any other languages.

"Yep!" he says. "Well . . . see ya."

And then Jason Stanley's gone, as suddenly as he appeared.

By the time I get to the wine bar, I've started to cry. (What's new?) When Rachel jumps up from our usual table, she looks stricken at the sight of me. "Are you okay, babe?"

"I'm going to quit my job," I say tearily.

"Oh . . . kay."

"I mean"—I sniff hard, wipe at my eyes—"not immediately, like in a movie. I'm not going to walk into Swapna's office and be, like, I quit! And then walk straight out of the office in a tight red dress with my hair down my back or anything."

"Well, that's good. Orange is better for your complexion."

"Either way, I have to find another job, before I can leave," I say. "But I think I just figured out why I've been so unhappy."

35

This Summer

I F YOU NEED me," Rachel says, "I'll go with you. I mean, I seriously will. I'll buy a ticket on the way to the airport, and I'll go with you."

Even as she says it, she looks like I'm holding out a giant cobra with human blood dripping off its teeth.

"I know." I squeeze her hand. "But then who will keep us up to date on everything happening in New York?"

"Oh, thank God," she says in a gust. "I was afraid you'd take me up on that for a minute."

She pulls me into a hug, kisses me on either cheek, and puts me into the cab.

My parents both come to pick me up from the Cincinnati airport. They're wearing matching I–heart symbol–New York T-shirts.

"Thought it would make you feel at home!" Mom says, laughing so hard at her joke that she's practically crying. I think it might be the first time she or Dad has acknowledged New York as my home, which makes me happy on one level and sad on another.

"I already feel at home here," I tell her, and she makes a big show of clutching her heart, and a squeak of emotion sneaks out of her. "By the way," she says as we bustle across the parking lot, "I made buckeye cookies."

"So that's dinner, but what about breakfast?" I ask.

She titters. No one on the planet thinks I'm as funny as my mom does. It's like taking candy from a baby. Or *giving* candy to a baby.

"So, buddy," Dad says once we're in the car. "To what do we owe this honor? It's not even a bank holiday!"

"I just missed you guys," I say, "and Alex."

"Shoot," Dad grunts, putting on his turn signal. "Now you're gonna make *me* cry."

We go home first so I can change out of my plane clothes, give myself a pep talk, and bide my time. School's not out until two thirty.

Until then, the three of us sit on the porch, drinking homemade lemonade. Mom and Dad take turns talking about their plans for the garden next year. What all they'll be pulling up. What new flowers and trees they'll plant. The fact that Mom is trying to Marie Kondo the house but has only managed to get rid of three shoeboxes' worth of stuff so far.

"Progress is progress," Dad says, reaching out to rub her shoulder affectionately. "Have we told you about the privacy fence, buddy? The new next-door neighbor is a gossip, so we decided we needed a fence."

"He comes by to tell me what everyone on this cul-de-sac is up to, and doesn't have anything good to say!" Mom cries. "I'm sure he's saying the same kinds of things about us."

"Oh, I doubt it," I say. "Your lies will be *much* more colorful."

This delights Mom, obviously: candy, meet baby.

"Once we get the fence up," Dad says, "he'll tell everyone we're running a meth lab."

"Oh, stop." Mom smacks his arm, but they're both laughing. "We've got to video-call with the boys later. Parker wants to do a reading of the new screenplay he's working on."

I narrowly avoid a spit-take.

The last screenplay my brother's been brainstorming in the group text is a gritty dystopian Smurfs origin story with at least one sex scene. His reasoning is, someday he'd like to write a real movie, but by writing one that can't possibly get made, he's taking the pressure off himself during the learning process. Also I think he enjoys scandalizing his family.

At two fifteen, I ask to take the car and head up to my old high school. Only at that point, I realize the tank's empty. After the quick detour for gas, I pull into the school parking lot at two fifty. Two separate anxieties are warring for domination inside me: the one that's composed of terror at the thought of seeing Alex, saying what I need to say, and hoping he'll hear it, and the one that's all about being back here, a place I legitimately swore I'd never waste another second in.

I march up the concrete steps to the glass front doors, take one last deep breath, and—

The door doesn't budge. It's locked.

Right.

I sort of forgot that any random adult can't walk into a high school anymore. Definitely for the best, in every situation except this one. I knock on the door until a beaky resource officer with a halo of gray hair approaches and cracks the door a few inches. "Can I help you?"

"I'm here to see someone," I say. "A teacher—Alex Nilsen?"

"Name?" he asks.

"Alex Nilsen—"

"Your name," the officer says, correcting me.

"Oh, Poppy Wright."

He closes the door, disappearing for a second into the front office. A moment later, he returns. "Sorry, ma'am, we don't have you in our system. We can't let in unregistered guests."

"Could you just get him, then?" I try.

"Ma'am, I can't go track down—"

"Poppy?" someone says behind him.

Oh, wow! I think at first. *Someone recognizes me! What luck!*

And then the pretty, lean brunette steps up to the door. My stomach bottoms out.

"Sarah. Wow. Hi." I'd forgotten that I could potentially run into Sarah Torval here. Borderline monumental oversight.

She glances back at the resource officer. "I've got it, Mark," she says, and steps outside to talk to me, folding her arms across herself. She's wearing a cute purple dress and dark denim jacket, large silver earrings dancing from her ears; she has just a splash of freckles across her nose.

As ever, she is completely adorable in that kindergarten-teacher way. (Despite being a ninth-grade teacher, of course.)

"What are you doing here?" she asks, not *unkindly*, though definitely not warmly.

"Oh, um. Visiting my parents."

She arches a brow and glances at the redbrick building behind her. "At the high school?"

"No." I push the hair out of my eyes. "I mean, that's what I'm doing *here*. But what I'm doing *here* is . . . I was hoping, I mean . . . I wanted to talk to Alex?"

Her eye roll is minimal, but it stings.

I swallow an apple-sized knot. "I deserve that," I say. I take a breath. This won't be fun, but it's necessary. "I was really careless about everything, Sarah. I mean, my friendship with Alex, everything I expected from him while you were together. It wasn't fair to you. I know that now."

"Yeah," she says. "You *were* careless about it."

We're both silent for a beat.

Finally, she sighs. "We all made some bad decisions. I used to think that if you just went away, all my problems would be solved." She uncrosses her arms and recrosses them the other way. "And then you did—you basically disappeared after we went to Tuscany, and somehow, that was even worse for my relationship."

I sway from foot to foot. "I'm sorry. I wish I'd understood what I was feeling before it had a chance to hurt anyone."

She nods to herself, examines the perfectly painted toenails poking out of her tan leather sandals. "I wish so too," she says. "Or that he had. Or that *I* had. Really if *any* of us had really known how you two felt about each other, it would've saved me a lot of time and pain."

"Yeah," I agree. "So you and he aren't . . ."

She lets me wait for a few seconds, and I know it's not an accident. A semidevilish smile curls up her pink lips. "We aren't," she relents. "Thank God. But he's not here. He already left. I think he was talking about getting away for the weekend."

"Oh." My heart sinks. I glance back at my parents' minivan parked in the half-empty lot. "Well, thanks anyway."

She nods, and I start down the steps. "Poppy?"

I turn back, and the light's shining so bright on her that I have to shield my eyes to look at her. It makes her look like she's a saint, earning her halo by unwarranted kindness toward me. *I'll take it*, I think.

"Usually on Fridays," she says slowly, "teachers go to Birdies. It's a tradition." She moves, and the light lets up enough for me to meet her eyes. "If he hasn't left, he might be there."

"Thanks, Sarah."

"Please," she says. "You're doing the world a favor by taking Alex Nilsen off the market."

I laugh, but it's leaden in my stomach. "I'm not sure that's what he wants."

She shrugs. "Maybe not," she says. "But most of us are too scared to even ask what we want, in case we can't have it. Read that in this essay about something called 'millennial ennui.'"

I stifle a laugh of surprise, clear my throat. "Kind of a catchy name."

"Right?" she says. "Anyway. Good luck."

BIRDIES IS ACROSS the street from the school, and the two-minute drive over is about four hours too short to formulate a new plan.

The whole flight down, I practiced my impassioned speech with the thought that it would be said in private, in his classroom.

Now it's going to be in a bar full of teachers, including some whose classes I took (and skipped). If there's one place I have judged more harshly than the fluorescent-lit halls of East Linfield High School, it's the dark, cramped bar with the glowing neon BUDWEISER sign I'm entering right now.

All at once, the light of day is shut out and colorful dots dance in front of my eyes as they adjust to this dim place. There's a Rolling Stones song playing on the radio, and considering it's only three in the afternoon, the bar is already hopping with people in business casual, a sea of khakis and button-ups and cotton dresses in monochrome, not unlike Sarah's getup. Golf paraphernalia hangs on the walls—clubs and green Astroturf and framed pictures of golfers and golf courses.

I know there's a city in Illinois called Normal, but I'm guessing it doesn't hold a candle to this suburban corner of the universe.

There are mounted TVs turned up too loud, a scratchy radio playing underneath that, bursts of laughter and raised voices coming from the groups crowded around high-tops or lined up along either side of narrow rectangular tables.

And then I see him.

Taller than most, stiller than all, his shirtsleeves rolled to the elbows and boots resting on the metal rung of his chair, his shoulders hunched forward and his phone out, thumb slowly scrolling up his screen. My heart rises into my throat until I can *taste* it, all metallic and hot and pulsing too hard.

There's a part of me—fine, a majority—that wants to bolt, even after flying all the way here, but right then the door squeals open and Alex glances up, his eyes locking onto me.

We're looking at each other, and I imagine I look nearly as shocked as he does, like I didn't arrive specifically on a hot tip that he was here. I force myself to take a few steps toward him, then stop at the end of the table, where, gradually, the other teachers look up from their beers and white wines and vodka tonics to process the fact of me.

"Hi," Alex says, little more than a whisper.

"Hi," I say.

I wait for the rest to pour out. Nothing does.

"Who's your friend?" an old lady in a maroon turtleneck asks. I clock her for Delallo, even before I see the ELHS name badge she's still wearing around her neck.

"She's . . ." Alex's voice drops off. He stands from his chair. "Hi," he says again.

The rest of the table are exchanging uncomfortable looks, kind of scooting their chairs in, angling their backs away in an attempt to give us a level of privacy that's impossible at this point. Delallo, I notice, keeps one ear tilted almost *precisely* toward us.

"I came to the school," I manage.

"Oh," Alex says. "Okay."

"I had this plan." I rub my sweaty palms against my orange polyester bell-bottoms, wishing I wasn't dressed like a traffic cone. "I was going to show up to the school, because I wanted you to know that if there's one thing in this world that could get me to go there, it's you."

His eyes briefly pass over the table of teachers again. So far, my speech doesn't seem to be comforting him. His eyes cut to mine, then drop to a vague point on my left. "Yeah, I know you really hate it there," he murmurs.

"I do," I agree. "I have a lot of bad memories there, and I wanted to show up there, and just, like, *tell* you, that . . . that I would go anywhere for you, Alex."

"Poppy," he says, the word half sigh, half plea.

"No, wait," I say. "I know I have a fifty-fifty chance here, and there's so much of me that wants to not even say the rest of this, Alex, but I *need* to, so please, don't tell me yet if you need to break my heart. Okay? Let me say this before I lose the nerve."

His lips part for a moment, his green-gold eyes like storm-flooded rivers, brutal and rushing. He presses his mouth closed again and nods.

Feeling like I'm jumping off a cliff, unable to see what lies through the fog beneath me, I go on.

"I loved running my blog," I tell him. "I loved it so much, and I thought it was because I loved traveling—which I do. But in the last few years, everything changed. I wasn't happy. Traveling felt different. And maybe you were sort of right that I came at you like you were a Band-Aid that could fix everything. Or whatever—a fun destination to give me a dopamine rush and a new perspective."

His eyes drop. He won't look at me, and I feel like even if he was the one who said it first, my confirmation is eating him alive.

"I started therapy," I blurt out, trying to keep things moving. "And I was trying to figure out why it feels so different now, and I was listing all the differences between my life then and now, and it wasn't just you. I mean, you're the biggest one. You were on those trips, and then you weren't, but that wasn't the only change. All those trips we took, the best thing about them—other than doing it all with you—was the people."

His gaze lifts, narrowed in thought.

"I loved meeting new people," I explain. "I loved . . . feeling connected. Feeling *interesting*. Growing up here, I was so fucking lonely, and I always felt like there was something wrong with me. But I told myself if I went somewhere else, it would be different. There'd be other people like me."

"I know that," he says. "I know you hate it here, Poppy."

"I did," I say. "I hated it, so I escaped. And when Chicago didn't fix everything for me, I left there too. Once I started traveling, though, things finally felt better. I met people, and—I don't know, without the baggage of history or the fear of what would happen, it felt so much easier to open up to people. To make friends. I know it sounds pathetic, but all those little chance encounters we had—those made me less lonely. Those made me feel like I was someone people could love. And then I got the *R+R* job, and the trips changed; the people changed. I only met chefs and hotel managers, people wanting write-ups. I'd go on amazing trips, but I'd come home feeling empty. And now I realize it's because I wasn't connecting to anyone."

"I'm glad you figured it out," Alex says. "I want you to be happy."

"But here's the thing," I say. "Even if I quit my job and started taking the blog seriously again, went back to meeting all the Bucks and Litas and Mathildes of the world—it's not going to make me happy.

"I needed those people, because I felt alone. I thought I had to run hundreds of miles away from here to find some place to belong. I spent my whole life thinking anyone outside my family who got too close, saw too much, wouldn't want me anymore. The safest thing was those quick, serendipitous moments with strangers. That's all I thought I could have.

"And then there was you." My voice wobbles dangerously. I steel myself, straighten my spine. "I love you so much that I've spent twelve years putting as much distance between us as I could. I moved. I traveled. I dated other people. I talked about Sarah all the fucking time because I knew you had a crush on her, and it felt safer that way. Because the last person I could take being rejected by was you.

"And now I know that. I know it's not traveling that's gonna get me out of this slump and it's not a new job and it's sure as hell not chance encounters with water taxi drivers. All of that, every minute of it, has been running away from you, and I don't want to do that anymore.

"I love you, Alex Nilsen. Even if you don't give me a real chance, I'm always going to love you. And I'm scared to move back to Linfield because I don't know if I'd like it here, or if I'd be bored, or if I'd make any friends, and because I'm *terrified* to run into the people who made me feel like I didn't matter and for them to decide they were right about me.

"I want to stay in New York," I say. "I like it there, and I think you would too, but you asked me what I'd be willing to give up for you, and now I know the answer is: everything. There's nothing in this whole world that I've built in my head that I'm not prepared to let go of to build a new one with you. I'll go into East Linfield High—I don't just mean today. I mean if you want to stay here, I'll go to fucking high school basketball games with you. I'll wear hand-painted T-shirts with players' names on them—I'll learn the players' names! I won't just make them up! I'll go to your dad's house and drink diet soda and try my hardest not to cuss or talk about our sex life, and I'll babysit your nieces and nephew with you in Betty's house—I'll help you take down wallpaper! I *hate* taking down wallpaper!

"You're not a vacation, and you're not the answer to my career crisis, but when I'm in a crisis or I'm sick or I'm sad, you're the only thing I want. And when I'm happy, you make me so much happier. I still have a lot to figure out, but the one thing I know is, wherever you are, that's where I belong. I'll never belong anywhere like I belong with you. No matter what I'm feeling, I want you next to me. You're home to me, Alex. And I think I'm that for you too."

By the time I finish, I'm breathing hard. Alex's face is torqued with worry, but beyond that I can't read too many specifics. He doesn't say anything right away, and the silence—or lack of it (Pink Floyd has started to play over the speakers and a sports announcer is jabbering on one of the TVs overhead)—unfurls like a rug, stretching longer and longer between us until I feel like I'm on the opposite side of a very dark, beer-sticky mansion.

"And one more thing." I fish my phone out of my bag, open to the correct photo, and hold it out to him. He doesn't take the phone, just looks at the image on-screen without touching.

"What's this?" he says softly.

"That," I say, "is a houseplant I've kept alive since I got back from Palm Springs."

A quiet laugh leaks out of him.

"It's a snake plant," I say. "And apparently they're extremely hard to kill. Like, I could probably take a chainsaw to it and it would survive. But it's the longest I've kept anything alive, and I wanted you to see it. So you'd know. I'm serious."

He nods without saying anything, and I tuck my phone back into my bag.

"That's it," I say, a little bewildered. "That's the whole speech. You can talk now."

The corner of his mouth quirks, but the smile doesn't stay, and even while it's there, it holds nothing like mirth in its tight curve.

"Poppy." My name has never sounded quite so long or miserable.

"Alex," I say.

His hands go to his hips. He glances sidelong, though there's nothing there to look at, except an Astroturf wall and a faded photo of someone in a pom-pom-topped golf hat. When he looks back at me, there are tears in his eyes, but I know right away he won't let them fall. That's the kind of self-restraint Alex Nilsen has.

He could be starving in a desert, and if the wrong person held out a glass of water to him, he'd nod politely and say *no, thanks*.

I swallow the goiter in my throat. "You can say anything. Whatever you need to."

He lets out a breath, checks the floor, meets my eyes for barely an instant. "You know how I feel about you," he says softly, like even as he admits it, it's still a sort of secret.

"Yes." My heart has started racing. I think I do. At least I did. But I know how much I hurt him by not thinking through things. I don't totally understand it, maybe, but I've barely started to understand *myself*, so that's not all that surprising.

He swallows now, the muscles down the line of his jaw dancing with shadows. "I honestly don't know what to say," he replies. "You terrified me. It doesn't make any sense how quick my mind works with you. One second we're kissing and the next, I'm thinking about what our grandkids might be named. It doesn't make sense. I mean, look at us. *We* don't make sense. We've always known that, Poppy."

My heart is icing over, veins of cold working their way into its center.

Splitting it in half and me with it.

Now it's my turn to say his name like a plea, like a prayer. "Alex." It comes out thick. "I don't know what you're saying."

His eyes drop, his teeth worrying over his bottom lip. "I don't *want* you to give anything up," he says. "I want us to just make sense, and we don't, Poppy. I can't watch it fall apart again."

I'm nodding now. For a long time. It's like I can't stop accepting it, over and over again. Because this is what it feels like: like I'll have to spend the rest of my life accepting that Alex can't love me the way I love him.

"Okay," I whisper.

He says nothing.

"Okay," one more time. I tear my eyes from him as I feel the tears encroaching. I don't want to make him comfort me, not for this. I turn and barrel toward the door, forcing my feet forward, keeping my chin high and my backbone straight.

When I make it to the door, I can't help myself. I look back.

Alex is still frozen where I left him, and even if it kills me, I have to be honest right now. I have to say something I can't take back, to stop running and hiding myself from him.

"I don't regret telling you," I say. "I said I'd give anything up, risk anything for you, and I meant it." *Even my own heart.*

"I love you all the way, Alex," I say. "I couldn't have lived with myself if I hadn't at least told you."

And then I turn and step out into the brightly shining sun of the parking lot.

Only then do I really start to cry.

36

This Summer

'M HEAVING. WHEEZING. Splintering as I cross the parking lot.

One hand clamped over my mouth as sobs snap through me, slice and stab in every sharp little corner of my lungs.

It's both hard to keep moving and impossible to stop. I'm power walking to my parents' car, then leaning against it, head bowed, horrible sounds coming out of me, snot dripping down my face, the blue of the sky and its fluffy cumulous clouds and the rustling trees alongside the parking lot all turning into a summery blur, the whole world melting into a swirl of color.

And then there's a voice, spread thin by the breeze and the distance. It's coming from behind me, obviously it's his, and I don't want to look.

I think one more look at him might be the tipping point, the thing that breaks my heart forever, but he's saying my name.

"Poppy!" Once. Then again. "Poppy, wait."

I shove all the emotions down. Not to ignore them. Not to deny them, because it almost feels good to feel something so purely, to know without question what it is my body's experiencing. But because these are *my* feelings, not his. Not something for him to swoop in and shoulder, like he does almost compulsively.

I wipe my hands across my face and make myself breathe normally as I listen to his steps scuffing over asphalt. I turn as he's slowing from a jog, taking his last steps at a determined but casual pace until he stops, closing me in between the van and himself.

There's a lull before he speaks, a pause that's just for our breathing.

After another second of silence, he says, "I started seeing a therapist too."

Despite myself, I give a phlegmy laugh at the idea that he's chased me down just to say this. "That's good." I wipe at my face with the heel of my hand.

"She says . . ." He rakes his hands through his hair. "She thinks I'm afraid to be happy."

Why is he telling me this? one voice says in my head.

I hope he never stops talking, another says. Maybe we can keep talking forever. Maybe this conversation can span our entire lives, the way our text messages and phone calls seemed to for all those years.

I clear my throat. "Are you?"

He looks at me for a long moment, then gives the smallest shake of his head. "No," he says. "I know if I got on a plane with you back to New York, I would be so fucking happy. For as long as you'd have me, I'd be happy."

Again that kaleidoscopic swirl of colors blurs across my vision. I blink the tears back.

"And I want that so badly. I *do* regret every chance I missed to tell you how I felt, all the times I convinced myself I'd lose you if you really knew, or that we were too different. I want to just be happy with you. But I'm afraid of what comes after." His voice cracks.

"I'm afraid of you realizing I bore you. Or meeting someone else. Or being unhappy and staying. And . . ." His voice catches. "I'm afraid of loving you for our entire lives, and then having to say goodbye. I'm afraid of you dying, and the world feeling useless. I'm afraid I won't be able to keep getting out of bed if you're gone, and if we had kids, they'd have these horrible lives where their amazing mom is gone, and their dad can't look at them."

His hand passes over his eyes, catching some of the moisture there.

"Alex," I whisper. I don't know how to comfort him. I can't take any of his past pain away or promise it won't happen again. All I can do is tell him the truth, as I've seen it. As I *know* it: "You already went through that. You lost someone you loved, and you kept getting out of bed. You were there for the people in your life, and you *love* them, and they love you back. You've got all of that in your life still. None of it went away. It didn't end just because you lost one person."

"I know," he says. "I'm just . . ." His voice draws taut, and his huge shoulders shrug. "Scared."

I reach out for his hands instinctively, and he lets me draw him closer, folding his fingers up between my palms. "Then we've found something else to agree on besides hating it when people call boats 'she,'" I whisper. "It's fucking terrifying to be in love with each other."

He sniffs through a laugh, cups my jaw in his hands, and presses his forehead against mine, his eyes closing as his breath syncs with mine, our chests rising and falling like we're two waves in the same body of water. "I never want to live without this," he whispers, and I knot my fists into his shirt as if to keep him from slipping through my fingers.

The corners of his mouth twist as he breathes out, "*Tiny fighter.*"

His eyes slit open, and the flutter in my chest is so strong it almost hurts. I love him so much. I love him more than I did yesterday, and I already know tomorrow I'll love him even more, because every piece of him he gives me is another to fall in love with.

He locks his arms tight around my back, his damp eyes so clear and open I feel like I could dive into him, swim through his thoughts, float in the brain I love more than any other on the planet.

His hands move into my hair, smoothing it against my neck, his eyes moving back and forth over my face with such beautifully calm Alexian purpose. "You are, you know."

"A fighter?" I say.

"My home," he says, and kisses me.

We are, I think. *We're home.*

EPILOGUE

WE TAKE A bus tour of the city. We wear our matching I Heart New York sweatshirts and BeDazzled Big Apple hats. We carry a pair of binoculars and use them to lock onto anyone who bears even a passing resemblance to a celebrity.

So far we've spotted Dame Judy Dench, Denzel Washington, and young Jimmy Stewart. Our tour includes ferry passage to the Statue of Liberty, and when we get there, we ask a middle-aged woman to take our picture in front of the base, sun in our eyes and wind in our faces.

She sweetly asks, "Where y'all from?"

"Here," Alex says at the same time I say, "Ohio."

Halfway through the tour, we skip out and go to Cafe Lalo instead, determined to sit just where Meg Ryan and Tom Hanks did in *You've Got Mail*. It's cold out, and the city looks its best for us, springy pink and white blossoms skittering across the streets as we sip our cappuccinos. He's been here full-time for five months now, since the fall semester ended and he found a long-term substitute position here for the spring one.

I didn't know regular life could feel like this, like a vacation you don't have to go home from.

Of course, it's not always like this. Most weekends, Alex is tied up with working on his own writing or grading papers and planning lessons, and on weekdays, I only see him long enough for a groggy morning kiss (I sometimes fall back to sleep so fast I don't even remember it happening), and there's laundry and dirty dishes (which Alex insists we wash immediately after dinner) and taxes and dentist appointments and lost MetroCards.

But there are also discoveries, new parts of the man I love introduced to me daily.

For example, it turns out Alex can't fall asleep if we're spooning. He has to be wholly on his side of the bed, me on mine. Until the middle of the night, at which point I wake up overheated with his limbs flung over me and have to shove him off so I can cool down.

It's incredibly annoying, but the second I'm comfortable again, I find myself smiling in the dark, feeling so unbelievably lucky to sleep every night beside my favorite person in the world.

Even being uncomfortably warm is better with him.

Sometimes we put on music in the kitchen while we're (he's) cooking, and we dance. Not a sweet, swaying embrace like we're in some romantic movie, but ridiculous writhing, twirling until we're dizzy, laughing until we're snorting or crying. Sometimes we catch each other on camera and text the video to David and Tham, or Parker and Prince.

My brothers send back their own kitchen dancing videos.

David replies with some variation of Love you freaks or Apparently there's someone for everyone.

We're happy, and even when we're not, it's so much better than it was without him.

The last stop of our night playing tourist is Times Square. We saved the worst for last, but it's a rite of passage and Alex insists he wants to go.

"If you can still love me there," he says, "I'll know this is real."

"Alex," I say, "if I can't love you at Times Square, then I don't deserve you in a Used Bookstore."

He slips his hand through mine as we're coming out of the subway station. I think it has less to do with affection (public displays of which he's still not wild about) and more to do with a genuine fear of getting separated in the ridiculous crowd we're moving toward.

We last in the square, surrounded by flashing lights and street performers painted silver and jostling tourists, for all of three minutes. Just long enough to get some unflattering selfies of us looking overwhelmed. Then we do an about-face and march right back to the train platform.

Back at the apartment—our apartment—Alex kicks off his shoes, then arranges them perfectly on the mat (we have a mat; we are adults) next to mine.

I've got an article to finish writing in the morning, my first for my new job. I was dreading telling Swapna I was leaving, but she wasn't mad. In fact, she hugged me (it felt like being hugged by Beyoncé), and later that night a huge bottle of champagne was delivered to my and Alex's door.

Congratulations on your column, Poppy, the note read. *I've always known you were going places. X, Swapna.*

The irony of it all is, I *won't* be going places anymore, at least not for work. In a lot of other ways, though, my job won't be all that different—I'll still be going to restaurants and bars, writing about the new galleries and ice pop stands springing up around New York.

But People You Meet in New York will be different too, more human interest piece than review. I'll be exploring my own city but through the eyes of the people who love it, spending a day with someone in their favorite new spot, learning what makes it so special.

My first piece is about a new bowling alley in Brooklyn with an old-school feel. Alex went with me to scope the place out, and I knew as soon as I spotted Dolores in the next lane over, personalized gold ball and matching gloves and a halo of frizzy gray hair, that she was someone who could teach me things. A bucket of beer, a long conversation, and a bowling lesson later, and I had everything I needed for the article, but Alex and Dolores and I walked over to the hot dog place down the street anyway, hung out until nearly midnight.

The article's almost done, just needs a few finishing touches, but those can wait until the morning. I'm wiped out from our long day, and all I want to do is sink onto the couch with Alex.

"It's good to be home," he says, looping his arms around my back and pulling me flush to him.

I slip my hands up the back of his shirt and kiss him like I've been waiting to all day. "Home," I say, "is my favorite place."

"Mine too," he murmurs, easing me back against the wall.

Next summer, we will get away from the city. We will spend four days tromping around Norway, another four in Sweden. There will be no Icehotel. (He's a teacher, I'm a writer, and we're both millennials. There's no money for that.)

I'll leave a key for Rachel to water our plants, and after Sweden, we'll fly straight back to Linfield for the rest of Alex's summer break.

We'll stay in Betty's house while he fixes it up and I sit on the floor, eating Twizzlers and finding new ways to make him blush. We'll tear down wallpaper and choose new paint colors. We'll drink diet soda at dinner with his dad and brothers and the nieces and nephew. We'll sit on the porch with my parents looking out over the wasteland of Wright Family Cars Past. We'll try on our hometown the same way we've been trying on New York together. We'll see how it fits, where we want to be.

But I already know how I'll feel.

Wherever he is, that will be my favorite place.

"What?" he asks, the start of a smile tugging at his lips. "Why are you staring?"

"You're just . . ." I shake my head, searching for any word that could possibly encompass what I'm feeling. "*So* tall."

His smile is wide, unfettered, Naked Alex just for me. "I love you too, Poppy Wright."

Tomorrow we will love each other a little more, and the next day, and the next day.

And even on those days when one or both of us is having a hard time, we'll be here, where we are completely known, completely accepted, by the person whose every side we love wholeheartedly. I'm here with all the versions of him I've met over twelve years of vacations, and even if the point of life isn't just being happy, right now, I am. Down to the bones.

Acknowledgments

There are so many people this book would not exist without. First and foremost, I have to thank Parker Peevyhouse. I was on the phone with you when I figured out what I needed to write next. I don't think anything but that phone call could have created this book. Thank you, my friend.

Thank you also to my incredible editors, Amanda Bergeron and Sareer Khader. There are no words that can adequately describe what working with you both has meant. The time and care you took in helping me find not just *a book* but *the right book* is something most writers can only dream of. Sharing ownership and control of your work can be scary, but I've known every step of the way that I was in the very best of hands. Thank you for pushing me and my writing beyond its limits and for being such an incredible team to collaborate with.

A huge thank-you also to Jessica Mangicaro, Dache Rogers, and Danielle Keir. Without you, I'm not convinced anyone would even read this book, so thank you for using your talent and passion to advocate for my books. You make everything brighter.

Thank you also to everyone else at Berkley for creating such a warm, supportive home for me and my books, including but not limited to Claire Zion, Cindy Hwang, Lindsey Tulloch, Sheila

Moody, Andrea Monagle, Jessica McDonnell, Anthony Ramondo, Sandra Chiu, Jeanne-Marie Hudson, Craig Burke, Christine Ball, and Ivan Held. I feel *so* lucky every day to be working with you.

To my amazing agent, Taylor Haggerty, as well as to everyone else on the phenomenal Root Literary team—Holly Root, Melanie Figueroa, Molly O'Neill—thank you for being so involved, dedicated, and kind. And perhaps most importantly, thanks for the sparkling rosé.

Thank you also to Lana Popović Harper, Liz Tingue, and Marissa Grossman for being such a huge support to me from the very beginning.

My dear friends Brittany Cavallaro, Jeff Zentner, Riley Redgate, Bethany Morrow, Kerry Kletter, David Arnold, Justin Reynolds, Adriana Mather, Candice Montgomery, Eric Smith, Tehlor Kay Mejia, Anna Breslaw, Dahlia Adler, Jennifer Niven, Kimberly Jones, and Isabel Ibañez have been making my life (and writing) better for years, and I can't thank them enough.

To have the support of members of the book community and writers I so admire has been not only hugely meaningful to me on a personal level, but is largely *the* reason I'm still able to do this job I love so much. Special thanks to Siobhán Jones and the entire Book of the Month team, as well as Ashley Spivey, Zibby Owens, Robin Kall, Vilma Iris, Sarah True, Christina Lauren, Jasmine Guillory, Sally Thorne, Julia Whelan, Amy Reichert, Heather Cocks, Jessica Morgan, and Sarah MacLean. Your kindness and encouragement have been so important in my journey.

And as always, thank you to my family, for raising me to be both pretty weird and weirdly confident, and to my husband, for always stopping to kiss my head on the way to the kitchen. You are the best, and no one could deserve you.

People We Meet on Vacation

EMILY HENRY

Behind the Book

Every time I start to watch *When Harry Met Sally . . .* , it feels like the first time. Not because I don't remember every iconic scene in Nora Ephron's rom-com masterpiece— I do.

But because I hate Harry. Every time. I catch myself thinking, however briefly, *I don't remember him being this awful!* Or *Sally really carries this movie.* During their first scenes together, I find cynical, horny Harry almost unbearable. But then Ephron works her magic, and everything changes. A softer Harry emerges, the true Harry, a Harry capable of great love and tenderness, one who only needed some time to grow *up* and to grow *on* Sally, and you.

And together, over the course of minutes and years, Sally and I fall in love with the last person we expected to.

When I started *People We Meet on Vacation*, I didn't set out to write a homage to one of my favorite romantic comedies. But perhaps it was Ephron who left this indelible mark on me, planted a seed of ardent appreciation for characters who grate and irritate and infuriate, until the moment they suddenly don't. Not only because they've changed, but because *you've* begun to see the full picture of who they are.

And *that* was what I set out to write in this book. Two characters with no obvious reason to like each other, let alone love each other. Two people with so little in common that romance never seemed to be on the table, and thus friendship could blossom. That once-in-a-lifetime kind of true, bone-deep, unconditional friendship that becomes such a part of your DNA that you could never feel quite like yourself again without it. Alex and Poppy, Poppy and Alex.

On the surface, of course, this is a book about vacations, written in a time before COVID-19, when weekends away and transcontinental flights felt much more within reach than they do these days. But as with Harry—and with Alex—the surface image of a thing is rarely the truth, at least not all of it.

This is, ultimately, a book about home. About finding it, about staying in it, about wrapping your arms tightly around it and breathing it in until it fills up your lungs. It's about a world built for two, the magical Venn diagram formed by a special friendship: You, Me, and the sacred overlap called Us.

So, while we might not all be able to hop on an airplane or stuff ourselves into a Greyhound seat, scour Groupon for discounted country-music-themed motels and questionably safe water taxi services, I hope this book carries you somewhere magical. I hope it lets you feel ocean breezes in your hair and smell spilled beer on a karaoke bar's floor. And then I hope it brings you back. That it brings you *home*, and fills you with ferocious gratitude for the people you love.

Because, really, it's less about the places we go than the people we meet along the way. But most of all, it's about the ones who stay, who *become* home.

Discussion Questions

1. When they first meet, Alex and Poppy are immediately put off by each other. Have you ever made a friend after a bad first impression?

2. What's something you do on vacation that you're unlikely to do in your daily life? Is there a certain comfort in anonymity?

3. Have you ever met a goal and found that your reaction wasn't quite what you expected?

4. What is your *worst* vacation memory? Your best?

5. Poppy is going through professional burnout. Have you ever experienced that kind of fatigue? How did you get through it?

6. Which vacation of Alex and Poppy's would you most want to take? Which would you least want to take?

7. Having grown up in a small town, Poppy struggles to break free of her reputation—or at least struggles to be-

lieve she can do so. When have you felt misunderstood, and how did you get past it?

8. Why do you think it takes Poppy and Alex so long to admit their feelings to each other?

9. Rachel has a lot to say about contentment versus purpose. In your own life, do you prize one above the other? Are these ideas mutually exclusive, or can you have both?

10. Do you think Poppy and Alex are going to make it?

What's in Emily's Carry-On?

Evvie Drake Starts Over by Linda Holmes

The Invisible Husband of Frick Island by Colleen Oakley

The Boyfriend Project by Farrah Rochon

The Marriage Game by Sara Desai

Eliza Starts a Rumor by Jane L. Rosen

Royal Holiday by Jasmine Guillory

One to Watch by Kate Stayman-London

East Coast Girls by Kerry Kletter

Luster by Raven Leilani

Last Tang Standing by Lauren Ho

Something to Talk About by Meryl Wilsner

Queenie by Candice Carty-Williams

Emily Henry writes stories about love and family for both teens and adults. She studied creative writing at Hope College and the New York Center for Art & Media Studies, and now spends most of her time in Cincinnati, Ohio, and the part of Kentucky just beneath it.

CONNECT ONLINE

EmilyHenryWrites